To Larry, 9/4/14

Please continue to be a Source of
interest and amusement to The
people you meet.

*[signature]*

# WET BRAIN

## Mark C. Hull

authorHOUSE®

*AuthorHouse™*
*1663 Liberty Drive*
*Bloomington, IN 47403*
*www.authorhouse.com*
*Phone: 1-800-839-8640*

*First published by AuthorHouse      08/22/2011*

*ISBN: 978-1-4567-5330-6 (sc)*
*ISBN: 978-1-4567-5329-0 (hc)*
*ISBN: 978-1-4567-5328-3 (ebk)*

*Library of Congress Control Number: 2011903846*

*Printed in the United States of America*

*Any people depicted in stock imagery provided by Thinkstock are models, and such images are being used for illustrative purposes only.*
*Certain stock imagery © Thinkstock.*

*This book is printed on acid-free paper.*

*Because of the dynamic nature of the Internet, any web addresses or links contained in this book may have changed since publication and may no longer be valid. The views expressed in this work are solely those of the author and do not necessarily reflect the views of the publisher, and the publisher hereby disclaims any responsibility for them.*

*Cover art by Melody Lockerman*

For Dean

PART 1

# SON OF SAMSARA

# CHAPTER 1

Serial killers always thought they were so much smarter than everyone else. Therefore I was generally suspicious of people who claimed to know everything. In fact my clear strategy of defense was to challenge excessive egotism. The wisdom that knows nothing other than itself quickly becomes ignorance, I would argue. He who knows less ends up knowing more. I felt a responsibility to peel away a braggart's vanity by illustrating that any accumulated information was bound by its own limits, that pride in facts and statistics actually became a liability, a form of desperate hubris. It was a good rule. Like I said, serial killers always thought they were so much smarter than everyone else.

The other rule I followed, which was a little less intensive, was never take a bar bet. If someone in a bar bets that they can resurrect the dead they will probably be able to do it. So when a suspicious looking man sitting at the bar offered to bet me that he could resurrect the dead, I was inclined to believe him. He had the nonchalance of the agreeable sadist. He offered the bet like a withered widow might offer tainted candy to a neighborhood child, the old woman at the end of the block acquitted of her late husband's murder by a lucky technicality. The man at the bar was relentless about his own superiority, which was a violation of my first rule. I was inclined to suspect him. He just looked like the type. You know...the type.

The real reason I found him so suspicious was that there was nothing suspicious about him. He was neither tall nor short, fat nor slim, handsome nor ugly--the type of person that passes by unnoticed everyday. He was the visible invisible. His plain shirt was buttoned straight up to his collar. Subconscious attempt at concealment. Like I said, he looked like the type.

"Excuse me Mr. Bartender. Can you please get me a glass of plain water and a salt shaker?" he asked me, his hands still clasped out in front of him. I got him what he wanted. As I got close to his hands I detected a slight buzzing sound.

"Before you start performing miracles, I am going to get a second witness," I told him. "A man with just the right levels of skepticism and blind faith. A beacon in search of the flotsam of modern mythos. Also if I have to restrain you it'll be easier."

"Take your time," he said, carefully opening his hands to pinch hold of the fly he had caught. I had noticed the fly before--circling, landing, enjoying the sticky spoils of some clumsy spill that resembled an enormous red amoeba. Now the fly was trapped between the thumb and forefinger of the suspiciously normal man in front of me, who pushed the insect deep into the glass of water. "I am not going anywhere and neither is our little drowning friend here."

I stepped out to get reinforcements. Of course I probably didn't need any, seeing as this suspicious looking man was one of the most normal I had ever seen, but these were the types you had to watch out for. If there was one thing that made me nervous it was adherence to strict conformity. These were the dangerous ones. To underestimate the caliber of a man's radical plainness was a big mistake, since there would be no sympathy in the event that he somehow got the best of you.

I walked into the back alley, scanning the dim surroundings looking for my friend and co-worker. It didn't take long to pinpoint his exact location. He was in a supine lean against the far wall next to a linen dumpster and some stacked chairs, engaged in conversation with an anonymous girl—a young thing, doe-eyed and unaffected. She was possessed of a kind of charming banality that was offset by an even more charming apathy. She had comically large breasts.

Zanz Alva was my only friend, which made him my best friend. This lack of alternate cohorts made our solidarity effortless, like the comfortable confidence a candidate has who is running unopposed for office. I admired the faith he had in himself. It was a faith that could not be diminished in any way by his casual neglect of the more prominent elements of his appearance. He had long hair, slumped mannerisms and was dripping down into the middle of himself like an old window pane that becomes wider at the bottom, slightly viscous with the ages.

The girl he was talking to seemed uncertain of him.

He was also quite unmoved by rejection, counting it as a nearsighted deficiency on the part of the pursued. I think he looked forward to it, in fact. It was Zanz's sustained belief that the imprisonment of the soul, the blinding of reason, and the shackles of servitude were directly linked to desire. Because of this he always attempted to seduce those whom he had developed a mild distaste for. I moved within earshot of his conversation.

"...You see I spent some time in the Seventies running domestic counter-intelligence—going undercover to infiltrate extremist groups, although I retired on disability after I was employed to seduce one of the female leaders of the Symbionese Liberation Army. I was the unsung hero who located the group's urban bunker, narrowly escaping with my life after that two hour shooting catastrophe between the leftist soldiers and the Los Angeles police department."

"I bet you've got some stories," the girl said with a cynical tone. Zanz took a drag of his cigarette, nodded.

"Sworn to secrecy, although apparently my conscience allows for cathartic mumblings during sleep. If you'd like we can go to my place later on and you can hear all about it."

"You know take this as a compliment," the girl offered, "but you don't look near old enough to have done all of that way back then."

"Due to a combination of herbal supplements and meditation I have retained a very youthful exterior."

"How old *are* you?"

"One hundred six years old."

"Zanz," I called out.

"I'm on break," he barked back at me, not once taking his eyes off of the girl.

"Some guy with very suspicious normalcy is talking about raising the dead."

"So let him," he snapped, waving me off.

"You might want to witness this. As I understand it these things don't happen very often. I think Lazarus was the last one I've heard of and that was in Jesus's time."

"Lazarus," Zanz huffed. "Do you know what his last words were the second time he died?"

"What?"

"Six of one, a half dozen of the other! It's in the bible. Come on, let's go," he shouted, flicking his cigarette off into an oily puddle. "Till next time, my young friend," he said with a respectful bow in the girl's direction. "We shall continue our conversation under more favorable circumstances."

❡

"Symbionese Liberation Army?" I chided as we made our way back behind the bar. "One hundred six years old? How do you keep up with that type of lying?"

"I couldn't help it," he shrugged. "I was watching a television program last week about historic police blunders. Like any good storyteller I am bound by the principles of verisimilitude to incorporate elements of reality into weaving a heroic image of myself to women. I've decided that next week I will be at Ruby Ridge and I'm thinking Waco for the first of the month."

It wasn't long before we were back in the middle of that violent maelstrom of thunderous chatter that swept up around us as we arrived at the nerve center—the source of power and control for all those seeking divine intoxication, inspiration, self-vindication--the bar.

"Toby...Zanz...Toby...Zanz..." ping-ponged back and forth around us. I freshened a couple of drinks for those who appeared desperate while Zanz turned on me in ripe frustration.

"Now Toby what the hell is so important that I need to be ripped away from the company of that young woman? You know we've been friends for a long time and I cannot have you taking advantage of it by carelessly sabotaging the seduction process."

"Some guy says he can raise the dead."

"If he acts up we'll just introduce him to my billy club," Zanz said, referring to the thick end of a pool cue we kept behind the bar. "After we beat him he'll have to raise himself from the dead." Zanz looked around. "Where is he?"

"He's over there."

"Are you kidding? You are nervous about that guy?" he laughed.

"Damn it, those are the ones that you never see coming," I argued. "He's probably a walking time bomb."

"You've got to stop reading all of those serial killer books," Zanz admonished, which was true, although I hated that he always pointed it out. For years I had grappled with a vague understanding that I would be murdered in the very near future for going through life feeling very guilty for reasons I could never exactly figure out. I was sure that my unreasonable fear of personal harm radiated off of me, which meant that one day somebody with tepid homicidal tendencies would probably be inspired to take me out, just because. More recently I had become obsessed with serial killer profiles in order to have a focused, reasonable anxiety. It made me feel better—provided the chaos with a backbone. There was a serial killer somewhere in my future, that I was sure of. The only thing that was going to save me would be my ability to correctly predict a natural born killer based on my study of past maniacs.

"You have no respect for random, freak occurrence," I condemned.

"Correction," Zanz replied. "I have no *fear* of random, freak occurrence. I'm telling you that this guy has no supernatural powers. Raise the dead? He probably has trouble getting an erection after a few drinks."

"Who the hell buttons their shirt all the way up to the collar?"

"No sense in speculation," he argued. "We are wasting valuable life seconds. Mr. Toby Sinclair, let us go bear witness." Zanz and I stepped in front of the man who still had the fly submerged in the glass of water. He looked up and smiled.

"Are you ready?" he asked. We told him that we were. He pulled the fly from the water and laid it atop the bar. We leaned in. The fly was laying on its side, unmoving, dead we supposed, a victim of drowning. I knew this guy had homicidal tendencies. Insect today, hooker tomorrow. The man introduced himself as Clem Harris and produced a business card. The card said Clem Harris. Beneath the name was the inscription, Happiest Man Alive. There was no contact information listed. Clem announced that he was a trafficker of the mysterious. He was a conduit of mankind's insatiable desire for redemption. He was a heartbreaker. He was always beneficial to his precise moment and location, he said. I took all this to mean he was a closet serial killer and fought the urge to accuse him of it.

"Can we check its pulse?" Zanz asked stoically, still studying the fly.

"Has he been under water the whole time?" I asked.

"Since you left me," Clem said. "We can put him back under if you . want."

"How long can a fly hold his breath for?" I asked.

"The lungs are tiny," Zanz pointed out. "It can't be for long."

"Do they even breathe at all?" I asked. Zanz and Clem looked at me like I had shit coming out of my ears. "Are they aquatic in some capacity?" I clarified.

"For Christ's sake the thing is called a fly not a swim," Zanz said, slightly irritated. Clem picked up the salt shaker and began pouring salt on the fly until its entire body was covered.

"Now we have some time to talk," he said, placing the salt shaker back on the bar and folding his hands in front of him. "Let me start off by reiterating what it says on my card. I am the happiest man alive."

"You know this for certain?"

"Count no man happy until he is kaput," Zanz said.

"I have been reborn, like our little fly is about to be reborn," Clem said. "But here is the critical point...not to be reborn but to appreciate the possibility of rebirth. If you are not grateful for this life your only hope is to be grateful for the next one. I'm not talking about life after death. I am talking about living after dying."

"Are you saying you can live until life instead of dying until death?" I asked.

"A shift in perspective is what I mean. A shift in perspective and the world is at my feet, just like it will be at the fly's feet in a few short minutes. Do you think our fly understands this? Do you imagine yourself as the fly? What is the first thing you do when you awake?"

"Whatever a fly does to celebrate?" I shrugged.

"Find a big steaming pile of..." the bar phone started to ring, cutting Zanz's suggestion off. Sometimes a ringing phone is an old friend. Sometimes it is a new nemesis. Sometimes it is an anonymous badgering and sometimes it is a nasty and tragic horror. Rarely, though, is it all of these things at once. At the time our bar phone was just a ringing phone. I ignored it. That was my third rule.

"Why are you the happiest man alive?" Zanz asked.

"I quit my job today. Picked up the business cards on the way over here."

"What did you used to do?"

"Bartender."

Now I was really annoyed. I imagined that he was rubbing it in and thought I might have to pull the billy club out and beat him with it anyway. My dissatisfaction with my job was usually pretty evident. When I had begun this job it was to be for a maximum transitional period of six months only, while I cooled off from the whole college dropout thing and started to troll for a respectable, progressive, socially aware position of guaranteed tenure where I could work feverishly for a few short decades, enjoy a host of benefits, retire early, and then die in my beach chair on some fair island just below the Tropic of Cancer. However, due to procrastination, apathy, beer, and general mistrust of the average person the years flipped by like pages of a calendar in a windstorm, and I found myself stuck in a routine that was becoming more and more difficult to get out of, although even if I did I had no idea where I would go. To make things worse genetics had inflicted plainness upon me, and as my age and intake of alcohol increased, so did my waistline. Furthermore I had been told by my former psychic advisor that I had underdeveloped chi, dim chakras, and a lazy aura, not to mention a hairline in frantic retreat. It was all part of the disappointment. This man was making fun of it. Where was the billy club?

Zanz, ever savvy to life's subtle machinations, pointed out that the fly was starting to move. sure enough it began to beat its little legs. A wing shook. Then the other wing shook. It stood up. I never believed until that moment that an insect could actually look bewildered, but it was as obvious as if the little fellow had expressed it verbally. Seconds later it was in the air, flying its chaotic path like nothing had happened to it.

"My boss was getting on my nerves," Clem said, wiping the salt residue off his hands. "He is getting a divorce and has decided to get serious in his career as a motivational speaker. Suddenly he has to work his new age magic out on me every chance he gets. I couldn't take it anymore. I quit and told him that I hoped he was plagued by clowns."

"Is that some new insult?" I asked, pondering the ways in which that might be taken as an offense. Finding none, I dismissed it.

"You gentlemen have a good evening," Clem said, giving us a wave. "If you ever need me just think the happiest thought you can and I will be there. That's how sombitchin' happy I am. Let us have a drink before I go."

"Truth!" Zanz shouted.

"What is that?" Clem asked.

"What we are all in search of."

Truth was our code name for Zanz's homemade peach brandy. It was kept in an unmarked bottle behind the bar, chilled on ice for our pleasure. It was terrible. Going down the throat it was like hydrochloric acid laced with cyanide—the kind of noble cyanide that patriots choose instead of dishonor. Even though it probably caused blindness over long-term use we drank it regularly. After years of searching we concluded that it was the only Truth we were ever apt to find. The inebriated condition it provoked was something that could not be falsified through any argument, whatsoever. We put the shots to bed. I immediately had the normal spasm, but to avoid injury it was best to just move with it.

After we had shaken the drink off and bid goodbye to our odd acquaintance we proceeded to perform the usual functions—refill the glasses, clean the ashtrays, answer profound life questions from the desperate and the frustrated. We got back to work.

"What the hell are we doing here?" I said to Zanz as a parade of empty glasses appeared around us and we busied ourselves to fill them all back up.

"We work here," Zanz explained easily. "It would stand to reason."

"I'm not talking about us two bartenders, behind this humble bar, in the year of our Lord, 2000's, Anno Domini, fresh millennium, whatever. I'm talking about humanity, the planet, the universe? Why set it into motion?"

"It is in motion for our specific pleasure and entertainment."

Even with the hard evidence of modern physics and astronomy, Zanz had still been able to retain the antiquated belief that not only was he at the center of the universe but all of those heavenly bodies spinning and circling overhead did so precisely for his direct benefit.

"I mean this job was alright when we were younger," I continued, "grabbing some quick money and biding our time before we conquered the world. But now we're almost into our thirties and we're not conquering anything. When are we ever going to get out of here and do something worthwhile?"

"Might I remind you that we have the best job ever? Let the lifeless drones cut themselves on the rough edges of the real world. You've got the plush lifestyle. You've got your hand on the pulse. You are a halfway bright guy Toby, I don't know why I have to keep explaining this to you. Let me die behind this bar and count me happy forever more." At that point he was beyond reach. Disgusted, I studied my watch. It took me a moment to realize it had stopped. Ah, who was I kidding? Time didn't matter to the condemned. Life behind bars. I threw the timepiece into the garbage. The bar phone began to ring again.

"Hey Toby," Zanz barked. "Answer that, will you."

I let the phone ring because nothing good ever comes from a ringing bar phone. It usually just means more work of some kind. Somebody lost a credit card or got food poisoning. Somebody wants to ask a host of inane questions. Somebody is looking for an errant spouse. Somebody wants to engage the bartender in a series of confused and ill-conceived points about the meaninglessness of life, the existence or absence of God or what time the place closes. At the very moment the bar phone was ringing I had no idea who was on the other end. It would turn out to be a man named Baron Corley. He would turn out to be the human shape of vague doom.

Reluctantly I answered the phone.

"Yes, quickly, I'm looking for somebody!" said the voice.

"Are you looking for somebody on your end of the phone or on mine?" I asked.

"What? Are you playing games with me?"

"No sir," I explained. "I was just wondering if you were looking for somebody at your end of the line and were calling to tell me about the progress of your search, in which case I would wish you the best of luck. The other option is that you are calling to find somebody on my end of the line, in which case I would have to look, since you are on your end and would be unable to look. The third option is that you are somewhere right in front of me, in which case you are out of your mind, in which case I wish you a life without excessive drool."

"Stop screwing around," the voice hammered. "This is important."

"I'm only trying to help," I insisted.

"Why the hell would I be calling to tell you about somebody I'm looking for where I am? I don't even know you and furthermore after this conversation I don't want to. Of course I'm looking for somebody on your end of the line, and of course I'm not there, or else I wouldn't be wasting my time talking to you. I'm not there and that's why I called and that's why you answered. What kind of fucking idiot am I talking to?"

"Five foot ten. Brown hair. Born into unremarkable circumstance."

"Zanz Alva. I need to talk to Zanz Alva." The voice finally gave it up. I flinched, feeling a little embarrassed. It was a personal call. A male voice looking for Zanz? A male voice that gave the impression that the mouth it came from liked to chew on shards of glass.

"May I ask who is calling please?" I inquired.

"How do I know I can trust you?"

"Is it really that big of a deal?"

"I hope one day to be able to kill you for saying that!"

"Hold please," I said, putting the phone down. I shuffled over to Zanz.

"You have a phone call," I said.

"Who is it?"

"I imagine somebody making a big deal over nothing."

Zanz slid over to the other side of the bar and picked up the phone. He was on it for less than a minute and for the duration of the conversation his expression was relaxed and unchanged. He hung up the phone. I knew it was nothing. People were always making a big deal out of nothing.

9

# CHAPTER 2

"Apparently he has killed someone and he needs a place to lie low," Zanz said while wiping down the bar, more concerned with whatever stain he was working at than the statement he had just made. "There is also a body that needs to be buried, I think. That is where we come in. We should be prepared for some heavy lifting. Dead weight can be tough."

"Explain this to me again," I said, my voice echoing through the empty bar as I stacked the chairs. "He killed somebody and he wants us to help him bury the body? Who is he and who did he kill? What does it have to do with us?"

"I am not sure. Details were fuzzy. I wouldn't ask you to help Toby but I'm figuring it is at least a three-man job. Like I said, dead weight can be murder."

"That is not funny."

"It just came out that way."

"Why would we want to help a murderer?"

"Not everybody who kills a person is a murderer," Zanz said.

"I am pretty sure that is the definition."

"Haven't you ever heard of justifiable homicide?"

"Why doesn't he go to the police?"

"Sometimes the police aren't very understanding. Nosy little buggers. They come up with all sorts of ways to trick you. Everybody's guilty to a cop. Most of the time it is just easier to take care of these things by yourself. If you've done nothing wrong then it doesn't matter."

"I can't bury a body!"

"All right, fine, you can carry the shovels."

"Who is this guy again?"

"His name is Baron Corley. He's my father, kind of. He is and he isn't. Taught me everything I know."

"I didn't know you had a father," I said. "You know what I mean by that."

"The old man sounded like he was neck deep in some mess."

"When you say 'old'," I asked, "do you mean 'old' as in known a long time or 'old' as in age?"

"Quantitatively he's around sixty," Zanz clarified. "But to measure the amount of living he's packed into those years in terms of experience, hazard and chaos I'd say he's," Zanz paused to calculate, "oh about two hundred and seventy years old. Everything I know I learned from him. He's a character alright. A full throttle terror. He's also a compulsive matrimonialist," my friend furthered. "He's been married and divorced so many time even he doesn't have an accurate number."

"You say he's back in town. Where is he back in town from?"

"He didn't say. It sounded like he was in a hurry. Usually when a person kills another person they tend to be in a hurry, for one reason or another. Stop looking so worried Toby. You are going to love him."

"When's the last time you saw him?"

"It's been awhile. He's always heading off somewhere or other. He doesn't like to stay in one place for very long. The last time he was passing through Atlanta on his way to the west coast. He was about to get married or about to get divorced. I can't remember which and after awhile it doesn't even matter anymore. For him they are both reasons to celebrate." Zanz dropped his shoulders into an otiose shrug. "Let's do a couple of shots of Truth in honor of Baron's return."

We drank even though we never really needed a reason.

&#8729;&#8729;

I can't say that I was pleased with the sudden turn of events. It was one thing to silently accuse the vast majority of people I came across everyday of being crazed killers based on outdated fashion choices and smug behavior. It was another thing to be waiting for Zanz's father or friend or whatever, already a confessed murderer. I wasn't quite sure how to handle it. My eye for miscreants was always calculated to look for what was absent, to find what was not there, what had been carefully hidden. Serial killers are experts at blending in, appearing normal, hiding their latent homicidal tendencies. This man's was already on display. My usual paranoia was useless because so far he had already admitted to killing, which effectively neutralized whatever paranoia I might've heaped on him. Now it was just a matter of waiting. A three-man job to bury a body. How did Zanz know? Who was his father? Was he a father at all? For the first time I considered the possibility that there were things about Zanz I might not be aware of. Of course I, like everyone else had heard of Zanz's supposed involvement in the Dunham Carriage House scandal a few years back, but as far as I knew he had been cleared of those charges. A man cleared of such serious charges would do well to stay out of trouble in the future. Anyway it was the twenty-first century. These were not good times to be an accessory to murder. Forensic science was too sophisticated. These days if a person farted during the commission of a crime some laboratory egghead could trace the stink back to the offender. I didn't want any trouble and yet I felt that was exactly what was on the horizon. Like the fly from before, was I already caught between fate's thumb and forefinger, ready to submerge, life unto death unto life? I would have to proceed cautiously.

I felt a tickle of dread and an undercurrent of nervous excitement.

"I've said it before and I'll say it again," Zanz preached to the empty restaurant as he wiped down the liquor bottles, happily working away. "We have the best job since the concept was invented. Here we are, us bartenders, caught somewhere between stardom and ordinary work, afforded the luxury of an occupation that facilitates every other occupation in society. It is like the idea of the *lectore* in cigar making."

"Huh?" I asked, distracted as I was.

"The *lectore* is a person who serves a very important role in the making of cigars. You've got these men and women sitting all day in these large tobacco factories rolling, shaping and sealing cigars. The *lectore's* job is to sit in the middle of the room and read aloud the daily paper to the staff of cigar rollers. He may also read short stories, magazine articles, anything to keep the morale and productivity of the cigar rollers high. The *lectore* is crucial to making cigars, however he does not have a hand in any of the actual cigar making. Now take this and reference it to the idea of the modern day bartender. We are in position to maintain the sanity of everybody that comes up to our bar. We tell stories, we show them tricks, we listen to their problems and when it is all over they can go back to whatever it is that they do for a living with a fresh and rested outlook. In this fashion the bartender becomes all things, advancing the accomplishments in fields ranging from surgery, to jurisprudence, to finance. We provide fuel for the Big Machine."

"It makes sense," I conceded. "But at this point in my life it would also make sense that the world is actually flat and balanced precariously on the back of a Giant Turtle whose head sometimes comes up in the vicinity of the Bermuda Triangle and swallows up passing ships. That type of thing also makes sense right now."

"What's under the turtle?"

"Don't start that crap again."

"This is a job of possibility," he went on. "We can leave anytime we want, free to move onto greatness. Not very many people can boast that happiness. They are too locked into their own circumstance. The idea of possibility keeps men young. The recipe is simple. Take two parts freedom, one part independence, top with equal parts latitude, longitude and temporality, then shake vigorously. There...you have it. Garnish with a nice slice of fiji apple."

Zanz was full of existential recipes that he would rattle off periodically to help illustrate in ways us bartenders could understand about how individual factors of the human condition could come together to form strange and interesting behavioral concoctions.

"Is there a name for that one?"

"Turtles all the way down," he said.

A chilly wind, source unknown, swept through the restaurant.

"Well I'll be damned," Zanz murmured. I looked up to see a figure approaching the front door whose silhouette alone provoked in me a heavy shudder. He came through the door with the look of an individual in an ongoing, decades long scrap with life. He had a salt and peppered beard and his walk was more of a lurch, a series of forward falls in which he caught himself at the last minute. Atop his head was a brown fedora. He was wearing a pair of tinted prescription glasses, the calling card of solitary, creepy men with strange obsessions. The kind who have jobs as night watchmen and steal women's underpants out of public laundromats. He was wearing an old brown sport coat buttoned in the center. There was no shirt under it. What the hell was that all about?

"Boys, let's have a drink," he grunted. "Anything. I don't care. Pour it into an ashtray. I'll drink from anything. Shoot it into my vein. Hurry up. I could be dead by sunrise." He fell onto one of the bar stools, pulled out a cigarette and lit up.

"It has been a long time, Baron," Zanz said, walking over to where the man was slumped. "How have you been?" Baron's worn face broke open into a greasy scowl.

"How do I look?"

"Why don't you tell me how you've been and then we'll iron out any discrepancies if we need to," Zanz said uncomfortably.

"Look we'll have plenty of time to catch up once I get a few things settled."

"Does this have something to do with one of your ex-wives?" Zanz asked.

"I suppose," he sighed, "if I studied the cause and effect long enough I could piece together a correlation. Put the smashed portrait of my life into a workable theme and they would certainly be a part of it. I see my ex-wives as a roving mob sometimes, in my dreams, bonded by hatred and indignation. The mob carries torches, crowbars and noose-shaped ropes. It could even be rope-shaped nooses for all I know. Terrifying."

"How many times have you been through it?" I asked. "You know, marriage?"

"Six up, six down the last time I counted," Baron responded instantly.

"When was the last time you counted?"

"The summer of '77. I remember it well. That was the year of David Berkowitz. The Son of Sam killings."

"Interesting way to log it," I told him.

"I try to abstain, really I do," he gave out innocently. "But these women have all wanted contractual reassurance, and who can blame them, given how historically unreliable mankind is." Zanz took a moment to introduce Baron and I. The worn-looking man steadied himself and gave me a hard look.

"Are you the wise ass?" he pointedly accused.

"About the only part of me that is, sir," I said. He continued studying me for longer than decorum would've considered appropriate. I realized that I was fidgeting. He remained motionless. He watched me from behind those tinted prescription glasses, crude brown, like a janitor might watch high school cheerleading practice, half hidden behind some bleachers, the lusty rattle of the custodial keychain on his belt loop signifying his dark approval.

"I'm taking an interest in you, kid," he said to me.

"I never really thought I was interesting," I said. "I consider myself a little on the boring side."

"Is that what you think the opposite of boredom is, lively and interesting?" he questioned sharply. "Do you think the opposite of boredom is fun and excitement, that type of thing?"

"I guess so," I answered, continuing to fidget. "I don't know."

"Sure, the opposite of boring could conceivably be lively and interesting," Baron shrugged, pulling his fedora off and setting it atop the bar, revealing the crown of a head that couldn't decide whether it wanted to go completely bald or have extremely long hair. He took another drag off his cigarette and flicked the ash onto the floor. "But the opposite of boredom could also be relentless torment in which a person is thrown ass over teakettle into a tragedy so ripe with horror that the peace of death is the only available alternative." He had me there. With no real comeback at hand I remained fidgeting.

"Drinks damn it, drinks!" Baron thundered.

"What should we drink, Baron, anything you want?" Zanz promised with a wave towards each end of the bar.

"You better have some Truth back there," he said. "That was my own personal recipe I gave you. Father to son. Never leave home without it."

Zanz held up the bottle of brown sludge.

"Hot Damn! The very thing!" shouted Baron. "Not meant for the general population. It is meticulously crafted for men of fortitude who have proven themselves by drinking deadly amounts while carrying on thoughtful, philosophical arguments intended to enlighten as well as entertain."

"Where have you been?" Zanz asked as he poured the drinks.

"I had to leave California pretty quickly," Baron admitted, swallowing his in one gulp.

"You know," I informed him after cringing with disgusted satisfaction at the effects of the peach brandy, "ten percent of all known serial killers in the last part of the twentieth century were from southern California."

"It is because of the smog. Makes people crazy."

"You said trouble. Is that what we are talking about here?" asked Zanz after shaking off his cringe. I could see Baron was having difficulty deciding on a proper explanation. His face exuded confusion, as if all the details of his travels weren't even entirely clear to him. This was the inevitable degradation brought on by years of heavy drinking. It was immediately evident that he had been under the thumb of the bottle for years. His nose had gin-blossomed into full maturity, and his hands suffered from mild swelling and visible tremors. He had the periodic sway of a man constantly trying to regain his balance. I didn't know if I was looking at a real man or a portent of myself in about thirty years.

"I'd rather not get into it right away," Baron answered finally. "Life, as of late, has been a strange ride. This coming from a man who was once hunted by a Tanzanian Witch Doctor, convinced that my psoriasis contained magical properties."

"That sounds like a good story," I said.

"Yes but now is not the time for stories. Now is the time for more drinks. Remember to pour straight into the glass. I don't like spillage. Do it quickly. I'm closing in on sixty and my clock has yet to start spinning in the opposite direction. Cheap liquor, fast food and faster women. Never an issue of taste. We need the whole experience. Sense overload. Delusions of grandeur. Serious hallucinations. We want to converse with the dead."

"So Baron," I said. "Do you still believe in the idea of marriage after being through it so often?"

"First of all, call me dad," he instructed acerbically.

"Okay dad!"

"But don't make a habit of it. Second of all..." He paused. "Where was I?"

"Your thoughts on marriage," I reminded as Zanz put out another round of drinks.

"Oh yes. You see an old therapist of mine once told me the problem may be that I've never really gotten over my first wife," he described absently as he drank his brandy. "Damn, she was a looker boy. Just all ass and tits and ass."

"You said 'ass' twice," I pointed out.

"Yeah but she had enough ass that you could mention it again after you mentioned the tits."

"That must've been nice."

"Yeah, but when you wake up one morning to find that she has cleaned out your accounts, taken off with the gardener, destroyed your credit rating, run over your champion terrier, set fire to your house, framed you for murder, cut off your manhood and made a voodoo doll out of it, drove your car into the pool and worst of all did it with the lame excuse that she needed to find herself, then you will know the suffering of the damned."

"She sounds like a live wire."

"I am exaggerating," Baron admitted. "She did however tell me before she left that she needed to find herself. I told her to save a little time she didn't need to check the kitchen or the closet where we keep the cleaning supplies. Don't worry though, I got even."

"How's that?" I asked.

"I smacked her in the back of the head with a shovel and buried her ass and her tits and her ass in the basement."

He laughed hard at that one, all phlegm and spleen.

"Ha, ha," I laughed along nervously. "That's a good one."

"Just kidding," Baron said.

"Of course," I said with an empty laugh.

"I had to put her in a compost heap."

"Toby you look a little green," Zanz observed as he cleaned up the empty glasses. "Those shots really got to you."

"Yes. Shots."

℘

The wearied, mysterious Baron Corley explained in a quick and evasive manner that he had traveled the country in a five day sleepless burn from the California desert, down through the dirt and glitz of Las Vegas, across the never-ending horizon of Highway 40, through the arid dust of the Midwest, down the swampland of the bayou, finally arriving in Atlanta, the jewel of the South. He had done so, primarily, for a set of keys. The keys were to a cabin that Zanz owned deep in the woods about a half hour west of the city. Zanz had actually been given the cabin as part of one of the most generous gratuities ever bestowed on a bartender. The kind benefactor was a terminally ill bar customer, an elderly codger with stage four leukemia who had put the quiet bungalow in Zanz's name before slipping into death, his only other wish being that he wanted to be placed in his casket face down so his family could kiss his stiff, wrinkled ass on their way past him in the viewing room.

Baron needed the cabin for a place to lie low. He was on the run, but his reticence prevented me from finding out exactly what from. Zanz was ready to put a plan into action. First, Zanz needed to borrow my car so he could run to his apartment to get the keys to the cabin. This had me worried for two reasons. The first was that Zanz did not own a car because the vehicles he attempted to drive had a nasty habit of having inanimate objects jump into the car's path. Trees, telephone poles, buildings, parked cars, bodies of water had all maliciously thrown themselves in the trajectory of Zanz's stellar, linear driving, and so over the years he had developed a nasty habit of borrowing cars, and even worse than this habit was the habit of not returning them to the proper place or to the proper owner after he was done with them. Zanz had left quickly with a wink for me not to

17

worry, that he could tell Baron had really taken a shine to me and that we would get along very well together in his absence.

Which brings me to the second reason I was worried. I had been left alone with Baron—a situation I hoped would never find cause to repeat itself again. Not that the man in the threadbare sport jacket, tinted glasses and fedora was paying me any mind at all. On the contrary I was being ignored. He seemed, instead, extremely preoccupied with something that may or may not have been out the front window. He would jump off his bar stool and walk to get a better look out the window at whatever it was he had been brooding over, then come back to his seat, walk over to the window again, then come back. Dissatisfied and strangely pertinacious, he repeated the process a few more times. I quietly watched him for any signs of abrupt hostility or casual explanation. He offered nothing.

It was time to go.

# Chapter 3

I led Baron out the back door of the restaurant and down the quiet alleyway. Alleyways were a consistent source of fear for me. Murderers hung out in alleyways because of the usual desolation and quiet. The natural shadows of an alley at night are perfect for lurking. It gave a killer time to think, to consider their kills, to plot, calculate and stay out of sight. To lurk, as it were. The murderer's bonus of the umbra of an alley was the unexpected thrill of being able to pounce on a lonely victim. If some staggering drunk tries to save time by cutting through the alley, then the lurking killer discovers he is the joyous recipient of a victim, a thrilling gift that he is now able to chop to pieces, perform sadistic experiments on, cannibalize, so forth. These were my natural and persistent thoughts when I encountered an alley.

"I enjoy alleys," said Baron, taking in the loose garbage, rats, dumpsters and darkness. "Quiet. Dignified. You can really hear yourself think in an alley." We emerged into the back parking lot where we were greeted by one lone automobile. The car was an enormous monstrosity—a sun-bleached, rusted, Fleetwood Brougham. Baron studied it with the precision of a neurosurgeon about to slice through some critical part of brain lobe. He seemed unsure, unsteady, and slightly afraid about something concerning the car directly or indirectly. I could've sworn he was staring specifically at the trunk. He was on the verge of doing something. I could tell. I was not prepared, though, for him to make a rather abrasive speech to the car.

"Behave yourself," he declared. "Be quiet like we agreed on. You are in a resting state. This is your only power and you better use it if you think you can save yourself. Don't go all falling apart. Don't get any funny ideas either. I won't be far. I'm giving you two hours. After that we do things my way." With that Baron spun on his heels and headed towards the street. I followed.

"Have you had the car for long?" I asked as we walked across the street to a nearby bar to wait for Zanz, who hopefully would be arriving soon with the keys to his cabin but more importantly with my car in one piece.

"I've had it about six days."

"You seem to have a unique relationship with it."

"Piece of shit. It is lucky I care at all."

"What was all that about ordering it to behave itself?"

"I'm on a schedule," Baron responded, avoiding the question. "We are supposed to meet some people here."

"We?"

"The car and I."

"Here?"

"I don't think they'll be showing up, but you never know."

"Do you want to call to confirm the meeting?"

"What makes you think I want to meet these people?"

"Isn't that what a meeting is usually for? To actually meet with somebody."

"First round is on me," Baron said, opening the big oak doors. We walked into the bar and for the first time since I met Baron I was at ease. The bar was crowded and there was safety in numbers, after all. The noise, lights, and stale beer smell swept over me.

We took a seat at a table by the window. Baron adjusted his chair in such a way that he could see the rear end of his crappy Cadillac F. B. across the street. It was behaving, as far as I could tell, exactly as it had been instructed to.

"Let's see how she does now," Baron grunted.

"Are you expecting the car to do something?"

"I specifically warned it not to, if you will remember from about three minutes ago."

The waitress arrived to take our order. I smiled at her. The smile dropped immediately as Baron engaged her with an abrupt, rude, heavy-handed approach that, quite honestly, I should've seen coming.

"Hey honey," Baron threw at her, "do you have any specials other than that round behind of yours?" I froze in embarrassment. The waitress looked from him to me as if I was supposed to corroborate the fact that she heard correctly.

"His brain is infested," I said. "He's due back to the hospital in an hour."

"Infested with what?"

"That is what the tests are for."

"Why don't you bring us a few beers," said Baron, "that is if you aren't too busy polishing the owner's knob back in the office." She looked at me again. I shrugged. The waitress went away. Baron turned to look up and down the street.

"Do you mind not being such an asshole," I said.

"She likes me, I can tell."

"You have a loose grip on reality, I can tell."

"Did you know," Baron went on, "that the first pregnancy achieved by artificial insemination of frozen sperm took place in the Fifties?" He paused. "And play doh was marketed to children as a toy after failing in its original purpose as wall paper cleaner." I nodded, appreciating the useless datum. "I lost my virginity in the early Sixties," he furthered. "In a church vestry to the organ player, whose title after that took on a whole new meaning." Baron sat back with a contented radiance that suggested he had bested me. I was not quick to comment, wanting to appear sufficiently absorbed. Quick responses suggest an impetuous mind. Lagged responses suggest a moron. I tried to slip in through the middle somewhere.

"Did you also enjoy setting fires when you were a child?" I said. "How about torturing small animals? Were you a chronic bed wetter?"

"Don't clutter my mind," Baron growled. "I have a lot on it."

"Like where to bury the body?"

"What did you say?"

"Do you want to tell me about it? If I am going to help you I should know something about it."

"Look, kid. I don't have to tell you shit," Baron warned. "You help us and keep your mouth shut. And if anybody comes around asking questions, I mean anybody at all, no matter who they say they are, no matter what they say I've done, you haven't seen me, you don't know me, you have no idea who I am or where I might be. Don't even venture a guess. Just act as confused as you look." His attention again turned across the street to his car.

The waitress dropped our beers off, which was nice of her to do. I half expected her to throw them at us. I thanked her and she moved on to the rest of the crowd who were shooting pool, standing in loose circles, shouting and laughing. In the back a drunk duo were throwing darts, hitting everything except the board. The pinball machine's lights danced and throbbed as some eager player threw his hips into it in an absurd show of copulation, the only sex he would be involved in for the evening.

Baron continued to ramble. His train of thought was all over the place and it didn't take long to tune him out completely. Instead I studied his hands as he gripped his beer. They were big hands, too big for his arms almost, tough looking, predatory curvature like the talons of an eagle. Every wrinkle and blotch on them a personal marker of wayward lifestyle, bruises from bar brawls, sinewy scar made by a jagged beer bottle, clawed at from a hysterical woman, whatever behavior he might define himself by. The rest of him could best be described as thin durability. The skin hung off his upper ribcage, naked and withered and taunting me from between the lapels of his sport jacket.

His core personality was tough to pin down, or maybe there was no core, just a handful of mimicked characters. He bounced quickly from arrogance to charm with a hint of childish beseeching, a need for approval. He said he hadn't slept in three weeks. He said some motherfuckers were after him and if he got caught this time he'd be going down for the count. I reminded myself that under California's three-strike-rule a person with three felony charges went to jail for life.

The waitress came by to see about another round of beers. On this pass Baron made it a point to ask the waitress if she had crabs, after which he clarified that he was asking about seafood. While not amused she tolerated him well enough, answering his question with polite severity. Then he told her that ten minutes in the back of his car with him and she'd be explaining to her parole officer that she was totally rehabilitated. I slunk down in the chair as far as I could go and reminded her about his mental infestation. The waitress brought another round of beers. Baron grunted out either a remark of gratitude or another insult. He picked up his rambling in a totally different era of his life, talking about his adventures as a ferryboat bartender, although he seemed to be suffering from retrograde amnesia, because he couldn't remember where the boat was or exactly how he had come to get the job in the first place. He could remember minor details though, one story in particular about a foggy morning when the bay was rather choppy and some kid had shit his pants so badly that a man seated not far from the child went into cardiac arrest and died.

"I wonder how Zanz is doing?" I interrupted, noticing that the night was getting late, or the morning was getting early, or however it was defined at this strange junction of fast approaching daybreak. The definitions were varied. I had heard of nautical twilight and civil twilight and there was another that had to do with astronomy, all sorts of ways that the day approaches the horizon. Basically I was tired and about ready to give Baron the slip when Zanz came walking in, brandishing the keys to his cabin. My car keys were nowhere to be seen.

"Is my car in one piece?" I asked.

"No," he said, "but I took the scrap metal from the wreck and made a little shanty out of it for the homeless people in the neighborhood. You should be relieved what is left of your car has gone to such a worthy cause."

"Where is my car?"

"You see that street?" Zanz said, pointing out the window. "You are going to want to ignore that street. Don't look at it or even think about it. Walk right past it to that other street." He pointed up the block. "Make a right at the roadkill and continue on until you see a woman waving from her porch. Follow the direction her thumb takes. Walk twenty yards for every person you've ever wronged, of course if you've wronged an Englishman you'll have to convert to meters. Then answer the age-old paradox of ...Is God all powerful enough to create another God that is even more powerful. If you decide yes, make a left. If you decide no, keep straight. Finally you'll come to a bearded man dressed in lavender robes who will be levitating over a Tibetan prayer rug. He will allow you one question. You can ask for your keys, but be aware that he might just tell you they've been inside you the whole time. But such is the frustration when dealing with sages."

"For the last time where is my car?"

"In the lot across the street."

The waitress arrived again. I told Baron that I would take care of the check since he had taken care of the offensive language and I wanted to do my share. He told me that was very nice of me. The waitress told Baron it was a pleasure serving him, wishing him the best of luck in surviving the car crash she had wished on him just a short time before.

"I know how it is," Baron said, putting his hand on her shoulder. "You've got this goddamn job. Your husband is in prison and your kids are busy knocking over pharmacies. You watch your soap operas, drink your beer, clean your son's room in the hopes that you might be able to find a loose joint that you can smoke for a little while, wondering where it all went, where it all is going to go. I understand, darling. One of these days I'm coming back for you."

*

After a quiet meeting at the corner of the bar between Zanz and Baron they took off, leaving me alone at my table in the corner, with strict instructions that I was to wait for them to come pick me up, giving me a time frame of about two hours or so. They took off in Baron's jalopy. The big Cadillac Fleetwood Brougham went roaring down the street.

His car had been very well-behaved, I had to admit, and wondered if it would have done otherwise without Baron's rebuke. I asked Zanz what he wanted me to do in the meantime and he suggested I stay put and get drunk. This was finally a part of the plan I fully agreed with and remained where I was. A table in a busy bar on a Friday night (now technically Saturday morning) was hard to come by and so I sat and waited and wondered. I realized I had never actually seen a dead person, never seen a body devoid of soul, and went cold at the prospect. How would a man like Baron have contained this corpse we were supposed to be burying? I wondered if it would smell and I wondered if it would look horrible and I wondered if it would try to grab me when I least expected it. I considered the circumstance of this supposed corpse's supposed life. He or she could've been good, or bad, or innocent or guilty, or mad, or compassionate, a mother, a brother, a sister, a father. The victim of deliberate homicide, accident or natural expiration. I had never even seen my parents in their death. My mother had disappeared on a capsized boat and my father's tragic blasting furnace accident prevented anything more than a somber and compact urn. Death, it seemed, ran quite strongly in my family and yet I had not stared into its face. Soon enough.

I ordered another beer and waited.

# CHAPTER 4

Some made the case that global warming and holes in the ozone layer were due to carbon emissions, industrial pollution, the clearing of natural vegetation, so forth. However I had my own theory on the destruction of the planet--too much bullshit conversation. I calculated in a way that was not at all a proper calculation that if all the hot air that was released from every bar in the world continued to attack our environment, the Earth would turn into the Sun in just under the next twenty years or so. For example a bitter old man behind me was loudly proclaiming his distaste for new, low calorie 'queer beers' as he called them, and harkened back to the good old days of "...Ballantine, Hentagehouse, Potosi, Elm Grove, Dale Stale Ale, Hudepohl, Edelweiss, Billy Beer, Fatima, Duquesne, Old Chicago, Falstaff, Big Cat..." the kind of beer that he vowed, "...put hair on yer pecker..." although when I thought about it I decided it was much more favorable to drink beer that didn't turn one's phallus into a pine fur. The old man was eventually drowned out by another drooling drunk in an argument about which city was the duct tape capital of the world. Apparently it was either Avon, Ohio or Paduca, Kentucky. Yes, we were all doomed. The only thing that would save the planet was to release as much cool air as possible. Because I was feeling environmentally conscious I opened another ice cold beer. It was the right thing to do, after all.

A familiar face caught my eye. He was shuffling toward my table. At first I thought it was one of the local homeless coming at me to test his exciting new panhandling lines but as he got closer I recognized him—one of the neighborhood scoundrels that, even though he sometimes got under my skin like a splinter, was too much fun to ever really get mad at.

Skid Row Paul.

Skid Row Paul lived a few blocks away. There was always the unpleasant smell of dirty socks wafting off him. He wore the same clothes habitually and his hair was completely unkempt. He had no job, as far as I knew, and never had a penny to his name. That being said, I didn't understand how he managed to afford an apartment, a cleaning crew, weekly massages and the luxury of getting his hair cut and styled from a swishy hair styling genius who repeatedly gave him the kind of avant-garde coiffure that made infants in strollers cry madly when he walked past them.

"Toby, you foolish young man," Skid Row Paul proclaimed, dropping down into the chair next to me. "Sitting alone on this fine evening when you could be spending time with a brilliant and engaging denizen of this community."

"Hey you," I reprimanded. "You got so drunk last night you left without paying your bar tab. I had to cover for you."

"I'm fully prepared to get that drunk again. It obviously saves me money."

"I don't take kindly to deadbeats, Paul. Even ones I like."

"Come on, Toby. I'm part of that tiny yet crucial category of bar customer that, while economically fruitless, provides a certain sense of spirit and character that other people are drawn to. Remember the reason the bar is considered edgy and hip is because of deadbeats like me. You know these days it is cool to mingle with low society. It appeals to the bourgeois sense of controlled danger. I'm providing you with a service. You can charge the chumps." He looked me over. "Well then are you going to buy me a drink, or are you going to let me just sit here and die of sobriety?"

"What do you want?"

"Give me a shot of bourbon and a beer."

"I count *two* drinks."

"You are a mathematical genius."

I called the waitress back over to the table and paid for my tab up to that point, tipping heavily so that I might remove any memory of Baron's harassment. My method worked and she quickly brought another round of beers and a small glass of bourbon for my insolent friend Paul, who finished it off quickly for fear it might be repossessed before he could enjoy it. I hadn't noticed Paul in the bar before he approached me but it was clear that he had been there for awhile, studying my table companion and trying to figure out from my obvious discomfort, Baron's shattered demeanor and the blatant awkwardness that screamed out between us the nature and reason for the unlikely stranger that had been sitting across from me.

"So who was the old guy sitting with you a little while ago? He looked like a real shit heel."

"You are one to talk!"

"My look is a calculated one," Paul defended. "I take great pains to put this appearance together because I like to know who my friends are. I could tell that guy was something else. He was slapped together like a gypsy commune. He looked crumpled, if you know what I mean, not only his clothes but his posture. It was obvious to the whole place that you were nervous about him."

"He is Zanz's father, but not really. Whatever that means. I'm supposed to wait here while they drive out to Zanz's cabin. They are coming back to pick me up so I can help them with something."

"With what?"

"You wouldn't believe it. I don't believe it. That is half the reason I agreed to wait."

"Zanz is a very secretive individual," Paul said. "He knows some shady people. That was what got him into trouble with that Dunham Carriage House thing a couple of years back."

"That was just a rumor that he was involved," I said.

"Bullshit."

"No formal charges were ever filed."

"Well whoever that shit heel was he better watch himself," Paul sneered. "There is only room for one drunken bum in this part of town and that is me."

"His name is Baron Corley," I offered. "I have to admit I don't get a good feeling about him."

"You don't get a good feeling about anybody, Toby. You know the old saying of 'A friend is just a stranger you haven't met?' If it was modified to fit you it would be 'A stranger is just a serial killer who hasn't murdered you yet'."

"It is good to be cautious."

"Cautious yes, but you are way beyond harmless caution. Remember when you quit going to therapy because you were convinced your therapist murdered her patients and planted them in the rose garden behind the clinic? Or you wouldn't let the repair man into your house because his fly was open and he had a handkerchief in his back pocket? You insisted it was some code for sodomy. Or the time you parked a half mile away from your place because you suspected you were being followed by the car in front of you?"

"He kept looking in the rearview mirror at me," I said.

"The guy with the leg cast in the supermarket parking lot that asked you to help him fold up his wheelchair so he could get into his car?"

"The oldest trick in the book!"

"The girl scout trying to sell you poison cookies?"

"Okay, okay," I conceded. "What about the guy that was in my tree with the binoculars all those times?"

"He was a professional ornithologist!" Paul said. "He was a bird expert. He had published books on the subject."

"How convenient that a pervert also happens to be a bird watcher," I said. "Okay maybe I was a bit hasty in my judgment those half a dozen times but this Baron fellow is a strange guy. He had a conversation with his car for Christ's sake."

"What do you mean?"

"Before we got here. We were across the street in the parking lot. He openly addressed his car. He kind of threatened it and warned it not to do anything foolish."

"What did the car say?"

"It didn't say anything on account of it being a car. Cars don't talk."

"I thought maybe it was one of those talking cars. Like that show. That show with that guy and his talking car."

"I think there was somebody in the trunk of the car. A person, maybe a woman. In my mind I could see her, bound and gagged. I could see the tears spilling out from under her blindfold. I could see the tape over her mouth sucking back and forth over silent sobs. This is what I had mentally crafted. I don't think I am that far off."

"A lot of people have that kind of relationship with their cars," Paul said. "Talking to them, petting them, babying them. Cars become like family members. Hell there are all sorts of things people will talk to. My grandmother used to talk to her sewing machine. She even named it Mildred and consulted it when she picked her lotto numbers. The day my grandmother died the sewing machine broke and could never be repaired."

I lapsed into silence, drunk as I was, feeling myself going over the continental shelf break, as I liked to refer to it. When I thought about the process of getting drunk I began to notice similarities between the gradual decline of intoxication, and the falling slope of the Earth's crust as it runs from the seashore into the depths of the ocean. For the first part of the night, as I travel away from the "shore" of sobriety, the gradient is relatively mild—that is, I can drink at a moderate rate and my slide into drunkenness is gradual. Eventually, though, I reach what is known, geographically speaking as the "shelf break", in which it only takes one step to plunge over the side, and down the "continental slope", if I may follow this analogy to its exhaustive end, where my awareness and motor coordination quickly sink, at angles upwards of sixty degrees, into the dark abyss—saturated and oblivious. I was heading straight down.

"I need to get out of my job," I said. "I need to do something else. I need to be somebody else."

"At least you have a job," Paul gave back. "I can't land a job to save my life." He shrugged. "Everywhere I go to apply I always hear the same old line."

"The 'No job without a college degree' line?"

"The 'It is against our policy to hire registered sex offenders' line. The college thing usually doesn't even come up after that one." Paul continued drinking his beer, smirking from his poorly crafted joke. Paul never bothered to look for a job. In fact he would run screaming if one happened in his direction. He took a unique pride in not doing anything for a living--believing that unemployment was an acceptable social position, only of course for a fellow with just the right credentials.

"Don't worry about it," Paul said, "after all you are a medical student, right?"

"Leave me alone about that. I'm not proud of it but at this point there is no turning back. My Uncle Jimmy would die of heartbreak if he found out the truth."

"Come on, Toby, your only living relative thinks you are in medical school when in fact you have been a bartender the whole time. You can't keep it up forever. I know he lives five states away give or take, but even a sea sponge living off the coast of Australia will eventually figure out what you have been up to."

"The ruse keeps him happy," I shrugged. "Why toy with another man's happiness?"

"Doesn't he own a bar himself?"

"Yes. He is the one who taught me how to be a bartender so I would see how shameless and screwy the occupation was and thus I would never want to do it."

"I think his plan may have backfired."

29

"He isn't a rational human being," I said. "In dealing with my uncle I am not afforded reasonable lines of logic. He is a pill popper and a drunk. He is a fifty-year-old bachelor who left school in the ninth grade, figuring he would pick up the rest as he went along. He went through a period of heavy anabolic steroid use. He regularly accuses people of odd perversions such as 'frottage', which is the habit of sniffing the upholstery of a recently vacated seat in a public place. He likes to wear a bathrobe and crash helmet when he walks his cat around the neighborhood, yes, you heard me, his cat. While teaching me how to drive he made me plunge one of his old cars into a nearby lake so he could show me how to escape from a sinking automobile. He is convinced his whole house is bugged by a government agency intent on obtaining the blueprints to an old invention of his—an ambiguous contraption known only as "The Omega Machine". He likes to engage strangers in public with odd hand signals in order to see who shows any signs of familiarity. He once sent himself to the hospital because he ate a bunch of silica gel packets like the kind found in shoe boxes. Do Not Eat--it said on the package, but no little package was going to tell Jimmy what to do. This is the type of mind I am dealing with."

"You better tell him before it is too late," Paul warned. "I think this is the source of a lot of your discontent. When you admit that you are a bartender to your Uncle Jimmy you will also in some way have to admit it to yourself. A tremendous weight will be lifted off your shoulders."

"What are you my therapist now?"

"At least you don't have to worry about me burying you in the rose garden." He paused, giving me a sly smile. "Or do you?"

He finished his beer and gave me a hard slap on the back. He said he was heading home. I invited him to wait a little longer but he said he was getting sleepy. I offered to buy him another beer and he said he would take a rain check, which annoyed me because now I would have to buy him a beer the next time I ran into him. As for me I had reached a point in the deep night that I referred to as *involuntary defeasance*. It was my own term concocted to express the pathetic emptiness that renders a person helpless to do anything other than sit and drink, knowing the only way to pry out of the void is to be acted on by an outside force. In this case, it meant that I was stuck here until Zanz and Baron came to get me. Over the years I had tried to figure out the source of this tricky phenomenon that removed all my powers of freewill but had always failed. I was, however, keenly aware of the symptoms—disgruntled comments, slumped posture, shifty eyes, bad conversation. It held everybody in its grip.

The talk around me was flat, had nothing to do with anything. People spoke blankly about how the summer was almost over, how the holidays were coming, how time burns through us all, and of course the weather. One man behind me was talking about the effects of colloidal silver on skin tone. He insisted it turns any son of a bitch bluer than a set of balls in a lumberjack colony. Another voice vowed that when Jesus returned it would be in the form of an atom bomb. It was the kind of talk that would make everybody appear, on paper at least, that there was some significant chromosome missing. Nobody spoke of their own shortcomings or the immediate future since both were slippery traps that could aggravate the fragile condition, force people to endure the hard truths about themselves— the kind that are not designed to be self-serving.

The bar was closing. The lights came on. The chairs were turned upside down on the tables, the smell of bleach and disinfectant rose up, the games and machines were turned off, the magic went away, the people reluctant to give up on it. They were herded into the street like cattle. I understood. Friday night party people were in a constant state of regression, trying to get back to that state of childish glee when the world was mysterious, not understood and better because of it. They were trying to get to that place before adulthood replaced nap time with over time, before science filled their mysterious skies with the dead planets and the nothingness, permanently obstructing the view of heaven. This was the reprieve from real life. This was the glamour mirage, the cultivation of the noble and the special, the embracing of the magic that the weekend promised and sometimes occasionally delivered. We were all looking for the greatest night of our lives every time we stepped out of the house, even if we didn't realize it. A location could be located, plans could be planned, but the magic itself was entirely unreliable. Sometimes it happened and sometimes it didn't. It could occur anywhere and at anytime. The trick was to be prepared so at those odd, unexpected moments when it whipped up the pursuer's only responsibility was to move with it, to ride it like a pack of wild horses. Sometimes you got trampled. Sometimes you made it to the sunrise.

A blaring horn knocked me out of my thoughts. I looked through the window to see the old Fleetwood Brougham waiting for me. Baron was at the wheel and Zanz was in the shotgun seat. The car wasn't so much idling as it was wheezing and straining like an old man on the toilet. Zanz had brought some of his peach brandy and offered me the bottle as I got into the back seat. I took a few swigs, and then I took a few more when I realized what was in the back seat with me. There were three shovels.

# CHAPTER 5

We were heading south, south of good deeds, south of reason, south to the world's molten heart, where a famous troublemaker is fabled to reside. We were heading south toward a chore I still wasn't certain I could go through with yet was unable to refuse. I was heading south toward the twilight of innocence. The luminous twinkle of the city had long since vanished, replaced by the dark woods all around us, split through the middle by a lumpy road that the Brougham roared down, pounding through the hallucinatory night.

The blue light creeping through the woods on either side gave the surrounding stretch of trees a haunted, skeletal presence. Flickering illusions brought on by fatigue caused me to see all sizes and shapes of strange images that would disappear as I tried to focus on them. I still had the bottle of Truth clutched in my hand, Zanz's peach brandy. I drank it even though it was a raging inferno that peeled my throat open. It was still helping me feel better. I passed the bottle up to Zanz who drank and then passed it to Baron who did the same. It went back to Zanz and then came back to me. I drank it even though it was like acid. The Truth hurts. It did this morning. The brandy had me sweating profusely, so I was sticking to the cracked leather of the car's upholstery. Baron and Zanz were speaking to each other in mute haste up front. The radio pumped waves of audio fuzz and hillbilly music through the car. I preferred the audio fuzz.

I wasn't sure where we were but I knew we were well outside the city when the billboards began turning evangelical. "Repent Now!" "Sin Today! Hell to Pay!" "It's 8:00 p.m., do you know where God is?" and other threatening messages that made me a bit nervous, not for the intended reasons, but rather because they suggested humanity could option to disregard a Supreme Being, which meant there was a glitch in omniscience—like a very, very, very smart person playing extended peek-a-boo with a bunch of infants. My own faith was well intact but fallible. It had the desire but lacked the conviction. My experience as a bartender was primarily responsible for throwing my belief system into a bit of a trap. If the Sovereign of the Universe didn't know exactly what everybody was doing at every given second then we were all up shit creek. However if the Sovereign of the Universe did know exactly what everybody was doing at every given second (which meant that other than checking in like a probation officer on Sunday morning He was also overseeing Friday night) then I needed to seriously ponder the larger significance of two debutantes trying to pull each other's hair out because they had both shown up to the bar wearing identical outfits, or a paranoid glue-head barricading himself in the women's bathroom because the collective sound of people blinking was driving him mad. Hopefully it was all part of the plan, I supposed, and as long as the plan was outside the feeble grip of my consciousness, then at least my faith had a chance. There was another billboard that read, "God is Watching". All I could think of was that I damned well hoped so.

"The road should be coming up any minute," Zanz said.

"How do we know we haven't passed it?" asked Baron.

"Because there is a set of high tension wires before it. We haven't passed those yet."

"When should we pass them?"

"Any minute now."

"Did you guys make it to the cabin alright?" I called from the back.

"Yes," said Zanz. Baron shot him a look of caution. "Everything is being taken care of."

"And now a body?" I asked. They exchanged looks again.

"No Toby," Zanz said. "I was mistaken."

"We aren't burying a body?" I felt myself relaxing a little bit.

"I think we've got company," Baron cautioned as he studied his rearview mirror. I turned to look out the back window through the rural distance and noticed the headlights. There was no way to tell what kind of car it was, but that didn't matter. Not only had Baron made up his mind that the car was following us, he also adopted the hysterical certainty that it was the police. I kept my eyes pinned on the two small points of light in the distance.

"I knew it. It's the police!" Baron exclaimed angrily. I continued studying the road behind us. The headlights began to take further shape, adopted borders and edges, distinct lines of being, gradually swelling with imminent proximity, it began to look like what it was. A car. "Shit!" Baron yelled. "I was afraid of this." He gripped the wheel in fear. I was beginning to feel it too—this pronounced force of quiet insistence steadily rising, emanating through the capacious car, contagious terror and at that moment I knew Baron was guilty of something terrible and that terrible thing was in the car. It was in the trunk. It had always been in the trunk. What the hell was going on?

"Everybody be calm!" Baron ordered, not taking his eyes from the rearview mirror.

"Baron, why would a car be following us?" I asked. "Just because he is behind us doesn't mean he is following."

"It looks like he's following to me," Baron said.

"Well maybe he's behind us for no other reason than the coincidental fact that we happen to be in front of him," I contested, petitioning a very base form of logic that, considering the circumstances, was entirely inappropriate.

"Don't bother me with semantics!" Baron chastised, with his foot firmly on the brake pedal. "They're gaining on us."

"That's because you are slowing the car down, Baron," I pointed out.

"Well I have to do something," he defended. "I might as well do something he doesn't expect."

"How do we know what he expects us to do? We don't even know who he is."

"Let's not take any chances," Zanz interrupted. "Can we tell what kind of car it is?"

"It looks like a plain white Crown Victoria," I guessed squinting to decipher all the detail.

"That's a cop car," Baron said.

"Not necessarily."

"Are those lights on top or a bicycle rack?"

"We'll know if they start to flash."

"Actually," Zanz said, turning forward in his seat to secure his bearings, "our turn is coming up on the left. It is past these high tension wires. That's the way we want to go." In response to this Baron sped the car up.

"What are you doing?" I called out.

"I'm going to pass our turnoff," Baron shot back, bent as he was over the steering wheel in sharp concentration. The car banked left, holding the road tenuously as we blew through a blur of pine trees, maples, magnolias, and three separate carcasses of unidentifiable road kill. We zoomed past our intended route—an inconspicuous, unmarked side road.

"That was it," Zanz pointed with a shrug as Baron ignored him. The white Crown Victoria was right behind us now. Try as I might, the nascent glow of the early morning daylight prevented me from identifying the nature of the vehicle. If it was a cop car it was unmarked. We broke out into a clearing—dewey fields on either side as far as the eye could see. The shoulder of the road leveled out on either side in a mixture of pebbles and Georgia red clay.

"Everybody hold on," Baron screamed. "I'm going to show you that in times of crisis there is nothing this piece of shit car can't handle."

Before I could raise any sane objection I was thrown to the side in a violent spasm as Baron jerked the wheel. The car itself howled and in a cloud of tire smoke, exhaust, red dust, steel grinding on steel, the decrepit boat did a complete about-face and came to rest pointing in the opposite direction we had been traveling in. As I had been pinned to the back seat during our spin through a fantastic G-force I had caught a glimpse of a carload of wrinkled faces watching us with a mixture of horror and fascination through the glass of the Crown Victoria as they slowly passed us. The car was full of senior citizens who, from their expressions alone, thought our stunt quite spectacular. The automobile and its elderly passengers quickly disappeared into the distance and out of sight.

"That was close," said Baron as he pressed the pedal to the floor and we took off back in the direction we had come from.

"Are you sure you are okay, Baron?" I called to the front after catching my breath. He performed a symbolic brush off with his hand. I sat back in exhaustion. The day was already becoming more than I could deal with. I had no business being outside. I needed rest and water, some painkillers and perhaps a hug wouldn't hurt. Baron eventually found the thin, country road that we had passed moments earlier to avoid being conspicuous (job well done there) and in no time we were cruising under a calming canopy of high trees that painted the unmarked pavement in a latticework of shadow and blue light.

"This is it." Zanz motioned towards the foliage as we bounced over an old set of defunct railroad tracks. Baron pulled the car into the high grass on the shoulder and turned the overworked engine off. We piled out of the car and reassembled behind it, waiting while Baron picked through his ring of keys to find the correct one for the lock on his trunk.

"You could fit six bodies in this trunk, if you had to," Baron bragged proudly as he tried key after key in the uncompromising lock, each time flicking the impostor to the other side of the chain and inserting the next in line.

"Why would you need to fit six bodies in the trunk of a car?" I asked.

"Exactly!" Baron said. "You may never need to, but it is nice knowing that a man has *options*." I backed away from the trunk, not sure whether I wanted to be close to it when it finally opened. Would it be a mangled corpse—one of Baron's ex-wives staring up at us vacantly, at which time he would tell us we were now just as guilty as he was and we better help him get rid of the body and keep our stupid mouths shut. Maybe it was a collection of 'snuff' films, Baron's personal inventory of documented sex-violence against women. It could be some cursed artifact that, once exposed, sealed the doom of everyone present and their entire lineage. Hell I didn't care if it was a blow up doll with a puncture wound, I was going to keep a little distance.

The silence around us was so overwhelming that it began to play tricks on our ears. "Quiet! Quiet!" Baron hushed, straightening himself up and searching the woods for the source of audible illusion. "Did you guys just hear something?" Zanz and I both stood motionless, pointing our heads in different directions. There was nothing but trees and sky. We both shrugged. "Okay," Baron said, finally plunging the correct key into the lock. The enormous metal door unlatched. It let out a mighty whine as Baron raised it up. I leered in cautiously.

This sounds redundant, but there was a trunk in the trunk. It was one of those wooden, flat top steamer trunks upholstered at the corners with black leather. It was about four feet long by one and a half feet—high and wide. A little too small to hide a body in—unless of course it had been chopped to pieces. The center hasp lock had an additional combination padlock around it. Somewhere in the spin of all those numbers was the secret. We all stared in.

"What's in it?" I asked.

"A bunch of junk," Baron said. "It's what it represents that has me spooked. I've seen some weird shit but this takes the cake. Let's just say that it is a collection of very bad energy."

"Like a swirling mist? Heavy atoms? Radioactivity?"

"Have you ever been around somebody or something that just didn't feel right to you?" Baron asked me.

"All the time," I said, giving him a hard look.

"Trust me that this stuff in here is trouble. The quicker we get rid of it the better off we will be." He then turned to Zanz. "Okay," he directed. "You grab one side and I'll grab the other. Let's get this thing out of there. Heave Ho!" They lifted the trunk out and walked it to the edge of the woods, Baron all the while yelling encouraging words like 'careful' and 'steady' across the top of the trunk to Zanz, who gingerly stepped through the high grass while trying to maintain his balance. The two men, saturated to their ears with peach brandy, were inches away from toppling over each other.

"Toby, close the car up," Baron instructed. "Then go around and grab the shovels out of the back seat. Oh yeah, and don't forget the bottle of Truth!" I went to slam the top of the trunk down but something that caught my eye caused me to stop. In the far corner of the trunk was a piece of duct tape, all twisted and stretched out. It looked sinister, like it had been used to bind something. Not something, I thought to myself, somebody. I reached out to grab it, but paused in fear. Did I really want to touch it? Would it somehow become part of me if I did? Would I be linked to its possibilities? It was harmless and yet it wasn't. I grew agitated by its ambiguity. Should I touch it? I had to. But first I leaned out of the trunk to secretly glance at Baron, who was moving away, motioning towards the woods with his head, oblivious to everything except finding the correct direction. Zanz was nodding back to Baron. I leaned back into the trunk and grabbed the piece of silver tape, turning it over in my hands, acquainting myself with its dormant potential, trying to experience its purpose. As I scrutinized it I noticed that embedded in its sticky adhesive were four or five hairs, long and soft, with a feminine wave to them. A light breeze made the hairs dance in my hand.

"Hey kid let's move it!" Baron called. I straightened up like I had been shot. The tape with the hairs stuck to it fell out of my hands and back into the trunk. "Come on," he ordered. I slammed the top down, went and gathered the shovels, the bottle of peach brandy and ran to catch up. They were following the old railroad tracks.

"Let's hurry up and get this thing out of sight," Baron commanded further. They lumbered down along the path. I followed with the shovels, the clear mental picture of the tape with the hairs in it nagging me. I could tell from the adhesive not only the woman herself but the whole struggle, her pleas for her life, her children, Baron's complete refusal to see her as anything other than an inanimate plaything. Him stuffing her into the back and driving off with her, deceitfully promising her she would be alright, her whimpers in the cavernous trunk space. This was the woman he had been speaking to when he shouted at the car. A woman with long wavy hair.

"What is in that steamer trunk again?" I asked.

"It makes men do crazy things," said Baron.

"Like a woman. Like a woman makes men do crazy things?"

"Toby would you shut up," said Zanz. We continued walking. The train tracks ended and the crest we were following sloped down into a narrow path cluttered with a gauntlet of thin branches that whipped back at me as Baron and Zanz struggled through them with the cumbersome cargo.

"What were you guys doing at the cabin this morning?" I asked.

"Had to drop something off," said Zanz. "I got Baron set up. He is going to be staying there for awhile."

"Not much to do out there," I said.

"I've got plenty to do," said Baron. "Let's put this damn thing down for a minute." They dropped the trunk callously to the ground. Baron took the bottle of peach brandy I had been holding and took a long drink from it. He passed it to Zanz who took a drink. Zanz passed it back to me. I dropped the shovels and drank, getting down what I could. My stomach started to churn. It was now obvious that I was going to puke. It was just a question of when.

"This just seems so screwed up!" I blurted.

"Hey, hey," said Baron. "I thought we could trust you, man. We are bound into a very valuable allegiance. Do you know how much trouble we could all be in right now? This thing," he kicked at the steamer trunk on the ground, "brings with it some serious shit. The wrong people find out where it is and we are all dead. Painfully dead. So don't go busting my balls. Just trust me when I say that we need to get rid of it quickly!"

"Look," I said, "I am not involved in this."

"That is not what it looks like from here."

"Well you know what it looks like from here, a souse trying to cover up a murder."

"You think whatever you want," Baron said. "If you are part of this then you are part of that too!"

"The hell you say!"

"Alright!" Zanz said, breaking it up. "Let's get moving. Enough jabbering."

Not wanting to give up the argument, I was about to bring up the twisted duct tape with the hair in it that I had found in the car when a rustling of leaves and the heavy crunch of footsteps moving towards us made me bite my lip. My legs turned to marble. My feet dug themselves into the cold ground. My spine melted. I urinated in my pants a little bit. From the woods emerged a couple of hikers, a man and a woman, debouched from behind some trees, their faces stretched high and wide in astonishment. I was still holding the bottle of brandy. In a feeble effort of concealment I put it behind my back, as if this was the only thing that would've aroused their suspicion. The two hikers were thin, muscular, tanned. They had backpacks. The woman had a handful of mixed nuts and gorp which was frozen at her lips as she took in this wasted scene of three foul smelling men, the old trunk and the shovels lying in the trail next to it. She was good-looking and all-American. She shrunk carefully behind her male counterpart, studying all three of us in turn--the angularity, the prominent features, rough height and weight. She would make an excellent witness. The jurors would feel that they could trust her.

"We were just walking through from our campsite," the male hiker said slowly.

"Yes, very good," Baron said. "Don't let us interrupt."

"Are you guys lost?" the hiker asked.

"Just resting."

"Are you alright? I couldn't help but overhear some conversation," said the man. The woman slowly tugged on his sleeve, a gesture that cautioned him not to get too curious. There was gorp sticking to her lip.

"What did you hear?" asked Zanz. "A lot of echo around here." It was then that I noticed Zanz lightly tapping the side of his pants. There was a bulge at the bottom of his shirt. He had taken his billy club from the bar and brought it with him.

"Nothing," said the hiker. "Just wanted to make sure you are okay."

"We are okay."

"Okay."

"Got the ashes of my granddad in here," Baron said with forced friendliness as the two hikers studied the trunk. "Also some of his heirlooms. He always wanted to be sprinkled into the Chattahoochee River. We are here to honor the old man's wishes."

"I understand," said the male hiker. "But this river up ahead is the Flint River. You'd have to go north for the Chattahoochee."

"Well I am pretty sure that he won't know the fucking difference,"

40

smiled Baron. "Would either of you care for some peach brandy? It was his favorite." Baron motioned towards me. I took a step backwards.

"No thank you," the female hiker said, pulling her companion along. "Good luck." They walked off. I anticipated Baron running after them, yanking some stick from the ground and bludgeoning them to death so as not to leave any witnesses. But he just rubbed his head and looked around like he had no idea how he had come to be in this spot at this moment. He looked like the last time he recalled he was ten years younger, give or take, sitting under some overpass in Culver City, curling up next to the freeway and now, years later, he had been whisked instantaneously to this remote woods. My feet came unstuck from the ground. With the bottle shaking in my hand I took another quick swig to calm my nerves.

"Other than meatloaf and bread, are there any other rock bands named after food?" Baron asked.

"What?"

"I can't think of any," Baron said, rubbing his forehead, overcome with the gravity of his new problem. "All I can think of are meatloaf and bread."

"Are you out of your mind?" I said. "Who cares? Let's get the hell out of here."

"What about peaches and herb?" said Zanz. This put Baron at considerable ease. Zanz then turned to me to plead his case. "I tell you this, Toby," Zanz said. "Current estimates of this planet's population are somewhere around six and a half billion people. Of those people there are roughly..." he paused to consider some difficult calculation, "...*two* whose safety I put before my own." He looked between Baron and I. "As it happens those two are standing in front of me right now. Which means I have a responsibility to protect both of you from all the other crazies that might try to take you down. If Baron is not safe, I am not safe. If you are in danger Toby, I am in danger. This level of commitment relies on the faith that your struggles are noble struggles. We do not do this kind of thing in vain. I must assume that if I am needed by one of you then it is for something important and if that is the case then my responsibility is to assist to the best of my ability. I'm asking you to honor the force of this loyalty by extending your own to somebody who needs your help today."

My head was spinning. My wretched condition was worsening. I was getting drunk all over again but this was a drunk mired in painful fatigue. I didn't know who or what to believe, but it did no good to just stand there.

41

I decided to get it all over with, remembering that famous existentialist story where the guy shoots the other guy because it is hot and sunny out.

"Alright, alright," I sighed. "Come on, the sooner we get this thing over with the sooner we can get out of here." I cradled the shovels to my chest and continued walking. Zanz and Baron gripped the handles of the trunk and, after a motivational one-two-three count, heaved it up and continued on the way. The walk through the woods became a short series of infinite distances. I could only motivate myself to continue by fixing on a point no more than five yards away and convincing myself that if I could only make it to that spot everything would be okay. Then I would force my mind to dwell on some terrific daydream such as sitting on a yacht in the Mediterranean or by a fireplace in a remote chalet where outside the window big snowflakes painted the hillside white. Before I knew it I would be trudging past my arbitrary destination, and I would pick another marker and repeat the whole damned process again.

It wasn't long (or maybe it was) before I could make out the sound of the steady tide of the river in the approaching distance. The sunrise was a bloodshot eye. My stomach was churning and I was getting the dry heaves.

"We're almost there," Zanz said. I picked up the pace, energized by something other than never ending wilderness. I fought the urge to drop the shovels, run through the woods to the riverbank and throw myself into the water.

We snaked our way down a thin gully until we came to a cluster of boulders. Baron and Zanz carefully steered themselves down towards these natural markers while I called to each of them to watch for small weeds and stumps that threatened to trip them up and send them tumbling the rest of the way. As the ground leveled and the sweet brown gush of the diluvial torrents of the Flint River came into view, we stopped upon a well-hidden plot of earth about a hundred feet from the riverbank.

We had made it.

I fell to the ground.

Zanz and Baron immediately grabbed the shovels I had cast aside and began digging out a substantial hole. It was hot and I felt like dying. I couldn't take it anymore. I got up, walked a couple of paces away and threw up in some bushes. The fetid smell of peach brandy burned through the forest like napalm.

"Look alive son!" Baron commanded.

After a minute of dissipating dry heaves I joined back up with them, grabbing a shovel and beginning to dig. The individual holes all three of us were working on eventually gave way to one sizable chunk. Baron had taken off his jacket and was going with all his might, bare chested, murmuring something under his breath that I couldn't quite catch. He was insane, that I was sure of and in the event this turned out to be a felony and we were all prosecuted for our part no jury would ever believe he knew what he was doing at the time of the commission of the crime. I would be a different story.

Zanz was stoic as usual, singing something about loading sixteen tons and not having a thing to show for it, although the exact song made it seem a little more fun and worthwhile. With the hole completed and some careful maneuvering we dropped the trunk in and started to fill it back up, which seemed to go by a whole lot quicker. Pretty soon the hole was nothing more than a flat patch of dirt.

"Well that's that," Baron sighed with relief. "Now we can forget about the whole thing." He shook his fist at the treetops. "Let's see them get me now!" He dropped his shovel, staggered off into some ferns and dropped down. "Bring it on you ratty sons of bitches."

Zanz and I dropped our shovels. We looked out at the river, the trees, the morning sun. It was more than I could bear. Hit by an impulse that I was powerless to deny, I burst into a full gallop with the last of my energy, ran towards the river and jumped into the cold water fully clothed, sinking like an anvil to the murky bottom, trying to cleanse myself of whatever wickedness I had just been a party to. There was something about a river in its eternal movement that carried forgiveness, enlightenment, majesty. A rolling torrent of natural ablution. Mark Twain knew it. Oscar Hammerstein Junior knew it. Langston Hughes knew it. I knew it.

I managed with some difficulty to resurface, flailing, doing my best not to drown. Eventually I had to cling to a moss covered rock downstream and wait for Zanz to rescue me with the aid of an outstretched shovel.

# CHAPTER 6

HANGOVER...

SCIENTIFIC DEFINITION: Intense dehydration, pain and fatigue due to systematic poisoning of the body from alcohol, metabolites, and congeners.

EXISTENTIAL DEFINITION: The inevitable consequence of an alcoholic's Icarus Syndrome.

LAYMEN DEFINITION: Punishment for trying to sober up.

The reports of missing women began to work their way into the national news. The stories could have been there the whole time but I had only started to take notice after the burial of the steamer trunk days ago, the incident being a trigger that pulled my usual blind absorption into the bigger scope of American consciousness, that slick machine of astonish and forget. My uneasiness over helping Baron had become adhesive, and the nature of adhesion being what it is, my uneasiness had been brushing up against things to cling to. So I became aware of the ongoing reports of missing women.

Bodies were popping up, all female, in Oklahoma, Colorado, Nevada, etc. Buried in shallow graves and dug up by animals, found by hikers and farmers in rural pastures and along desert roads. Elements of the crime suggested a single perpetrator. The women resembled one another, there were similarities in the use of certain ligatures, common causes of death. Strangulation was evident because the hyoid bone had been broken, which is always a clear indication. The critical details of the murders were withheld from the public. The details only a killer would know.

Thus I had been on a rather serious drinking binge, not quite knowing how to handle what I thought I knew about Baron and not knowing anything definitive in the first place and not wanting to know anything and hoping nobody would find out either way. It was a blinding summer morning. I was in the backyard of my landlady's picturesque Southern mansion. I rented the small carriage house tucked into the far corner of the property. A clean, simple living environment believed to be haunted. During the renovation of the carriage house my landlady had found a child's shoe in the wall, which was the way, she said, you could always tell. Other than a few creaks and rattles this tortured soul and I got along fine.

This morning I had woken up with a deadly hangover and a litter of empty bottles on my night stand, wondering if the two had something to do with one another. A pounding headache pulsed behind my eyeballs. I couldn't feel my legs. This was serious shit. My hangovers were subject to the same Saffir-Simpson classification system that gauged how deadly a tropical storm or hurricane was. Normally, they never went over a class two. However today I could definitely feel a class four coming on. The only way to combat this level of hangover was for me to strip down to my under shorts, head out into the yard and drop myself into the Koi fishpond my landlady had installed to bring an element of serenity to her yard. I stretched out in the cool water and reached for the hose coiled at the edge of the grass. I doused my head and drank from the spigot while the Koi fish lined up around me, a curious, floating army, their mouths moving in exaggerated oval expressions, seeming to say, why, why, why? The great seekers of cause, these fish were. The biggest one sidled up to me, brushing against my arm, a natural, bestial comfort, a comfort not between humans but of life between life. I appreciated the gesture. A Koi fish's growth depends on the size of its habitat. A serial killer's growth depends on the degree and heinous nature of the crimes. Some of them had the whole of remembered history to stretch out in.

I worked fast to get some water back into my system, dousing my face again, spewing a raining geyser from my mouth. Hydration and Intoxication are contrary modes of a common art form. Something I was either plunging into or recovering from. Even through all of this I still held fast to the notion that I was a responsible drinker, always smartly stopping just short of death.

"Hey puddle head," a voice called out from somewhere above me.

"Not now. I am dying in your pond."

"I'm talking to you puddle head."

"I am out of the office today."

"Puddle head I am not your secretary."

"I am going to expire right here in your pond, Nona. In the name of the Father, Son, Holy Spirit. I'd say it in Latin but I can only remember the first part."

"Since when are you a troublemaker, puddle head? A woman comes by the house today and says you are in trouble. Are you listening? Get out of my pond. You are driving me to the wall."

"I am driving you *up* the wall, Nona. You have to go *up* it, not just stand in front of it if you are trying to express frustration."

"My patience is thickening, puddle head."

"The Koi fish will take care of my remains. You will have fish food for weeks. By the way your patience is thinning."

Nona, my Filipino landlady had been brought to the United States years ago by marrying an army lieutenant and then divorcing him as soon as she touched down on the land of opportunity. Since then she had used her family connections to set up a mail order bride service out of her house to help lonely American men find happiness with petite Filipino women who wondered, when they arrived, why all American men were wrinkled and/or fat. This was not the virile masculine culture they had seen on American soap operas. A fellow had been convicted a few years ago of murdering three of these mail order brides once he got hold of them. Three is the magic number that transforms a murderer into a serial killer, provided they fit the necessary patterns.

Nona's hold on the English language went in and out. I was fond of her habit of screwing up common sayings and colloquialisms. I often wondered whether she was legitimately confused or just did it to amuse me. I also took pride in her endless source of insulting nicknames for me, figuring that if she took the time to come up with them it meant she was emotionally invested, which is valuable regardless of the way it manifests. At the very least I figured I would not get evicted.

The only slight strangeness of living in Nona's backyard was that every once in awhile a nervous man would be milling around waiting to be connected with his long distance wife-to-be by telephone and because of the time difference between America and the Philippines it happened at all sorts of strange hours. The nervous groom would be pacing around the Koi fish pond, working up the nerve to say 'I do' and then kiss the bride...in about four to six weeks after all the paperwork had been filed. Some men wore suits to the phone call and I had even seen a few wearing tuxedos.

"I could care less how you feel," Nona said. "You have creepy people bothering me. This woman left a message for you. She was on my doorstep dressed in a bathrobe."

"First of all you have to say that you could *not* care less. If you are trying to say that you don't give a shit and you could care less then chances are you would." I sat up. "What are you talking about? What woman in a bathrobe?"

"She wants to meet with you," said Nona, handing me a slip of paper that I handled carefully so it wouldn't become wet and illegible.

"What did she want?"

"She said you were in trouble and that she could help you. She said you were in over your head. Said you were in a situation with her husband."

"Who is her husband?"

"I don't remember but he had a funny name."

"Baron?"

"Why not." She knelt down and checked my pupils. "Why have you been drinking so much these past few days?"

"The ghost child in the carriage house did this to me," I said. "He opens beers and pours them in my mouth while I sleep. Then he takes my bedroom closet and puts it where the toilet is supposed to be."

"Stick that hose in your ear," Nona commanded. "I want to see the water shoot out from the other side of your empty head."

"That was a sophisticated put-down, Nona. You are coming along fine."

"I wrote down her address and the time she wants to meet," said Nona. "I would be careful though. She is crazy and you are a puddle head. Never a good mix."

I studied the address. The woman didn't live far but I noticed the time on the piece of paper said twelve a.m., which I assumed Nona had gotten wrong, figuring however strange a woman roaming around in a bathrobe might be she would not want to meet at midnight but rather at noon. It was almost that time so I pulled myself out of the fish pond just as a tentative old man in a blue suit and white carnation waved to Nona from the back fence. The wedding bells were ringing. A man was never too old for love if it was convenient and for the right price. I got dressed and drove over to the address on the piece of paper, wondering how the hell this woman had found me so quickly, eager to find out what she knew, eager to dispel any accusations, eager to see what kind of woman would marry Baron Corley.

The relentless summer sun brought a fresh wave of nausea over me and again my malaise kicked up to a level where death seemed a fine alternative. God, the hangover was so bad that it wasn't even confined to the inside of my aching skull, or in my tired muscles. It was actually *out* in the world. It hung in the trees, it grayed the skies, it caused people to appear frightening, alien, purplish and bug-eyed—horrible grotesques crawling their way desperately through an earth scorched by flame and sin. Even the plants and trees were slumped in the intense heat. Buildings were in gross decay and the bridges sagged wearily. Men in orange vests stood out on the blacktop with murder in their eyes—the series of telephone poles on either side of the street like a line of crucifixes. Sad songs poured out of my radio. I switched stations but that only succeeded in finding songs all the more mournful. A woman in the car next to me was beating her kids from the front seat because they were ugly. She beat them with the guilty knowledge that she had made them so, had donated half her ugliness to these twisted little brats, which made her beat harder.

I considered stopping off at the nearest bar for a quick beer to lighten my mood. I thought better of it because I couldn't find a bar and I was almost out of gas. It was at times like this that I had to consider if I was an alcoholic or not? It was a valid question but one I would have to answer with an emphatic no. The reason I say no is because I had learned a word recently. Dipsomaniac. The definition is a person with an insatiable, often periodic craving for alcoholic beverages. Easy to drop the word 'maniac' and add the suffix 'phile'. Dipsophile. Dipsophile sounded almost scholarly. So much nicer than alcoholic and not as loaded. Don't be surprised if the word pops up again.

❦

I found the house in a quiet neighborhood near the old abandoned mill, which of course would be where I'd find it. The street was lined with shotgun houses, some in disrepair, some with cheerful renovations. Some looked like drug dens. The house I was going to was the most rundown on the block. I got out of the car, walked to the front door. There was a note on the door. On it was handwritten, "I said twelve a.m.! That means midnight. Can't you read?"

I looked back down at the message Nona had taken, shrugged, got in my car and went back to my carriage house since I had about twelve hours to spare. Sitting at my desk I took out my big scrapbook, studying newspaper clippings, books, criminal profiles of famous serial killers, most of the men looking normal, some almost charming, others terrifying and insane. But it was all the same face when it came down to it. Gacy. Dahlmer. Manson. Lucas. Panzram. Constanzo. Bonin. Rader. Ridgway and the rest.

I reread some of the more grotesque escapades, trying to get at the mind of Baron Corley.

A series of dead women to coincide with his drive across country. A man constantly on the move. What was his method? Prowl the truck stops. Kidnap the convenience store workers, counting on the fact that most of the closed circuit cameras had very poor quality. Introduce himself as a feeble, stranded traveler. Pretend he was a cop. Offer to drive the drunk girl at the roadside bar home.

He wouldn't be one of the notoriously handsome ones like Ted Bundy or Paul Bernardo. His method of operation would be markedly different from the too-good-to-be-true lothario. He would have to adopt more of a pitiful, innocuous strategy like Harvey Glatman or Robert Garrow, first gaining the woman's trust through some authoritative pretense before getting them alone and acting out his sadistic perversions. Honing his technique he would have his torture kit readily available. He would use handcuffs, offer to show a little trick with them. Slip these on, watch how I can take them off with a simple sleight of hand. Once restrained he would go into action. Threaten them, burn them with matches, use hypodermic needles to make painful injections with bleach and other chemicals. Take polaroid pictures for his own gratification years down the line. If caught he would plead to keep these sadistic snapshots in his jail cell. The judge would tell him no. His lawyers would sneak a few in.

My phone rang.

"Hello?" I said.

"Hey you little shit," came a gravelly voice on the other end. It was my Uncle Jimmy. He was drunk. I could see him, clear as day, standing behind his bar in Long Island, working on his fifth rum and soda, deciding in his inebriation that it was the perfect time to call his only nephew to either rattle off some half-cocked wisdom or ask me a medical question, since because of my ongoing deceit he had been operating under the false assumption that I was in medical school for the last four years. I had sunk so deep into my own lie that it was impossible for me to come clean. Jimmy was all I had and I was all he had. Although we lived in different cities we still counted on each other, not for any one thing but to be there for anything, the more trivial the better. Our tests of each other's loyalty was never more serious than when nothing important was going on. Jimmy was hardheaded and brusque. He liked to be the smartest man in the room without all the exhaustion of being the smartest man in the room, believing any argument could be won through sheer belligerence and volume. He was like a chess master who labels himself as such once he has a decent idea of how all the pieces move on the board. A vastly inept and premature sense of personal genius. He could always pick the board up and knock his opponent unconscious with it if things started to get weird.

"Hello Uncle Jimmy," I sighed. "I haven't talked to you in awhile."

"You know I'm always going to call you a little shit," he promised. "Even when you are a hotshot doctor."

"I know Uncle Jimmy, I like it."

"I'll still be smarter than you even when you are a hotshot doctor."

"I know."

"I hope I didn't call you too late. I figured with the time change and all you'd still be up."

"Jimmy, there is no time change from New York to Atlanta."

"Yes there is."

"And it is late afternoon."

"Yes, it is here, that's why I wasn't sure."

"What's going on?"

"Are you still coming for a visit?" he asked. "All the guys can't wait to see you. We're going to have a lot of fun. You little shit."

"Yes we are."

"I promise I won't let them hassle you. I told them they weren't allowed to bother you with their medical problems. But since you are so close to being a doctor, maybe you can answer some of their questions and get them off my ass."

"No problem, Uncle Jimmy."

"All the bar regulars have been asking for you. They've been on my ass. What's happening with Toby? When are we going to see Toby? I tell them, hey fellas, go faulk yourselves. He'll get here when he gets here."

"Thanks Uncle Jimmy."

"So when are you getting here?"

"Three weeks."

"We'll have fun," he repeated, "it will do you some good to get away from your studies. Get you into a nice filthy bar with a lot of belligerents. It'll get you out of the hospital. It'll be a nice change of environment. The guys at the bar will be on your ass instead of mine."

"I can't wait," I said.

"Toby, my ass has been itching lately. It usually happens at night. What do you think it is? Hemorrhoids?"

"Maybe it is the bar regulars?" I said.

"Hey you little shit, I'm serious."

"Have you been drinking a lot of coffee Uncle Jimmy?"

"No."

"How much?"

"Only about three pots a day."

"Well it could be the ketones from the coffee. You might want to cut back."

"It doesn't happen all the time, but boy when it does, watch out. It's like a fire down there."

"It could also be the tannins from red wine."

"Red wine?"

"Have you been drinking a lot of red wine, Uncle Jimmy?"

"Tannins. Ketones. How did you get so faulkin smart?"

"Good genetics, eh Uncle Jimmy?"

"That's my boy. You little shit."

"Yes."

"I love you. I'll see you in a couple of weeks."

"Love you too, Uncle Jimmy. I hope your ass feels better."

I hung up the phone, wondering just what the hell I was doing with myself.

స

At the stroke of midnight I drove back to my appointed meeting. I thought about calling Zanz to let him know what I was doing but sensed he might try to get involved and I didn't want any distraction. This woman might get spooked into silence if I brought someone with me. I wanted her undivided attention. I parked in front of her house, checked and rechecked the address then walked to the front door. The house was pitch black except for one window that reflected the dancing light of a television. I knocked on the front door, noticing that her handwritten message from before had been removed. I stood back. Silence. I knocked again. More silence. I knocked a third time. The porch light came on. The door opened. A squinty-eyed woman stuck her head out.

"I hope I didn't disturb you, ma'am. I am..."

"Oh, don't be silly," the woman waved off with a scowl. "You didn't disturb me. I don't *sleep* at night. That's what the daytime is for. All that sunlight will kill you. No, I like to stay inside during the day, sleep, smoke cigarettes and yell at my plants. The night is what roaming around is for, aimlessly, like a goddamned vampire to socialize with the killers and rapists. The daytime is full of boring people. Dull people. People that work and make money and have full lives. Who wants that? I sure as hell don't, right?" She slammed the door in my face. Sensing the woman to be quite deranged I knocked once more to at least justify my presence before I left. The door opened.

"I just wanted to let you know that you asked me..."

"If you don't get off of my porch I'm going to call the police. Only it won't be to report a disturbance. It will be to report that I have shot a subnormal in the gut for hassling me in the dead of night. He was exhibiting mild retardation and poor posture. They will label it a mercy killing. I'll be given some type of award for eliminating an undesirable. Society will be that much sharper because of me. This is the last warning. Get the fuck out of here." The door performed a repeat slam.

"Screw this," I murmured turning to go. The door opened back up. The woman leaned her head out.

"What do you want, anyway?"

"Nothing," I said. "I am leaving you alone."

"You come all the way out here to knock on my door in the middle of the night, and now I am asking you what you want, and you are just giving up?" She seemed offended.

"You asked me to come over. You left a message with my landlady this morning. I am in the right place, yes? Are you Baron Corley's wife?" Her entire demeanor changed. She relaxed, straightened up a bit, actually appeared younger.

"Well don't just stay there like a lump in a colon. Come on in!"

I was whisked inside, and the door was shut and bolted. Then I was shot, dismembered, boiled alive, eaten and that was pretty much the end of me.

# CHAPTER 7

Okay, maybe I wasn't shot, dismembered, boiled alive and eaten, but I will say that if I had been shot, dismembered, boiled alive and eaten it might've made things a little more comfortable. We faced off for a long while in the front room, this shabby woman and I. She had a strong sense of interior design, the strongest thing being the festering odor of stale smoke, booze and a peculiar, androgynous musk. Heavy drapes blocked most of the windows. Cigarettes were put out on the linoleum floor. An iron chandelier was tastefully placed on an old chair in the corner instead of the usual, overdone, hang-it-from-the-ceiling type of thing. The woman introduced herself as Raylene Corley. Three-a-Day Ray, she said she was known as, but didn't offer any examples of the three things on any given day she might've been known for and I sure as shit wasn't going to ask. It had to be something generally destructive to produce the burned out wraith standing in front of me.

Ray obviously felt the importance of consistency and so her fashion sense mimicked her decorating sense. Her big toes protruded shamelessly through her tube socks, giving them a quality of comic neglect. She had an old pair of flannel pajama bottoms on that disappeared into a plump, pink robe. Her left hand was tucked into the pocket of her robe. Her right hand danced through her hair like a bony tarantula, hair that could've been the prototype for tumbleweed. Her lips were curled down and asymmetrical. Her eyes were heavy and had a cloudiness behind them that suggested pathos, inebriation, or cataracts. Three nervous breakdowns a day?

"Would you care for a drink?" she asked.

"I'd drink for a care."

"I've got some Scotch and some vodka."

"We are going to get along fine, Three-a-Day Ray."

53

"Just call me Ray."

"You got it."

I walked over to an antique salver sitting atop an Oriental hutch. There was a bird cage with a small yellow bird in it watching me from its perch.

"Nice bird," I said.

"His name is Jack," Ray muttered. "He mocks me with his silence."

"There might be something useful in that."

"I'm thinking about getting a dog," Ray threatened specifically towards Jack in his birdcage. "That will teach you, little bastard. Introduce some danger and then save you from it." She turned back to me. "I bet he'll appreciate me then."

I thought she made a good point as I turned back to pour myself a Scotch. I poured a healthy dose, healthy as in a lot not healthy as in a moderate amount. I was about to take a sip when I noticed Ray eyeing me. Three packs of smokes a day?

"Now now, don't offer to make me a drink," she hissed, producing from out of nowhere a glass that was about three-quarter full. "Hell, it's just my house. I obviously wouldn't care at all for a cocktail. Sobriety rules. Long Live Sobriety. Don't worry about me."

"Can I make you a drink?" I asked.

"Wow, I thought you'd never ask. You would think that you were a bartender or something." She drained the rest of her drink and then handed me the empty glass. "Vodka with plenty of ice. Use this same glass. It's seasoned with the vapors."

"Where are the ice cubes?" I asked.

"I keep them in the oven," she answered. I paused. She then looked pensive, and slowly said, "Oh no, that's right. That didn't work out so well, so I moved them to the freezer." Her right arm shot up and her thin dagger of a finger pointed the way to the other room. Sheepishly I walked through some hanging beads into the adjacent kitchen. I opened the freezer door and in my usual attitude of morbid expectation, assumed there would be an array of severed body parts—purple hands with freezer burn around the fingers, a collection of nipples all stuck together like pepperoni, a frozen eyeball—the furtive crimes of a deranged spinster. However, to my paradoxical chagrin and relief, there was only a box of baking soda and a bag of crushed ice. I packed the glass full, returned to the front room, filled it with vodka and handed it to Ray. She swiped it with firm ingratitude.

54

Three bottles of vodka a day Ray. I should've checked the refrigerator for a severed head.

"So how did you find me?" I asked, settling into a chair.

"I just know things," she said.

"Are you a medium?"

"Not quite."

"Medium rare?"

"Stupid looking is bad enough. You have to make stupid jokes too?" She put her drink down on a side table. "You don't think I'm connected in this town. You don't think that when my ex-husband comes riding back to the city that I won't know immediately. I've got friends here. He passes the city limits. I get a phone call. He stops for gas. I get a phone call. Of course I don't need a phone call to know where he is going. He is going to see that no good Zanz Alva."

"Now wait a second, Zanz is my friend."

"Don't you think I know that too?"

"What else do you know?"

"There is going to be trouble for you if you get involved with those two."

Ray sunk into her couch and lit another cigarette, content to be in such bad shape, a natural warrior against her own vice. She pulled open a photo album and settled on a page of Baron, a collage whose unifying theme was a beer in every picture, either handheld or littered in the background. She ran her fingers over this page, over younger days of her lost spouse. Her hand pressed down hard in a gesture of sad recollection of a love affair that might have worked out in an alternate lifetime, lamenting a failed destiny destroyed by the trappings of suspicion, substance abuse, wounded feelings, infidelity. The mechanical ruins of authentic emotion.

"You know they framed that poor man who supposedly attacked that girl in the carriage house behind the Dunham mansion," Raylene said. "It was Zanz's idea. Baron helped him. Zanz owes him one."

"I live in a carriage house," I said out of a reflexive response to defend the practice of renting these small bungalows, the old covered stable areas that adorn many of the restoration mansions in the city. "It is a cheap living situation. Nothing to be ashamed of."

"Who said anything about being ashamed? I am telling you what they did to that man. Framing him in death. I hear he didn't have anything to do with it. "

"I don't know much about it," I said. "I think the dead man's name was Munchik."

"Zanz doesn't tell you these things?"

"It's always a subject that is awkward to approach."

"Zanz got Baron involved. Only Zanz knows why he did it. That poor Evelyn Goss. Beaten and disfigured. Never even caught the guy. Then going and framing a deceased man. Why go through all that trouble?"

"Look Evelyn Goss, the late Munchik, that is all in the past," I said. "But something has come up recently that I am very concerned about. The reason I agreed to come over here tonight was because I wanted to ask you some things about Baron. I have been a witness to some behavior I can't make sense of. I thought you might be able to help. You help me and I can help you with whatever you want out of this."

"What do you want to know?" said Ray.

"Did Baron tend to keep odd hours during your marriage? Did he have large gaps in his weekly routine that he couldn't account for?"

"He was a bartender," Ray answered. "He always kept late hours. Due to his drinking there were plenty of gaps that he couldn't account for."

"Was he a secretive man?" I asked. "Did he have storage facilities or lock boxes that you were forbidden to see or inquire about?"

"A man has a right to his privacy," Ray responded absently.

"Did he ever develop unhealthy attachments to items of clothing or jewelry that weren't yours? Did he take long walks at night or show a peculiar interest in unsuspecting female neighbors?"

"Baron was a good man," Ray reflected. "But even good people have their imperfections."

"Like forgetting to take out the garbage or flogging you when you talked back to him?"

"He had a terrible jealous streak."

"Jealous?" I asked, getting up to refill my glass of Scotch. Jack the yellow bird was still silently at his perch, very unaffected.

"Oh yes, quite jealous." Ray nodded.

"Jealous jealous?" I repeated.

"Jealous jealous jealous."

"Can you give me an example?"

"He once beat up a man for asking me directions."

"That sounds excessive."

"The directions were how to get into my pants."

"I see. Tell me something Ray, did he ever make any admissions to you of criminal behavior?"

"A good wife isn't obliged to mention such things outside the sanctity of marriage." She blushed. "I will say that he liked women."

"Liked?"

"Loved. He was obsessed with them—as a species. All types. Tall. Short. Fat. Thin. Blonde. Brunette. White. Black. Asian. Christian. Jewish. Hindu. Rastafarian. Plain Jane. Dog ugly. It was a huge strain on our love for each other. I suspect he owned more pornography than I was aware of." Her face was a mixture of regret and wistful nostalgia. She sighed heavily and with a glassy eye, eyed my glass. "How do you like the Scotch?"

"It's good," I assured her. "But then again Scotch and I have always had a strong relationship built on mutual trust and understanding."

"It was Baron's favorite. I've had it all these years. I don't get many visitors."

"So why did you ask me to come over?"

"Because I want to get in touch with Baron. He needs me, even if he doesn't know it. He has got a bad case of wet brain."

"What is wet brain?" I asked.

"It is the terminal stages of alcoholism. Your mind turns into cream cheese. You lose your memory, motor skills. He needs me to take care of him. Do you know where he is staying?"

"Not exactly. I mean I know where he is but I can't draw you a map. It is hard to get to."

"Baron was very irresponsible," Ray confessed, and I could sense a change in her voice as she drew upon memories of the darker side of their relationship. "He only looked out for himself. That's not the way a man should act. The world needs men who care about others. Strong men. Men who are responsible and forthright. Men who provide for the important needs of loved ones. Things like food, shelter, and...*brakes*." Ray began to sob. To keep the situation calm I got up and refilled Ray's glass of vodka and set it on the side table. "Thank you," Ray said, dabbing at her eyes with her bathrobe sleeve. Three crying fits a day Ray.

"Some people just aren't right for marriage," I said.

"There is only a certain amount of abuse a person can take. But I still love him, even though I could only get so close to him and then there would be a wall guarding his inner self."

"I don't know him that well but from what Zanz has told me he is like a parent and a child. He's like a guide that lets you find your own way.

He's like an itch in an easy to reach spot. He's like a burden that tries to convince you of how light he actually is."

"Baron had no concept of what it was to be a responsible husband," Ray agreed. "He was uncontrollable, always moving at a million miles an hour, very careless. It was just a matter of time before his brakes went out. But it is not him. It is the wet brain."

"I suppose it is important to keep oneself in control," I added.

"Without brakes it's impossible to be in control," she chastised, eyeing me down the barrel of her nose to make sure I understood.

"Brakes. Yes. A grand metaphor. Quite right. Brakes."

"Baron was impossible to count on," she continued from her chair, still with the photo album in her lap. "He missed our first month anniversary by a month, our second month anniversary by two months, our third month anniversary by three months, and so on."

"So what you are saying is he only showed up for the wedding?"

"Exactly." Ray blew her nose.

"How did you meet him?" I asked.

"I just woke up one morning and he was beside me."

"It was a quick courtship?" I asked.

"No, I mean, one morning I woke up and this stranger was in my bed, naked. I screamed, ran out of the house and called the police. They came and hauled Baron off to jail and booked him for trespassing and they added sexual assault, as well as drunk and disorderly conduct. I had gone to sleep with my front door unlocked, and in the fevered grip of alcoholic's dementia he had wandered through my door, peeled off all his clothes and climbed into my bed." A sad smile crept over Ray's face. "The next day after he had posted bond he brought me flowers and apologized. Three days later I dropped the charges. Seven days later we were married. Things were okay for a little while. But then the drinking started. Then the other women. Then the drinking, other women." Ray sighed. "I did everything I could to keep him home, and for awhile it worked."

"Of course you did," I encouraged.

"But then he got loose and escaped."

"You can't say you didn't try."

"But it was only because I cared for him. I didn't want him to be so self- destructive. At the rate he was going he was apt to kill himself and I am sure he has only gotten worse. It is the wet brain. It makes you go crazy."

"Did he ever ask you to play dead in certain sexual situations?"

"What?"

"Forget it." A rush of heat stormed my body. My heart thumping like a speed bag pummeled by a prize fighter. The room drowning in gusts of furnace intensity, sweltering waves of fire. I pulled at the collar of my shirt. My mouth began to water. I felt nauseous. Tears ran down Ray's face. She rubbed at them with her frenetic right hand. Her whole left arm had not moved a muscle—shoved as it were, into the pocket of her bathrobe. She didn't notice or didn't care to notice my discomfort. "I loved Baron. But our relationship was too destructive. He caused me to lose things that I could never replace."

"Like your innocence?" I asked, wiping the running sweat from my face.

"I wish."

The air in the room was oppressive. I wasn't sure what the problem was, but I could feel myself getting ill. Something was not right. "I'm sorry," I apologized. "I don't feel well. I don't know what's wrong with me. Is it hot in here?" I gagged into the crook of my arm.

"Are you looking for sympathy?" Ray asked.

"I think I'm just looking for an answer."

"An answer to what?"

"An answer as to whether it is hot in here?" I said, trying to get hold of my cough as it rattled my ribcage.

"Baron caused me a great absence," Ray said.

"Like faith?" I asked.

"Not quite," she answered.

"God, I feel like I'm standing on the damn sun," I complained, soaked with sweat. The heat in the room was too much. Worse than that, something was very wrong with my body.

Spasms raced through my abdomen.

"Baron caused me the worst kind of pain one can possibly experience," Ray kept on.

"Like spiritual emptiness?" I asked.

"Something a little more here and now," Ray said.

"I give up," I said. Ray stood up, let the photo album drop with a thud to the ground and pulled the left sleeve of her bathrobe up to her shoulder. The arm was nothing but a nub. I continued to die in my chair.

"Does this bother you?" Ray asked me with an aggressive wave of the negative space of what used to be her left arm in my direction.

"No," I slurred.

"You look ill at ease," Ray accused.

"I don't know what's wrong with me!" I said.

"If I have to live with it for the rest of my life then you can endure it for a little while, eh?"

"It's not that. It's something else."

"What else?" Ray shouted.

"I don't know," I whimpered.

"You don't have to be so insulting!"

"It is not the arm, I swear."

"Baron!" Ray explained, slowly returning to her seat. "Like I said before, no brakes."

"Literally...no brakes?"

"It's not a goddamned metaphor," she yelled. "Does this look like a fucking figure of speech?" She waved her nub at me again. "Baron was supposed to get new brakes put on the car. Instead he drove to Biloxi and gambled all our money away. Of course he told me he got the brakes fixed, but when I went into that ditch I knew better." She came over and grabbed me with her one good arm. "You find out where he is and you come back and tell me. Bring me to him or bring him to me. If you don't, I know where to find you. You won't rest for a minute until I get what I want."

"I feel like I'm passing out," I cut in. Ray suddenly turned and looked at me, and a strange expression came over her face. Her expression of deranged wrath was replaced by a more complacent derangement—a lunacy of gross concern.

"Oh no!" Ray exclaimed. "I forgot about the Scotch."

Baron's favorite Scotch.

Three poisonings a day Ray.

My intense dry heaving interrupted all else. Eyes watering. Wretched spasms. Skin blistering and frigid at the same time. Blotches of gray everywhere. A loud horn was sounding in the distance—loud and getting louder. I stood up on two very weak, shaking legs and began to walk, but where I was going I didn't even know. I just felt I needed to move, to escape, to get out of the darkness creeping towards me. The last thing I remember seeing was the decanter filled with Baron's favorite Scotch. I was its unlucky victim. I felt betrayed by the Scotch, whatever was mixed in the Scotch. How could it have let this happen to me after all we had been through? Scotch was supposed to be salvation, not condemnation. I broke through the front door, walked across the porch and went down the three steps to the walkway and the gray was no longer blotchy patches but a tumid cloud racing for me. I went to the ground, trying to decide whether to be annoyed at death or just go with it.

# CHAPTER 8

The bleeding room fell into focus, taking its time to assign things its proper shape and contour. I could make out the white paper partitions, the medical machines, the bed next to me with an inert body lying in it. A fat-bottomed nurse was shamelessly pointing her posterior in my direction as she orally probed the man in it—a man who looked like he had been dead for weeks. Then my nose came alive. I could smell the sterility of it all. The odor of death and medication, flatulence and illness. My hearing came back. I could hear the beeps of the machines, the general commotion of the hallway, the groans of waning life, the nurse's baby talk to my malfunctioning, supine roommate. At the foot of my bed were two people. One was Zanz. The other was a doctor-type studying a clipboard. The doctor-type was in fact a doctor. He didn't seem at all surprised that I had awoken. It was as if he had done it himself—brought me out of the ether by a flick of his golfing, BMW driving, Wall Street Journal flipping hands.

"Mr. Sinclair," the doctor said grimly, "you have ten minutes to live. Confess your sins and tell us where the money is."

"What money?"

"It is always worth a try."

"Do I really have ten minutes to live?" I asked, sitting up.

"I told him to say that," Zanz waved off. "By the way, have you lost your mind? What possessed you to go to that woman's house last night? Did you know what kind of situation you were in? I don't know about you Toby. I suspect though that if we gave your family tree a good hard shake some inbreeders would definitely drop out. Mumble and drool on themselves. Crawl around and sniff each other. Great-grandpa and his trusted sister great-grandma."

I was in a hospital gown. There was a cemetery on the hill outside my hospital window. I looked down on it, feeling relieved. You knew you were screwed when you had to look up to see a cemetery. I turned my attention to the hallway outside of my room. Carts with various life saving ingredients were being wheeled back and forth. A Dr. So and So was being paged to radiology. It seemed that I had escaped death this time, which unfortunately meant I was still a bartender ripe with mild anxiety and alienation. A commotion arose in the hallway. People were being told to step aside. Somebody important must be coming. Perhaps it was the man that invented medication, or a socially concerned pop singer here to shake hands with invalids and assure us that we are "...the real heroes". However it was none of that. It was Baron. His fedora was aslant and he looked like he was going to die of breathlessness.

"Jesus," Baron exclaimed, "how does anyone find anything in this hornets' nest?" The nurse at the bed beside me scowled at him. The dead man under her awoke. He approached me. "You are alive!"

"No thanks to his own idiotic scheming," Zanz said.

"If you weren't in such a fragile condition I'd box your ears," Baron snapped. "You are taking your life into your own hands when you spend time with any of my ex-wives."

"I am sorry. I thought I was doing the right thing. She told me I was in trouble."

"You were in trouble the moment you set foot in her house." Baron began pacing and chewing on his thumb. "This means she knows I am in town. She could ruin everything. Did you tell her where I was?" He came over and shook me by the gown, tearing it down the middle. "Did you?"

"No. Zanz's cabin is hard to get to. Dirt roads with no names, just some natural landmarks. I couldn't tell her even if I wanted to."

"What did you talk about? Tell me everything."

"Mostly talked about you. She said she misses you. Wants to be the one to take care of you. She says you aren't in control of yourself. She says your mind is shot." Baron paused and took this in. His eyes darted around the room and went a bit blank.

"I once swallowed a penny to find out how long it takes to get from sucker to pucker, if you know what I mean. The penny was never found."

After admitting this Baron studied the doctor for any expertise he might be able to apply. None was forthcoming. I fell back on the bed. The doctor was still glancing at the medical chart. I turned to him in the hopes that he would shed some light as to what had happened to me. He sensed this and to illustrate his importance he let the silence linger for a few moments.

"It seems," he eventually gave, "that you had a significant amount of the drug Disulfiram in your system, Mr. Sinclair." He dropped the pages on the clipboard and looked up at me. "Do you happen to take any type of alcohol aversion therapy?" The doctor let the laughter subside before he continued. "Disulfiram is a drug that is given to clinical alcoholics as a deterrent to drinking. If a person ingests this drug and then drinks alcohol they will get very ill. Too much of it is absolutely deadly."

"How was I rescued?" I asked them.

"It was nothing short of a miracle," Zanz broke in. "First, it is written in the *Hagakure* that the proper decision is best made within seven or so breaths. Acting in such a way will bring efficient and decisive closure to most situations, before the paralysis of indecision seeps into the bones, freezing them up while the window of opportunity seals itself off. Extended from this type of reasoning is the idea that the crucial matters of one's life are but a couple of whip cracks among the vast horizon of reflection and projection, and the individual who recognizes and seizes these opportunities will surely elevate to a great and powerful man."

"Get on with it," I said.

"I just happened to be coming out of the house up the block when you stumbled off her porch. Say what you will about that neighborhood but it is always a good place to score some smoke when the hash pipe dries up. I was heading up the street with a quarter bag of dank-dank-dank when I noticed the commotion. I couldn't believe my eyes when I saw you, but then this demonic woman was chasing after you. You went to the ground. In a split second I was at your side. We began to fight over your limp corpse. Let me tell you for a one-armed woman she has got some strength. I wrestled her into the house and barricaded her into a closet with her prosthetic arm that just happened to be sitting on a nearby table, relishing the irony." Zanz leaned back with a smile. "The recipe for escaping disaster is simple," he added. "Take one part imagination, two parts diversion, fill with favorable opportunity. Add just a splash of bravado for color and garnish with a prosthetic arm." Everybody in the room agreed that the recipe was sound. Only the doctor remained cool, fixing his hair in the reflection of the window.

"How did you use a prosthetic arm to secure a closet door?" I asked.

"There there, Toby," Zanz said, patting my leg. "You've been through a lot. It is time to rest."

"And another thing," I continued, turning to Baron. "What did you do to that woman? You ruined her life when you married her."

"Listen Toby, when you are facing criminal trespassing charges, you do what you have to do."

"You caused her to lose an arm! An arm? Most men cause a woman to lose faith. Not an actual body part!"

"That was not my fault," he denied. "Her car hydroplaned off that embankment fair and square."

"I kinda liked her," I admitted. "I don't think she tried to poison me on purpose. In a way it is your fault Baron. If she hadn't hated you so much I'd be fine."

"She loved me," Baron said. "That kind of powerful love is the only thing that could breed such serious hate." He turned to the doctor. "What do you think doc? Are you a psychology man?"

"Not when it comes to women."

"I like you, friend. What's your name?"

"You can call me Doctor Eddie."

"Wait a second. Eddie Fernwitz?"

The doctor stared at Baron for a moment, surprised, as he tried to figure out what part of his past would allow for this drunken monstrosity to lumber through it. "Yes."

"Shit man, it is me, Baron Corley. Bertha's ex-husband."

"Well I'll be damned," Doctor Eddie said tossing the clipboard he had been studying onto my bed where it bounced off my knee. He gave Baron a smile and a hug as they exchanged the usual pleasantries about how fast time goes by, how small the world is, how interesting coincidence can be. I was ripe with malaise, exhaustion and a sudden throbbing in my knee so I didn't pay much attention to the reunion. Instead I considered the fact that Baron had an ex-wife named Bertha. I pictured the ruddy expansive girth of this woman based on her name, along with her medical issues, based on her name. Rheumatoid arthritis, sciatica, diabetes, the fact that she hadn't seen her feet in years. I thought about her ill-temper and chronic cough, again based on her name. Women weren't named Bertha anymore. Bertha was the name given to torpedoes, elephant guns, warships and battle tanks. I took all of this into consideration imagining Bertha, and boy was she a beauty.

"Whatever happened to Bertha?" Doctor Eddie asked.

"Disappeared," said Baron. "Mysterious circumstances."

"She was always one of those, wasn't she?"

With the newfound familiarity Doctor Eddie assured us that if we ever needed medical attention, a bogus doctor's note or a prescription we should come and see him. Baron introduced Zanz and I as his successors, noting that the younger generation of today will need two to live up to one of his generation. Zanz pointed out that with Baron's reputation it would take two of us just to live him down. Doctor Eddie heartily agreed but did it in such a way that suggested we were all fucking idiots for not holding an advanced medical degree. Some nuance in the doctor's laugh convinced me of this. Perhaps, though, I had misinterpreted the doctor's demeanor due to my sensitivity of the medical profession in general, since on some level I was supposed to be there, had told Uncle Jimmy, my closest living relative that I *was* there—that I had been studying medicine for years, and now my proximity to an actual doctor had caused my poorly crafted fiction to cower in naked shame. I was in the bed. I was sick and dependent. Doctor Eddie was powerful. He understood and manipulated life. He knew complex biochemical reactions like Krebs cycle and genetic recombination. He could explain about the different types of cholesterol, or why examination rooms are always so chilly. He represented everything that I had fought so hard to fabricate and avoid. He was the reprehensible reminder of my failure. At about twenty years my senior he was better looking and had more hair.

I was upsetting myself, so I turned my attention away from Baron, Doctor Eddie and Zanz and mused at the bigger ramifications of my current situation. I could, I suppose, pick and choose from a string of possibilities as to exactly what the night before had meant for me, considering I had landed in the hospital. If there were indeed supernatural forces at hand, then while I had been sorely mistreated by them it still gave me a small sense of comfort to know that there was something out there pulling the strings, some kind of overriding direction, an explanation outside of normal chance and circumstance. Of course the other explanation was that I was the unlucky victim of chaos whose interest only lies in perpetuating random, inexplicable phenomena.

I thought about Ray. I wanted to go back and make sure she was alright, hoping that Zanz hadn't roughed her up too much and then realizing that would be impossible given the shape she was in. I had taken a shine to the woman. I remembered her warning, that I would be in trouble for hanging out with these two. Was she right? Was this the start of a calculated downhill slide, the eventual diffusion outward of atoms and molecules that would doom me to the ravages of an empty universe?

One thing was for certain, however. Alcohol Aversion Therapy is for the birds. I vowed never to come within a mile of Disulfiram ever again. I could breathe relief, however, in knowing that type of stuff was for alcoholics, and not dipsophiles like myself.

It was mid-afternoon by the time I was discharged. Zanz, Baron and I were walking down the steps outside the hospital. I heard Zanz ask Baron how things were going for him at the cabin. Baron said that it was a big mess but that he always cleaned up his messes. He said he had to hurry up and get back because she was tied up in the basement and the last thing he wanted was for her to get loose and run screaming through the woods to another cabin. There would definitely be a lot of explaining to do if that happened. I slowed my pace up, let them pass me. In the daylight it was evident that Baron had scratch marks around his neck and face. Zanz told Baron to wait. He would go and fetch the Fleetwood Brougham for the old man. I stood out on the curb with Baron, still feeling ill from the poison, or feeling ill from Baron, not quite sure of the source of nausea.

"If that crazy woman contacts you again you better consult with me first," Baron warned.

"How do I get in touch with you? You are out in the middle of nowhere."

"You don't. That is why I am out at the cabin. I can't risk anybody finding me. Something happens you tell Zanz. He'll know what to do. There are times when the weight of a problem can only be seen clearly after the fact. Now I can clearly see that I am in a delicate situation. In fact there are a couple of delicate situations, each ready to shatter against each other if I'm not as careful as possible. That's why I'm staying out of sight. You tell Zanz if anybody asks about me. Don't do anything else."

"When we were coming out of the hospital just now I overheard you say something about a woman tied up in the basement?"

Baron lowered his eyes.

"If this is all going to work out then isolation is essential," he said. "I'm able to work in absolute secrecy while keeping an eye out for undesirables." He lit a cigarette. There was an air of desperation about him. He was skittish, harboring an obvious burden, yet still maintaining a flippant confidence. His mouth tugged at his cigarette. An old woman wearing a surgical mask and rubber gloves shuffled past us toward the hospital. I wondered if she knew something that I didn't know. "At night out in the woods you can listen to the coyotes," Baron spoke hollowly. "Their song comes through the darkness. A primitive call. Beautiful and dangerous. Sometimes I call back, knowing somehow that we understand each other's nature."

"So is there a woman out there with you?"

"I'm completely alone," he answered. "In a sense I'm not understood and this makes for some of the worst loneliness I've ever felt."

"But to be understood, or misunderstood for that matter, you must be with somebody else," I said.

"In a sense yes, and in a sense no," he argued.

"That makes no sense."

"Sometimes you have to keep a woman. You see. For their own good. If you love them sometimes you have to make them love you. If it is for their own good."

"So you have a woman at the cabin?"

"Let's leave it at that."

"Who is she?"

"A woman I can't live without. Let's leave it at that."

"What makes you think you can just hold a woman against her will?"

"She doesn't know what is good for her. I do. Let's leave it at that."

"But what the..."

"You are not leaving it at that! When the time comes you may have occasion to meet her. But not until the time is right. Once again I will try to leave it at that."

"Will I be able to shake hands with her or will I just be carrying her in a trunk to the middle of the woods?"

"Would you stop being so morbid?" he yelled. "I'm going to slaughter her. Is that what you want to hear? I'm going to torture her until she can't take it and then I'm going to torture her some more and then I'll kill her. I'll find another one just like her and do the same thing. It is the only way I can achieve orgasm. Is that what you want to hear? I'm a normal man with strange fantasies that are impossible to ignore. I dream of death. I like to watch the dying eyes, knowing my face is the last thing they will see. It is the release of the power struggle. Is this what you want to hear?"

The Fleetwood Brougham roared up next to us, followed by a blue mist of whatever cancerous vapors the defective car was spewing out. Cursing and grumbling Baron got into his car and took off.

"I don't want him around me anymore," I told Zanz. "Whatever he is up to I don't want to be a part of it."

"Remember you said that the next time some crazy lady invites you to come romping in her house in the dead of the night."

By the time I got back to my small carriage house apartment I was ready to sleep for days on end. I had dropped Zanz off at his carriage house on the way home, it being a couple of miles up the road from mine. This was a community of carriage house living, a whole subculture dwelling, a network of one-bedroom apartments behind the grandeur of large homes. A secret society. A hidden treasure behind the empty splendor of reconstruction mansions. That was why there was such outrage when Evelyn Goss was attacked in her carriage house. It could have been any of us, it seemed. Zanz was particularly affected. He swore he would find the person responsible. Weeks later a man named Munchik was dead. His fingerprints were found in Evelyn's apartment. The case remained open, however it was generally agreed that the man responsible had gotten his divine justice.

Zanz and I considered living together but decided against it due to the idea of *conditioned response*, which put simply, is a response to indirect stimuli. The most famous example is, of course, Pavlov's dogs, who would salivate when hearing a bell, because they associated the bell with food. When I saw Zanz I began to crave a drink. Therein lies the connection. It was bad enough at work with his deathly peach brandy, but in order to keep ourselves from drinking around the clock it became necessary to effect a calculated amount of separation so we didn't succumb to an early death from total liver failure.

We decided to live separately.

# CHAPTER 9

A popular question posed to bartenders is, "What's the strangest, weirdest, most fucked up thing you've ever seen?" The question had been posed to me yet again. I was back at work. I recounted the story to kill some time.

"It was a normal day," I began. "A woman had arrived at the bar early on in the shift. She was a normal woman but you could tell there was something wrong. She was twitchy. She had a pile of mail with her that she proceeded to sort through. The letters were shaking in her hand. She ordered a glass of wine and because people will confide almost anything to a bartender, she admitted to me that she had been having a rough week."

"How come?"

"The reason, of course," I continued, "is that she had been having an affair with her best friend's husband, and through feelings of extraordinary guilt had ended the affair about a week prior. The husband did not take the news very well. He pleaded and begged for her to reconsider but she refused him. Well unfortunately her best friend had called her a couple of days before, hysterical. Apparently the husband had hanged himself in the family garage."

"Poor son of a bitch," was the collective sentiment.

"That's not all, though," I said. "He had cut his dick off before he hanged himself, or maybe he had just cut his dick off, realized how stupid that was and then decided to hang himself because, well, I guess you are in kind of a difficult situation at that point. There is always a lot of explaining to do when you cut your dick off. I told the woman that it was a shame but the man was obviously disturbed. I walked off to continue setting up, leaving the woman with her mail. About a minute later here comes this deafening shriek, bloodcurdling and full of terror. The woman runs out of the restaurant screaming. I go over to her pile of mail and I see a padded manila envelope. I looked inside, carefully, mind you."

"What was in it?"

"Let's just say that our suicide made Van Gogh look like a gutless wonder." My customers were dumbfounded. The men hunched over as if to protect themselves from a similar fate.

"No shit."

"A package in the package."

"Was it really the man's...thing?"

"I didn't scrutinize it too carefully," I said. "I think it reminded me of a thumb with blood on it. There was also a blood-spattered note in the bag. It read 'Something to Remember Me By.'"

"So what did you do?"

"Nothing. Called the cops. It took several years for the jokes to wear off about leaving a tip."

"Did that really happen?"

"Sure as air, fire and water. Legend has it that the ghost of that severed forelimb still haunts this very bar." The customers all searched the rafters nervously. I took an order for a vodka and tonic, accidentally put soda in it and hoped nobody would know the difference.

Zanz, meanwhile, was busy at the other end of the bar telling a group of eager listeners about his part in the pre-dawn raid of Barker Ranch that helped capture Charles Manson in 1969. And to think Zanz did all that when he was eighty-four years old. He had already done a few shots of Truth which always helped give his embellishments a brilliant luster. Zanz was flipping his billy club in his hand and showing different striking motions. He was demonstrating how he had taken out 'Tex' Watson, a Manson disciple, after he had mouthed off. The fact that this particular Manson disciple had not been at the ranch with Manson hardly mattered to Zanz, who was not going to let mere facts get in the way of a decent fabrication.

It was about this time that Skid Row Paul came in and sat down. He looked miserable and broken, even for him. He had stopped by to collect on the beer I had promised him the other night. A couple of customers slid away from him, sensing his personal space somewhat toxic and distancing themselves to save their own.

"Hey Paul. What's up?"

"Hangover," Paul whimpered, pounding his head on the bar. "I've been crying like a baby all day and I don't even know why. I hate everything. Life sucks and everything is ugly. You are ugly and she is ugly and he is ugly and I am ugly. The roses and the babies and the puppies and the rainbows, ugly, ugly, ugly, ugly. This whole place is a cesspool and we would all be better off if the Earth swallowed us up and shit us into Hell."

"Paul you know I can't have you in here acting miserable like this," I said. "You are going to destroy the atmosphere of happy abandon that these paying customers are clinging to."

"Then give me a drink so I can pull myself from my misery."

"Here is a beer. I'll go fetch some of Zanz's peach brandy."

"If you are pouring I am drinking."

I returned and poured him a shot of Truth. He took it and the color came back into his cheeks. I poured him another and the life came back into his face. I poured him another and the shape came back into his spine. I poured him another and the bullshit came back out of his mouth.

"Toby do you know what I like about you?"

"What?"

"Not much so listen up."

"I am all ears."

"As a man of the street I have certain advantages when it comes to information and with information comes opportunity. Now you know that when I have information relevant to you that I let you in on it right away. What has to happen now is the system has to work in the opposite direction. If everybody wants information all the time then the balance is thrown off. So I need information to keep your credit for receiving information in check."

"What do you want to know?"

"That shit heel you were with the other night. Baron, yes? Corley, right? I want to know what he is in town for?"

"Why?"

"I have my reasons. He is a man people might be interested in. Like I said with information comes opportunity."

"Why don't you ask Zanz. I am sworn to secrecy."

"No, you are not," Paul said. "Zanz is sworn to secrecy. You are involved but you aren't committed. You told me his name. Baron Corley. As soon as you say the name I start hearing things. I have a feeling Zanz is protecting him for some reason. I'm thinking it has something to do with Evelyn Goss. I think her assailant might still be out there, or maybe he is back in town or maybe he has been here the whole time." Zanz walked over to us and Paul got tight lipped.

"Hey Paul."

"Zanz!" Paul exclaimed. "How is the night going?"

"Not the dumbest crowd I'll ever see, although I have been accused of being too optimistic. No, just the normal--the oily people, the quiet people, the cheapskates, the generous, the downtrodden, the whiners, the lobotomized, the overly happy, the overly sad, the obnoxious, the desperate, the searchers. People who find value in the meaningless. All of us."

"Has the Buddha become jaded?" Paul asked.

"Nonsense," Zanz waved off. "In the purest sense this job is an exercise in Zen movement and I am Zanz the Zenist. It takes a special skill, a series of efficient movements that make it possible for one man to tend to the whim of hundreds. Handy with the Brandy. Making the pay with the Dubonnet. Grabba the Grappa."

"He is talking big," I said.

"The secret is calm composure," Zanz continued, dropping into a fighting stance. "Focus. The hands go for the bottles even before the mind instructs them. The true bar guru operates under the current of consciousness and therefore exudes ease and finesse. Grace and style. Truly Gods among men."

"Of course," I countered, "that is until we are caught by the inevitability of our own excess. But by that time hopefully the bar crowd is too drunk to care."

A few girls came up to the bar to smoke. Zanz paused to light each cigarette, except for the last girl, who had to be told that the cigarette was in her mouth the wrong way. She took it out, pondered it for a minute and then stuck the filter end in her mouth, still wondering if she had made the correct adjustment. I always reveled in being able to witness the lost elegance of the totally wasted—manifest in things like backwards cigarettes, skirts tucked into panty hose, or a straight line plummet to the floor after misjudging the distance of one's ass from the bar stool. Small perks with large entertainment value.

"Zanz, I hear you got a friend in town," Paul said.

"What did you hear?" Zanz answered, remaining cool.

"I heard him with my own eyes. Saw him with my own nose. Smelled him with my own ears."

"Auditory-Ocular-Olfactoryism. By the way when is the last time you showered?"

"Is he a good friend?" Paul said. "This friend of yours. A real good friend? A help-you-break-the-law kind of friend?"

"Paul I don't have any other kind of friend."

"Is this at all related to Evelyn and the Dunham carriage house?"

"That is too far gone to have any relevance to anything."

We drank more of Zanz's peach brandy.

"Skid Row Paul, there is news that is reported and news that is created," Zanz said. "I think you are trying to create something because you can't figure out the nothing. The nothing that concerns you anyway."

"I'm a busybody," Paul said. "Everything concerns me."

"The recipe is simple," Zanz said. "You take a glass, fill it with ice and add two parts curiosity, one part too much free time, top with angst and shake vigorously. No garnish. The absence of it is a perfect metaphor."

"I just don't want to be left out of the action," Skid Row Paul shrugged. Zanz walked away. Paul seized the opportunity, leaned in and whispered, "so now are you going to tell me what you guys were up to the other night?"

I poured him a shot and poured one for myself. After we drank I told him about the woods and the steamer trunk. With a certain dramatic flare I told him about the duct tape with the woman's hair I found in the back of the Fleetwood Brougham and I told him about Baron's hysterical flight from a car full of old people. I told him about the hikers and I told him about burying the trunk. I left out the part when I jumped into the river and almost drowned. Skid Row Paul looked like he was ready to leap out of his own filth by the time I was done. I gave him another dose of the peach brandy, somewhat relieved to have unloaded the burden of this strange secret to somebody.

"Let me get back to you on all this," he said. "I think there is an opportunity here. I just have to find it. I don't know what this Baron Corley has over Zanz but it is something serious. I have a feeling that Munchik was framed."

"Munchik is dead. What does it matter?"

"It might not matter to Munchik but it will matter to Baron. A matter that could involve money."

I went back to the other side of the bar and dropped the bottle of Truth near Zanz, knowing that he got skittish when it was out of his reach for too long. I saw the girl almost immediately as she walked to the bar and sat down. She was wearing a tank top and jeans, looking both casual and provocative, but there was something more to her, an unnameable gravity tugging at the very core of my gender. I lapsed into a hopeful daydream, and as with any good hopeful daydream things went into slow motion—black and white, even, like that Alain Resnais movie. The backdrop of the establishment morphed into a classical mix of gauche excess. White marble. Noble columns. Vaulted ceiling. The barflies and drunkards morphed into gentile women of high society, captains of industry. A big band played lazy ballads while men in tuxedos and women in flapper frocks slid easily and gracefully around the dance floor. The luminous darling that had caused my hallucination sat at the bar in a thin black evening dress, no longer casual, hair cascading in ripples around delicate shoulders, the elegant sweep of a graceful swan-like neck, high cheek bones, dark eyes, elbow length gloves, smoking with a French cigarette holder of course, the gray smoke itself cutting across her silhouette, disappearing dreamily. She turns toward me, and although there is an absence of color, I can still feel her rich red lips, smell her roses and tobacco, even as she beckons me over to her. I get up, powerless to do otherwise. I am beside her. She motions for me to lean in, and whispers, and even then I can feel the lips on the small hairs of my ear, sweet breath, as she speaks of Oscar Wilde, William Thackeray, Prosper Merimee, with glib remarks pertaining to topics of stylized vacancy. She takes my hand in hers, moving it towards her, laying it just below her clavicle to feel the pulse, the pulse that matches mine perfectly…"

"Toby, I'm talking to you!" Zanz blasted. I popped out of my reverie. I was back at work.

"What were you saying?"

"Did you ever notice," he said, "that when a customer explains to us some verbal disagreement they had in the recent past, they always fill in the other person's response with 'duh duh duhs, blah blah blahs, rah rah rahs,' and so on, but when the person explaining the argument fills in their own retorts it is always the smartest, sharpest, most sensible answer possible? There is a whole world of anonymous debaters out there losing arguments with gibberish. I'm not sure what to make of it but it is one of those realizations that demands further contemplation. What is wrong with you?"

"I am very much taken by that girl at the end of the bar," I admitted. Zanz craned his neck to see and then turned on me with disappointment in his eyes.

"You go after a girl like that and you are stoking the furnace of your own private hell."

"But she's beautiful," I said.

"That kind of beauty is a liability," Zanz argued.

"You have to admit that she is stunning," I insisted.

"I'm admitting nothing."

"She's beautiful, damn it."

"No she's not. Not when you take the depravity into consideration."

"High cheekbones, piercing eyes, perfect symmetry."

"She appears scaly, red, and she's got a set of horns protruding from her forehead."

"Her skin like the untouched desert sand under a full moon Persian sky. Her hair dipped in the redness of the setting sun on the horizon."

"She's blessed with the natural talent of stealing a man's soul. It is plainly evident."

"Look at the way she defies gravity."

"Obviously no attention span."

"...large, red lips..."

"..the color of sin!"

"An angel on Earth!"

"A devil in the city," he sighed. "What you need are girls like the ones over on this side." He motioned to the other end of the bar. "Subtle. Sturdy. Women who feel they have to win the orgasm."

I left Zanz and returned to my side of the bar. With nerves of steel I approached my new customer and asked if she would like anything to drink, noting that Skid Row Paul had already switched his bar seat to be next to her. She glanced at him, gave a small wrinkle of a smile and turned away. That was all Paul needed.

"In the DNA of love I am adenine and you are thymine," he said, unleashing his game. "A perfect match."

"You are a charmer, aren't you," she replied absently.

"Darn," Paul said. "You aren't supposed to realize I'm a charmer because then you are going to think I lack sincerity. I'm trying to be sincere when I'm really only charming. If you see through the sincerity then I am no longer charming but a wolf and a scoundrel and oh my God you are wearing striped socks and I am incredibly turned on by that and if that isn't sincere then I don't know what is."

"These are my lucky socks," she said, staring right at me. I nodded, unable because of my position behind the bar to see anything lower than her midriff, taking it for granted that she was wearing striped socks and indeed they were her lucky ones.

"How high do they go under your jeans?" Paul asked. "Are they ankle length? Mid calf? Thigh high, please for God's sake. If you tell me they go all the way up to your thighs I will never ask the Lord above for anything ever again."

"Paul, you are scaring her," I said.

"She is scaring me. The potential length of her striped socks has my angina all worked up."

"What is it like to have one of those?"

"I said *angina*."

"What if I told you I had the animal sensibilities of a female praying mantis?" she said. "I could bite your head off."

"I promise I will continue the death thrusting," Paul said. "Do we have a deal?"

I got her a drink. At this distance the whole of the experience that was her was irresistibly suffocating. It was a privilege to be caught in the radius of her perfume. It was an honor for her attention. Her handshake was an accolade. Every part of her was its own reward. I hesitated to assign her any obvious or trite descriptions, deciding not to go on about the interplay of roundness and leanness, the graceful cleft of this or that, the playful and inconspicuous freckles—each a tiny constellation of wonder spread across her skin. She was a being of endless possibility—heal the sick, raise the dead, feed the hungry—you name it.

"Are you drinking tonight?" she asked.

"Alas, yes," I said. "I'm not ready to begin the long, daunting process of sobering up, like the mountaineer laments the inevitable descent from his perch atop the snowy peak, where he stands at the foot of heaven, filled with the natural mystic. The view from here is exhilarating."

"My name is Star," she introduced.

"Parents hippies?" Paul asked.

"Worked at a planetarium. I'm in Atlanta seven years now. Recently divorced. I sold medical supplies and I hated it. Now I work for a hotel."

"Have you ever found a dead body in a room?" I asked.

"Toby, don't be rude!" Paul chastised.

"No. But I wouldn't mind it," Star shrugged. "The hotel is required to give me the rest of the day off as part of a grievance package. Nothing could brighten my day like finding a corpse hanging from a shower head. I see those vacant eyes staring at me and I'd only be able to think of one thing...quittin' time."

"You are like the first line of law enforcement," I remarked. "Discovery is a crucial part of the trade."

"Let us get back to the socks if we could," Skid Row Paul suggested.

"What if I told you I am a very dominant person in bed?" Star pointedly told Paul.

"I am all for it."

"You have to let me do whatever I want."

"Sure."

"What a relief. Some men are so uptight about penetration. Don't worry. I'll be gentle."

"Toby," said Skid Row Paul, his face both pleasant and hysterical, "I just remembered I have a very important meeting with a very important person to discuss very important things."

"I think he or she is waiting for you at that other place that is not here," I said.

"Very good." Skid Row Paul got up and left.

"That was well done," I said, turning to Star.

"What is your name?" she said.

"Toby."

"Toby I'm going to ask you a question but don't feel you have to say yes."

"Okay."

"Do you want to see the Poor Man's Porno Show?"

"Why not?"

"Get me a spoon and some coffee grounds." I got her what she needed, legitimately curious. "Okay." She took a pinch of coffee grinds and stuck it in the fleshy crack where the base of her thumb met the base of her index finger. Then she took the spoon and held it in front of it. "Now look at the image reflected in the outside of the spoon," she said, tilting the convex side of the spoon back and forth between the thumb and forefinger. Sure enough, the reflection looked like a woman's spread legs moving up and down, the coffee grinds providing the perfect replica of a big tuft of dark pubic hair.

"Now I have seen everything."

"Why don't you come meet me across the street for a drink when you get out of work?" she asked.

"Okay."

"Well then you ain't seen nothing yet."

All the people on Zanz's side of the bar were as drunk as an Irish wedding, Zanz included. The bottle of peach brandy was empty. Zanz was standing on top of the bar giving an impromptu speech of Shakespearean proportions, or so it felt to him, I'm sure. The Truth was pumping through his veins. "If I've said it once I've said it a thousand times, that to live without purpose is not to live. If there is one thing that I have learned, in my seventy-eight years on this planet, is that to live without a shining beacon pointed at the glittering diamond of all your aspirations, desires, and loves is to meander through the sewers of existence while filthy, diseased creatures gnaw at your soul."

"Yes!" said the crowd.

"Passion is the fuel that ignites the dying embers of sterile intelligence. You look for things to live by… things to cling to. Mantras. Religion. Philosophy. The vicious cycle of brooding self-analysis. You break things down and deconstruct them. What's wrong with your life? Is this chaotic event heaped upon chaotic event or is life a preordained set of circumstances leading us to some higher and loftier purpose? Well folks you can take your chaos and shove it."

"Yes!" the crowd agreed.

"The more you slice and dice up your existence, trying to find that seed of truth, the further you will be removing yourself from it. Don't waste your time on analysis of a tiny drop of water. You need to swim in the ocean of life, rocking gently on the waves, feeling the saltiness on your lips, giving yourself up to the hypnotic dance of the ocean gently swelling and then falling away. Sometimes it rages violently, and sometimes it is placid like a photo. But I assure you that these variations are the dynamics that serve to increase your capacity for happiness. Do not waste time on a few seconds, on a little minutiae, but ride on the vast rise and fall of time, in which you are given the brief opportunity to enjoy its magnificence."

"That sounds like a metaphor for sex," somebody remarked.

Zanz made a wry face and jumped down from the bar. "Unfortunately I have a congenital affliction that erodes my capacity for metaphor, simile, analogy, and abstract connections—although this same affliction allows me to hold an erection for hours. Apparently it has something to do with uneven blood distribution."

"Here's to uneven blood distribution!" somebody shouted.

"Cheers."

"Do you do anything besides this?" a girl asked Zanz.

"I'm a self-employed dipsophile," he replied.
"Are you hiring?"

℘

There is a great source of pride that people have in being the last customer—like the survivor of a tontine, ready to reap the benefits that the others had forfeited by dropping off prematurely, gloating in the knowledge that they have bested all the other patrons in stamina, drinking prowess and attrition. So it was that Skid Row Paul had won the prestigious if not precarious honor this particular night, which was even more impressive considering he had no money to spend and yet had continued drinking all night long. His was a complex technique of bribery, bartering and plain old begging, which, by the end of the night had rewarded him with the removal of all the hatred and misery that he had heaped upon me when he had first shown up.

"I love you guys," Skid Row Paul said, slobbering on himself. "I love everybody. Everybody in the whole world is beautiful. The world is beautiful. You guys are the best. Life is the best. This world is the best. I'm so glad to be here, with you guys, my best friends, in this life, with you guys, my friends. If anybody tries to mess with you guys, you just let Paul know. I'll kill them. I'll kill everybody. Because I love you guys. I love everybody. How much you ask? Well I'm glad you did. Take everybody in the world….put 'em together…that's how much I love you guys."

Zanz and a group who wanted to continue drinking were making plans for the rest of the night. They were working out the logistics of a system called 'caravanning'. This was the practice of figuring who was the least drunk of the crowd and then nominating that person to drive the car at the head of the line of cars driven by the rest of the crowd. So instead of the least drunk person driving everybody home they would all be driving with the least drunk person in the lead, relying on a creative technicality. The car in front drives. The rest of them *follow*.

I told Zanz that I was cutting out early. Sensing my motive he waved me off and warned me that I was taking my life into my hands by going to meet Star. I told him to go fuck himself and that a death of this kind was well worth it. I walked across the street, in proud possession of a powerful intoxication. All things conspiring to lift me from my normal gloom. She was sitting at a table, smiled and waved me over. She was curvy in all the right places, revealed in all the right places, tucked away in all

79

the right places. Her expertise in her own concealment and exposure was thrilling.

"You made it."

I got a round of beers. Star asked me about myself. I told her that I would be as vague as possible to make it easy for us to be compatible. I considered myself warm, clever, outgoing but not too much... rational, genuine, caring. I had paradoxical qualities of structured spontaneity. I was occasionally dependable and completely convinced I would always be uncertain. I enjoyed "...things...". I tended to be passionate about "favorable circumstance". I also took pleasure in the accumulation of "personal satisfaction". Star said that we were made for each other, at least for tonight, which in a very practical way, is all anybody ever has anyway.

"I moved down to Atlanta originally to look after my younger sister," she said. "Funny where life takes you. Then I met my husband, or my ex-husband. I keep referring to him as my husband when I shouldn't. Husband is easier to say than ex-husband."

"It is one syllable but it seems like so much more," I said.

"Where was I?"

"Funny where life takes you," I said.

"Oh yes. It is funny where life takes you, except when it takes you to my ex-husband. There is nothing funny about that."

"You seem to be getting used to the prefix."

"I am a fast learner," she said. "But back to the reason I came down here. My sister. Wild as wild can be. Smoked, drank, snorted, injected. If there is another way to ingest she would've found it. Get this, her middle name is Chastity but she turned out to be a real whore."

"Foul irony," I said, "have you no conscience?"

"Do you want to know what my middle name is?" asked Star.

"Let me guess, it is Whore but you are pure as a newborn's tear drops."

"I finally got her some help," said Star. "Do you want to hear the reason she said she abused herself for so long? She said she was afraid to go to bed. She was afraid to give up on the night. She could never bring herself to climb into bed and wait for sleep. This was terrifying for her. She had to dope herself up, or stay out for as long as possible, or do whatever until sleep had overtaken her. She was desperate to outlast her awareness." Star sat back and took a pull off her beer. "Family can be a bit loony, can't they?"

"I have an uncle who supports your theory," I said. "Your sister will be alright. Hopefully she will emerge as a woman of strength and integrity who develops a deep disdain for frightened hypocrites, quick to condemn what they secretly desire. Perhaps the relaxed morality of her past will strengthen her character, saving her from future peril. I don't trust anybody who hasn't gone crazy at least once. I also don't condemn the butterfly for once being a caterpillar."

"You have a good outlook."

"If you only have one thing you better make it good," I said.

"Now I just have to deal with my husband."

"You relapsed," I pointed out.

"Maybe that is another reason I leave the 'ex' out. He still thinks we're married. He stalks me. Everywhere I turn he is there. Flattering on one hand. Ridiculous on another. I'm going to have to dress up like a clown to scare him off."

"What do you mean?"

"He has a thing."

"A thing?"

"A clown thing. Long story. Doesn't matter."

"I guess there is something wrong with everybody if you look hard enough."

She chuckled to herself, sipped her drink, crossed her legs so that her foot brushed mine and then gave me a warm gaze from across the table. She was crystallizing before my eyes, to borrow an idea from Stendahl. Her voice was getting softer and sultrier, her face was gaining in aesthetic momentum, soaking in hot radiance, a superconductor of the Godhead—soft, plentiful, coy, dirty. Skid Row Paul's musing about the length of her socks was starting to get to me. I found myself trying to guess.

"Toby," she asked, "what is it you want more than anything else in the world?"

I sensed a trap. Instinct warned me that the question had been posed only so Star would have a chance to give her own fanciful answer. I decided to answer anyway. I thought carefully. What was it that I wanted? I would usually say 'nothing', but that was impossible, wasn't it? Everybody wanted something. Hell it could be love, enlightenment, money, wicker furniture that doesn't make that awful wicker furniture wheezing sound when you sit in it—whatever. I guess I could say I wanted it all, but that was just as much of a cop-out as saying I wanted nothing. True, I wanted out of my current lifestyle, out of my current job as a bartender, but that was more of what I didn't want. I had no alternative. Perhaps, more than anything I just wanted to know that everything works out in the end. I decided that was a good enough answer. I looked at her deeply, the words came out very carefully. I believed in those words, wanted to give them gravity, a delving depth, a sacred place in the moment.

"I guess more than anything I…"

"Do you want to know what I want?"

"I knew you were going to do that."

"Then why did you try to answer?"

"What I was going to say was more than anything else in the world I wanted to know what you want."

"For you to walk me to my apartment."

"If I must."


Statistically women serial killers are a rare breed. Most tend to be older than Star, have either a very poor or a very rich background--either extreme, a perfect environment for the development of an alienated sociopath. Most use drugs habitually. Common forms of homicide for female killers are poisoning or smothering, although a woman like Aileen Wuornos or Mary Ann Cotton just blew the brains out of their victims with a gun. Elizabeth Bathory, the Hungarian Countess, would drain her victims of their blood for use in her beauty rituals. I was pondering all this because during our walk Star had told me that she wanted to do something crazy and that was why she was with me. I started to think this whole thing was a setup. She was too beautiful for a guy like me. What if her husband or boyfriend was waiting at her apartment to knock me over the head, steal my money and dismember me in the bathtub. It would be a smart move because bartenders always had loose, untraceable cash on them, as I did. I got nervous. Or maybe she would just kill me herself? A female serial killer. The Bartender Killer. I hadn't heard of any other bartenders going missing. Maybe I would be the first. If I was going to be the first at anything I might as well be the first victim. These thoughts got stronger inside my head and still I continued strolling with her, even as she mentioned that she wanted to do something illegal as part of her recent liberation from her husband. Was this how it was for all victims? Did they have victim's reasoning, to understand and label themselves as victims, no longer as human beings, to resign themselves to a brutal death, to relinquish control over themselves to somebody who wanted to inflict pain.

Her apartment was on the second floor. Small. Neat. Beautiful view of the city. Star wasted no time. She began to peel off her clothes leaving a trail, I suppose, that I was meant to follow. The socks were knee high.

"I hope you don't think I do this all the time?" she said as she sat down to remove them.

"Take me home with you? No I'm pretty sure this is my first time here so I have no doubt you are telling the truth." She stood up, matter-of-fact and naked in the middle of the room.

"Well?" she asked, motioning towards my clothes. "Well come on, take it off." I pulled off my garments quickly and awkwardly, doing the one-legged dance as I wrestled with a shoe that might as well have been welded to my foot. She went to a nearby desk and retrieved a handful of condoms. A handful? Who did she think I was, Priapus himself? By the time I got done undressing I was winded. I sat down, defeated—heart pounding, breath heavy. Star pounced. At this close range I could see that she had an impressive mural tattooed in the region between her navel and her nethers. It was a cartoonish representation of constellations across the night sky and although my astronomy was lacking, they all seemed to be accounted for. Cassiopeia, Orion, Big Dipper, Ursa Minor, Labia Majora.

I'll spare the details, but in no time we got going. Exaggerated cries exploded from Star, which I thought were a bit contrived, but who was I to ruin her fun. Anyway, the sword was jammed into the scabbard. The key slid into the lock. The nut was tightened into the bolt. Gun tucked in holster. The train disappeared into the tunnel. The drill forged its way down the shaft. The bucket dipped in the well. All metaphor converging in the warm womb of the midnight heaven.

Just like that, it was all over.


We lay there in her bed in the darkness listening to the symphony of the late night city play in the distance. The skyline was a candlelight city, a city of fantasy. I was sipping on Star's last beer and she was smoking a cigarette. A glass ashtray was planted over her bellybutton. The bellybutton was strangely shaped, a warped sea mollusk trapped under a glass bottom boat.

"I really had a great time tonight," I told her.

"Yes," she murmured.

"Now what?"

"I don't think that far ahead."

"You never told me your middle name?"

"Grace."

"That figures."

"Why?"

"You are an unmerited blessing. I don't feel like I deserve you. Don't take this the wrong way but I think I love you."

"Don't take this the wrong way," she countered, lifting the ashtray from her stomach, putting it on her night stand and propping herself up on one elbow. "But I can't have you sleeping over. I'm not a sleep over kind of person. I'm not a morning person. I'm at my worst at daybreak. You understand?"

"You want me to leave?"

"It's not you, It's just…my policy. It's not a bad thing to have a policy. Policies keep things running smoothly."

"I'd really like to see you again, though," I said.

"Sure."

"How about tomorrow?"

"Tomorrow is not good for me, Toby. How about next week?"

"Well, next week is okay, I guess. Can we see each other in the meantime? If we see each other in the meantime it might not count as a formal meeting. It could be a frivolous counterpoint to actually seeing each other. The negative space that brings out the distinct edges of actual togetherness. If we spent some haphazard time together it might solidify the context and meaning of our next date. We could pretend we don't like each other. Would that be okay? We won't be allowed to advance the course of our relationship in this interim togetherness. It will help keep us in check, this seeing each other in the meantime. You asked me what I want more than anything else in the world? I want this dumb argument to be convincing."

"Listen," she said. "Are you working this weekend?"

"Yes."

"Well then, I'll come by for a drink."

"Do you promise?" I asked.

"If it will make you leave happily?"

"Yes it would," I answered.

"As long as it will make you leave?" she continued.

"Leave happily?" I finished.

"Leave?" she nodded. I nodded. We kept nodding. I felt we understood each other. There was a lot of nodding to support this. Head forward. Head back. A universal symbol of agreement and accord. Mutual nodding.

"Sounds great," I said, grabbing my clothes and dressing. Star walked me to the door in all her glorious nudity. "I'll see you next week."

The door closed. A series of harmonious clicks ascended the jamb as the dead bolts were all snapped into the locked position. As I was walking back to my car I had the strange sensation I was being followed.

# Chapter 10

In my opinion, to be prepared for disaster is in a sense to avoid it. This differs strongly from Zanz's opinion that to be prepared for disaster is to expect it and to expect it is to hasten the occurrence. Regardless, general feelings of danger are useless if there is no specific evidence available. If there had been any ominous indications or subtle warnings of the events of this night they were completely lost on me at the time. This bar shift found me in an extremely good mood. In fact as I stood there behind the bar I was in shock. The reason?

In my hand I was holding an honest to goodness business card from a very important looking man that had offered me an entry level job in a rapidly expanding business company. His name was Abe Farrell. His title was something like, senior director of regional district management processing…something…system associate…guru…consultant guy. Whatever it was, it was certainly long and distinguished, a complex role full of gross responsibility and grand benefits, a stark opposition to the emptiness of life as I knew it. While this man, this tall and urbane man, this Abe Farrell had been sitting at the bar he had been plagued by countless calls on his cellular telephone. Each caller got a healthy dose of his loud and commanding authority. He spoke of constant travel, exciting and challenging work environments—general, self-importance. I had also noticed, in the short intervals that he was not on his phone, that he had been studying me critically. At first it had made me a bit nervous but I did my best to ignore it and continued on with my normal bar intelligence, bar diplomacy, and bar troubleshooting abilities.

Mr. Abe Farrell, in his polished and dapper manner was studying my performance and was impressed enough to offer me a job, an alternative, a career—asylum in the cushy world of cutthroat business. He inquired as to whether I had a decent suit. I told him of course I did. I left out the fact that I hadn't worn it since high school. He then asked if I had a resume. I explained that it would need a bit of polishing but it would do. I left out the fact that I had never done anything worthy of a resume. However, the one that I would be plagiarizing would certainly be acceptable to get me in the door at least. The man was slick—I might even go so far as to say unctuous. I could tell he was a bit of a bastard too, but characteristics like these were not just forgivable vices in big business. They were indispensable virtues.

"The resume is mostly a formality," Abe promised. "I'll make sure there are no problems. Just dress well and be at your best."

"Yes sir. Thank you sir."

"Don't make me look stupid, now. I have confidence in you. If you betray that confidence I won't hesitate to break you. Be down at the office first thing Monday morning. That gives you only a few days to get prepared. Can you handle it?"

"Thank you for the opportunity, Mr. Farrell sir."

"Call me Abe," he demanded. "Let's just hope you've got what it takes. I always trust my intuition and it is telling me that you are bound for success." I must say I was both surprised and impressed with myself for exuding this. "Now look at this guy over here," Abe pointed across to the other side of the bar at Zanz, who was leaning forward casually engaged in conversation. "I can tell right off the bat that he is never going to make anything of himself," the businessman elaborated. "He has no ambition. He's got no drive. But I can tell you are the type of person that is never satisfied. You are always looking to better yourself, or to become something more than you were the day before." I had never had it explained to me quite like that. "We're looking for somebody with practical, common sense," he continued. "Someone that isn't afraid to take chances. Someone that's got a set of balls on them."

I reached down to make sure I was in possession of the proper *criteria*. Yes, they were there. Abe got back on his telephone and started firing away. I walked over to Zanz's end of the bar, wanting to share with my friend the good news. He was in the middle of a story.

"I was one of the cameramen with the U.S. envoy who made it out alive when Jim Jones commanded all his followers to drink that cyanide koolaid in the South American jungle. We were ambushed at the Port Katuma airstrip. I escaped into the brush, slightly wounded in the leg from guerilla gunfire. I survived on various plants until I was rescued. I was seventy-four years old at the time but the doctor that removed the bullet said I had the body of a man half that age."

"Zanz," I said, "I just got offered a job." He looked disgusted. He straightened himself up and grabbed the card out of my hand. He studied it for a minute and then threw it back at me.

"Toby you have a job. This is a job."

"But I got offered a job with a future."

"The future is a fabrication," he insisted. "The future has been packaged and sold to you by assholes like this guy." He pointed to the card. "It is a con. It is a fallacy to keep you locked in desire. I suspect, however, that all will work out as it should."

"I thought you might just wish me good luck."

"Toby you are forbidden to take seriously anything that some drunk promises you at a bar. You know this."

"You make promises to people all the time when you are here and I know you are usually stone drunk. Are you saying I shouldn't believe you?"

"Now you are thinking critically," he said.

"How about we do a shot of Truth?" I asked.

"Now you are thinking brilliantly! You pour. I just made a new batch."

They were gone almost before they hit the glass underneath them.

"Did you ever notice," he pondered freely, "that most things born out of artistic purity eventually get raped by mediocrity?"

"I think it arises from the human problem of wanting to devour and ultimately destroy the very things that inspire us most."

"Sometimes we're too Nietzschean for our own good."

"I suppose."

"Let's do another shot."

"Sounds good."


Despite Zanz's rigid skepticism I was enthusiastic about the possibility of a different job. To do something else, to break free of this slavish servitude, to get this stagnant mass of flesh on the right track and make something of myself was a bright light on the horizon. Toby Sinclair—Sales Rep, Marketing Guy, Salesman. Wearer of suits and ties. "*My Company* specializes in sound investing, portfolio management, securing futures." I told myself this even though I had no idea what any of it meant. I repeated the sentence with an emphasis on *My Company*. Yes mine. I repeated just that phrase. *My fucking Company.* I tried it again without the expletive. *My Company.* Those two words were very comforting. They instilled a profound sense of belonging, a sense of identity, a sense of pride. No more working in smoky bars. I would be switching to a healthy environment that promoted clean living. Alcohol would not be within reach. My whole lifestyle stood to change drastically. I could lose weight, have more energy, and not be constantly racking my degraded brain for the elusive names of common things like that feeling you get when you are angry because someone has wronged you, or that sticky stuff one uses to connect things together. Instead I would be able to quickly and confidently rattle off... *indignation, glue.* I pictured myself in my office, pacing at my desk, at the copy machine, on the phone, trying to get the toaster in the office kitchen to work properly, out for happy hour with my fellow employees as we compared recent sales commissions. I envisioned, quite clearly, forbidden flirtations with Jan from accounting, Suzanne from product development, Lee Anne from human resources. If they had different names—so be it. I could not be bothered with triviality. It was all so lucid. Things were working out just as they ought to be. In my mind I had already quit being a bottle jockey. I had moved on.

"Hey bartender who do you have to fuck to get a drink around here?"

Well, not yet.

It wasn't long before Skid Row Paul arrived. Ever his usual filthy self, he was wearing a filthy sport coat and a crusty bow tie. He seemed uptight and impatient.

"Hey big spender, why are you all dressed up?" I asked.

"I wonder if my friend in the striped socks will be here again tonight? I have decided I will let her penetrate me."

"Sorry Paul, I took her home last night."

"You don't have to lie to me."

"The penetration thing was just a joke."

"The only thing that is a joke is a guy like you being with a girl like her."

"I have burns on my ears from where those striped socks were rubbing."

"I see nothing," he said, leaning over the bar to scrutinize. "There is no trauma to your ears. If you are lying about that then you are lying about everything."

"They were thigh high Paul."

"Who wears thigh highs with jeans? Impossible. You are a fat liar."

"It is true . . .or is it?"

"It is the summer. Too hot for such an outfit."

"She's got an intricate tattoo on her belly."

"It says 'Toby Sinclair is a big fat liar'. Give me a beer."

"Are you going to pay for it?"

"Of course. I'm just not going to use money."

"What is the currency?"

"Information!" He hunkered down. "Do you think you could find the spot where you buried that steamer trunk in the woods?"

"I think so," I said. "I still have nightmares about it. I keep dreaming a corpse pulls itself out of the ground and runs after me. I try to run but it isn't fast enough. That type of thing."

"Was there an odor?" Skid Row Paul asked. "When you were walking with it? Did you smell anything?"

"I don't know if I was really smelling or imagining."

"Were there flies?"

"It was the woods Paul, there were flies everywhere."

"Was there a kind of lolling and thumping in the trunk when it was shifted, the kind of lolling and thumping sound you might expect from a body sliding back and forth in a box?"

"No, not that I can recall. It wasn't that big. Even a small woman would've had to be shoved in."

"Take me out there," Skid Row Paul said. "I'll dig it up. You can wait in the car. I'll do it. I have a strong stomach. We find out what is in the trunk. We blackmail him. We make him pay or we call the police and he goes to jail."

"He'll know I'm the one who let it slip and then he'll come after me."

"You said there were hikers that saw you, right?"

"Well yes."

"I'll claim to be that hiker. We can blame it on the hiker."

"I don't know."

"Toby. There might be a body and there might not. All I am saying is that something is out there. Something of value to somebody and we can use it. We have a way to disguise ourselves. We don't have to be us. We can be the hikers. I'll draft a note. I'll allude to the fact that I came across him and two others in the woods. Depending on what is in the trunk. I'll leave clues in the note. He'll know I mean business. It is perfect. The hikers take the fall and we get the money."

"This is not a joke or a profit making scheme," I cautioned.

"A guy like me has to get it where he can. My mind is made up. We'll blackmail him and we'll get him to tell us what really happened to Evelyn Goss that night. If not we go to the police. It is a brilliant scheme."

"Have you ever heard of a man named Gary Heidnick?" I asked Skid Row Paul.

"Is he a bar customer?"

"He was a wealthy investor who lived in Philadelphia in the late Eighties. He kidnapped about a dozen young women or so and kept them under his house. Not only that, he made them all sleep in a hole. He would cover the hole with plywood and sandbags. He tortured them and raped them. When one of them would finally die he would feed her to the rest of his hostages."

"Why are you telling me this?" Paul said with a twisted look on his face.

"I am just saying that the conniving human mind is capable of this type of horror. People can do these things. This is not just an opportunity to make some money or put the screws to somebody. I just don't want to land in the middle of something horrific."

"You want to know what is in the trunk as badly as I do."

"I do and I don't," I said. "It is a terrible position to be in."

I had to get back to work. There was a man snapping his fingers at me. Physically he was a big fellow. Big head. Big body. A fattened up, plush-looking man with a hefty set of jowls. His features bordered on gruesome. His skin was orange from too much tanning or too much vitamin C or something. He was wearing a shiny gray suit. He kept snapping his fingers at me, even when I was right in front of him.

"Well now that I've got your attention *finally*," the man said. "Why don't you get me a couple of drinks, bartender." He pulled out a wad of bills and thumbed through them.

"What can I get for you?"

"Tell me something bartender," he declared, still flipping through his roll of money. "How do you become a bartender?"

"I don't know. How does anyone become anything?" I shrugged back.

"I guess just let life stick you somewhere, and hope that somewhere is behind a bar."

"That's the wrong answer," he corrected. "The right answer is that you can get a job as a bartender, but it takes a lot more to *become* a bartender. To become a bartender you need to have a commitment to service, an eagerness to provide people with a unique bar experience, and the abilities with which to accomplish these tasks. You are living a lie. Did you know that?" He paused to let this sink in. "You should take my seminar. It would make you *become* a bartender."

"You still haven't ordered a drink," I pointed out.

"How much money do you make here a night, on average? Give me a solid figure, bartender."

"What the hell kind of question is that?"

"I could show you how to double it by using time-tested sales techniques." He looked me over carefully. "Let me ask you a simple question. Do you want to be...or do you want to be better?"

"Would you like a drink?"

"What are you doing behind that bar besides standing there like a fool?" He recoiled innocently before I had a chance to respond. "I'm not trying to be mean, really I am not. I'm just trying to tell you the reality—your reality. You should take my seminar. I will give you a reality makeover."

"Would you care to actually order a drink?"

"I thought you'd never ask!" he exclaimed. "I want two vodkas—with two cubes of ice."

"Is that one cube per drink or two cubes in each?"

"Do you want to know how much money I make a year?"

"Not really," I sighed.

"Wrong answer, bartender," he barked.

"Two cubes in each or two cubes total?"

"Of course you want to know how much money I make," he went on. "I make high six figures. But that is just a reflection of my attitude. Attitude dictates circumstance. Repeat...ATTITUDE DICTATES CIRCUMSTANCE." He calmed himself and continued. "Now when you tell me how much money you make, I will explain why your attitude allows for such a paltry number. Then you can take my seminar, where I'll teach you how to fix that attitude. You'll have an attitude makeover."

"I'll make at least a dollar, tonight. You never know," I muttered, as I scooped up a nearby dollar that somebody had left on the bar.

"You know I ordered some drinks and they still aren't here."

I grabbed the ice scoop, put two glasses out, made the executive decision to put two ice cubes in each glass and poured the vodka. The man turned away from me to regard a group of women approaching the bar. The new cluster of women, aware they were being watched, took up rehearsed poses designed to portray ambiguous signals of modesty and lechery.

"Alright ladies, who wants to fuck a millionaire?" the man said to the girls. They snickered. "Wrong answer. Everybody does!"

He picked up one of the two drinks he had ordered and threw a hundred dollar bill down. I grabbed the money and walked over to the register. Zanz was his usual oblivious self at the other end of the bar telling some fool story. Being a prisoner of war in Vietnam or orchestrating the overthrow of some Latin American, democratically elected president. I made change, returned to where he stood and threw the money down.

"This drink is terrible," he complained, waving his glass at me.

"What could possibly be wrong with it?"

"For starters there is too much ice in it."

"You mean rocks," I said.

"Yes rocks, too many rocks."

"I agree there are too many rocks in it."

"Yes. Too many rocks in the drink."

"I was talking about the rocks in your head."

"I could ask to speak to the manager for that comment. But I am not one to dwell." He sat back, quieted, picked up his money and counted it. Buzzing with frustration, I marched to the other side of the bar where Zanz appeared to be having the time of his life.

"…About ten years ago some of you might recall the marriage of Japan's Prince Naruhito to Princess Masako. What some of you may not know is on the day of the wedding a group of Japanese bio-terrorists under the order of cult leader Shoko Asahara drove around the city spraying a virulent form of botulism into the air, hoping to infect and kill thousands. Not one single illness was reported that day. Do you know why? Because I had infiltrated the group, and working under strict cover within the cult's laboratories had successfully replaced the deadly botulism with a harmless variant."

"Unbelievable," someone said.

"There should be a nationally recognized holiday," someone else said.

"What's wrong Toby?" said Zanz. "You don't look good."

"I've had about all I can stand over there. I'm dealing with one of those people that only get quiet and nice after you insult them. So far he has demeaned my job performance, my income, my ambition and my attitude. I almost feel bad to tell him that he's running out of criteria." Zanz looked over at the orange man, laughed and shook his head.

"Some people will only be nice to you if you mistreat them," Zanz said. "It is an unfortunate phenomenon, a regrettable characteristic of some people's social conditioning. Use it to your advantage. Tell him he looks like a tomato. A halfwit tomato. Tell him halfwit tomatoes get smashed for their own good."

On the bar television there was an update about another woman that had gone missing in Oklahoma. There was a picture of her on the screen-- mid-thirties, long brunette hair, smiling innocently at what looked like a backyard barbecue with the anonymous arm of some family member who had been amputated out of the photograph slung casually around her neck. There was a substantial reward for information leading to her whereabouts. I thought about Skid Row Paul's plan. Get a reward. Make some easy money. Quit my job. Go buy a boat and sail around the world. Publish the memoirs. Die of drink.

The television then announced it would be airing an investigative report the next day concerning the recent arising of small, secret organizations in rural parts of the country known amongst its members as The Gilded Dawn. The groups are rumored to operate under various fronts. Despite their assertions that they are a harmless ecumenical religious community there has been growing concern that this may be the birth of a cluster of dangerous new cults, as one former member under a request for anonymity has agreed to tell her story with shocking revelations of bizarre grave robbing practices, brain washing, perverse sexual rituals--all in the name of a mysterious alien entity. I made a special note to tune in for that one. Although cults weren't my specialty there was still something morbidly intriguing about them, tending to lack only through the sheer number of their groups a certain unadulterated essence of brute horror that the lone serial killer is in possession of. Also, cults tended to murder their own, while serial killers murdered everyone else. I went back to my side of the bar. The orange man was ready to dole out more insults.

"I bet you think you are something pretty special, don't you bartender?" the man said.

"I would be mistaken if I did though, right?"

"Get me another drink, bartender."

I poured him another drink. One ice cube. I cashed it out and gave him his change. He didn't leave a tip. There was a curious calmness to him. The eyes were empty. He made no move to take his drink. He let it sit there.

"Do you want to do this for the rest of your life?" he asked. "Is this where you see yourself in the future? Doing this?"

"Yes. Standing here. Talking to you. Only in the distant future we'll be great friends. We'll go on a speaking tour to promote our finest invention, a tasty low fat custard."

"You aren't a bartender anyway."

"Why do you keep calling me bartender then?"

"To prove a point," he said.

"Are you going to drink that drink?" I asked.

"I'm just saying that some people are bartenders, some people are not," he clarified after looking at his glass for a moment. "Just like some people are leaders and some are not. Some are followers." He looked me squarely in the face. "And the leaders have a responsibility to teach those who are followers."

"And?"

"My grandfather, who was a prisoner of war, used to tell me that to suffer is to defy submission," the man said. "A man can suffer all the way to his own glory, but can never submit towards the same end. Remember this if and when you find yourself in a position of suffering, bartender."

"Your one ice cube is melting," I pointed out.

"Take care of yourself," he said before disappearing into the crowd, leaving his untouched drink on the bar. Ever the conservationist, I knocked it back real smooth.


The restaurant was empty and silent. The music was off. The lights were on. Zanz was busy unclogging the drain in the sink. I was stretched out on the bar, lying face up, thinking about what Skid Row Paul had offered, thinking about Baron, about the possibility of stealing the trunk back, about everything. I felt alone in the universe. Nobody else seemed to comprehend the gravity of the situation. Skid Row Paul was eager to cash in. Zanz was treating the whole thing as if he had helped Baron rake some leaves. And still the women were turning up missing. The Fleetwood Brougham could be rolling down any street right now, trolling the city, looking for that precise woman to excite the fever of murder in him. A particular walk. A certain shape of the face. A hairstyle. Pull past her and park the car. Get everything ready. Ask for directions. Pull a gun. Tell her to be quiet and everything will be alright. Close the lid on the trunk.

I saw it all very clearly. I saw what nobody else did and it provoked in me a heavy solipsism. I was the sole inhabitant of my contained universe. Vast galaxies clustered in the outer reaches of my feet. Space debris in my pocket, heavy matter at my fingertips. I was a lonely God unto myself and decided that I too, if afforded the capability, may create a race of tiny beings for my personal amusement, hide myself from them, torture them, give them addictions, loved ones that didn't love them back, cause them to go mad with speculation about me. It would, after all, be fun…for me.

"I can hear the squeaky wheels of your mind turning," said Zanz from under the sink.

"I'd oil them up but the bottle of Truth is empty."

"I think I'm perfecting the recipe. Either that or we're becoming clinical."

"I have to put together some kind of resume for my job interview Monday," I said. "I don't know the first thing about it. It'll be good for a laugh."

"I don't want to tell you that you're making a mistake," he replied. "But I will. You want to throw away paradise? Being a bartender is a privilege. In your wildest dreams could you think that this type of magic would descend upon you, bless you, keep you, reward your life with all the richness you've always felt you deserved but never quite knew how to harness? This place is your good fortune. The hallmark of wisdom lies in not squandering this unique chance to reach your highest potential. Let the bar exist through you. It is an extension of yourself. When a person sits at the bar they are entering your being. You make them happy. Soon they come to understand their intoxication as a function of your goodwill. Then comes their love. Then comes their money. You need to realize what you are part of, to understand a bar on this level of intimacy. You need to appreciate the sacred, social responsibility a bartender undertakes every time he walks into his workspace."

"But it'll be easier to tell my Uncle Jimmy I'm not in medical school if I don't have to admit that I am a bartender too. The cumulative shock could kill him."

"You want him to be disappointed so badly," Zanz said. "You'll probably keel over when you see that you've been making a big deal out of nothing."

"I guess it is just my way."

96

"That's a good guess." He stood up, wiped his hands on his jeans. "I think she's all cleared out. Come on, let's get out of here." I jumped down off the bar. "You know you have my support in all this, Toby," Zanz said. "The proper path is always the one chosen, by definition. I suggest tomorrow that you take a careful look at the quest for your own authenticity. The real thread of it lies in your past, not in your imagined future. Reflect on your life up to this point in order to gain some insight on what you need to do from here."

"I suppose."

"Go on ahead. I have to take a piss."

I stepped out into the back alley, waited for Zanz. From that point things happened in a mad flash. I noticed the sheen of the suit, heard the whistle of the pine board as it struck me in the head. I went to the ground, deafened by the blow. He struck me in the ribcage and the air raced out of my lungs, effectively silencing me. I curled up to protect my vital organs. His foot caught the left side of my face and I bit my tongue. I could taste the blood as it ran out of my mouth and nose. There was a crude heaving by the man, taunts and peals of vicious laughter, groans and cries of my own in my ears as I was repeatedly knocked from one side of the alley to the other with the board, his foot, his fist. Kicked in the head again. My hands went to my face and when I pulled them away there was blood everywhere. The beating lasted forever and was over in seconds. Footsteps went running into the night. I crawled a few shaky feet before collapsing.

PART 2

# "THE HARLEQUINS! THE HARLEQUINS!"

# CHAPTER 11

Let me just say, in my defense, that I did try to reschedule my job interview. I had personally called Abe Farrell after I had been beaten stupid in the back alley. The call, apparently, couldn't have been more poorly timed, but for reasons that weren't very clear. Mr. Farrell had answered the phone out of breath and incredibly bothered. I wasn't sure what the average executive was engaged in on an average Sunday afternoon, but four scenarios came to mind. The first was that perhaps I had caught Mr. Farrell on the toilet trying to pass a kidney stone. A second theory was that he answered the phone while in the process of being forced into submission by a leather-clad dominatrix who was busy burying her stiletto heel into his groin. Yet another possibility was that he was being tortured in his own home by anarchist youths looking for the combination to his bedroom wall safe—youths who periodically shocked him with mild electrodes. Lastly, Abe Farrell could've come home and found some buck naked man on top of his buck naked wife, chased him out of the house and down the road, and it was this terrific pursuit that I had interrupted with my phone call. Whatever. Point being, the man was distressed.

"Yes," he uttered breathlessly.

"Mr. Farrell, this is Toby Sinclair."

"You kinda…caught me at a bad time…"

"I was just wondering if I could reschedule the job interview, sir?"

"Damn it. I knew you bartenders were unreliable screw ups. Well I guess that's what I get for trying to put my faith in someone. I already set it up. This is going to make me look bad. You don't want to make me look bad, right? *Ouch*."

"I guess not."

"Well then you make it to that fucking interview...*gasp*...or just forget the whole thing. What's going to happen if you get hired?" He took a second to groan. "Are you going to run around with excuses and procrastination? We don't make money with excuses and procrastination. We make money by making money, and that is what this whole thing is about. M-O-N-E-Y. Now you get your ass down to that fucking interview tomorrow or I'm going to personally come down to that bar of yours and rip your spine out. No one screws with....Ahhhhh..(*heavy breathing*)... Abe Farrell."

"Mr. Farrell, are you okay?" I asked.

"That remains to be seen," he wheezed. "But you will not be okay if I hear that you didn't make it to that interview. Don't be a loser for once."

Click.


I adjusted my jacket and tie and slumped back in the cracked leather seat of the cab I was riding in as my driver did his best to murder us both while engaging me in frivolous conversation about the future of the city of Atlanta. Perhaps he was explaining the city's future because he understood that I wouldn't make it to the end of the cab ride alive. I was taking a cab because my face was so swollen that my peripheral vision was compromised and because downtown parking is about as frustrating as it gets. The cab itself, seasoned with a fine mixture of dents, scratches and scrapes, snaked through the congested morning traffic. To make matters worse my cabbie, who had gotten his expert training on the unforgiving avenues of New York City so he said, would turn around almost completely to engage me in a face-to-face dialogue as he continued to steer and accelerate, eventually turning forward just as the back bumper of a braking car came rushing at us, and he himself would lock up at the last second, honk his horn, and accuse the person in front of us of not knowing how to drive.

"You don't sound like you are from around here," the cabbie said as he turned to me. "You sound like you are from up North."

"New York."

"I'm from Staten Island," he erupted proudly.

"It's a small world," I said.

"It is round in pictures but flat on the surface," he said, weaving the car out of a near miss with a delivery van. He leaned on the horn—key of F—apparently, as my driver explained that notes in the key of F are generally regarded as the most abrasive.

"You learn something new everyday," I said.

"I also forget a lot of shit," he said. "If I keep learning one day I'm going to wake up and wonder how to tie my shoes."

I was on my way to my first real job rejection, which would immediately follow my first real job interview. The reason for my impending failure? I looked like a punch drunk sailor afflicted with a nasty case of leprosy. My face was beaten to a pulp. I tried to reconstruct the whole fight as it happened but couldn't. It had been beaten out of me. It had been run out of my head with all that blood. The orange man in the suit coming at me with the pine board. That was all I remembered.

Zanz had found me. He had shaken me back into a workable consciousness. The first thing I asked him was if I was alive. "Yes," he said. "Not that it will make you feel any better but yes." I told him I couldn't feel my legs. He told me to put my hands on them. He got me to my feet and into my car and drove me back to the hospital to see Doctor Eddie. Every bump in the road sent bolts of pain through my midsection. My head swam like images in a fun house mirror. My right temple was going like a bass drum. Glancing in the side mirror I saw that the right side of my face was swollen out like an eggplant. My bottom lip was as big as a sausage and running blood. I had abrasions up and down my arms and an actual shoe print along my ribs. Doctor Eddie performed the standard tests, pointing out that it hadn't been a very good week for me. He told me I had a concussion. I asked if that was bad. He said I might experience some dizziness, a dull throb, some memory lapses. I remarked that it was kind of like a hangover and Doctor Eddie brightened, suddenly aware of a rather profound biological connection. I was given painkillers and ordered to rest.

"It looks like you got yourself into some trouble," my cab driver continued, noting how raw and ragged my face was in the morning sunlight. "This city has got some bad elements in it. Some people don't respect this city because they all come from someplace else. This city is an air plant—no roots. It'll take two or three more generations for the carpetbaggers to really dig in and accept this place as home."

"I suppose."

"How many of them were there?" the cabbie asked. "How many got you?"

"Just one."

"How much did he get you for?"

"It wasn't a robbery," I said. This made the cabbie extremely curious and he turned around to let me know it by the bright expression on his face.

"You mean to tell me you *was* the target of a personal vendetta?"

"He was a customer of mine."

"From the looks of it a dissatisfied customer."

"I guess he is sensitive to insult."

"If I were you I'd learn how to fight or get better insults."

We reached the correct address.

"Alright, sir," the cabbie exclaimed as he pulled up to the bustling sidewalk. The building in front of me shot into the heavens, where I suppose, the gods sat around behind big mahogany desks at the top and gambled with the fate of the world. I checked the address with the one I had been given. This was the place. I reached for my wallet but stopped suddenly when I heard the price for the ride. "Four hundred dollars," the cabbie winked, his eyes begging to be understood.

"Four hundred dollars?" I said. "You can't be serious."

"I'll run anybody over for four hundred dollars," he explained. "Find out where they live and make it look like a fucking accident. Anybody at all—well, no kids. I won't run over kids for any amount of money. But anybody over eighteen and I'll use my cab to make a speed bump out of them, especially if they are troublemakers."

"How much for *this* cab ride?" I asked. "Just the ride."

"Give me twenty bucks and we'll call it even," he said. "But if you ever need anything else, just ask for old Shep." I paid, grabbed my small leather folder from the seat next to me and headed through the revolving doors. There was a bum standing in front of the building with a plastic coffee cup extended towards pedestrians. He looked me up and down, deliberating on whether to share the spoils of his change cup with me.

I followed the signs to the human resources department, tenth floor (next to accounting, hardware, men's furnishings). I did my best to ignore the odd stares from super-civilized men and women who seemed strangely fascinated and appalled at my appearance. These people were interspersed with others walking at a rapid clip, too busy to notice what city they were in, much less a beat up guy in a suit two sizes too small for him. Still others were congregated about with their coffee mugs, talking about working out or made-for-television movies. The environment was a pressure cooker. The air was too thin at this altitude. Fiery bursts of shouting erupted from around corners, and went away just as fast. Too many flesh eaters in too cramped a space—that was the problem. There was an implicit acceptance of a common hatred under the guise of healthy Darwinism. I could read it on everybody's faces, see it in the mannerisms, feel it in the polite deception that people used to address one another. I pondered the way of things. Is it either nothing or madness? Could a person run with the pack and not be forced to kill for it? I doubted I would find out.

I located the correct receptionist, broke her out of some halfhearted daydream, gave my name, told her I had been referred by Abe Farrell and I was to meet with a "...Ms. Glakstatter."

The receptionist looked up at me and emitted a small, dainty yelp. My hand went gingerly to my face as it fell into a lopsided, puffy smile.

"I had a bit of an accident over the weekend," I laughed. She didn't share my laughter or anything else, frozen as she was in propriety and taste. It was getting brutally warm. I asked her if I could have a seat. She insisted. It was obvious I made her nervous, and her nervousness fed mine. I fidgeted with my tie and it came off in my hand.

"Clip on," I explained.

She smiled and began to collate documents to escape further awkwardness. It wasn't enough. She found it more useful to knock her coffee cup to the floor and throw herself over it, scrubbing at the spill with a wad of napkins kept on hand for just such a diversion. It was beautifully choreographed. I took a seat in the small waiting room, as far away from the diligent receptionist as possible.

There were crinkled business magazines scattered around the coffee table, a small plant and a Lucite paperweight that doubled as an Announcement for Excellence in Strategic Accounting (or something). Motivational posters hung in dime store frames, showing men and women in various stages of adventurous accomplishment—climbing mountains, shooting rapids, jumping out of planes—and under them all were various phrases of limitless optimism. Cute, I thought, but I myself would've appreciated posters of a more mundane realism that the average worker could really relate to, instead of showcasing activities largely unknown to a sleep-deprived middle manager suffering from a ninety-hour workweek, streamlined work force and budget cuts.

Some examples:

Perhaps a picture of a cemetery with the caption, "Thankfully, someday the problems of today will all be over."

Perhaps a picture of an old man in drag with the caption, "Everybody's got something they would pay dearly to keep secret."

Perhaps a picture of a man on a surfboard with the caption, "Statistically this man is much more likely to get eaten by a shark than you are."

I opened my small leather binder and browsed through the resume that I had put together. It was full of exaggerations, extrapolations, and outright fabrications. My objective was to obtain a position in a competitive, successful, work environment in order to estublish (sic) a long term career in the field of market trend analysis and project coordination. Just vague enough to be dead on. I lied and said I graduated college with a 3.8 because if a person is going to lie they should go all the way. I enjoyed backgammon and camping and was an Eagle Scout. I knew what a computer looked like and I took criticism well. I won a hamburger eating contest when I was eleven. There was a new person on this sheet of paper, brought into existence out of oblivion. If the interviewer tried to get specific with me I would blame my reticence on the obvious beating I had endured and of course my tireless modesty.

"Is that damned coffee stain almost out?" I asked the receptionist. It was suddenly very important that I know the cleanup status.

"Almost," her voice rang out from behind the desk.

"Mr. Sinclair!" The name was shot in my direction. I looked up to see the frightful apparition known in these hallowed halls, I supposed, as Ms. Glakstatter. She was a big old spinster. Her girth was tastefully covered up with a floral muumuu, one hundred percent rayon, I suspected. More preferable than the boring old, A-line style, that's for sure. She stood in a very unfriendly manner and spoke coldly. Her face sagged heavily behind an enormously thick set of glasses. "Follow me please," she rattled off. I kept up behind her, studying her feet as she walked. She was wearing a pair of heels that were ill-designed to support a sizable woman. They buckled considerably with each step taken. We walked into an office and the door was shut. I took a seat in front of her desk, even though she didn't offer it, and tried to relax. Ms. Glakstatter took a seat at her desk and shuffled some papers around. The room was decorated with pictures of cats and Jesus.

"Well now, let's see here," she began. "It looks like you got a hold of some trouble."

"Trouble got a hold of me."

"Can I see your curriculum vitae?" she asked. I handed her the resume and she took her time perusing it. "Mmm, mmm, mmm," she groaned. There was some crusty peanut butter on her top lip. I normally wasn't a fan of the substance, but in this situation it took on an air of personal offense, as if Ms. Glakstatter had placed it there to make me uncomfortable.

Then, without warning, she sneezed all over the resume. The smell of old peanut butter exploded in the room, a goddamned toxic gust of internal decomposition.

"The only redeemable thing about this resume is that it caught most of my snot." She crumpled up the paper and told me that she was going to file it under T, as in T-rash. "Let's start out with a general question. What have you been doing all these years?"

"Just trying to figure it out, I guess," I said.

"I am sitting on the edge of my seat to find out what you have figured out, given the amount of time you've allotted yourself."

"With all due respect ma'am it is dangerous for a woman of your build to sit on the edge of anything."

"Mr. Abe Farrell," she said with a lamenting sigh, "is forever burdening me with you types of people. He thinks he's going to find the diamond in the hedgerow, the streetwise genius that can take his practical talents and apply them to the world of corporate finance. Well, that's nice in theory, but this is not a Franz Kafka movie."

"I think you mean, Frank Capra," I said.

"I'm telling you from my experience that it doesn't occur. Look at yourself? You've been sitting on your butt for years now, just waiting for someone to give you a free ride. You have no initiative and no drive. What about the people that have worked here for years, struggled to accomplish something for themselves and their employers? It is an insult to their years of hard work for you to come in here with no experience and suddenly be given a position. There is a lot of trust involved in this type of work environment and you types of people are not worthy of that trust. Once a person is employed here they are no longer just an individual, but a representative of the greater good, which of course is the corporation—and its shareholders."

There had to be some kind of sign to this. It was all too coincidental that I hadn't been in a fight since middle school and I find myself arbitrarily beaten the day before my first job interview. I shouldn't have said anything about the job offer to Zanz. To speak frivolously about future expectation is the quickest way to rob it of its momentum—like a racer trying to break a land speed record by calling a victory press conference a hundred yards from the finish line, or trying to sprint through a tornado with a fully deployed parachute hanging from your back. Communication for the benefit of an ego is a serious energy burner.

Of course I wouldn't be hired, but it was evident that Ms. Glakstatter was going to continue with the interview, probably because she didn't want to be sued for discrimination, or some type of legal nuance that didn't allow for my ejection before all of the necessary paperwork was in place. However, because I understood this, I suddenly felt free to speak my mind without fear of consequence. Let's give her a dose of naked honesty.

"We'll start off with your thoughts on sales ability," she began. "Describe to me your selling style."

"I find a delicate balance of threat and intimidation to be most effective."

Her eyes grew wide in indecision at whether to be furious, horrified, or insulted. Perhaps she would call security, or yell rape. However, Ms. Glakstatter kept her cool, although she began to heave like a great rhino, and I was sure that another of those peanut butter sneezes would be heading my way and without my resume to deflect it I could find myself in serious trouble. I ducked. Her stubby hand went up against her nose and the sneeze imploded. Her bulk rippled.

"Let's continue," she said. "What is the most important thing you learned in your last job?"

"I learned that nobody likes a snitch," I said. She eyed me, cleared her throat and continued on.

"Tell me about a selling experience that really changed your life?"

"My soul to the devil," I responded. "Things haven't been the same since."

"What are your strong points?"

"I would say my strongest point is the inability to admit any weak ones."

"What do you think is a fair policy regarding tardiness?"

"Laissez-faire."

"What do you value in a job?"

"Being worshipped."

"How do you communicate with someone who is not a good listener?"

"A good hard shake usually does the trick."

"Well, I think that will be quite enough," she finished. "Hopefully someday you'll find what you are looking for. My only advice is don't expect the world to come knocking at your door."

"Knowing me, Ms. Glakstatter, I'd answer the door and tell it to go fuck itself."

"Well now, no need for profanity. Profanity is an ignoramus's retreat," she chastised with a steady handshake, glancing off to a smudge on the drab wallpaper that she had been meaning to take care of for weeks now. I turned and walked out of the office.


I got out to the sidewalk, never happier to breathe in good old dirty, city air. I had developed a mild headache, probably due to the waning concussion. Doctor Eddie was right—a concussion was kind of like a hangover. I decided to apply my peculiar expertise in hangover management to the treatment of my concussion. I walked into the closest bar, sat down, unclipped my tie, and ordered a beer.

"We're not open yet," the girl behind the bar yawned. "We don't open for another thirty minutes." She adjusted her glasses and gave me a more focused glance. "Hey wait a second, aren't you a bartender?"

"Yes," I answered.

"I almost didn't recognize you with your face like that. Did you get beat up?"

"You should see the other guy," I said.

"Well, if he's not dead then I'm afraid he won." She looked around to make sure the coast was clear and opened a bottle of beer for me.

"Industry courtesy. Just take that one," she smiled. She walked off to finish her opening side work. I threw down a ten and took a long hard swig. Cheers to the winners of the world, wherever they were at that particular moment. I was halfway through the bottle when the urge to sob uncontrollably was finally more than I could endure. I politely buried my head down in the arm of my sport coat and let it all go.

# CHAPTER 12

The sealed document came in the mail today.

Jury Duty!

Greetings! This is your summons for jury duty. Please see reverse side for confidential jury information. Ques: Are you a citizen of the U.S.? Ans. Yes. Ques: Are you now a resident of Fulton County? Ans: Yes. Ques: Have you ever been a party to a lawsuit? Ans: No. Ques: Have you ever been a victim of a crime? Ans: Yes. Ques: if YES, what type of crime? Ans: Theft. Theft of innocence by a parade of vicious women. Theft of patience by virulent strains of bureaucracy. Theft of optimism by a callous, uncaring, and smug society. Theft of temperance by alcohol. Theft of empathy through alienation. Theft of endeavor through constant failure. Theft of peace through the greed of the few. Theft of tranquility due to my own sense of indefiniteness.

I sat at my small kitchen table and filled out, as honestly as possible, the preliminary questions for my upcoming civic responsibility of objectively and impartially passing judgment on people that were definitely guilty as sin itself. My date of attendance was weeks away. I wondered what it would be like to sit on the jury of a man accused of being a bona fide serial killer? Sequestered for months. Agonizing testimony. Heartbreaking victim impact statements. Gruesome crime photos. Many of the more charismatic serial killers actually have throngs of groupies, women who claim to understand and love the broken child behind the ruthless slasher. One of the jurors in the Night Stalker trial baked him cookies and them married him or something.

I tacked a reminder of the jury date up on my calendar, sealed up the questionnaire and continued my midday breakfast of cold pizza, lo mein noodles and a 22-ounce of Schlitz Blue Bull malt liquor. If anything my choice of drink was always adaptive. I tended to drink sake at sushi restaurants, ouzo at Greek restaurants, strega at Italian restaurants, Irish whiskey at pubs, at sporting events I settled in with cheap domestic beer, and when I was relaxing in my apartment I drank malt liquor.

I finished my breakfast, added the empty plate to the apex of the dirty pile already in the sink, went to the mailbox, put the red flag up and deposited my questionnaire. Nona, my landlady was on her porch. She asked me who had kicked my face in.

"I've been telling everybody you did it because I was late on the rent."

"Somebody knocked you off your long horse?"

"It's *high* horse, Nona."

I walked to Zanz's carriage house, taking advantage of the crisp day and tree-shaded sidewalk. I was meeting him there in order to discuss nothing at all. No topics would be discussed. We would make no specific plans. Our chat would be vague. It would serve no purpose. It would be of absolutely no consequence. We had no agenda. We were going to discuss nothing.

The staircase leading to the second story of Zanz's carriage house looked solid, sturdy and dependable. It was peculiar, then, to see him throw himself out the side window and drop into a pile of mulch. He got up and dusted himself off.

"What was that for?" I asked.

"To avoid an explanation I do not have, to a girl I do not know, for certain things that may or may not have happened."

"It's that awful peach brandy," I told him. "One time I woke up in the lobby of a funeral parlor wearing nothing but a pinafore, boa, and tights. Don't ask."

"This girl wanted to test me. You see everybody knows I make my own peach brandy but I also make a terrific potency tea that I save for nights that are full of heavy drinking and sexual promise."

"What are the ingredients of this magical tea?" I asked.

"Well it's got sea horses, snake skin, Komodo dragon claw and a rare white ginseng root grown in a remote Chinese province, whose garden soil is enriched with the remains of three martial emperors of the Han dynasty."

"Sounds tasty."

"If you ever want to be a believer I'll loan you some," Zanz offered.

"But it's got to be diluted or you'll be standing around with an erection for two days straight."

Zanz showed me the piece of paper with the man's picture on it. It stopped me cold in my footsteps. "Where did you get this?" I asked.

"I am surprised you would ask that," said Zanz. "You know how in tune I am with the universe, with the forces outside of visible perception. The mystical, karmic pathways of return. The universe itself is in a constant state of revolution. All things move in a circle. Everything that moves away will eventually be back. I knew I recognized that tomato fellow from the bar. I receive his junk mail advertising his motivational speeches."

He went by the alias Doctor B. Right. The same man that had attacked me was staring up from the paper I was holding. Hurry now! While supplies last! Order your copy today! Doctor. B. Right has all the answers. Learn how to increase profits! Learn how to identify and motivate problem employees! Learn to deal with all different personality types: The Complainer. The Blamer. The Slacker. The Excuse Monger. Eliminate tardiness, apathy, inertia. Learn how to turn a new customer into a repeat customer! Change your life! Change your attitude! Live success. Order now!

There was a toll free number at the bottom. Zanz said his copy was on rush delivery.

We walked down to Skid Row Paul's dilapidated apartment complex, again, to discuss nothing at all. Paul's rented dwelling was a small corner in an old, run down, brick building that had most likely been a motor lodge in the Fifties. It boasted a courtyard just beyond the rusted gates. The concrete slabs were cracked and uneven and overrun with tall weeds. In the middle of it all was the deep belly of a neglected concrete swimming pool, empty except for a thin, green algae puddle at the bottom of the low end. It was a plausible anachronism for me to imagine that the entire property had been meticulously designed around Paul's filthiness, almost a quarter of a century before my unhygienic friend had even been born.

Skid Row Paul was sitting in the old courtyard playing chess with one of the neighborhood crazies, an old man who called himself 'The Aegis' and who claimed to be a direct descendant of Jack the Ripper, of all people. When prompted he would always insist that 'Uncle Jack' had gotten a bad rap from history. The notorious killer was nothing more than a medical philanthropist who had botched a couple of abortions. Since The Aegis was against the practice himself, he made it his life goal to impregnate as many hookers as he could get his hands on in order to even the score. It was commonly known that he wore a diaper to maintain a healthy sperm count. The Aegis would go into a blind rage when someone suggested that the diaper was for incontinence. He soiled himself often.

The Aegis's knowledge of chess was one of the only things unaffected by the marbles in his head. The two were both bent forward in concentration. As The Aegis captured Paul's knight he explained in gory detail exactly how the knight had been slaughtered, how his guts had spilled from his belly, how the knight's skin had gone white as his blood poured out into the field, how he had died whimpering like a sick animal, and how he finally had to chop the knight's head off to be merciful. Paul nodded and made his move. I had watched these two play chess many times before. The Aegis never gave a shit if his king was checkmated. All he was concerned about was long, sweeping strikes intended to embarrass and humiliate Paul's pieces in order to lower the rank's general morale. He would come out like a beast and run kamikaze missions—describing as he did so the brutal slaying of the bishops, knights, the soldierly rape of the queen, torture of the rooks, all the pawns, until Paul would use whatever sparse pieces he had leftover to frugally checkmate from a safe distance. Then, as The Aegis's king was there paralyzed, he would announce that his king, rather than be taken, has turned his weapon on himself, mortally wounded, daring God to restore him back to life, collapsing with a smile on his face, a leader of consummate action, ridding himself of his bothersome pluralities of fear, happiness, desire, disgust, action and lamentation. Death has moved the regal sovereign into the final victory, the removal of all physical restriction and the unification of his soul into one, unwavering vital essence. Yes, The Aegis would say, take that you bitch.

Then they would start again.

"Paul," Zanz said, "we have something for you."

"What might that be?" Paul said, still studying the chess board.

"We want you to find somebody."

"Aha!" the Aegis cried. "I have just crushed your pawn's head with a mighty swing from my spiked mace. Most of his face has been torn off."

"That doesn't matter pops because you are in check."

The Aegis looked down at the board. "Son of a bitch." He backed the monarch up a square.

"Checkmate!" Paul said, sliding his rook to the appropriate file.

"That is what you think!" he laughed. "My king has just chewed through a poison capsule that has been hidden under his tongue the whole time. He has signed his land over to his second cousin, an Earl of a distant

Shire who is right now assembling a fighting regiment that will conquer the far sides of your kingdom. As you can see, I have successfully destroyed your entire army. Your doom is imminent."

"Hey pops," Skid Row Paul said. "Take a walk."

"I've got to get moving, anyway. Need to attend to my life calling. Got me a girl named Wetness. This is a girl that does not like to be kept waiting." The old man staggered off.

Paul began to clear the chess pieces off the board. "Have a seat." We sat down. "What the hell happened to your face, Toby?"

"That is why we are here," Zanz said. "Keeping it as quiet as you can, we want you to find the guy that did this." Zanz prompted me to explain that I was jumped in the back alley. We gave Paul the pamphlet with the picture on it. I then reminded him about the girl with the striped socks. I told him that the man in the pamphlet was her husband.

"I warned Toby it was going to turn out bad for him," Zanz said.

"I see," Skid Row Paul said, looking over the picture. "Is this all I have to go on?"

"For now."

"Why don't you just go talk to the wife?"

"She is the one that got me into this in the first place," I said, pointing to my face.

"Plus we don't want anybody to be able to pin a motive on us when we get him," Zanz said.

"Why don't you go to the police?" Paul asked.

"I'm sure they have their hands full," I said.

"That would take all the fun out of it," Zanz said.

Zanz told Paul that he wanted to know where to find Doctor B. Right and then we would take it from there. He had consulted Baron, he said, on an effective form of revenge, knowing that Baron had an appetite for that kind of thing. Zanz pulled another piece of paper out of his pocket. On it were handwritten instructions from Baron. Two ideas that he thought would be acceptable for the orange-faced motivational speaker. The first idea was to rent a garage in a poor part of town. Then we would take our man Doctor B. Right there and shoot him up the ass with a .22 revolver. We would place a telephone at the far end of the garage and tell him that if he can make it to the phone he can call for help. Then we would watch him wriggle wounded across the floor like a slug towards the phone. But if and when he reached the phone he would pick it up only to find no dial tone. The phone, in fact, would not be plugged in. Then we would shoot him in the head, light his remains on fire and bury him in some rural stretch of land. Baron's second idea was to rent a garage in a poor part of town. Then we would kidnap our man and take him there. This plan also called for us to kidnap an innocent transient. We would shoot both of them up the ass with a .22 revolver and leave them there to bleed on the cold cement floor. Then Baron would explain to them, as they lie there writhing in agony, that the one who lives longest will be taken to the hospital. Then we could all stand back and watch as they try and kill each other in order to allow themselves to live. When one finally succeeds, we shoot the other in the head. Then we would light their remains on fire and bury them in some rural stretch of land. After Zanz finished reading Baron's suggestions he ate the scrap of paper.

"Is all that really necessary?" I asked uneasily.

"I think it is more of an idea of what Baron is prepared to do. A show of loyalty. The final decision will be left up to us."

"I'll find him," Paul said. "But I am going to want something in return." Paul looked specifically at me with a smile. "But we can talk about that after I deliver. Now if you will excuse me, I have a quarry to hunt." He folded the pamphlet up and put it in his pocket.


Zanz insisted I try some of his potency tea along with his new batch of peach brandy. On the way past his house he had given me a liter of both in unmarked plastic bottles. Drink as much of the peach brandy as you want, he said. But the tea could only be taken at two or three ounces at a time. When I got home I put both in the refrigerator. Later in the evening while I was inspecting my waning bruises in the mirror the telephone rang. It was my Uncle Jimmy.

"You don't scare me," he said. "You think I am the type to be intimidated? Show your balls around me and I'll blow them off with a shotgun."

"Uncle Jimmy who are you talking to?"

"Whoever is listening in to this conversation."

"You mean me?"

"No. The others."

"Jimmy you have to stop being so paranoid."

"I got nothing to hide," Jimmy said. "My life is an open book. Unfortunately I'm surrounded by faulkin illiterates."

"I'll be seeing you in a couple of weeks. I already have the plane ticket."

"Good," he said. "Toby, by the way, what does cancer feel like?"

"I don't know what it feels like."

"Shit! I have cancer."

"Why would you say that?"

"Cause I have this pain but I'm not sure what it feels like. It is hard to describe."

"Where is it?"

"Here."

"We are on the phone, Jimmy. I can't see where 'here' is."

"I want to die with dignity, Toby, you little shit!"

"I'm sure you are fine."

"God wants me dead."

"He would've killed you already," I said. "Plus you don't believe in God."

"That's why he wants me dead."

"Go put on a pot of coffee and sober up," I said. "I'll see you soon. Don't go performing any weird surgery on yourself either. I want you in one piece when I see you."

"You don't scare me," he erupted again. "You think I am the type to be intimidated? Show your balls around me and I'll blow them off with a shotgun..."

Then again, it might already be too late.

# CHAPTER 13

The brutal summer in Atlanta affords its citizens a rather heavy malaise--what with the sticky humidity and rolling heat. The air is no longer emptiness but something that must be fought off. The heat is like a drug—it makes people sleepy, ill-tempered, reclusive, soft in the head. The disruptive nature of this type of oppression is everywhere. Cars and trucks break down more often, crime goes up, elderly citizens die specifically to complain to the good Lord himself about the frickin' weather. We were passing through the high point of the summer heat wave. July had expired and now it was August's turn to pummel us with record-breaking temperatures. Luckily bartenders are surrounded by ice, and this cool asylum provides us a happy relief.

My face had gone back to its normal shape, my bruises faded to a subtle shade that people either didn't notice or just didn't make mention of because of how slight the blemishing. I was bored, seated on the ice well, stuck in conversation with a young, towheaded white man, a little overzealous, eager to be my friend for some reason. There was a striking intensity about him but not one specific feature lent itself to this overall characteristic. He was somehow pulling off an erroneous perception of himself right before my eyes.

He was talking with fledgling excitement about an artists' community he had just moved into right outside the city. The living experience had been blowing his mind. He couldn't believe that I hadn't heard of it and wanted me to be his guest for one of their parties. He said there were really good looking women always in and out of the place and because they were 'art types' they didn't mind a little casual sex. They insisted on it, in fact. The only rules for the premises were absolute freedom. I told him I had never heard of such a thing but it sounded like fun. He told me he would send me an invitation next time they had a party. I wrote down my address and said that would be fine and to send it on over. He could tell I was a 'fountainhead', he said. All the people living in his new home were 'fountainheads', the source of the life flow, the birth movers of the world.

"I don't see myself as a fountainhead," I insisted. "I'm more like the rippling pool at the bottom of the fountain to which all things spill, the shimmering receptacle that naturally reflects the fountainhead along with the sky, sun, nearby buildings, faces of pedestrians staring into me, casting pennies into my wake. My ripples are playful of the reality they reflect but there is nothing within me that isn't already part of the surrounding environment." I told this to him mainly to shut him up, but after I said it he began slapping himself and telling me that anybody who talked like that had to be a fountainhead.

I wandered over to Zanz's side of the bar to heap my charming brand of complaining on him. He was in the middle of a story about his role as an undercover CIA agent responsible for training the Mexican militia group 'Los Pepes' in order to help them take down the famed drug kingpin Pablo Escobar.

"Zanz, when will people realize that we are full of the worst kind of bullshit—the dull and impractical kind? One of these days we will be exposed for the phonies that we are."

"The impractical kind is the best kind of bullshit," corrected Zanz. "It is its own work of art. The very fact that it is unnecessary is a testament to its strength. If I am somehow given a degree of power and respect for being able to convey ridiculous ideas to mediocre minds, then it is required that I exploit it."

"And you have no remorse?"

"You have to wean yourself off a guilt-based ethic," Zanz recommended. "Stop feeling the need to apologize for your own existence. Instead, embrace your existence. Put value in your intelligence and humble charm, instead of putting value into banal things that are momentarily out of your reach like titles and large sums of money. There are different forms of wealth, Toby—alternative commodities. I'm reminded of the story about the thief who inadvertently breaks into the scholar's house. Upon realizing his mistake he looks around and says, 'shit this place is worthless. There's nothing in here but *books*.'"

"A beautiful allegory. Another booze creation."

"You act like the thief and the scholar combined," he continued. "You have so much at your disposal that you believe is absolutely worthless."

I remained quiet, allowing him to assume that I was letting this all sink in, absorbing his advice, allowing it to manipulate and improve on my attitude. Instead I felt myself becoming plagued with something oddly irrelevant, yet pressing just the same.

"So what happened to the scholar?" I asked after a moment. Zanz looked at me in disbelief.

"What the hell do you mean what happened to the scholar?" he gasped.

"From your little anecdote? Was the scholar home at the time of the robbery? Was he bound and gagged? Did he get shot surprising the thief, perhaps? Or how about his wife? Was he with his wife? Maybe he was with somebody else's wife? Maybe the scholar was out of town? Did the thief vandalize the place in frustration after he realized there was nothing of value? If the scholar was away, what was he doing? Were there children involved? There is a lot you left out, Zanz. Is the scholar okay? I'm sure he must feel violated on some level. What are the measures he can take to prevent this type of crime in the future? You know in America an armed burglary occurs once every twenty seconds."

Zanz raised his hands to the sky in anger. "Do you see what I have to deal with!" he said to God.

"Is that true about a burglary once every twenty seconds?" a customer asked.

"I don't know," I shrugged. "I said it because it sounded alarming."

"The scholar was out of town on sabbatical," Zanz finally conceded. "The thief took a few minor valuables, pawned them, and was eventually shot dead a few weeks later by sheriff's deputies as they tried to apprehend him on an unrelated warrant."

"Thank you."

A customer spilled his drink on himself. I threw a couple of towels down. Zanz did a quick check on the rest of the customers. Other than one or two refills everybody was doing fine—mingling and preening—offering the best of themselves while their more twisted characteristics lie dormant. Saying what they thought people wanted to hear. Begging to be appreciated. My new friend at the end of the bar was happily describing the sexual habits of the girls in his new living arrangement, I figured. Something about his jerky mannerisms convinced me.

"I wonder how Skid Row Paul is making out with Doctor B. Right?"

Zanz mused. "That one is a bloodhound, he is. He'll sniff the bastard out."

"We aren't going to kill the orange man, are we?" I asked.

"Something between humiliation and outright death seems appropriate."

"I am nervous," I said.

"We are doing this for you," Zanz answered.

"I don't necessarily believe that," I countered. "I don't really know why we are doing this, other than sheer cause and effect, like a ball rebounding off a wall. It's just a law of movement."

"You aren't making any sense," Zanz said. "If we aren't doing this for you then we have to do it for the rest of the people that could be victims. You know they are out there. You think this is the first time he's done something like this? He's an irrational freak. Beating people for no good reason."

"I don't want to use anybody else's misery as my motivation, though," I said. "If I harbor their anger for my own personal grudge it means that on some level I'm glad that they suffered, if only so I could act with a clear conscience. Wow. I think I just detected a terrible character flaw within myself."

"So let me get this straight, you twisted bitch," Zanz said. "You don't want to get back at him for what he did to you and you feel like if you encourage your retribution through the pain of other victims you are somehow exploiting it? You are crazy, Toby. Any pain and misery this phony doctor has caused is going to be there regardless of what you do. But if we can maneuver ourselves into a position to prevent him from doing this stuff in the future then we have to act. Where is your sense of collective responsibility?"

"I'm just saying that justification for my own grievances should not rely on anybody else's pain," I said, trying to continue my part of the argument. It was such a mystifying nuance, however, that I wasn't even sure exactly what I meant.

"You are an idiot," he sighed.

"I am delirious poetry and my flesh is the parchment it is written on," I answered. He rolled his eyes and walked away. With nothing pressing to attend to I turned to the bar television to watch the national news. There was a story about a woman from southern California who had recently married the very same man who had shot her and held her captive in his barn for a week. She admitted that she fell in love with him because he was

120

so kind and considerate to nurse her wounds. Indeed, the fact that he had created them seemed almost rude to point out. They had been married in a prison ceremony. Goddamned southern California, I thought to myself. What is it about that place? People are crazy out there. The region just bred characteristics deleterious to normal human functioning. Hell Hollywood alone was proof of that. I wanted a shot of Truth. My hand was inches away from the bottle of peach brandy when the scream erupted. It was a woman's frantic voice.

"Help! Somebody! That man has my purse! Somebody stop him. THAT MAN HAS MY PURSE!"

I looked up to see a hooded figure heading away from the bar at a fast clip towards the front door. The woman's screams continued. Unfortunately for the victim, not only did nobody try to stop the assailant, the sparse crowd actually, unconsciously, cleared a path right to the door for him. But this particular thief, quick and confident, did not count on the fact that almost thirty years prior to the robbery a woman had given birth to a greased lightning son of a bitch named Zanz Alva. In a matter of seconds he had grabbed his billy club, jumped up onto the beer cooler, and was poised to throw. His eyes were steady as he did some quick calculations that no doubt mirrored some mathematical word problem usually found on standardized college entrance exams.

Something like this:

A thief in possession of a stolen handbag is hurrying away from the scene of a crime at a velocity of eight feet per second towards the exit of a drinking establishment. It will take him three and a quarter seconds to reach the door. Meanwhile, a club wrapped in duct tape is to be thrown at the man's cervical vertebrae. It takes two and a quarter seconds to line up the strike. The club has a second and a half to reach its target before the thief is out of the building. What is the required velocity of the club in order to reach the man before he escapes?

Answer:) Using the equation $Vc = Vt$ multiplied by the total time involved (total t), factoring in the two and a quarter seconds used for aim, divided by the club's flight time, we arrive at a resultant velocity of twenty one and a half feet per second. Congratulations, you are now ready for a life of grand disappointment.

"I got em," Zanz assured me, aiming through the crowd.

"Don't throw it!" I warned. "You are going to miss and kill the blood relative of some high-powered attorney."

"No, no," Zanz waved away, "he is in the cross hairs." He let his billy

121

club go, throwing as hard as he could. It sailed inches away from a dozen or so heads, tumbling over itself as it rocketed towards the fleeing man, the purse tucked tightly under his arm. I held my breath. Fought the temptation to look away. For a brief moment it looked like the impossible was about to become reality. Alas no. The club sailed right past the thief's head. All was lost.

Alas no!

In an amazing move that Zanz would later claim was planned perfectly, the club hit the wall, ricocheted off a lighting sconce and caught the thief right across the bridge of the nose. He cried out, blinded as he was, just a few feet from the front door. He dropped the purse and clutched his face. The crowd was stunned into retarded paralysis. Zanz and I raced out from behind the bar—he was in the lead, fully intent on consummating his valor. He dove at the thief and they both went careening out the front door. I myself, in a more passive role, snatched up the purse and the billy club from the floor. The crowd slowly came alive again, parting the way for a young, handsome Asian couple. They raced up to me. The woman had tears in her eyes. Her husband had insanity in his.

"You saved my purse, you saved my purse," she stuttered, throwing her arms around me. I nodded and tried to gently pry her off but she was rather tenacious, as was her husband, who was slowly cutting off my windpipe with his iron embrace.

"You have samurai aim," the man lauded. "You are a deadly weapon." Other customers quickly accumulated around us, loading praise upon me for my quick thinking, precision calculation, and careful throw. It dawned on me that because everybody was watching the thief, nobody had actually seen Zanz throw the club. By the time everybody had gotten caught up to what was going on I had the club in my hand and so the natural assumption was that I was the thrower. I was paraded back to the bar, all the while trying to fight off the congratulations and accolades since I had nothing to do with foiling the robbery, but the rabid, impressed crowd only interpreted my continual head shakes as humility and this pushed them further into a cheering seizure. It was interesting to note that if anybody had bothered to look over their shoulders they would've seen Zanz out in front, on the sidewalk, trying to ram the purse snatcher's head into a metal newspaper vending machine.

"I will bring you something very special for this," the Asian man assured me as I marched back behind the bar in phony triumph. "You have brought honor on yourself and us," he added. "You are a great man."

What the hell, I thought, I might as well take the credit, if only to see what it felt like to be a great man. It was a moment of pure joy, both for the crowd who were still congratulating me, and for myself—their momentary hero. This type of thing would surely never happen to me again, unless of course apathy, moping about, or the ability to boil water became rare and virtuous assets.

People all around the bar reached out to touch me, shared stories of other forms of witnessed heroism, embellished accounts of their own achievements. One woman asked me if I could teach her my throwing style. They were all fascinated and enthralled. They questioned the root of human inequity. They pondered among themselves why people did what they did. Was it heredity or environment? Was it out of necessity or thrill? These lingering questions, baffling as they were, made the celebration of my valor that much more intense. They held onto the moment, their rapture burning out of control. It was time to celebrate, and nobody was going to tell these people, least of all me, who they were allowed to glorify and who they weren't. For myself the adoration was exhausting. People tried to outdo each other's compliments, tried to outmatch and outwit previous praises. Then one man, who looked like he should know, announced heartily that I was a *true* Christian, and that right now Jesus Christ himself was weeping with pride from my act of selflessness. This ethereal compliment brought a whole new dimension to the event. It provided a magnitude of scope and splendor that almost embarrassed the crowd for failing to realize it before and inevitably it pushed them all into quiet reflection. When it became evident that this man's admission could not be improved upon, most people shuffled away and settled back down.

"You see!" shouted my towheaded, art colony resident/friend. "You are a fountainhead. This whole thing has me going crazy. I knew there was a reason I came in here tonight. It is you. You are the reason. I have to introduce you to the man who runs the art community. He will want to meet you. He has to meet you."

"Just invite me when you have a party," I said.

"Oh I will invite you. Hell we won't even need to invite you. We'll have a party in your honor. You will have any woman you want. Jeremiah will see to it. When I tell him what happened here tonight he is going to know that you are a fountainhead."

"Who is Jeremiah?"

"Who isn't Jeremiah," he said. "Jeremiah is the guy who runs the premises. But he is so much more. He tells me things that change me. He is a brilliant man. The girls do anything he says. You have got to come to the party. It will change your life."

"Does this art community have a name?"

"No, no," he shook his head. "Because once we have a name we become that name. And we aren't trying to make ourselves smaller but make ourselves bigger...and the name...we are bigger than...we outgrow the name as soon as we have one..." he shook his head again to clear away the confused thought. "He explains it better than I can. You talk to him and he'll explain it perfectly. You just promise you'll come to our party."

"I'll come to your party," I said.

"You are going to be at the party?"

"The party will be attended by me, myself."

"If the party is there so will you?"

"I don't know how many other ways we can put this," I said.

"God I'm freaking out right now."

# CHAPTER 14

I was bent over tying up the scraggly lace on my work boot when I felt the tap on my shoulder. The restaurant was closed and I thought I had locked the door. There was the polite utterance of "Excuse me, please." I stood up to see the same, young Asian gentleman who had been so incredibly grateful to me for his misconception that I had anything to do with getting his wife's purse back. In fact, I could tell from his wide smile that he had lost none of his gratitude. Both his hands were behind him. I surmised, correctly as it turns out, that he was holding something behind his back.

"Do you remember me?" he asked.

"From a few hours ago?"

"I told you I had something special to give you for your bravery and kindness, and so I have come to keep my word."

"It was nothing, really," I brushed off.

"You must accept my gift or it will bring shame to me!" he cried. I wasn't too familiar with his cultural rules and conditions concerning the settling of accounts, but I assured him that in America we have no problem taking things off other peoples' hands. This pleased him immensely. He carefully brought the object of concealment out from behind his back. It was a large, unmarked glass bottle, its contents readily visible. The air left my lungs as I struggled to make sure my eyes weren't deceiving me. A heavy, life-altering seriousness descended.

"Holy shit," I remarked slowly. "What is that?"

"It is called *soju*," he explained, setting the bottle on top of the bar. "Very good. Very strong. A high grade derivative of Japanese *sake*. It is whiskey made from rice. You must drink it. It is only for men of power."

I looked inside the bottle, unconcerned with the clear liquid in it. I was taken, however, with the enormous cobra snake that was coiled inside the bottle soaking in that clear liquid. Its placid, fanned out head, its blank eyes staring at me, its tiny forked tongue floating limply out of its mouth.

"Is that a real cobra snake floating in there?" I asked him.

"Yes it is."

"Is it dead?"

"Even more dangerous in death than it was in life."

"Where did you get that?"

"Let's drink."

"Toby I was wondering if you..." Zanz had emerged from the bathroom but was now frozen in place as his eyes settled on the large bottle.

"You will drink it, yes?" said the Asian man. Zanz and I looked at each other and silently decided it wasn't a good idea. We knew at that point that our answer was obviously going to be yes. I had sampled mescal with a worm in it, but this was ridiculous. The dead snake took up half the space inside the bottle. Should we do it or shouldn't we? Was it a matter of personal caution? If so what the hell was personal caution? We had never heeded that in the past. Why should this be any different. Zanz went over to the bottle, unscrewed the top and peered inside.

"What do you think it tastes like?" I whispered.

"There is, I believe, only one way to find out," he answered.

"Do you think the venom is still in it?" I asked.

"Man I hope so," he nodded.

"Three glasses!" the Asian man cried out.


So there we were, each holding a glass of some high-octane preservative. I took one last look at the cobra and its dead expression from inside the bottle, tipped my glass to it and threw it back. Zanz did the same. My throat went into spasms, seized up, tried to block itself off. I couldn't breathe. I knew at that point that I was going to die, and only then did I weigh the consequences of this ridiculous decision. Zanz was ashen. The Asian man was standing there completely unaffected, inoculated as he was from years of drinking this shit. Why would he do this to us? We had helped him, after all. But now, as it was all too late, I understood his logic. By saving his wife's purse we had actually shamed this little man and now his only successful redemption would be to kill us off so we wouldn't be around as a constant reminder of his ineptitude at protecting his wife's belongings. I wondered why I hadn't seen this coming. The grim reaper drove his red chariot right to the front door and pulled on the reins of his winged, black steeds.

"Should we drink some water?" I asked, shocked that I could talk. The grip on my neck loosened. Fresh air filled my lungs. The grim reaper gave me the finger, whipped at his steeds, and took off into the sky. "Or maybe we should induce vomiting?"

"That's ridiculous," Zanz argued as he got a hold of himself. "The only way to make it better is to do another shot!"

"What?"

"Yes!"

"You are wise," the Asian man said as he refilled our glasses. "We must keep drinking." The second round was far better. My tongue could now decipher the general flavor. It was kind of gritty, robust, snaky. We had another. I inspected my glass for any signs of corrosion. How bad could this *soju* stuff really be? I supposed the effects of drinking it could possibly manifest in the long term. Years would pass. I would be leading a rather normal life, riding with my pregnant wife to the hospital, her contractions minutes apart. After enduring a twenty-hour labor, I would enter the room, where my flushed and exhausted woman would be lying there holding our beautiful, scaly, lizard child.

"Is it a boy or a girl?" I would ask my doting spouse.

"Well, it fertilizes its own eggs, so kind of both," she would answer.

Our Asian malefactor turned benefactor bid us goodnight for the evening. He shook our hands, gave a gracious bow, told us we could keep the bottle. We thanked him in turn for showing us our own mortality and hoped for his family's general success. He walked out the door.

"More for us," Zanz said as he refilled the glasses. He put the bottle back down. The cobra's head was now jutting out from the surface of the liquid. This pleased Zanz. "We must keep drinking until we have released our snake from his briny prison."

"Maybe for once we should entertain the possibility of some kind of moderation?" I suggested.

"Hell no," Zanz said. "This elixir has made me mighty—like a thundercloud. We have been given a rare opportunity here. For a sense of consistency and closure, as well as for the poetic responsibility, we must drink the entire bottle." I understood. This type of thing was a once in a lifetime possibility for guys like us. No matter what resulted from the experience, the only real tragedy would be the haphazard appreciation of so unique an affair by allowing it to peter out over an extended period of time.

Down the pipe it went.


"You know, I think it was easier in the Nineties," Zanz reasoned as we sat at the bar drinking our snake juice. "In the Nineties there was this impending dread about the new millennium. It gave people motivation to do something because it was all closing down. Now, as we have passed into the millennium, it all seems a bit too wide, too overwhelming. Like fresh, fallen snow all the way out to the horizon. No tracks to follow. Complete and terrifying freedom. We have roughly another thousand years to go before we feel the push again."

"Could you ever imagine that a creature with no arms and legs can move at speeds of twenty miles an hour?" I pondered, tapping at the bottle where the snake was slumped.

"It is a magical world," Zanz said. "And to think that people debate the existence of a fine and friendly God."

"Do you hear a rattling sound?"

"Cobras don't have rattlers."

"I think we are going to succeed in drinking the bottle," I said.

"Did you have any doubt that we would fail?"

"Don't knock failure," I said. "Failure is safe haven, after all. It's a solid force field against expectation, risk, and change. It's complacent and unpretentious. It is pure and unmasked, the thorns of my rose, protecting me and preventing my escape."

"I think you are getting a little too drunk," Zanz said as he wobbled, then steadied himself.

"This snake has taught me something," I said. "He is my friend. I'm beginning to understand about original sin. Excessive pride. I guess we can tack on gluttony as well." I filled our glasses up again. "This is a fall from grace, that is what it is. Exactly what is expected of mankind. I now understand the stakes of Civilization's first big decision. Here's to chasing the fruit of the tree of knowledge." We clinked glasses.

"Bad for the soul but surprisingly high in fiber and vitamin C," Zanz pointed out.

"Is it any wonder that a snake is involved in all this?"

"It seems fitting," he nodded.

"Why do we do this to ourselves?"

"I hate to tell you Toby but men smarter than you and I have tried and failed to come up with an answer to that very question."

"I'm always one drink away from complete understanding."

The bar was getting swimmy as the level of the soju fell and more and more of the snake's body was freed from its watery tomb. The reptile was slumped against the glass like a drunk who has passed out in a telephone booth. I looked around the bar. It occurred to me, in my compromised condition, that a bar is more than a bar--it is a complex phenomenon of lights, colors, promise, chance, prospect, hope and hazard. There is a strange, hypnotic voodooism in the aesthetic of the different bottles, a substantial mysticism that extends to the bartenders, like an apothecary who by simply shuffling around his test tubes and bromides provokes a mood of tacit courtesy, and with small, knowing glances maintains the unsettling possibility that by mixing just the right ingredients an unfavorable customer may very well be turned into a warty toad or dog shit.

"I haven't heard or seen much of Baron," I said, going as long as I could without mentioning him.

"Which is exactly what you wanted."

"You aren't the least bit concerned with what he is doing out there in your cabin?"

"I am concerned but not how you mean," he said.

"Have you seen him?" I asked.

"I run supplies out to him. Bring him food. Tranquilizers. Handcuffs."

"Are you going to tell me who this woman is that he has out there?"

"I'm not sure," he said. "Something very strange happened to Baron out in the desert in California. It's something he hasn't been able to discuss, but I am going to let him come around. When he is ready he'll tell us. He needs to relax and feel safe for now."

"But is he holding her against her will?" I asked.

"Yes he is," said Zanz.

"And you approve?"

Zanz looked down. "I have no choice in the matter." He sighed and regarded the empty bottle with the reptile corpse in it. "It is time to go home."

If I felt a false sense of confidence for thinking we had bested the dangers of drinking the entire bottle of the snake juice, I was soon to be corrected as a wave of sickness overcame me as I was staggering towards my car in delusive victory, cursing myself for going along with the idea of drinking the entire bottle of soju. It was Zanz's fault and it was my fault. This was why it was dangerous for me to be around him too often. We were always inviting the elements of our destruction. Zanz would've argued that we had to do it to achieve greatness, and of course with greatness comes great suffering. To put it in terms of an intelligent argument: Would Edgar Allen Poe have been Edgar Allen Poe if he hadn't been Edgar Allen Poe? I think not. His existence in a historical context was defined by his suffering. An ominous prospect to be sure. We were destined to endure the pain of our artistry. I felt like I was going to be sick.

I sat down on my couch, figuring something was very strange about my apartment. There was too much music. It was far too loud. And there were too many people in my small apartment. Strange people. I didn't recognize one person. I tried to ask one of them what the hell they thought they were doing in my apartment but they just gave me a disgusted look and walked away. And it was too smoky in my apartment. My landlady would be upset that all these people that I didn't even know were smoking in my apartment. One of the reasons she had agreed to rent the carriage house to me was because I was a non-smoker. And all my furniture had been removed from my apartment. Removed and replaced with a bar and a dance floor. And the bartender had charged me for a drink, in my own home. It was then that I began to realize I might not be home. Now I had to figure out where the hell I was. It started to come back to me. I had been walking towards my car, but then I had walked past it down the road looking for something I couldn't figure out--a lumbering, whiskey-sodden freak. I stopped at the door of a club. An unfriendly bouncer blocked my way.

"Can I help you?"

"I would like to go into your establishment," I said hazily.

"Get lost," he said. I walked away, thought about it, and turned and walked back to the door.

"Excuse me sir?" I inquired.

"Can I help you?" the bouncer asked.

"I was just wondering why I can't go into your establishment?"

"Get lost," he said. I walked away, thought about it and turned and walked back to the door.

"Excuse me sir?"

"Can I help you?"

"Am I being turned away because I am a nobody? Because I am too short? Do I lack the proper wardrobe? Is it because I am dissatisfied with myself? Do you find me inferior? Is it because I am in debt, because my belief system is in shambles? Go ahead and give it to me straight. I can take it!"

"Get lost."

"You know, for somebody who is always asking if you can help me you aren't doing a very good job of it."

Finally the girl at the cash register right inside the door just told the bouncer to let me in. I was making the place look bad by staggering around in circles outside of it. I wandered in, a mismatched addition to the club in my dirty work clothes, sweaty, smelling of alcohol, rotten and reptilian. I had never heard of the place. The club was hot, dark and smoky which I would've loved if it had been a cup of coffee. I needed some sobering elements. The room itself was filled with strange looking men smoking pungent cigarettes, whispering freakish come-ons in unfamiliar languages to scantily clad women. The whole crowd all appeared so unimpressed with anything that it became an odd form of self-loathing, as if they hated themselves for having to endure their own superiority. The crowd cross-pollinated bizarre viewpoints, got high, tried to seduce that beautiful, special someone who in the harsh light of the following morning resembles a science fiction villain, an oozing creature with marked deformity.

I sat back on the couch watching the lights go whipping by like a dream, glad to be ignored, trying to sober up, happy to be the alienated observer in my own personal outcome. A lone figure appeared, tall and nacreous, wearing the darkness, pale like a tormented ghost, floating towards me. She took a seat on the couch and grabbed me by the scruff of my neck. Now I recognized her. It was Raylene Corley, Three-a-Day Ray, Baron's ex-wife, scorned woman, recluse. She looked exactly as she did the first time I met her at her house. Crazy hair, pink bathrobe, the only difference being the old running sneakers she was wearing.

"I told you I could find you!" she yelled, still holding me by the neck.

"How the hell did you get in here?" I asked. "You are wearing a bathrobe."

"They want interesting people in this place. I just look interesting."

"You are certainly that."

"Which doesn't explain how you got in here," she said.

"By being a nuisance."

"Figures." She looked me over. "You were supposed to do something for me," she reminded.

"What?"

"Powder my ass!" she scowled. "What do you mean what? You were supposed to find my husband."

"Best to leave him alone," I said. "We don't want you losing your other arm now do we?" I pulled her hand from my neck. She sat back, studying me.

"Are you going to buy me a drink?" she asked.

"Here," I said. "You can have mine."

She took it and sniffed at the rim of the glass. "What is it?"

"You'll love it. It's alcohol." I rubbed my eyes. "I can't drink anymore tonight. I just got done drinking a poison even worse than the one you fed me."

"I never apologized for that," she said.

"Okay."

"And I never will!"

I felt like I was molting. I felt my tongue being cleaved at the tip. I kept hearing a hissing sound. I wondered if I should make my way to a hospital for some anti-venom. I decided that if I unhinged my jaw I could easily fit two or three people into my alimentary canal, the people all around me that were talking, drinking, feeling each other up, engaging in air copulation with themselves on the dance floor.

"Where have you been?" Ray shouted. "I thought we were friends."

"Do you always poison your friends?"

"That was an accident." She blushed with childish contrition. "I like to refer to it as making an impression."

"I was going to come see you," I said. "As a matter of fact we are closing in on three in the morning. That's prime time for you."

"I thought you might be dead. I was worried."

"About me?"

"About being prosecuted for murder. So yeah, I was worried about you in a way."

"I like you Ray," I told her. "Don't know why but I do."

"Don't go getting soft on me you twerp," she spat. "I like you too...for now...that could change at any second. Don't get too comfortable."

"Okay."

"Do you want to dance?" she asked me.

"Are you serious?"

"When I make a joke you will laugh. That is how you will know it is a fucking joke. Check yourself. Are you laughing? No. Good. You can now be convinced I am serious."

"Okay, I guess."

The club must've been closing soon because the music was getting slow. Moody and atmospheric with a soulful, echoing voice rising and falling wordlessly in the background. Ray made me take hold of the cuff on the limp sleeve of her left arm. Her right arm gripped my shoulder. Not much of a dancer, I let her lead me around the floor. Deft and graceful, her running sneakers glided around the room. Her eyes were pleasant and concentrated. The lines in her face faded. She was enjoying herself. In another life, one without pain, she would've been beautiful.

"I've been meaning to ask...why do they call you Three-a-Day Ray?"

"Because nobody on earth could handle four a day."

"Thank you for clearing it up."

"You don't seem too sure of yourself," she continued. "I can tell from the way you dance. You can tell a lot from the way a person dances. You have a hard time making up your mind. It is the uncertainty factor that drives your tragic comedy."

"I'm going through a phase," I said.

"The moon goes through phases," she shot back as she made me twirl the limp sleeve of her robe while she performed a subtle pirouette. "People just make vague excuses about their situations. I can tell there is no such thing as happiness for you. You can achieve something but you won't because you will be proving to yourself that even with achievement you will be just as miserable as you were before."

"What is this, therapy?"

She gave a shrug, continued moving me in small circles.

"You can try to avoid me but you know it won't work," she said. "I'm not going to give up on you until you take me to Baron."

"Why do you care about him?"

"That is my business."

"I don't know what to do," I admitted.

"See, uncertainty again! Who is good and who is bad? What are the right choices to make. You know what it is going to say on your gravestone. 'Still Deciding!'"

"It is getting a little complex."

"You are afraid that if you take me to him you will betray your friends. But if you don't take me to him you may find yourself in a worse spot because of it. So just sit there in your uncertainty. I like it. Looks good on you."

"He is not alone, Ray."

"I don't care. When I make up my mind to do something nobody stops me. He is a wanted man. For fraud. Embezzlement. He used to make his living emptying the bank accounts of lonely women. Be that as it may I still love him. Our souls are in love, you see, but it is our bodies that have caused all the trouble. I have the solution."

"I don't understand," I said.

"Remove the bodies and our souls will be in union. Eternal union."

"You are going to kill him and kill yourself?"

"Did I use that word? You may think me somewhat stupid but I do have that word in my vocabulary and know how to use it if I need to convey what the word means!" She pulled me closer and got her lips right up to my ear. Her one arm was like an iron brace. "The word kill only applies to those who fail to acknowledge the afterlife. I can tell you aren't a believer. It is the way you dance. I can tell you don't believe in heaven."

"You are making me a little uneasy, Ray," I grunted, trying to shake the rigid hold of her half embrace.

"I would love to help you get some backbone," Ray offered in a tone that suggested she could hardly tolerate the prospect. "But like a medical procedure what is beneficial may also be extremely uncomfortable."

"What are you talking about?"

"I had a vision last night," she whispered, ceasing to move, just holding me fast. "A gruesome one. Blood and carnage. Beasts ripping each other apart. You were there. But for some reason these creatures didn't harm you."

"Was this a dream?" I asked.

"No for Christ's sake. Dream is also a word I have in my limited, halfwit vocabulary. I would've used this word if I wanted to convey a sleep impression. I used the word 'vision'. After these beasts were done killing each other a big pool of crimson spread out and a phoenix arose, red with eyes of hellfire, bigger than anything you've ever seen, feeding on the corpses. That was when I saw you again, covered in blood. But it wasn't your blood. It was the blood of the others. That doesn't mean, however, that you weren't in pain. You were in terrible pain. The pain was a cowardly ache in your gut, hemorrhaging inside. It is the bleeding ulcer of your self-deception. Thanks for the drink and the dance. Get home safely. Take care of yourself. If you don't help me find my husband I'm going to have to kill you."

Ray gave me a pinch on the cheek (gluteal) and left me standing in the middle of the dance floor as she hurried on to wherever. The other patrons, standing in the shadowy folds of the dimness, no longer regarded me as a luckless inferior. They were now all terrified of me. I was the lone survivor of a dangerous dance with a hideous harpy, after all. They had narrowly escaped, themselves. A stylish gentleman held the door for me as I walked out into the street and another offered me an umbrella to shield me from a sudden downpour. I declined and stood in the middle of the road, a beggar's baptism in the sour city rain. Cars went by and were obliged to miss me. A woman hurried to my side and wiped my wet brow with a napkin before carefully placing it back in her purse. I danced a free-form jig through the sizzling thunderstorm. A couple of entranced penitents mimicked my moves. When I reached my car these eager strangers stole my keys away from me. I was driven home in my own car and placed like a swaddled infant on my couch and bade goodnight as the Koi swam through my murky dreams.

# CHAPTER 15

I woke up so bleeding hungover that I was blind, deaf, and dumb. My eyelids were crusted shut, my mouth and throat were like sandpaper. A class five hurricane. Whatever, I shouldn't have expected anything less from an alcohol that preserves perfectly a large dead cobra snake. I came to the conclusion that I was lying on my couch. The circumstances surrounding how I got there were unknown. As was my normal habit I tried to remember the last thing from the night before. Three-a-Day Ray in her bathrobe talking about death and carnage, which I must admit was rather peculiar, even for that time of night in that part of town.

I stood up and walked cautiously, arms flailing out in front of me as I moved blindly through my apartment towards the bathroom. I felt I was making progress until running smack into a premature wall, deciding then that it was best to try a different direction. I hit another wall, fell forward and wound up in the closet. I wrestled with some hanging clothes, beat them into submission, and freed myself. I stepped out of the closet and worked at my eyelids with my hands to pry them open, and after a moment they conceded. Blinding light poured into my skull—a burning incandescence. I could make out blurred shapes, and there was some type of vague commotion...someone was knocking at my door. Probably my landlady. I found the bathroom, slammed the toilet seat up and let loose stomach juice and bile until there was nothing left but empty heaves. I then went to the sink and splashed some cold water on my face. This prompted my vision to return, although when I looked at myself in the mirror I kind of hoped it would go away again. My eyes were so red they were glowing, my face was white like death—sagging, puffy, hopeless—but also comfortingly pathetic.

My throat was so dry that it was making it difficult to breathe, so I stumbled into the kitchen and opened the refrigerator, grabbed the first thing I got my hands on. I chugged and chugged. I stumbled back to the couch. The knocking at the door persisted. I yelled for Nona to come back later, I was in no shape to deal with another human being. the knocking got louder. There was no way to concentrate with this racket. I went over to the door and opened it, just a few inches. Through the crack I could see that it was the same man I had been talking to at the bar the night before, the one who was thrilled to be in my company. The blonde-haired man who lived at the art community. I tried to figure out a polite way to ask him what the hell he was doing at my doorstep.

"What the hell are you doing at my doorstep?"

"I am here to take you to Jeremiah."

"I don't understand," I said.

"He wants to see you."

"I gave you my address because I thought you were going to send me an invitation to a party. Later. Much later. Maybe never. But definitely not now."

"Yes. The party will happen," he said. "But when I told Jeremiah about your heroics he insisted that I bring you to him, and when he insists, I deliver."

"This is not a good time," I said.

"It is the perfect time. It is THE time. I am sorry but you have to come with me. When you meet him you'll know it was what you had to do."

"Absolutely not!"

"Don't be a slave to negativity," he said through the crack in the door. "Right now your polarities are reversed. You are in the 'anti'."

"I am in the hangover," I said.

"You won't be for long," the man promised. "Jeremiah. He has these abilities. He can align you properly. You are fighting with yourself right now. He will establish you righteously back into yourself. You will be in accord. The cosmic energy will rush through you. It will bring euphoria. You will feel better than you've ever felt in your whole life. Higher. Confident. Free from your self-infliction. I told him you were a fountainhead and he ordered me to come get you. His will is my will and if I fail he fails and he never fails."

"You are saying that this Jeremiah person can cure a hangover?" I asked, my resistance fading.

"Like water putting out a fire," said the man. "Like a peaceful God calming the restless thunderstorms of the sun."

"Does it have to be now?"

"Yes it has to be now."

I was about to continue the argument, but something very strange pulled my attention away from my uninvited guest. There was a bubbling in my loins. I glanced down. Highly irregular. I told him to wait outside a moment and slammed the door in his face. I ran to the bathroom and locked myself in. A sharp pain sliced through my pelvis, bending me over the sink. The throbbing was getting worse. The sharp pain was getting sharper. That was when I realized that, when I had reached for something to drink in my refrigerator, I had drunk Zanz's potency tea. All of it. Every drop of the seahorses and ginseng and emperor remains and mystery root and whatever else.

"Don't be nervous," the man yelled from the other side of the bathroom door. "Today is the first day of your new life. By the way my name is Zephyr. What is yours?"

"I told you to wait outside," I shouted.

"Whatever happens from this point is no longer within your limited will. You have already been absorbed. Do yourself the greatest favor of your life and submit to your newfound splendor."

There were signs of internal trauma in my groin. The pure rigidity of my most cherished of body parts was like nothing I had ever experienced or imagined. It had shot skyward with all the pressure of a hot springs geyser. Debilitating cramps were on the attack. I pulled down my pants to *survey the damage*.

"What is your name?" he repeated.

"Toby!" I called out.

"Our names are almost identical," said Zephyr from the other side of the door.

"Using what alphabet system?" I said.

"They both have an airy quality."

"Look, Zephyr, there is a new element to this situation," I explained through the door, feeling like a fool for having to do so. "I'm getting sick."

"I am trying to heal you," he said. "His will is my will and if I fail he fails and he never fails."

"If you don't leave I may have to call the police," I said.

"There is no earthly force that can keep you from meeting Jeremiah today," said Zephyr. It sounded like he was weeping. "All your pain ends today. All your doubt ends today. All your misgivings end today. All your velleities end today. Can you believe it? I don't even know what that word means but it is somehow appropriate. That is how I know Jeremiah is speaking through me."

Quite honestly I was afraid to touch my stiffness. It was discolored, misshapen, and quivering like a plucked guitar string. I babbled a series of futile apologies to my manhood and dug under the sink for some kind of adhesive. I found some old electrical tape and fastened myself to my leg, knowing that this almost ensured our relationship would never be the same again. There was a definite breach of agreement, something that couldn't be hammered out in court, a personal betrayal that would haunt me for the rest of my life. I wound the adhesive around my leg, speaking words of encouragement, forgiveness and redemption. I gave a general reminder that we were in this together. I spoke of happier times and promised that they would soon be here again. I was having a hard time concentrating. All the blood had left my cranium to swell my genitals like a baboon's behind.

"Who are you talking to?" asked Zephyr.

"Give me a minute," I said.

"This is a glorious day."

"I can't believe this is happening," I said as I fell to the floor, no longer able to use my legs. The bathroom door was kicked open. Zephyr's hysterical weeping face hovered over me.

"I can't either but we must believe, brother. Let me help you. Get up. You will be healed. This is Jeremiah's way of making you come see him. He will remove the pain. This is a glorious, glorious day."


Zephyr was driving my car. I was doubled over in the passenger seat, leaning towards the door. The streets of the city were strangely vacated. The buildings leered down like decaying monsters. People were absent from the streets and the sidewalks, hiding in a collective all-permeating shame of my absurd situation. Zephyr was making light-hearted small talk but I wasn't paying attention. Wild thoughts of teenage obsession beat through me—middle school librarians and high school english teachers, neighborhood housewives bent over their gardens, cheerleaders, sorority girls following ancient traditions of sleepovers and heavy petting, while I sat there sweating like a sex felon whose barred jail window just happens to overlook a nudist colony.

Zephyr drove further than I thought, to a plot of rural abandon. It was all woods and small fields. We passed a few mobile homes. A man with no shirt and a long beard waved at us. A couple of dirty looking children were busy climbing an old tree. When my car passed them they stared, frozen on the various limbs. Only their eyes moved, following my car as it lurched and clanked on the uneven dirt. Not at all what I expected. I would be out of there as soon as possible. I had to get to a hospital soon or I was afraid they would have to amputate.

The car emerged into a clearing where a long, nondescript, two-story, slapped together building sat plainly in the middle of an open field. A few rusted out, wheelless old cars wasting away in the tall grass surrounding the building lent the whole thing a sense of proper abandon. There were some smaller structures in the distance, and a field in which rows of vegetation were tended to by a handful of hunched gardeners holding small baskets. Zephyr pulled the car up to the front door of the main building and shut the ignition off, tossing me the keys. The jewel of my anatomy felt like it was going to rocket off. I took a few deep breaths and pulled myself out of the car. I tried to walk as naturally as possible, which was difficult at first due to the pain and the electrical tape, but I made some quick adjustments and eventually my walk fell into an old west swagger that hopefully wouldn't arouse suspicion.

We walked through the main doors into a small foyer. Not much to the place. The walls were particle board and sheet rock, the floors warped linoleum and worn carpet, the air dankness and body odor. In an adjacent room an old phone on a nearby desk was flashing a tiny red light—its pulse blending a poly-rhythm with the one in my pants. I felt this was supposed to mean something and tried to figure out how to properly interpret it. Other than that the place seemed deserted. I followed Zephyr down a long hallway.

"He's waiting for you," Zephyr said with chimerical drowsiness.

"Jeremiah?"

"Father Jeremiah," he said.

"Fine."

"We've had quite a year," he boasted from over his shoulder as he led me down a dim hallway with a series of small rooms on either side. None of the rooms had doors. Some had sheets hung for privacy, some didn't. They all felt empty.

At the end of the hallway there was a large oil rendering of a man who would turn out to be Father Jeremiah. The background of the painting was eerily naturalistic—big, happy sun over his shoulder, mountains in the distance, children holding hands in a circle, a field of rich vegetation stretched around them. It struck me as the type of verdant utopia found in children's biblical illustrations and on salad dressing labels.

"We expect to really get the word out in the upcoming months," my guide went on. "Radio commercials. Conventions. It is all part of Father's plan." He turned back to make sure I was still there. I gave him a nod and a smile and when he turned back I surreptitiously adjusted myself.

At the end of the hallway was Jeremiah's office, significantly more spacious but as cheaply decorated as the rest of the building. The silver haired patriarch was behind a large desk in a matching black sweat suit. Another man about my age was sitting across from him in a wheelchair. The wheelchair fellow appeared hostile.

"Father," the wheelchair man cried from across the desk. "We need to have a meeting concerning scroll seventeen. There are some things in it that I strongly disagree with. It could cause problems for us down the line! WE NEED TO DO IT SOON!"

"Fine, fine, Jim Donald," Jeremiah eased, looking up at my guide and I standing in the doorway. "We shall talk about that later." Jeremiah stood up and spread his arms. "Hello Toby, welcome. Zephyr has told me all about you." He came around the desk and gave me a hug. He then introduced me to the man in the wheelchair. "And this is Jim Donald." I told him it was nice to meet him. Jim Donald said nothing, just shook my hand limply and avoided eye contact. Scroll seventeen must've been a son of a bitch. He wheeled himself out of the office. Zephyr floated out behind him like the winds he was named after. I jumped into a chair and leaned over to quell the uprising in my trousers.

"Make yourself comfortable," Jeremiah said. "Can I get you anything?"

"No thank you," I murmured. There was nothing he could provide that would comfort me. The rage in my pants was going full blast with no signs of easing up. Jeremiah continued talking to me, motioning with his hands, explaining something about giving me an extensive tour of the facilities, including a visit to the laboratory, the hydroponic gardens, the artesian water well system, his on-site mansion to meet some of his wives. I tried to appear amiable and listen carefully to what he had to say. Unfortunately Jeremiah's calm voice had to compete with the army of Japanese Taiko drums pounding themselves through my crotch.

"It seems immediately evident that you are a fountainhead," Jeremiah went on. "I think you will find that when you take a walk around the community you will be inspired. You will meet people just like yourself. This place offers you a chance to change your life. For the better!"

"It seems like a very nice place," I told him. "A little off the beaten path."

"Yes but it is a whole world unto itself. I think you would find yourself a perfect match for it."

"I see."

"An environment of fountainheads. Of men and women who want a new and better world," he added.

"Yup." I glanced around casually, not at anything in particular, but to keep the meeting, if that's what this could be called, free and easy. I glanced out a window. A woman was bathing an infant in a portable cooler under a tree. I turned back to Jeremiah. He was concentrating on me, his manner completely confident and comfortable, a mood of quiet poise.

"How long has this place been around?" I asked.

"I've owned the land for some time. I started the community about five years ago, although there has been a sudden emergence, if you will. We think it is due to the new millennium and our exciting philosophy."

"What is your philosophy?"

"It is the belief in and hope for the future," he answered, leaning back with his hands clasped under his chin. "What we are trying to promote, our mission if you will, is for total physical, mental, and social well-being. Self-actualization. Peace and Understanding. Vitality. This type of undertaking is an around the clock endeavor."

"And how do you promote this type of living?" I asked. His smile widened.

"You simply have to allow yourself to begin the path," he said.

"Sounds interesting," I said with a slight moan as the problem in my pants continued its ruthless throb.

"More than interesting, it is the start of a whole new life," Jeremiah confidently announced, sitting back in his chair. "Understanding life through devotion, commitment. It makes things simple. Makes things clear." He motioned somewhere off to the side. "I've got some printed information you can take with you when you leave."

"Thank you."

"So tell me about yourself, Toby. I want to know about YOU," he said, leaning back in his desk chair. "What is Toby all about? I want some insight to your personal habits and tendencies, or the wants of your soul, for that matter." He leaned forward and stared right at me. "Now I want you to tell me something personal, something close to you, something in your past that may have deeply affected you. Your parents, for instance. Tell me about them."

I went to speak but a painful spasm ripped through my gut. "Died," I managed to get out.

"How tragic!" Jeremiah offered, falling dramatically back from his desk. His gaze was hypnotic. "You must've felt so alone. You must have had a very tough time."

"Sure," I spit out, tightening up my abdominal muscles and letting out a low groan, leaning all the more forward. My erection was getting worse. Erections, by nature, want to become non-erections. They usually insist on only one solution. Jeremiah stared at me.

"I see," he nodded with a glimmer in his eyes, an indication of a mind hard at work. I wondered if he thought me a more likely candidate for inclusion into his community because of my orphaning. A man-child with no real definite sense of self. Easily manipulated. There could be an inheritance involved. "I'm certainly not trying to put any undue pressure upon your shoulders," he explained. "We want you to be here of your own freewill. We want you to have all the facts."

"Of course," I nodded.

"How else can you be an effective part of our community?" he furthered. "How else can you understand and embrace our ideals and transmit these ideals to others who are lost and miserable? How else can you truly be on the path to vitality, the vitality of life?"

"Of course," I repeated due to a mind numbing lack of words.

"All of our fountainheads--men, women and children--are all committed to each other's unfettered happiness," he bragged. "People who almost lose themselves in their devotion, but find something much more valuable. In time if you were to join our family you would come to know this level of experience. You would be able to say without hesitation that you'd be confident in taking a bullet for me, and I would have to be able to say the same!"

"You'd have to be able to say that you were confident I'd take a bullet for you?" I asked.

"Hmm," Jeremiah said. "I understand a great many things, Toby. You don't get to be my age and in my position without being able to pick out and discern the finer points of human nature. For instance I can tell you have deep periods of depression and isolation. You are dissatisfied.

What happened to your childhood optimism? Where have all your dreams gone?" He stood up from his chair, walked around behind it, gripped the back. "Look no further, son. All you've ever wanted is right here." He spread his arms wide, inviting me to look around, as if my lost hopes and dreams were tangible packages that had mistakenly been delivered to his office after a shipping screw up.

"You are not married, Toby, am I correct?" he said.

"No."

"Well, that's alright. There are plenty of women."

"In the world or on this property?" I asked.

"There are plenty of women in the world," he answered, "but there are plenty of good women right here."

"On the property?"

"Wholesome women."

"I assume, of course, you mean on the property."

"Vital women."

"Property women?"

"We'd have no problems finding you a suitable partner," he finished confidently. "I personally oversee all...partnerships." The mere mention of the word *partnerships* sent my nether regions into priming contractions, as if my body was ready to respond with a demonstrative gesture to this man of what my potential partners were in store for. My breathing, yet again, locked up. Sweat poured out of me. Jeremiah sensed that something was wrong.

"Are you okay, Toby? You look distressed."

"I'll be alright," I wheezed amiably.

"I know this is a lot to take in," he went on as I clenched and hoped for the best. "Our world here is multi-faceted. We have our line of marketed herbal remedies, we have our beliefs, we have a recording studio, a ropes course, our gun collection and shooting range. We watch movies in the cafeteria on Friday night. We offer courses in social revelation, psychophysics, psychometry, theology and anatomy. We have our fun. I'm offering you a way to live your dreams, to be the person you've always wanted to be. In today's society it is hard to find happiness. Turn on the television, Toby. Watch any talk show. The modern nuclear family is out of touch with the needs of its younger members. This perpetuates itself into generations of misery. Fathers against sons. Daughters running wild to spite their mothers. Who else do we look to? The government?" He let out a laugh. "Uncle Sam is a paranoid monster with no real leadership.

Celebrities are depraved money-grubbers. All the role models are doing drugs and videotaping themselves in the middle of fornication. There needs to be a restructuring of the elements in charge of our well-being. You talk to people all the time, don't you Toby? You seem like a friendly fellow. Does anybody ever come across as truly happy? I mean, genuinely radiant? Apathy, intolerance, distrust, desperate egoism and depravity around every corner, and you are going to tell me that any person out there has the slightest chance to feel good about themselves?" Jeremiah leaned back on a bookshelf and shook his head in pity. "That is why our community is going to be a revelation. We speak the truth and we deliver the happiness you deserve. We are a group dedicated to the principles of strong trust, friendship, cooperation, love, brotherhood, and above all else the total absence of any and all perversions."

"Perversions?" I asked as my erection and I poked our heads up. The word sparked a sudden guilt. After all here he was about to rant about perversion and here I was secretly harboring the very symbol of that offense. My host assumed a whole new level of seriousness. He leaned down from where he stood and fixed his eyes on me. I felt, in a very specific way, that I was about to explode.

"Oh yes, Toby. Perversion. It's the worst thing there is. If there is one factor that leads to the ultimate ruin of mind, body and soul it is perversion. That bloated, bulgy, distended, ugly affliction that rots out lives. The very thing that causes a person to veer from what is good."

"I see," I moaned.

"Perversion is a terrific throb, an unyielding pressure that leads to ultimate degradation when we use ourselves irresponsibly and selfishly. It pushes people into swollen-headed, cocksure wickedness. It ruins lives with its elephantine powers of corruption." The contractions were growing more forceful. I didn't know how much longer I could hold on. I was heavy with the imminent release of the primordial soup, if you will. I needed to escape. I hugged my knees in a kind of crash position.

"…the surging, pulsing, madness of it all," my silver haired host wailed hotly. "The weighty disaster that follows any perverted misuse of our bodies and minds. I, Father Jeremiah, personally vow to stamp it out. The plumpish evil, the stubby swell of man's innermost filth. The terrifically thickset, inflated sense of primal appetite that is the scourge of our very species, the downfall of our humanity!"

I had the profound hunch, from my fetal position, that I was going absolutely mad. Furthermore I couldn't truly tell if this guy was really using all of these queer adjectives or had my erection simply jarred the auditory part of my brain into manipulating his harangue to suit and understand the severity of my current problem. One thing was certain—there wasn't a second to lose. This was the last chance to interrupt him before total evacuation.

"May I be excused for a moment?" I cut in. "I have to hit the restroom." He pulled himself back from his diatribe, flustered and disoriented. He looked around, ran his fingers through his hair and straightened out his sweatshirt.

"No problem," he said. "It's at the end of the hallway."

I waddled like a penguin through the deserted corridor. I sensed that Jeremiah was watching me from behind, standing in the doorway of his office, completely convinced that there was something amiss, but unable to properly put his finger on it.

Nevertheless I made it to the empty restroom and hobbled down the line of toilets until I came to the last one—the handicapped stall. It would provide plenty of room for the execution of my hideous plan. I slammed the door shut, unzipped my pants, yanked everything down to my knees and took stock of the situation. The tape had been stretched out considerably, and what with all the movement and shifting on my part was almost completely undone. I unhooked myself from its sticky grip. My appendage immediately shot towards the ceiling, its color a festering, agonizing, dark purple. It could tear in half at any moment, showing no signs of letting up on its campaign to break itself out of its own skin.

I began to, I'm ashamed to admit, quite clinically remove the problem. In my defense, this was no moment of gratuitous onanism. I had no depraved, mental daydreams of cheap, lascivious encounters with strange whores. I took to the task simply as a matter of personal maintenance, like lancing a boil or applying direct pressure to a bleeding wound. My breathing was slow and steady. The only other sound was the occasional drip of a nearby leaky faucet. I increased the frequency of stroke and shut my eyes, murmuring pathetic pleas to the empty silence of my tiled confines. It was only a matter of seconds. Every inch of my body began to shake uncontrollably. I knew I was in store for something I had never even been close to experiencing in the past. An eruption of life altering proportions. The rest of the world faded away, a heavy drone filled my ears, fanciful colors of orange fire danced on the insides of my eyelids. I can't even remember, in retrospect, if I heard the main door of the restroom opening and then thudding shut, or the glide of the wheels, or the general presence of another being. I was too far gone in my own rapture, up on the balls of my feet, breathing rapidly, bracing for the inevitable.

Suddenly, quite rudely in fact, there was a banging on the stall door that caught me off guard, pulling me away from the precipice of my own ecstasy. I took a moment to lean forward enough, never ceasing stroking, to get a glimpse of two large wheels book-ending a pair of bent feet. It was a wheelchair, and in it, as sure as anything, was Jim Donald, the hatchet man of scroll seventeen.

"Come on buddy," he yelled from the other side, "this stall is reserved for the handicapped. I can see your feet. You don't look handicapped."

"I'm sorry, just a minute," I said and began working at it faster and faster.

"There are four empty stalls in this bathroom," Jim continued from the other side. "It is ridiculous that you have to use the one reserved for wheelchairs."

"One minute," I sang through heavy breath.

"Don't you think that I would be more than happy to be able to use a regular toilet? I have no choice. You have a choice. Do you also park in handicapped parking spaces? Do you sit in the reserved wheelchair space in movie theaters? If you want to be handicapped so bad come on out and let me break your neck. Then you'll be able to use all the handicapped facilities you want, you son of a bitch."

He had a good point, as I stood there, jerking like a monster, trying to get some relief. I was only half listening, though, as the heavy drone kicked up and the kaleidoscope again danced in front of my eyes. Nothing could stop me now. I bounded over the edge, letting it go, howling uncontrollably like a mountain cat. There was silence from the other side of the door. The wheelchair backed away. I didn't think it was going to end. The undulation went on and on. I felt I was going to have a stroke, or at least sustain some irreversible, neurological damage that would restrict the rest of my days to a life of soft foods and bedsores.

Shaking and out of breath, I carefully opened my eyes and was shocked at the sight. I'm not sure exactly what was in Zanz's tea, but not only did it provide one of the most incredibly solid erections but the amount of ... shall we say *albumin* it produced was something else entirely. I suddenly understood the geophysics of the tsunami. It was all over the place. Thick, dripping strands of genetic goop—enough for a billion, billion Toby

Sinclairs—heaven forbid. The thudding on the door started up again, along with forceful "Come on now's" and "Outta there's". I looked down. A bit more flaccid, color a bit more natural. Carefully, I re-inserted myself into the loop of electrical tape still attached to my leg, pulled my pants around it, toweled off as best I could and prepared to open the door. There was no time for cleanup. All was lost. The only thing left to do was get the hell out of this place as soon as possible. I took a deep breath and ripped the door open, coming face to face with Jim Donald. The paraplegic versus the pervert. Jimbo's face was a mixture of hostility and confusion. Something told him that I was up to no good, but that same something hadn't provided him with the sordid specifics. He would, I was certain, figure it all out soon enough.

"Excuse me," I murmured, racing around him towards the exit. He muttered something profane and rolled himself angrily into the stall. He slammed the metal door shut and locked it. As I stepped into the hallway I could hear him putting the clues together.

"What in the name of all that is good…"

The door closed on the ending of the exclamation.


"Everything okay?" Jeremiah asked as I returned to the seat in front of his desk.

"Sure," I smiled.

"I'm sorry I got a little out of control before," he apologized. "I don't want you to think that I would get perversion confused with sacred ritual. There is an important distinction. We are not indifferent or disrespectful to the more basic human inclinations here. It is just that our men and women don't practice them in vain. We have carefully monitored forms of release and exultation. There is supervision, order, meaning and context. This keeps out any perversion. You understand?"

"I get it."

"So what do you think, Toby? Of course you'll need time to think all of this over, but I believe you'd be a perfect addition to our little paradise here. You must take a careful look at yourself, and decide whether you are ready to leave everything else behind for this unique and gratifying opportunity. Why don't you come back next week and we can discuss the finer points of life here, like daily responsibilities and monetary contributions that may be required of you. Also," he paused carefully, "have you ever dealt with corpses?"

"Why?" I asked.

"It is a harmless inquiry."

"No." I answered. He gave a dismissive nod.

"Anything on your mind?"

"You said there were some pamphlets I could look through?" I asked, feeling the need to show at least a slight interest in the place.

Jeremiah smiled. He began to fish through his desk. "If you have any questions be sure to call me anytime." The clickety-clickety sound of spinning wheels came towards the office. I looked over my shoulder to see Jim Donald rolling himself down the hallway slowly, heading right for me, his narrow eyes piercing like a dagger, fixed directly on the back of my chair. I turned back to Father Jeremiah, who had paused in his search, sensing--knowing--that a problem was about to surface. A great perversion. I turned back to Jim Donald. There was no denying the rage cooking off of him as he glided closer and closer. I prepared to flee. He reached the doorway, and from this close vantage point I could see the wild detail of his hot pink face, awash with awe, hatred, humiliation. His nostrils flared, his eyes bulged. Large veins in his forehead and neck made his skin dance like a serpent.

"Jim Donald," Jeremiah said slowly from over my shoulder. "What's on your mind?"

I jumped up and shot towards the man in the wheelchair, who was too tongue-tied to express himself to his leader, and I took advantage of these precious seconds to try and liberate myself by vaulting clear over him, although I underestimated that consequent of Jim's leg infirmities he was rather strong in his arms and chest. He caught me in his iron grip and squeezed, and for a split second I thought the game was up. While I am not incredibly strong, I am rather blessed with squirminess, and it was this talent that freed me from the clutches and sent me bounding back through the front office out to my car, my wheels kicking up the dirt and pebbles at the half-dozen or so men congregating outside the front door, watching me go with looks of terminal disorientation through the dust as I tore away from the place for good.

# CHAPTER 16

It had been about a week since the cobra juice night and not that Zanz or I were ever really up for learning any lessons as a general rule—cursed to repeat our mistakes ad infinitum, we had at least agreed without much dialogue on the subject that next time when our beer, or wine, or any spirit for that matter comes with a big fat dead reptile in it—we will politely pass.

I still suffered from small twinges in my groin area from Zanz's tea, but luckily it had all pretty much subsided. Worse was the mental damage the tea had inflicted on my poor self, since I was afraid of ever getting an erection again. Just the thought of sexual arousal was enough to send me cowering into a corner, shivering, mad and pleading for my thoughts to turn to that of a eunuch's—impassive, sexless and uninterested in anything resembling the female form and its possibilities.

After my harrowing escape from the art community I drove immediately to the hospital to see Doctor Eddie, who luckily had just returned from lunch and was more than happy to show me into a secluded room, where I was more than happy to show him my affliction. He took stock of the whole thing, his thumb and forefinger digging at the cleft in his shaven chin, as I explained in stutters and stops how the whole thing had, "… popped up."

"You are a glutton for punishment," Dr. Eddie sighed with professional empathy as he dosed me with blood thinner, then sent for a hulking nurse with hairy knuckles to 'massage' the afflicted area to help remove some of the clotting, which she did with a strange degree of detachment and efficiency, all the while warning me that if these conservative measures failed they would have to use the BIG NEEDLES to alight. Her description of the BIG NEEDLES went some way to wilting it naturally, and soon enough I was as soft as ice cream under a heat lamp. I thanked the good doctor. He waved off my gratitude and remarked that it seemed odd that he hadn't heard from Baron in awhile. I considered telling him we'd hear all about him when the bodies started turning up, but I just bid him a good day and went home to sleep like a dead man.

Zanz and I were at my carriage house. We were waiting for Skid Row Paul to arrive. Zanz had received his rush delivery of Doctor B. Right's motivational lecture. We watched him on the television, the smug prick, doling out his wisdom, a gratuitous grin slapped across his face. I remembered that grin under different circumstances, seeing it for what it really was--a jealous, violent grin. On the screen next to him were two columns. In one column there were words like CONFIDENCE, SUCCESS, HAPPINESS and in the other column there were words like FEAR, SORROW, NEGATIVITY. His orange face and big teeth made me sick. His words gave me as hard a beating as he had in the alleyway.

"Friends," he said from the television screen. "I want to tell you something." He spread his hands out wide in front of his chest. "These columns represent the two ways in which we choose to live. One column is favorable. One column is not. So we see that these columns are more than words. They are things that we use everyday in the form of work, personal relationships, the search for love, the attitude and value you have in yourself. If we don't have value in ourselves then we occupy the column of fear, sorrow, negativity. But if we have value in ourselves we occupy the column of confidence, success, happiness. Now let us get into some effective methods that leading politicians, movie stars and pop singers have been using for years to make their dreams come true. I will now share with you some of these very special, time-tested techniques..."

"Put this on mute," I said. "I can't listen to this shit." Zanz hit the button and Doctor B. Right was immediately robbed of sound, of his mouth, of his offensive power. He was now just a two-dimensional marionette, smiling and gesturing, and I was free to assign him monologue of whatever I cared to imagine.

"Ladies and Gentlemen, I'd like to admit to the world that I too have had impure thoughts about the sexless, pale bodies of aliens, with their tiny probes, big bug eyes and expressionless faces, and I will not wallow in my shame for one more second about it!"

151

Or...

"Ladies and Gentlemen, I will now attempt, in the name of science and exploration, to stick forty sewing needles into the skin between my scrotum and anus."

Or...

"Ladies and Gentlemen, I had a speech prepared, but let's face it, why bother? I'd like to tell you, instead, as I look around the room tonight, that if I took a crap in a bucket right here on stage and then whizzed its steamy contents at you, well, let's just say that it would be the closest to greatness that any of you would probably ever come. I've never seen a group of morons so primed for failure in all of my life! Thank you."

Skid Row Paul came through the door with a smile on his face.

"That's the guy," he said, motioning towards the television set. He went directly into the refrigerator, pulled out the peach brandy and poured three glasses.

"I think you will be pleased," he said. "Cheers." We put them to bed.

"What have you got?" asked Zanz.

"Leads were slim at first. But patience, cunning and perseverance are trademarks of mine and they have paid off. Doctor B. Right's real name is Wally Wochalinsky. He is forty-two years old. When he is not on his lecture circuit he spends his time between Atlanta and Hilton Head, South Carolina. I found him by staking out his production company. Then with the help of a police officer friend of mine I got his home address from his car registration. I hung around his part of town for a couple of days. Talked to some of the neighbors. One busybody across the street told me that Wally keeps strange hours, always seems to have too much garbage and will water his lawn on days when he is not supposed to and that is why he has never been able to keep a good woman. I told her that I was a claims administrator for a class action lawsuit involving a product defect in Wally's car and that he could stand to win some money from the settlement. The neighbor was able to put me in touch with Wally's personal secretary. That's when I heard about his upcoming lecture at the Landmark Theater this Wednesday."

"He's giving a speech," I said. "Live?"

"Yes," said Paul.

"It would be a shame for us not to be there," said Zanz. "We could learn something useful."

"There is more," said Skid Row Paul. "But for that we are going to take a little field trip. I am going to introduce you to a man who used to work for Wally. He has some very interesting things to say about him. Let's take a walk."

"Where are we going?"

"To the basement bar of the Kadore Hotel," answered Paul.

We hit the street. Zanz was walking at a good pace in front of us. Paul and I were locked instep casually, basking in the fragrant summer afternoon.

"Our Doctor B. Right is a real freak," Paul continued. "I don't even want to tell you about all the weird things I came across."

"It is the ones that claim to know everything that are the most twisted," said Zanz from up ahead.

"There is a rumor that he has a fetish for hermaphrodite porno," said Paul, "and had to have a restraining order taken out by a second cousin of his, a Wynan Wochalinsky, who was undergoing hormone therapy treatment in order to eventually change genders without having to change first names. Wally wanted to produce a series of blue movies with this cousin, wanted the poor soul to keep both sets of dirty parts. I didn't find out whether the surgery had ever been performed, and I never did find out whether the gender change for old Wynan was from man to woman or woman to man."

"That was information we probably could've done without," I said.

"There is also the rumor that Wally has the ability to suck himself," Paul said as we walked down the block. "But I didn't feel the need to share that with you."

"You just did."

"I had to in order to prove to you that I wasn't going to. You asked for it. I hope you are disturbed for the rest of the day by that mental image."

"Skid Row Paul," I said, "I know you have a distaste for anything resembling a job, but you seem to harbor a natural inclination towards this type of work. Have you ever considered apprenticing for a private detective agency? Perhaps honing your skills?"

"I don't know," Skid Row Paul answered with a reluctant shake of his head. "I'm a sensitive person whose life is subject to intricate routines and customs that are essential to my well-being."

"Like sleeping late and wacking off?" Zanz offered from up ahead.

"Call it what you will," Paul maintained, "but a job just seems to be something that gets in the way of our natural born right to laziness."

We walked to the old building known as the Kadore Hotel, a crumbling relic of the mid-twentieth century that was once a grand hotel whose guests included statesmen, captains of industry, top entertainers of a forgotten era. Now it was just a pile of bricks in gradual disintegration, haunted by destitute creatures wandering aimlessly like lost phantoms, some mad with life and some with the stillness of premature death. There was a realness, though, a decrepit nobility and an endurance that shamed most of the newer facades around it. It taunted and challenged the rest of the city, and undeniably would only be taken down when it decided to implode on its own self.

"You know how I am going to be repaid for my troubles, right?" Paul whispered to me. "I delivered for you. Now you have to take me out to that spot where you buried the trunk."

"Okay, okay I will," I whispered back. "I am flying up to New York next week for a few days. I'll take you there when I get back."

The Kadore Hotel bar was in the back bottom of the building. Anybody could well imagine that if this old hotel had suddenly been turned into a giant human being, anatomically correct in every way, it should be obvious in what orifice the bar would be located, and surely with similar characteristics. We walked through the door, fashioned with the old red-padded vinyl and into the darkness, amidst rude murmurs from the surrounding gloom to turn the lights down. There were no windows and no clocks—no world outside. It was the last refuge for people too tired to even be angry, desperate or sad. We walked to the bar. There was one patron and he was fast asleep, a bottle of beer nestled in one limp hand.

What I would describe as a no-nonsense bartender came around the corner and stood in front of us with arms folded, silently waiting for our order. He had a dirty, ribbed muscle shirt on and a rag thrown over his shoulder. His fly was down.

"Is Clem Harris here?" asked Skid Row Paul. The bartender said nothing. His face twitched a little, and then out popped a mephitic cough that, once it got going, turned into a savage laugh. It was the laugh of a thousand cigarettes, bourbons, whores.

"That bum," he finally said. "He's always here, the bum." The use of the word *bum* twice in one sentence in this type of place didn't fare well for Clem Harris.

"Why is that name familiar?" I asked.

"We'll find him," said Skid Row Paul. The bartender grumbled and went back to where he had emerged from. Zanz and I followed Paul to a back row of tables, each with a sleeping drunk at it. Paul picked up the first head he came to and studied it. "Not him!" He let the head thud back onto the table. Next one. He picked the head up. "Not him!" The head came back down. At the third table our luck changed for the better, as Paul picked up the sleeping fella's head and nodded. "Here he is!" He slapped his face a couple of times and Clem woke up.

He blinked a couple of times, wiped the sleep from his eyes and then took to studying the three of us carefully. Now I recognized him. It was the same man who had revived the drowning fly a few weeks back. The suspiciously normal guy. I believe, now that I thought about it, that he claimed to be the Happiest Man in the World. He didn't look that way anymore. Right now he looked scared, unsure, out of place.

"Are you guys my friends?" he asked slowly.

"Yes," we said in unison.

"Good," he sighed, a smile spreading across his face. "Let's get some drinks going over here." He waved a shaky hand around the top of his head. "Billy boy, we need some boilermakers," he told the bartender. "Four of them. I've suddenly got friends and I intend to keep them. Put it on my tab."

The bartender got to work. Clem stood about halfway up from his seat and beckoned us, his friends, to sit around him.

"It is good to see you guys," he told us, nodding and shaking our hands. "I trust you've all been well?"

"Yes we have."

"That's good." He looked us over carefully. Clem Harris, the great resurrector of common flies.

"You remember us Clem?" Zanz asked.

"Of course I remember," Clem shot at us in surprised insult. "I always remember my friends. If you can't remember your friends then your life isn't worth shit. Through years of anonymous faces there are only a handful that I can count on. I'll never forget you guys....I'll never forget... I'll never...where the hell am I?"

"Kadore Hotel."

"What day is it?"

"Monday afternoon."

"You are kidding."

"We are your friends," said Zanz. "We wouldn't kid you."

The beers and shots were brought over. We raised our glasses. Clem had the honor of making the toast since he was buying. He raised the glass in his shaking hand. The whiskey went dribbling down the sides. If he didn't hurry up the glass was going to be empty.

155

"Here is to the Joker. Here is to the Ace. Here is to those who drink with style and grace. Here's to the brawlers, the proud and the few, and to the tea-totallers here is a hearty 'Fuck You'."

We drank. Clem got a little distant for a moment. I watched as his face started to fall slowly, to melt into sadness. He quickly broke down crying and since I was sitting closest to him, he buried his face into my shoulder. I put my arm around him and pulled him close. The wet heat of his tears soaked my shirt. When this episode had run its course he pulled his face back up and looked directly into mine. "Don't ever quit being a bartender," Clem warned me, specifically me, as if I had a sign on my head that said 'malcontent'.

"What?" I asked.

"You heard me. Don't ever leave its safety. You think you know what you are doing, but you have no idea. You'll wake up one day needing those people around you, making you feel you have a purpose, and there will be nothing but silence. You'll find yourself drinking Scotch out of a coffee thermos and trying to think up reasons not to kill yourself. Stay there. You don't know what it's like out past that bar. It's a death trap. The world is a horrible place." He started to sob again.

"But you were the self-proclaimed Happiest Man Alive a few weeks ago," I said, turning to search the others for support. Both Paul and Zanz simply made shooing motions with their hands, as if I was doing fine by myself, and any intervention by them would detract from the wonderful progress I was making. "You could look for a job using your people skills. You could volunteer for a hospital. You can join a rotary club."

"I'm considering becoming a serial killer," Clem admitted simply, and of course if we weren't such good friends the comment might've proved unsettling.

"What?" I asked again.

"The ultimate power," Clem brooded. "The power to manipulate and impose, to inspire fear, to control. The pinnacle of Godliness. His power can be my power. His whim can be my whim." He re-positioned his body to engage the whole table. "It is all about power," he explained. "I have seen, and now I know. Power and servitude. People in the world just trying to exercise what little power they have at their disposal. How many times have you had to endure some low-wage customer service representative giving you the runaround? You understand this. How many times have you made somebody wait on you just for the hell of it? We feel the need to flex the only powers that we have. Put somebody in a stranglehold. We can feel better about ourselves by mistreating others." Clem now had his arm around me. He gestured with his other hand towards the door. "Go outside this bar and look in the street. This is a poor neighborhood. Watch these transients and bums. All they do all day long is cross the street. They walk across it, get to the other side, and then the sons of bitches walk right back across. They only do it when there is oncoming traffic. They are exercising the only power they have, which is to slow down traffic, to make cars come to a crawl for them. No matter how expensive a car might be it *will* have to slow down for them." Clem took a sip off his beer before continuing. "Anytime somebody acts out this way, tries to assert themselves in somebody else's life, what they are really trying to say is, 'I would like very much to kill you'. I thought why not? Cut out the shit and start doing it. That was the rage I was feeling. Now it is a matter of exercising it in its purest form. I could have a city full of people cowering in fear. Afraid to leave their homes. Nightly curfews. Town meetings. There would be a historical convergence. I alone would define a place in time, arranged in a heavy awe-inspiring context that people would study for decades. I'd have to come up with a catchy moniker for myself like BTK, or better yet, the Night Stalker. That's the best one ever if you ask me." He took another sip from his bottle, implored us with sweeping glances for some reassurance. It was time to change the subject.

"Clem," said Skid Row Paul, "do you remember talking to me the other day. You were telling me about your old boss, Wally Wochalinsky, better known as Doctor B. Right. Can you tell my friends what you told me about him?"

"About the whole hermaphrodite thing?" asked Clem.

"No. Not that. Tell them about the clown thing."

"What's the clown thing?" I asked.

"He's got a problem with clowns," Clem said. "He is afraid of them. Well, not afraid of them like you or I might be afraid of snakes or spiders. He just has a firm conviction that clowns are harbingers of death."

"Why does he think that?" I asked.

"The two times he has seen a person die a clown has been present for no reason at all."

"Was he at the circus?" asked Zanz.

"No," said Clem. "One was a car accident. Standing with him in the crowd of onlookers was a clown. Appeared out of nowhere. Nobody else made mention of it which persuaded Wally that he was the only one that saw him. The second one was a woman who fell off a balcony at Mardi

Gras. Wally caught the clown looking out of a nearby window, only he wasn't looking at the dead woman. He was looking at Wally. After that Wally can't be around clowns because he knows somebody is going to die."

"Is it really that bad?" I asked.

"Coulrophobia," Clem said.

"Coulro...what?"

"Fear of clowns," Clem said. "It is not the clown itself. It is what it represents to Wally. Wild-colored keepers of the Gates of Hell."

"It's not so outlandish," shrugged Zanz. "Usually anything that occurs that brightly in nature is highly poisonous."

"Yes," Clem nodded. "I still can't figure it out, but hey it's a big world out there. Lots of potential for different kinds of madness. As John Wayne Gacy once said of his clown act, he said that clowns can get away with murder. Maybe he is partly responsible for the fear."

"Now that you mention it I remember his wife saying something about that," I said.

"I thought you guys might want to hear it from the source," said Skid Row Paul.

"So what does Wally do if he happens to see one?" Zanz asked Clem.

"His life is calculated to avoid them," said Clem. "But if he does happen to see one he gets the hell out of there as quick as he can."

"An involuntary fight-or-flight response," I said.

"And he is giving a speech at the Landmark Theater this Wednesday," said Paul.

"That reminds me, should we order another round?" Clem asked hopefully. "You guys are my friends. I should buy you another round."

"We'd love to Clem, but we've got to be going," Zanz replied hastily, gathering himself up. "But we'll be back soon. We promise."

"Maybe I can come see you guys where you work?" Clem offered, his voice becoming alarmed. He clasped his hands together and shook them at us. His eyes beseeched us to postpone our abandonment. "We can spend some time together?"

"By all means," Zanz assured him. "You come see us."

"Where do you guys work again?" Clem asked. We told him another place. "I'll have to stop by there," he suggested morosely.

"Anytime," we said.

"To see my friends," he added.

"Of course."

"Which are you guys?"

"Yes."

We walked quickly out the door, taking in the air as if we had been held underwater for the last twenty minutes. We reconvened at a safe distance from the old hotel and pondered this strange turn of events. A plan was needed. Put one together and then make some subtle adjustments for maximum effectiveness. Don't give off any premature excitement. In the waning moments of preparation, when all that could be done has been done, it is best to appear as casual as possible. To project an attitude of thoughtful deference is to invite the hand of good fortune.

"How about that?" Zanz mused, lighting up a cigarette.

"Fear of clowns," Skid Row Paul commented, absently kicking a stone down into a storm drain.

"That is something," I threw in, stopping to speculate about a set of initials immortalized in the sidewalk.

"Now the question is, how to exploit this information?" Zanz pondered aloud, watching a squirrel scurry inverted down the side of a tree.

"Yes, how?" echoed Paul as he coaxed a ladybug from the lapel of his jacket to the tip of his index finger.

We all stood there—three relaxed, easygoing guys harboring three relaxed, easygoing smiles.

# CHAPTER 17

"Give me a break, it's hard to drive with these big, goofy shoes on," Baron complained as he struggled to manage the pedals on his Fleetwood Brougham, missed due to his bulbous clown shoes, careened us through an intersection and narrowly missed two cars approaching from either side. The cars swerved to avoid us and might've been angered at our recklessness had the faces passing us not looked surprised to see the car occupied by four clowns, and were resigned to dismiss because of it that type of zany driving.

"Watch it," I yelled from the back. "You almost killed us."

"This car is a veritable tank," Baron confidently dismissed. "Any traffic accident the Fleetwood Brougham gets into would render us completely free of harm. That's the type of formidable machine you find yourself traveling so comfortably in at this moment."

Yes, I wondered, and how did I find myself traveling in Baron's car at that very moment? After all, Baron had not been part of the day's plan as he had disappeared for the better part of a month or so, only to arrive unexpectedly at Zanz's apartment while we were pulling ourselves into the clown suits we had rented the day before and following the step-by-step instructions for the application of the clown makeup. Some of the finer points of Baron's sudden appearance were a bit troublesome for me and without the benefit of an adequate explanation only became more troublesome. The fact that Zanz had bought Baron's story quite easily and without much thought about it made me all the more frustrated.

The most obvious point of my dismay was that he had shown up at Zanz's door covered in what looked like, and later turned out to be, blood. He had staggered in and collapsed on Zanz's couch looking harrowed, exhausted, twitchy, and crazed all at the same time. He had a guilty resonance and a hysterical look in his eyes and might I mention again, he was covered in blood. It was on his shirt, his pants, his jacket, puddled around his knees. I had inquired repeatedly as to what had happened, but Zanz, seeing that Baron was bordering on a state of hysteria, had gotten him up and taken him to the bathroom to change clothes, had thrown him into a steaming hot shower, and then had dosed him with a stash of sedatives and laid him out in the bedroom. When he returned he told us that there was probably a reasonable explanation and he was sure that when Baron awoke he would tell us all about it in calm detail.

We then recommenced quite casually, as if the disruption hadn't even occurred, to getting dressed. Skid Row Paul and Zanz took to discussing the plan. Paul was adamant that he be included after all the work he had done in flushing out Doctor B. Right. He wanted to see the whole thing through to completion. We decided that Paul would be a strong addition and welcomed his presence. Our plan was to infiltrate the Landmark Theater and secure front row seats for the speech, dressed as clowns. Yes, three clowns seated directly in Doctor B. Right's line of sight. We pondered his potential reactions, wondering whether he would freeze up, run screaming, take a hostage. Anything was possible. I must admit though, that while my friends were completely absorbed with Wally Wochalinsky, I found myself obsessed with Baron. The factors surrounding his arrival were impossible for me to dismiss. I applied a strong foundation of white face paint to my furrowed forehead.

I underwent the normal processes to figure out what could've happened to Baron, yet all my worrying did nothing more than churn my mind into a garbled mess, never getting closer to the truth, and in frustration trying that much harder to figure out what happened, or to be more precise, trying to think of something that could've befallen Baron besides the obvious conclusion—his abrupt arrival, blood soaked look and agitated demeanor were certainly the by-products of a vicious murderer.

If Baron Corley was a modern day killer, whose name was just waiting to be added to the annals of true crime—a name presently anonymous as John Wayne Gacy or David Berkowitz's once had been before their diabolical fame—if Baron was now part of that upstanding yet eccentric group of men who keep odd hours and quiet habits until their maniacal ways were found out, then it was going to mean terrible trouble for us all. What was the type of anguish these men caused, not only to their victims, but also to the people that knew them personally? The state of grief, shock, and disbelief that family and friends had to endure would be catastrophic. Not to mention the burdening of themselves with all of the killer's guilt, feeling as if they had a hand in creating victims through their own failure to realize, their own inability to recognize that someone so close to them could do such terrible things, a pain so thoroughly sickening and ironic. The killers themselves largely seem to express no genuine remorse. The guilt had to go somewhere. The blood would be on us. We were letting him get away with it, but why?

At the core of it, I suspected, were extreme personality fluctuations that made these men so hard to spot. In regards to case studies of historical serial homicide, it is easy to understand the perpetrator only in terms of his brutality, as if he is some hideous monster, deformed and grotesque that kills as he breathes, constantly and involuntarily. However, as with many a charismatic psychopath—H.H. Holmes, J.B. Jones, P.J. Knowles—there are indeed brief periods when they can appear both agreeable and likable—if only to further their appetite for blood. It was easy to simplify and dismiss these past offenders as pure homicide incarnate, but the trusting public, innocents like myself, needed to be aware of the downtime, the favorable and therefore dangerous personality characteristics that manifested when their brutality went into remission.

It was this mental schism that I feared had infected Baron, my friend's father-figure and confidante, insofar that at times he possessed a unique and inexplicable appeal, and sometimes went out of his way to be helpful. Had Jeffrey Dahlmer ever found a wallet at his job in the candy factory and turned it back in? Had Ted Bundy ever leapt from his tan Volkswagen Bug to help an old lady cross a street? One thing was for certain—whatever good deeds Baron had been responsible for in the past would all be largely eclipsed by what I had now decided was his uncontrollable urge to abduct and mutilate women—all kinds as his ex-wife might say. It didn't matter as long as he got the chance to bind them, carve them up, keep their organs for trophies, try repeatedly to achieve some impossible satisfaction as the corpses piled up in the basement of his personal charnel house out in the woods, with the flies and the stench and the filth and the eyes and the maniacal gluttony, the vain persistence. He had shown up covered in blood. It was too much blood to be explained away. There was something seriously wrong with Baron Corley.


I had chosen for my personal clown outfit an ensemble of big green and yellow overalls with a blue afro, red nose, white gloves and a paisley, mismatched shirt that was a little too tight for my body. For my face paint I had chosen a traditional look—a white face with garish embellishments of red and green around the eyes, red lip coloring, and two matching yellow dots adorning each cheekbone. I believed it reflected an exaggerated version of my own personality, delightful and modest, until Zanz pointed out upon completion that I looked incredibly feminine. Even though I was not pleased with his opinion, it would've been too much of a pain in the ass at that point to change it.

Skid Row Paul had opted for that ritzy, big top touch, wearing a clown's version of formal attire—oversized top hat, rainbow afro, oversized bow tie, red dinner jacket with tails, big yellow gloves. Paul's face paint was conventional and subdued, jester-ish and happy-go-lucky. Who would've ever thought this outlandish piece of culture could successfully champion a vast hamburger conglomerate?

Zanz, after hours of indecision, had decided on a motif that could best be characterized as a Satan Clown of sorts. His face was painted red with black accents around the eyes and mouth. His suit was a billowy one-piece, one side red the other black, topped by a ruffled red neck-piece with small, silvery baubles hanging around it. For that extra touch he had bought a set of fangs for his mouth, and on his red gloves had drawn small anarchy symbols on the palms. This, the shopkeeper had warned Zanz, made the gloves a nonrefundable purchase.

To get back to Baron's surprise arrival (covered in blood, I may reiterate) it was relatively early in the day—about a half hour after we had shown up with the costumes and the make-up. Zanz's secret stash of sleeping pills had ensured that when he finally got Baron into bed his slumber would be a heavy one, full of moans, groans, and a constant, heavy snore that rumbled through the open door of Zanz's bedroom the whole time we were dressing.

We had a strict schedule that day. Paul and I had arrived at Zanz's place in the early afternoon in order to suit up as mischievous harlequins and get down to the Landmark Theater so we could get a front row seat for Wally's seminar, in which Doctor B. Right was preparing to give a speech about pro-activity, confidence, goal-oriented success strategies, and ignoring three thug clowns sitting in the front row. He'd have to improvise on that last part of the speech though, since our appearance would be a surprise for him and hopefully, if all went according to calculation, an episode of terrified angst in which he would be paralyzed on stage. If he rushed at us, all the better. He was outnumbered and this time, we'd be prepared. This eventuality relied on the hope that Clem Harris had not over-stated Wally's condition. It all just seemed too bizarre to be made up.

It was almost time to go. I was adding the finishing touch of a red, squeaking ball to the tip of my nose when I became aware that the snoring had stopped and as I looked through the open doorway of Zanz's bedroom I could see that Baron was awake. He was pacing Zanz's room in his underwear with the telephone receiver on his ear, the base of it he carried in his other hand.

"How lucky for us to capitalize on Doctor B. Right's death fear of clowns," Skid Row Paul commented, completely unrecognizable in his big colorful outfit.

"I think I'm beginning to understand what might lie at the heart of the Coulrophobe's problem," Zanz furthered, inspecting the finer details of his devilish makeup job in the mirror. "Any type of face paint historically can be associated with fear, death, destruction. For centuries cultures have used various facial adornments to inspire fear in enemies and outsiders. It is used in religious ceremonies, hunting, and war. Consider the Huli Wigmen warrior tribe of New Guinea with their yellow and red ocher face paint—a savage gesture symbolically associated with death and destruction. Or Celtic nomads with their blue woad smeared across their faces and bodies, a mystic ritual designed to protect themselves in battle. Lest we forget the Native American Catawba tribe, soaked in black and white battle paintings. From the plant extracts of the earliest civilizations to the grease paint used by our modern militaries, it isn't hard to see why this masking can provoke skittish chemical reactions in certain people. We are taking the humanism out of the most primitive identity marker, our face. We are turning ourselves into creatures, we are removing ourselves from our own being, from our own conscience, free to act outside the accepted normalcy. A congruity of look and deed." Zanz sat back, pleased with both his reasoning and his makeup application.

"Everybody has a fear of something," I mused, rocking back and forth on each foot, trying to find some foolishly symmetrical mannerism to go along with my new look.

"I have a fear of rats," Skid Row Paul admitted. "A death fear. There is a recurring nightmare where I am in a high torque muscle car and one hundred yards away from me is a rat facing my direction. The object of it all seems to be that we will rush at each other full force, I in the muscle car, the rat on its little feet, and whoever dies as a result loses. I can't even bring myself to drive towards the little bugger. It's the tail mostly. Just seeing that long hairless tail fills my body with ice chips. In fact, in the dream I make a U turn, drive high speed in the opposite direction, and the whole horrific ordeal ends with me accidentally running over my mother."

"Have you had this dream analyzed?" I asked.

"Once."

"What was the verdict?"

"My fears were valid and running over my mother was not an accident."

By this time Baron had finished his phone conversation and had emerged from Zanz's bedroom, scratching his hairy belly, looking rested, groggy and thoughtful all at the same time. He had obviously slept off whatever terrible thing had haunted him upon his arrival. He came into the room, shot us a quick glance and then stepped into the kitchen to snoop around for some coffee. He froze. Slowly, he turned and faced us, an expression of immense confusion.

"Why the hell are you guys dressed like that?" he finally asked. We brought him up to speed. As we were explaining the situation Baron's face sunk into an insulted look. He couldn't believe we weren't going to include him. The most valuable asset we had and he wasn't even in on it. He said he had never felt so wronged in his life.

"Sorry, Baron," said Zanz.

"Well it doesn't matter now because I'm here, and I'm going with you," he adamantly told us. "We're going to destroy this son of a bitch."

"We are not going to kill him, Baron," I said. "Or bury his remains in a stretch of land. We just want to embarrass him."

"Relax Toby," Baron said. "We can rough him up a little. Something tasteful and subdued. You know, don't take this the wrong way but you generate a lot of anxiety. It's not healthy. I think you need to let out some aggression. When we finally have this shit head cornered I want you to really lean into the beating. I mean, let it go. Swing hard. Release. Let it pour out of you. Let it provoke its own special euphoria. Reach deep into yourself and harness the rage. Consolidate every sorrow and frustration you've ever had and put it into your knuckles. Don't be afraid to deliver a good ass-whipping. Give him an ass-whipping for every moment of your life that you felt let down, betrayed, lost. Don't be afraid to bleed this guy. Trust me. You'll feel like a new man. I know what I'm talking about."

There were a few elements that sheer chance had put in place—elements that pretty much insisted Baron be included in the plans. The first was that Zanz couldn't decide between a more traditional clown outfit and his vision of a combination Lucifer/Jester type of thing the day before when we were at the costume shop, so he had rented both. It was this other alternate outfit that Baron hurriedly climbed into with Zanz and I on either side of him pulling it up around his middle-aged girth, while Skid Row Paul nervously watched the clock tick away the waning, remaining hour we had allotted ourselves to get to the auditorium in plenty of time for a good seat.

In a flash Baron was fully dressed in a big, billowy one-piece jumpsuit flecked with neon dots of all colors. He had a large, yellow, high ruffled collar, a matching yellow afro topped with his usual worn, brown fedora. But it was his face that was by far the most eerie. Since time constraints prevented us from crafting a clown mask on him we simply used what leftover makeup we had to paint his face a pale, deathly green color, decayed and gruesome, like a Haitian Voodoo Priest. We then dripped red paint down one side of his face. It looked like the side of his head had been cracked open. He was right out of the darkest nightmare of the most terrified child on Earth. Instead of a honking nose he finished his outfit off with his tinted eyeglasses. We then jumped in his car and raced towards the Landmark Theater.

Four clown suits. Four men. There was no doubt in Zanz's mind that Baron's presence was predestined. It was this type of thing that the shortsighted might call coincidence, but Zanz would refer to it as *Teleological Approval.* In effect it meant that the universe was on our side. I was a bit put off by the addition of Baron for reasons already stated, yet had I known how the day would unfold, I would've had to agree that his presence was for the best.


"So Baron, you never told us what happened to you this morning?" I asked from the back seat. "You seemed in a bad state when you showed up to Zanz's place. What was that, red paint you were covered in?"

"I'm not going to lie to you Toby, it was blood."

"That was a lot of blood. You were drenched in it."

"Don't I know it," he said, his green face catching sight of me in the rearview mirror. "First off, I started out the morning by cutting myself shaving."

"What were you shaving, your aorta?" I asked.

"This is only the beginning of the story. I'm just trying to make you understand what kind of morning I had."

"Where did the rest of all that blood come from? Furthermore, why would you bring up cutting yourself shaving if the majority of the blood came from somewhere else? Add to that the fact that you have a beard?"

"Would you let him tell the story Toby?" Zanz yelled from the front seat.

"Because I know you like a thorough explanation, that's why," Baron said. "I had to come into the city to get some business taken care of."

"Marriage or divorce?"

"Don't change the subject," he said. "On my way into town there was a horrible accident on the highway. A school bus flipped over. I barely missed being hit myself. But I did what any Good Samaritan would do. I pulled over and rushed to see if I could help. I got to the driver first."

"Was he hurt bad?"

"No, he was fine," Baron said.

"So the children were all bleeding to death in the back?"

"There were no children on the bus," Baron explained.

"So it wasn't the driver's blood and it wasn't the kids' blood," I said, trying to piece the story together.

"There weren't any kids, so there couldn't have been any blood from them on account that they didn't exist," Baron said.

"Then whose blood was it?"

"I don't know," Baron shrugged.

"I'm not following."

"The bus that overturned was an American Red Cross bus. It was an old jalopy."

"I thought you said it was a school bus?" I said.

"I'm sure at one time it was. It had been repainted white with a red stripe around it. Blood Services Southern Region was printed in block on the red stripe. The front wheel must've come off or something. The bus flipped twice. About four big refrigerators shot out through the windows along with medical supplies, folding tables, cots, gauze pads, rubber tubing. It was a mess. It brought traffic to a grinding halt." Baron shifted lanes and continued his story. "One of the refrigerators had spilled about thirty pints of blood into a big puddle. As I was running to help I slipped and fell in it."

"And that's it?"

"No. Like I said I also cut myself shaving this morning. I was going to shave my beard but I interpreted the cut I sustained as a sign to keep the beard. God tells us stuff all the time, in his own way. It is up to us to listen. God likes my beard."

"That's very brave of you Baron," Zanz said. "To help that poor bus driver."

"That's all behind us," Baron shrugged off. "Let's concentrate on what lies ahead of us. Look, I see the Landmark Theater coming up on the right. Does anybody want a stick of gum?"

He produced a pack of gum and as a show of good faith offered it in turn to each one of us. Only I declined. "I like to chew gum in these types of situations," Baron added as the three of them chewed eagerly. "Helps to release any nervousness. Keeps you focused."

As a bartender I had heard many an implausible story, but the one that Baron had just rattled off was the biggest pile of crap I had ever heard in my life. I was getting agitated. I should've probably taken a slice of gum, but I decided that I couldn't accept anything from this man in good conscience because when the truth came out I didn't want to be accused of benefiting even the slightest from someone like Baron.

I noticed that from the time Skid Row Paul had been introduced to Baron that day he had been quiet--keeping a careful eye on him, curious and tentative. He had shot me some sly stares from the seat next to me in the back of the car, giving me small nods, begging me to be as excited as he was to venture out to the woods to get the steamer trunk. To Paul there was a whole world of potential in the ground out there, and he wanted the whole world.

"Damn it," Zanz said as we drove past the front of the theater where a line of people were waiting to get in. "We're already too late. We'll never get a good seat now."

"Bullshit," Baron spat, hooking a right down a side street and driving towards the back of the theater. "We're not going through the front. We're going through the back service entrance." He jammed on the gas. "Screw sitting in the audience. The real way to drive this guy to madness is to be standing in the wings of the stage while he's giving his speech. We want him to feel like we can almost reach out and grab him." Baron made another right down a narrow driveway behind the theater, past a set of loading docks, then made another right down a small alley. He hit the brakes, threw the car in park and shut the engine off.

"How are we going to get backstage?" I asked.

"There is a lot you don't know about me, Toby," he answered.

"I don't doubt it."

"I used to have a job at the Landmark Theater years ago," he said as we all spilled out of the car. "Back here is the service entrance that the staff uses. We can move through the place without arousing any suspicion."

I stretched myself towards the glaring, cloudless sky. The clown suit wasn't very breathable. I was pouring sweat by the gallon. Baron, Zanz and Skid Row Paul lined up next to each other at the foot of an iron staircase. The three of them were collectively such a picture of ridiculousness, what with all the colors and the wigs and the face paint that I started to get a headache from it all.

We climbed single file up the stairway. Baron was in the lead, Zanz was second, Skid Row Paul behind him, I myself bringing up the rear. At the top of the stairway was a large metal door with a small window in the middle of it. On the brick wall next to the door was a buzzer. Baron mashed it down. He then took a small step back, whistled a little tune, snapped his fingers and clapped his hands together.

"Let me do the talking," Baron said. "Whatever happens you guys play along, got it?" We nodded. Baron then pivoted himself back toward the door. Eventually, a face filled the entire pane of the small window, a face too big to be seen all at once. The door was pushed open and there, standing in the whole size of the doorway, was a blubbery security guard. He regarded us sluggishly and with a bureaucratic vacancy across his face—a fleshy expression deeply sunk into a suspicious and perplexed grimace. The fact that we were all dressed as clowns was probably the only reason he didn't banish us outright, wondering what type of appropriate protocol he should employ for this eventuality. He was wishing right now that he had paid more attention to the security training correspondence video. In his right hand was a rolled up skin magazine, and there was a whole potato chip stuck to the side of his blue uniform shirt. Other than that the man was fairly unremarkable. In a brilliant opening move Baron plucked the potato chip off the guard's shirt and ate it, crunching it at him in a deliberate flaunt. Then he leaned forward and spoke hurriedly into the guard's giant lobe of an ear.

It was impossible for me to hear exactly what Baron was saying, but his manner was feverish, agitated, filled with many gestures, what I might call willful thrusting. First he pointed inside the building, then at the security guard, then at himself, then down the line at us. All the while trying to find the angle, I supposed, the crux of this man's compassion. I steadied myself on the railing, looked over it. A man was feeding pigeons from a park bench in the distance—serene and oblivious to the struggle. Overhead the summer raged on like hell had relocated to the penthouse, and the heat, outfit and stress were making my legs weak. I looked back up at Baron who it appeared, was motioning again down the line of us. Now the security guard was gesturing back, shaking his jowls, and pointing back towards the street, which only made Baron point that much more toward the inside of the building. From the exchange of gestures it looked like lives were at stake. Baron motioned back down the line at us, back towards the inside of the theater, then back down our line. The guard slowly stopped gesturing. His head was now cocked thoughtfully at us. The rolled up skin magazine he was holding was now tapping lightly at his thigh. Baron kept jabbing the air in our direction while his lips moved at a frantic rate like a Pentecostal preacher in some kind of babbling state of rapture. After a moment I realized he was motioning directly at me. Zanz and Skid Row Paul stepped back. It was obvious. The guard was studying me, his meaty face rising out of a grimace up into a smile, but there was malevolence behind it, some kind of lurid intention that made me uncomfortable. The others just stood back as Baron had instructed them. Before long the guard nodded, stepped aside, and one by one we slipped into the inside of the theater. I, as the last clown in, was none too surprised to have my ass pinched by the guard as I passed him. He pulled the door closed.

"Wait here!" he commanded and hobbled off down a long hallway, at the end of which was an office of some kind.

"That guard just grabbed my ass," I complained in a whisper as we huddled up to figure out what to do next.

"I was afraid of that," Baron sighed.

"How did you convince him to let us in?" I asked.

"I tried to tell him we were part of the entertainment, but he didn't buy it sooooo…." Baron paused, adopted a shameful posture, and hung his head. He was stuck in the painful hesitance one may have before divulging a sin to a religious figure, "…I told him that our female clown had a thing for men in uniform," he finally confessed, beseeching me in his tone to understand. The other two turned to look at me.

"Female clown?" I gasped. "You son of a bitch. How could you tell him that?"

"I told you that you looked feminine," Zanz whispered.

"That shirt is so tight you can almost see your boobies," Skid Row Paul added. My arms went up to my chest bashfully. I felt molested.

"Inappropriate comment!"

"Hey we got in didn't we?" said Baron. "Now I suggest we find a place to hide, since the security guard is right now on his way to find a replacement so he can have his way with you, Toby." I stood up straight and looked back down the hall. The guard was talking to another man in identical dress, thin and hoary, who even from this distance looked entirely agreeable to whatever the fat security guard was explaining to him.

"I can't believe it!" I shouted. "What am I going to do?"

"Try to be inconspicuous."

"I'm in a fucking clown outfit!"

"We're wasting time," Baron waved off. "We've got to get down to the basement level. From there we can sneak over to the back stairwell and get backstage." He pulled his satin sleeve up and looked at his watch. "We've got to get going."

"Which way?" I cried.

"Get in the service elevator," Baron instructed, motioning behind me to a set of cargo doors, again with a small, dirty window in it. He leapt for the handle and yanked. The doors opened vertically to reveal a collapsible metal cage. Baron slid that open and we all piled into the tiny compartment.

"Hey, get out of there!" The cry rumbled down the hallway. I stuck my head out to see the guard rambling towards us, barreling down like a boulder. "You guys don't have authorization. You guys don't have..."

"Toby get your stupid head in," Zanz reprimanded, pulling me back from the elevator entrance. Baron heaved the outer doors shut and slid the metal safety grate across. He then hit the button for Basement Level B. The tiny compartment groaned and began its slow descent into the lower pit of the building. I watched the tiny window rise out of sight, momentarily filled with the red-faced, livid expression of the prurient security guard who eyeballed us with fury, until he was cut off by the ceiling of the elevator, dropping us down into the basement of the theater, where who-knows-what awaited us.

Due to the extremely foreign environment, the extended lapse of time since Baron had last set foot inside the building, not to mention the complete obliteration of the old man's memory due to years of acute alcohol abuse, finding our way through the underbelly of the theater was a frightful illustration of bumbling idiocy. Our small group, with Baron our confused leader, did many spins, perplexed pauses and backtracking as we hurried through room after room of dirt, brick, exposed pipes, stacks and stacks of house lights, folding chairs, mechanical monstrosities, and all the while Baron mumbling things like, "…I'm almost certain this room leads to…" "…No, no, that can't be right…" "…Let's just see what this corner has in store…" "…I know that this is a shortcut…" "…There used to be a stairway here, damn it…" "…This wall must've been put in recently…" as the clock ticked down the final minutes until the seminar. I was disoriented. There was no end in sight to the complex labyrinth we had stumbled into. Musty and gloomy, there was something about old basements that frightened me, as if these places were death's haven, the actual specter itself lurking with yellow eyes under a hooded cloak somewhere behind the crippled machinery and dark corners, waiting to pick us off one by one, starting with the last in line, which, of course, was me. We kept up single file through an old boiler room. It felt like a crematorium.

"Are you sure you know where you are going, Baron?" I called up to the head of the line, my voice cracking from the strain of it all. "I have this nagging feeling that we are absolutely lost."

"Toby," Baron called back cheerily as he adjusted the yellow tissue paper on his clown outfit, "my memory is a little shaky but I assure you it is all coming back to me. Maybe it would settle your nerves if I tell you the story of ex-wife number five."

"Alright. If it will help pass the time."

"Any man, divorced in the capacities that I have been, will tell you that there is a certain ruinous delectation involved in coming face to face with one of the previous wives. It arouses a kind of guilty lechery, and in such a fashion two old lovers can become new to each other again, although not in a purely loving way, but more a passive-aggressive revenge type of way. So it happened in this very theater where I was working in the early Eighties that one night, she shows up in front of me—Brandy Alexander, wife number six."

"I thought you said *five*?"

"If you say so," Baron shrugged. "There she is, standing, tall and glorious in front of me, wearing a dirty smock and showing the beginnings of dreadlocks in her long brown hair. She told me she was glad to see me, but not before I caught the initial expression of shock and annoyed surprise, since she had left me eight months earlier to join a free love commune, known back then as 'Hookers for Jesus'. One thing leads to another, as these situations often do, and it doesn't take long for her to offer to initiate me unto the powers of 'primal prayer', and so I took her down to this very basement, in order to investigate the 'plexus of loins and soul', as she put it. So there we were behind the air conditioning unit, her on the eternal path of understanding through sensual experience, I on a ten-minute cigarette break, humping like jack rabbits, when from one of the pockets of her smock she produces a small dropper and before I know it, squeezes its contents into my mouth, telling me that it was the final way to complete awareness."

"What was it?"

"Apparently it was the highly poisonous gland extract of the bouga toad," Baron muttered. "It wasn't until much later that I found out the actual source. What I do know is that it turned me into a zombie. The last thing I remembered was being right here in the basement. The next thing I knew it was almost a year later. I was in some kind of Mexican Internment Camp outside of Guadalajara. I had gout, chlamydia and psoriasis, not to mention a rather pounding headache. My scrotum had been ravaged. Do you know how bad off I must've been for that year not to have even noticed the pain involved in a ravaged scrotum? After I was released the U.S. Embassy shipped me off to a San Diego mental hospital. Terrible food. Plenty of board games."

"What is the point of this story?" I asked.

"Fine!" Baron shouted ruefully. "Don't heed the warning. But you better not come running to me the next time some smooth talking gal gets you sucking on a bouga toad."


Baron's story of love-gone-wrong-behind-the-air-conditioning-unit bled seamlessly into the room itself, the industrial physicality of it all, gears and motors and shafts all around as we traversed a grated walkway to the enormous air conditioning system—commodious like the inside of a dump truck. A large flywheel manipulated hundreds of tiny water jets that cooled the air as it came rushing through and back up a cement passageway leading to the main auditorium. It was because of this air flow design that we could hear, quite clearly from above, a thunderous round of applause as some anonymous voice announced proudly...

"Now, ladies and gentlemen, would you please welcome the King of Confidence, The Mayor of Mirth, The Paladin of Pride, The Emissary of Excellence, The Herald of Happiness, The Potentate of Peace, The Sovereign of Serenity, the Panjandrum of Panache, The One, The Only...

Doctor B. Right!" The applause continued for another ten seconds or so, until the familiar voice came booming over us—a voice that quickened our anger because of its urbane tone.

"THANK YOU THANK YOU THANK YOU ALL, GOOD EVENING LADIES AND GENTLEMEN, WELCOME." The applause died down. "I thought long and hard, about what to say this evening, and decided to start off, with a simple question. WHAT WOULD YOU DO IF YOU COULD WALK OUT OF THIS AUDITORIUM AND GET ANYTHING YOU WANTED IN LIFE?"

"It sounds like we are too late," I said, scratching my bright afro.

"We've got him right where we want him," Baron disagreed. "He's stuck on stage. Come on. Double time it." We hurried on. Finally due to dumb luck, we emerged from the basement. We spilled out into a series of crisscrossing hallways with arrows pointing every which way for House Keeping, Screening Room, Musicians Lounge, Stage Right, Stage Left, Restrooms, and Stairwells. The hallways were by and large empty, which made the walls shake with the echoing, voluble booms of the public address system above. It was both immediate and distant, causing the three in front of me to speed up their pace. I started to fall behind. Baron reached the end of the hallway and disappeared around a corner. Then Zanz. Skid Row Paul was next. I intended to match their movements, but as I went to follow I was halted by a hand, a large sweaty hand, falling heavily on my shoulder. It was the size of a catcher's mitt, and I was pulled back by the breathless, heaving size of him. The security guard who had let us in had finally caught up to his prize--me--and looked none too pleased by my reluctance to submit. He shoved me against the wall with one hand and with the other smoothed his shirt and straightened his hair. He produced a mint spray and gave his cavernous mouth a few blasts. He then leaned in and continued his aggressive courtship.

# CHAPER 18

My mouth, tongue, larynx--all vocal components--were locked into petrified silence and as such a decent explanation was difficult. The guard didn't seem to care either way. He was doing his best to move the mating ritual along. His preemptive explanation was that of a gentle and understanding rapist, and I imagined he thought that, if done just right, what may happen in the next couple minutes could've been his finest hour, the goddamn coulrophile.

"Alright baby," he said. "Don't be afraid. I am only a man in a lonely position of authority. You have your suit. I have mine. But underneath we are the same. Skin. Bone. Desire. The pulsing madness of throb and moisture. We are people. People need people. I can speak at length of the brutal nature of love, or I could just show you. I'm going to treat you good little lady, you can be sure of that. I'm going to treat you good, even if it don't feel like it at first." Where were the others? Had they not noticed in their eager haste that one of the group had gone missing? One thing was certain—I was on my own. The guard had said enough. He reached down and cupped my crotch, his eager expression twitching a bit. Something was obviously not quite right. His hand kneaded at the source of his dismay. Yes, there was a bit something extra—an appendage of formal insult. In his hand what should've been concave was a daunting convex. There was a protuberance where there should've been a cleft. An excurvature where there ought to have been a depression.

"Shit," I said.

The guard removed his hand from below my belt, crumpled his fingers into a clenched fist and aimed it square for my jaw. Spit and insult sprayed from his mouth. Regardless of what people thought, he said, he was no dupe. After he beat me up he would have his way with me, despite. He referred to himself with first name, last name and middle initial. He had not been born night prior, he said. Many species in the animal kingdom make no distinction anyhow, he said. I closed my eyes, braced for impact. Suddenly the guard cried out and went down to the floor. I opened my eyes. Zanz was standing over him.

"For a man of this size it is usually most efficient to strike at the knee," he explained. The guard whimpered from the ground. Zanz looked to either side of him. "No time to waste Toby. Get some fuel in your step." We took off down the hallway as the guard screamed for help from the floor, holding his knee gingerly in his hands with his leg bent out in a most unnatural position.

"Where are the others?" I managed to get out.

"I lost them when I doubled back for you."

"Where should we go?"

"Follow me!"

We crept down the corridor, eyes and ears alert, Zanz trying to silence the jingle of the baubles around his neck. As we approached an intersecting hallway, loud voices whipped up around the corner in a rising crescendo, louder and louder, closer and closer, the rapid click of heels on the tile. "How many were there?" "Did you see where they went?" "Dressed as clowns you say?"

Zanz froze and held up his hand. He looked quickly from side to side and spied a door that read, "Organ Pit Access. Authorized Personnel Only." He nodded and went for it. I followed.

"Are we authorized?" I whispered as we stepped out of the hallway and into the plain, empty room.

"Today we are," he answered slowly as the voices of our pursuers went past us on the other side of the door that had been carefully closed just in time, voices slowly fading away into silence.

"Where are we?" I whispered, pondering the strange room we had escaped into. There were no windows, a couple of doors. The proscenium arch of the main theater was visible high above us. Doctor B. Right's voice swelled clearly and sonorously. The murmur and shifting of the crowd was everywhere. The imminent hovering of a collective vibration.

"I can't believe this," Zanz marveled.

"Why?"

"We are in the orchestra pit."

"What?"

Zanz pointed up. About ten feet over our heads, standing at the lip of the stage, behind his podium, was Doctor B. Right in mid-speech. It began to make sense. We had stumbled into the orchestra pit, completely hidden from the audience overhead—from all the eyes that were currently on Wally Wochalinsky. We could easily, however, catch his attention, but only if he happened to lean over and look down into the sunken orchestra pit instead of keeping his bulged, frenzied eyes locked on the faces spread out in front of him across this theatrical abyss. Zanz and I stood there in absolute stillness, staring up at Wally, so close and yet still entirely unreachable. We were dumbstruck at the situation. So dumbstruck, in fact, that it seems necessary to switch the perspective from below the main stage to the audience above for the purpose of pure objectivity. Let the events themselves illustrate how this situation unfolds, since for the moment, Zanz and I are unable to do so. It is essential to raise like a ghost out of the confines of the orchestra pit, up into the comfort of an old theater seat—a good one with a clear, unobstructed view of Doctor B. Right—the man of the hour. Row D, seat 20... in between, perhaps, a drowsy woman and an uptight gentleman in a suit and tie picking his nose. Settle in. Get comfortable. The Doctor was just in the middle of a methodical, succinct, and important point on...

"...CHASMS LADIES AND GENTLEMEN." Bellowed. "Chasms..." Subdued. Dramatic pause. Meaty fingers drumming on the podium. A cough from somewhere in the balcony. "Spread out in front of me...spread out in front of everyone of you is an abyss. An emptiness. An absence. A chasm. But it is not just an ordinary chasm. Ladies and Gentlemen this chasm represents the chasm that is within us all. WHO HERE HAS FELT AN EMPTINESS AT TIMES IN THEIR LIFE?" Most hands go up. Wally himself has his hand raised. A connection. "That's a lot of people." Peering carefully into the audience. "A lot of emptiness. Lots of chasms. And we know that nothing fills a chasm. Why? Because then it ceases to be a chasm." A rhetorical silence. The audience puzzled and hesitant, but somehow still hopeful. "You are in the chasm, yet you are not. You are drawn to the chasm as part of the purely feminine metaphor. But there is danger in the chasm. The chasm is like broken glass under bare feet. It is the hole in the noose. It is the lingering reminder of all that is missing. It is hysteria. Agony. Ecstasy. Life and Death. Possession and Absence. You love the chasm and fear it. Its horror you hold like a shroud over your existence." A sneeze from somewhere in the audience. "And why are these chasms so dangerous? GRAVITY! Gravity is the chasm's sadistic partner.

If there were no such thing as gravity you could float right over the damn thing. The chasm is useless without gravity. Gravity is the firing squad. It's the lethal injection. It's the push over the edge. It casts you down into the subterranean, cracking your head open like an egg. It pins you to the lowest point possible, and keeps you there while it laughs and jeers. It's the devil's lasso." Dramatic pause. Wally takes a sip of water. "Now of course I'm not just talking about the physical law of gravity, but the gravity that is IN ALL OUR LIVES! I know some of you are thinking, what do I care about gravity? What does that have to do with me?" Someone's stomach performs a loud, embarrassing rumble. "Let me tell you that if you are under the impression that this idea doesn't extend into your personal life... well then I pity your existence. Life is gravity. You have gravity of family responsibilities, friends, social obligations, and let's not forget what kind of pressure love can put on a person. You can let these factors get out of control, but then don't be surprised when gravity shoves your FAT ASS right into the jaws of the chasm. Everything in your life will fall like the guts of an animal split open at its belly." A baby begins to cry in the back section. "So you are probably wondering now, Doctor Right, if all of heaven and earth are at the mercy of gravity, then how are we supposed to combat it? Maybe you are wondering, how are we to avoid these harmful, yawning valleys around life's every corner? There is some bad news, and there is some good news. The bad news is that nobody is ever going to be able to remove a chasm. They, unfortunately, are part of life. The good news though, is that we can use the chasm. We must make it a receptacle of all that is valueless. We can use gravity to get rid of all the negativity, while embracing all that is positive. How is this accomplished? For starters one must never be afraid to look into the chasm." He steps around the podium and removes the microphone from its holder. He leans forward. "Only when one stares into the chasm does one see..."

Wally froze.

White knuckled. A slick sheen of sweat. Coughs and murmurs throughout the audience. His eyes are locked on something below. Is this a dramatic pause? This must be part of the program. The motivational speaker still hasn't broken his stunned stillness. No one can regard a chasm with that much intensity. The motivational speaker must really believe what he is putting on. Very real expression. Very real fear. His face is swelling with horror. One can almost grow fearful by proxy. Everyone in the audience is transfixed. For one thing, he's very good. The fear is believable. It pushes out explosively. It hits the audience like the heat from a molten blast. A few laughs ripple through the audience. Wally has straightened up. His knees are shaking. His breathing is audible, quickened. He turns and starts walking silently towards the wings. Someone in the back applauds. Wally is no longer on the stage. He has broken into a fast walk. Heavy footsteps thudding toward backstage. Another set of footsteps race toward the podium from the opposite direction. The announcer appears and grabs the dangling microphone. He begs the audience to remain calm. He apologizes profusely, but is still so confused that the apology comes across as entirely insincere. What happened? He looks down into the orchestra pit for some explanation. But finds nothing. There is nobody down there. He doubts there ever was. Some of the crowd starts to boo. Others are cheering and laughing. He leans into the microphone to try to offer some half-cocked explanation, but can find no words.

He decides it is not time for the dissection of madness in the latently disturbed.

It is time, in fact, for a stiff drink.


When I was a budding adolescent I once read a book of case studies in clinical psychiatry. One patient in particular was a twenty-four-year-old man named, let's just call him Gerald M. Funchess, whose overbearing mother had sensed a problem with her son and had brought him in for observation.

The reason?

It seemed that for three hours a day Mr. Funchess would hang himself upside down in his bedroom. His other quirk (if you will) was to remove his feces from the toilet and smear himself with it. In extensive interviews it was brought to light that Gerald believed that organs in the human body had a tendency to slide down into the legs due to the fact that people stood upright for most of the day. He believed further that this problem was the reason people were so upset all the time. When Gerald felt his organs begin to slide he would hang himself upside down to get everything back to its normal place. Now, one might comment, who cares about hanging upside down when the other behavior includes rubbing shit on yourself. Answer... To Gerald it wasn't a matter of waste material. He believed his organs were shriveling up and falling out of him. He had believed that they had stopped working because he couldn't feel them vibrating inside of him, at least that was one of his constant complaints. So when something fell out of him he applied it...topically... in order to have it absorbed back into his body.

My recollection of the odd story concerning the unfortunate Gerald M. Funchess was the clearest thing in my mind, years later, as Wally stared down at Zanz and I in absolute madness from his podium. I think that I was searching for relief in the logic of something similarly baffling to me—a security in knowing that there were some things about human behavior I would just never understand, and bam there was Gerald M. Funchess. He had afforded Wally's "coulrophobia" a little bit of dignity.


Getting out from under the stage proved a bit troublesome. In our haste to flee the scene of the crime we again got caught in the theater's underground maze. Every door that we came to looked like an exit... in so far as it had hinges, knobs, was door-shaped and appeared somewhat open-able. We burst into two production offices and a bathroom before Zanz caught sight of a stairway with an exit sign over it. We ran up and out, spilling onto a side street.

"Guys!" a voice cried from our right. We both turned and there, at the far end of the street, was a small yet ferociously animated burst of color. It was Skid Row Paul. He was jumping up and down, waving his top hat in the air.

"We got him!" he yelled. "We've got him. He's running for the freeway."

We took off as fast as our awkward shoes would allow. To avoid tripping we adopted an exaggerated run in which our knees were coming up to our chest. Buffoonery at its finest. My heart was racing like a trip hammer. The paint from my face was mixing with sweat and running down into my eyes. I looked over at Zanz, whose face was melting likewise, and who was bug- eyed with a psychotic look of brainwashed exaltation. We caught up to Skid Row Paul, who was trying his best to keep track of Baron up ahead while making sure we were not left behind.

"Where did you guys disappear to back there?" Paul asked as we continued the pursuit—three strong—ignoring the bewildered stares of a guy in a pizza place, a woman depositing some mail, an old homeless man who applauded us as if we were in the home stretch of a marathon. "We turned around and you guys were gone."

"I was almost raped," I told him as we rounded another corner, where up ahead the last of our vigilante brigade was rushing full blast down the street, easily recognizable in his neon dot clustered jumpsuit. Baron was moving at a phenomenal speed, pumping his legs with the energy of a man half his age—spurred by anger, indignation, gratuitous homicide.

"Baron and I were waiting for you on the side of the stage," Paul interrupted between gasps. "Whatever you guys did I've never seen anybody with that much terror on their face. Wally went running by so fast he almost knocked me over."

"The recipe is simple," Zanz gave out, breaking away into a strong lead. "Over ice, take two parts traumatic experience, one part superstition, fill with inbreeding, and top with a quail egg."

I was faltering, falling back as much as Zanz was racing ahead, with Paul the center point of the axis of our abilities. My pace slowed into a pained stagger as I clutched my gut and tried not to throw up. It had been over a decade since I had gotten any exercise at all much less something of this kind of intensity, and of course I hadn't stretched properly. The daily probability of some sudden burst of unexpected vigor and stamina was close to nothing and so how could I really be prepared. I threw myself into a stationary shopping cart sitting up against an abandoned storefront just to have an alibi as to why it had taken me so long to catch up.

I settled into a hasty stroll to regain my breath, bothered by my physical inferiority. In the future I promised myself that I would avoid any situation involving fleeing or pursuit. These, after all, were primitive tendencies—the vestigial habits of our uncivilized ancestors. The future of evolution belonged to the individuals who could refrain from personal struggle and shop competitively.

I finally reached the other three. Zanz and Skid Row Paul had each taken a knee while Baron stalked back and forth between two driveways, his eyes intent, his nose up in the air, tracking like a timber wolf. "I know he's down one of these alleys. I'm just not sure which one."

"We'll split up then," Zanz suggested. "Paul and I will go down one. Baron and Toby go down the other."

"Why do I have to go with Baron?" I complained.

"By taking the average," Zanz said. "Baron was the fastest. You were the slowest."

"But I was hit by a shopping cart."

"Come on Toby," Baron encouraged as he began running down the far alley. "If we catch him I'll let you get the first punch."

Reluctantly I followed down our assigned stretch of pavement. It was quiet and empty. There were very few places Wally could hide. A chain-link fence topped with barbed wire ran the length of one side while a concrete bulwark separating us from a parking deck stretched along the other. Up ahead the driveway ended in a busy, four-lane road.

"He must've turned down that thoroughfare," Baron pointed, his pink skin showing through the green face paint as it gradually washed away in streaks from the sweat. "I can smell his fear."

"I can't smell anything over my own terrible odor," I admitted as we approached the intersection. "It's bad enough to raise the dead."

"Keep up kid," Baron said. "And watch out for the *traffic*."

Maybe it was this cautionary remark that threw me off balance. The suggestion that I take heed may have actually done more harm than anything. In addition I believed, up to that point, that I had mastered running in the clown shoes. Surprising then that at the very same moment my confidence and awareness were peaked that the tip of one shoe got caught in the generous hem of the clown pants, which sent me tumbling forward. I hit the pavement once, bounced and skidded right into oncoming traffic.

These types of flash catastrophes happen so quickly that there is no proper way to explain the exact sequence of events. The boom of the angry horn could've sounded even before I rolled into its lane, the pain before I even hit the cement, the white light at the end of the tunnel even before the tire crushed my big fat head. I do remember, with a harrowing sickness, not suspecting or dreading, or wondering, but absolutely knowing that I was going to die painfully. The grill of an old panel truck was coming right for me. Two rockabilly types were passing a joint in the smoke filled cab. The situational blend of speed, metal, disregard and clumsiness were the choice ingredients to the recipe of my doom. Everything was too late. Even if the truck applied the brakes (which I was certain they would not) it would've only resulted in them going over my carcass in a slower, more painful, yet considerate fashion. The bumper sped on. I tried to get up but my ankle was twisted and inert. The guy in the passenger seat now saw me and was elbowing the driver. The grill was aimed at my face—rapidly expanding as it closed the distance. The truck didn't slow down, but in a move of great courtesy the horn was blown for my sprawled out benefit. Their faces disappeared beyond the hood, close enough to overshadow everything else. My insides sank away below my gut, as if the whole of my viscera was trying to climb down into my legs towards my feet to get away from the worst part of the collision.

Too close to even be considered realistic in any pure sense, I found myself yanked by a tremendous force onto the sidewalk. The panel truck that had been right in front of me was now zooming by. The men in the cab shook their fists at my audacity—at the nerve I had to lie in front of their oncoming vehicle.

"Careful kid, you almost got splattered."

Shocked and shaking I looked up to see Baron standing over me. He sat me up gently on the sidewalk. "That was a close one, don't you think?"

I babbled something, an impotent and pitiful response against Baron's quick thinking and tremendous strength, as well as his cavalier attitude. Sweet, damnable fates, I said to myself. The murderous son of a bitch had saved my damn life.

"Hey you idiots, stop lying down on the job," Zanz yelled from a block up. "We are on his heels. Come on." Baron pulled me to my feet and we headed towards the chase, although my blood was going cold and my muscles were stiff with rigor mortis. (The panel truck had been so close that my body simply decided to proceed with the normal processes of decay.) I hobbled along unevenly. Something wasn't right. I glanced down. One of my shoes had come off. I looked out into the street. It was lying there ruined--pancake flat except for the tongue of the shoe, which was cocked up and out, giving the sky a kind of deranged grin. The only thing to do was pull the other one off and run in my socks. Zanz and Skid Row Paul had crossed the street that had nearly marked my final resting place, and Baron and I followed after a break in traffic.

We cut through a small alleyway to a quiet street with detour signs in front of it, big concrete barriers, large tractors, orange cones all over the place, yellow tape fluttering in the wind, a couple of empty buildings, and best of all, due to some city bureaucracy, not a worker in site. We ran towards the last building, an empty depressing façade, and regrouped on a quiet sidewalk. Somewhere close by was the Interstate. I could hear the gentle swish of constant traffic. The perimeter of the dead end was enclosed by a tall fence and beyond that a sloping decline directly into traffic. The only way out for Wally was to double back. He could go no further.

"We lost him again," Zanz said.

"He's around here somewhere," Baron nodded, confidently scanning the deserted area. "I can feel it."

Each of us stood at irregular distances from the other. Baron was centered with a meditative look on his face. Paul and Zanz were quietly craning their brightly colored heads to hear any change in sound—some type of human rustle that would give Wally's hideout away. All of our faces were melting fast. The paint was working its way down in smears of perspiration, making us look all the more horrendous. My hands and knees were burning with gray and red streaked abrasions.

I tried to calculate the amount of blocks since we had last seen Wally, the distance ratio, the average foot speed of a six foot, two hundred-or-so pound man, the wind direction and velocity, until I realized that I didn't know squat about math and all the numbers just fell into a mental jumble, and so I just sat back and thought about women and beer. It was Skid Row Paul who finally spoke up.

"That dumpster has feet," he muttered plainly. We all turned to look. A pair of polished black shoes were tapping themselves nervously at the far end of the street, cut off at the ankles by a brown metal bin filled with rubble and city filth. We walked towards our man. I was still clutching my clown shoe. We fanned out around our prey to close off every possible angle of escape. The feet stopped tapping. Seconds later the entire man emerged, wild-eyed and soaking wet, in a wounded two-footed gallop. Wally continued his waning marathon.

He turned and ran for the mouth of a small alley, the only path not blocked by a clown. He ran down into it as if the high brick walls on either side could somehow make him disappear. We ran after him. Baron held a strong lead. As we neared the other end of the alleyway the thin woven lines of a chain-link fence came into focus. Wally's escape was entirely blocked off, yet he continued towards it, slowing to a standstill when he realized all was futile. He turned towards us and dropped his head, still, except for the mad heaving of his shoulders up and down, his head hanging limply in front of him, his body expanding and deflating with every gasp of hopeless breath. We were five feet from him. We had him as he had gotten me—in an alley. The circumstances were fitting. He had surrendered to the inevitable ending.

Baron walked up and stood in front of Wally, a.k.a. Doctor B. Right.

There have been many pioneers in the field of the 'backhand' throughout history. People who with just the right motion, technique, pivot, and speed have elevated the backhand into something of an exquisite execution of force. Some are in the field of tennis (John McEnroe), badminton (Sony Dwi Kuncoro), racquetball (Jason Mannino) and music (Ike Turner). These men would've applauded the form, torque, and crack of Baron's hand as it walloped Wally's head. The motivational speaker hit the pavement with a thud. Zanz and Skid Row Paul followed. They descended upon the crumpled heap, swinging, thrashing and stomping like mad. I remained frozen in place watching with disgust and pity for the whole damn thing. I have never liked conflict, and even though I was the one who had suffered, which prompted me in quieter times to believe I could take part in the retaliation, I knew in that moment that I could do nothing but stand idly by.

Physical hostility is a process. It has a cumulative effect. So it was that Baron, Paul and Zanz had begun the beating with a hint of timidity, thumping him around his meaty midsection until they got impatient with his injuries. Baron's foot caught Wally right in the mouth, sending a mixture of spit and blood against the wall next to him. Then a fist to the eye, the eye rising purple, the recoil of the wounded man's head against the pavement, blood spraying from unseen places, and all the while the garbled pathetic pleas, weeping and gurgling, no mercy, no mercy, no mercy. Wally was folding in on himself like a fetus. It was like watching reverse footage of a flower un-blooming, closing itself up, shrinking back into the ground, collapsing into a seedling.

I looked away. I couldn't stomach it any longer. Instead my gaze crept through the chain-link fence beyond into the street.

Holy Crap, I said to myself.

I rushed over and pulled Skid Row Paul away from the brawl, who tried to fight me off initially, until his eyes came to rest on the very thing that had caught my attention. Now Zanz too, had noticed it, and slowly backed away from the crumpled mess that lay at his feet. Only Baron remained, striking, muttering, cursing. It was Zanz who pulled Baron off, as the old man continued to fight in vain with the air in front of him, until he looked up and saw it as well.

In the street beyond the alley, staring back at us, congregated in the rear end of a school bus, were a dozen wide-eyed children with expressions of rapt horror. One little girl was sobbing. Their general puzzlement, at least what could be assumed from their faces, was of a strikingly similar nature. I could tell that some of them were dealing with uncertainty for the very first time. This singular sight was prompting other more general life questions that their limited experience was not able to properly deal with at that point.

Why is there bad?

How long is forever?

Does God have to pee like us?

It was an almost Dostoevskian purging, with the added foolishness of four grown men standing around in clown outfits. The back of the bus pulled away—an unseen red light had no doubt gone green. Sadness and exhaustion descended on our group. The children had equipped us with a raw innocence that had drawn us back into childhood ourselves. We all needed to go home and sit in quiet contemplation of what had just happened. Baron kicked the whimpering motivational speaker one last time before we all walked away.

We had just created about a dozen new Coulrophobes.

# CHAPTER 19

To properly celebrate the culmination of our entire summer Baron insisted we adjourn to a unique environment, one that would truly stand to represent as he called it, "...Our towering achievements of the hot season." He insisted that we must recognize and take advantage of quiet times or "fulcrum moments", points of calm reflection between periods of struggle that allow us to put everything into perspective. Zanz had provided a couple of bottles of his peach brandy, which was the defining incentive. We had adjourned--Zanz, Baron and I--under a ripened grape sky, to the roof of the Kadore Hotel the evening before I was set to leave for New York to visit my Uncle Jimmy.

This part of the building was usually strictly off-limits, but Baron had bribed the desk clerk, mentioned to her that he knew such-and-such who was a friend of so-and-so, and promised her a personal escort to the dialysis clinic anytime she wished. The clerk, with gloomy resignation, took us to the top floor, up an iron custodial staircase, and as we settled in on the exposed tar mentioned that it would be kind of us to "...refrain from suicide".

The bottles were set down between us. We got into the first one. Baron said we needed this type of private venue so we wouldn't be disturbed by lingering strangers, the type that detract from conversation by providing an abundance of curiosity with an overwhelming shortage of brains.

We started drinking. The Truth went around and around. There was an intermingling of joy and sadness in the air. We took turns sharing haphazard conversation, old stories, bizarre thoughts, while the zigzagging streets down below us emitted honks and zooms, the veins and arteries of the world, white lights coming, red lights going, the steady heartbeat of an alive city. The artificial light twinkled resplendently around us. It was a city seen at night from an elevated distance that conjured some type of clean, unattainable magnificence. It was always something greater than the streets below. On the streets the façade is lifted. On the streets there is the filth and the hustle. I wasn't sure of the exact statistics but I figured it was infinitely less likely to get mugged at the top of a building than at the bottom.

Speaking of the bottom, I wondered if our pal Clem Harris was still down in the Kadore Hotel bar, somewhere below us, brooding in the bowels, waiting for us to return? Well, in a sense we had, perhaps for the last time, in this type of satisfied mood. I could feel the winds changing, an impending chill associated with the end of the summer. For some reason I felt that life itself was entering a new phase, evolving from something frivolous to something serious and foreboding.

Baron had a happy, stoned look on his face, which was covered with his normal constituent parts of fedora, tinted glasses and graying beard. There was something peaceful about him. He no longer seemed delirious. No longer seemed beyond reach. Zanz was sitting closest to the edge of the roof wistfully smoking a cigarette, thinking of nothing and everything at the same time. He was completely dissolved in the environment, sensitive to it like a nerve ending, but also exuding wise indifference, a blank welcoming.

I was lying on my back, staring at the capitalized KADORE letters as they ascended the metal latticework of the hotel roof's defunct radio tower stretching into the night sky overhead, looking more like a big oil geyser. It was a stately relic, now emitting only the frequency of history. I was reading the sign backwards, from the ground up, enunciating slowly, morphing the words to suit me. "Ee—Row—Dake, Ee—Rah—Dake, Ee—Raw—Take, Ee—Ra—Tic. Hey. Kadore backwards spells 'Erotic', kind of." Instead of sitting up to drink my peach brandy I kept trying to pour it into my mouth from my lying position. It spilled all over my face, burning it.

I had invited Skid Row Paul to this rooftop gathering but he wanted no part of it. He made me swear to him that I would get in touch as soon as I returned from my trip to New York. I was going to make good on my promise and take him to the steamer trunk.

In the aftermath of Doctor B. Right's motivational seminar, some facts had come to light. Skid Row Paul, always with his ear to the ground, had found out that Wally had taken a leave of absence from his lecture circuit, and was probably resting comfortably in some hospital, babbling like an infant, colicky only when hungry or when his diaper needed to be changed.

There was still some talk about Wally's hasty exit during his speech--all kinds of theories. Some blamed the record summer temperatures. Others assumed that Wally had seen an apparition noted to inhabit the halls of the Landmark Theater. Apparently one or two audience members in the front row had chanced to lean over and glance down into the orchestra pit to see a couple of clowns fleeing, and wondered to a few people if *that* could have had something to do with it. Thankfully this theory was quickly dismissed, since the eyewitness accounts were flimsy and unsupported, and mitigated by the fact that the eyewitnesses happened to be heavy alcoholics and the so-called 'clown theory' was eventually rejected as the bleary-eyed invention of a couple of attention-seeking drunks. I wondered aloud if we had destroyed Wally's life or if he would ever be the same? Zanz pointed out that the man is a professional motivational speaker, and as such he is trained to embrace the optimistic side of everything.

"Here's to the bartenders," Zanz cheered.

"And the barflies," said Baron with a raise of his cup.

"And the flies that hang around the bar flies," I added.

"That was some beautiful thing we pulled off the other day," Baron said. "It made me wish for the old times, back when I had half the age, three times the women, and about one-sixteenth of the aches." He took another sip off his cup, studied the rim. "You boys had a lot of guts to do all that. I'm proud of you. You did the right thing. You've got to take it straight to these fools."

"Are you nervous about going to see your Uncle Jimmy tomorrow?" Zanz asked me.

"It could be the drink talking, but I don't feel nervous."

"It is definitely the drink talking. Are you finally going to tell him that you are not in medical school?"

"Yes," I said. "It is time he found out."

"Glad to see you are coming around," said Zanz. He turned to Baron. "Toby's uncle thinks he has been in medical school these past four years."

"Make sure you get a couple of drinks in him before you tell him," said Baron.

"I can't remember a time when he didn't have a couple of drinks in him."

"What inspired you to come clean?" asked Zanz.

"Honestly I think I'd have to credit Doctor B. Right with giving me a new perspective," I said. Baron and Zanz choked on their brandy.

"Did I hear that right?" said Baron.

"I was affected by watching you guys beat him the other day. I don't know exactly what happened but as you pummeled him I suddenly had an incredible feeling of being present in myself for the first time. My circumstance was real. Everything was here and now. Just like that the fear got displaced. Wally's breakdown became the receptacle for my apprehension. I wasn't allowed to feel victimized in his presence. His situation was too pathetic. I became elevated in my own struggles. If we ever run into him again remind me to thank him."

"Toby," Zanz said. "I can say this because we are friends. You are a weird bastard."

"Look, you know I'm weird, I know I'm weird. It is just that sometimes I still marvel at the specifics of it."

"Where does your uncle live?" asked Baron.

"Long Island, New York," I said.

"You are from Long Island?" Baron exclaimed with a wide smile. "I used to be a bartender on the Bridgeport ferry. What a coincidence."

"My uncle's bar is up the hill from that ferry," I said. This information pleased Baron, like I was now a descendant from some lineage of middle class, drunken Irish royalty.

"If you have time you should go take a ride on the ferry. Tell them you know me. They'll give you a couple of free drinks."

"Thanks Baron," I said, a little ill at ease with what I had to say next. "I also want to thank you for dragging me out of the road the other day. You have some strength for an old man."

"Quick thinking, Baron," said Zanz.

"You make a better clown than you do a speed bump," he said, rubbing at his chin and falling back into silence. Down below a car backfired. A woman screamed. Sirens went by. It was a tough thing for me to admit. I didn't want to be grateful to him because I knew something about him that he didn't want me to know.

He had been lying.

I had scoured the local news the other morning for some type of report concerning a massive traffic accident involving a Red Cross blood bus from the day before. There was nothing remotely similar to support Baron's claim as to why he had been covered in blood when he showed up at Zanz's. There was no major accident, no biohazard spill, no emergency, no traffic delays.

Nothing.

Baron had saved me. Why couldn't it have been Zanz, or Skid Row Paul, or some other wandering stranger who saw the chance to save a life. It was Baron. There were four clown suits. He had saved me. There was no accident involving an American Red Cross truck. He had plucked me like a feather out of the road. There was woman's hair on the electrical tape in his trunk. He wanted Wally beaten down for what he had done to me. We buried his steamer trunk in the woods. He was the closest thing to a father Zanz had. He admitted to holding a woman captive. He came to visit me in the hospital.

It was too much blood.

"I wouldn't be surprised," Zanz mused as he slid over to get more brandy, "to find out the number of times I had been an inch from death and didn't even know it."

"I wouldn't be surprised if I won the lottery, without even playing it," said Baron.

"I wouldn't be surprised to sit down at the controls of a rocket ship and realize I knew exactly how to fly it," shrugged Zanz.

"I wouldn't be surprised at the true amount of misinformation fed to me on a regular basis," I added, as the non sequitur went around and around.

"I wouldn't be surprised if in twenty years time, everybody's head had swelled to the size of a grapefruit on one side from cell phone use."

" I wouldn't be surprised if I started shitting precious gemstones."

"I wouldn't be surprised if a cop gave me a ticket for being ugly in public."

"I wouldn't be surprised if rising gas prices soon made it too expensive to get lost."

"I wouldn't be surprised if Satan had a terrible childhood."

"I wouldn't be surprised if the only word correctly spelled incorrectly is the word 'incorrectly'."

"I wouldn't be surprised if everybody did it for the money."

"I wouldn't be surprised if someone tried to sell me a marijuana cigarette while in line at the post office."

"I wouldn't be surprised if we actually drank all this brandy," Zanz suddenly realized. We studied the empty bottles. Tomorrow morning was not going to be a good one.

"I guess it's time to go," I said, pulling myself up to a standing position and then reeling back to the ground. Zanz stood up, wandered over to the edge of the roof and took a piss off the side.

"I feel like a giant pissing on a miniature city!" he exclaimed. "You guys have to try this."

"Have a safe trip," Baron said to me as he got to his feet. "And don't go getting married while you are up there. That happened to me last time."

"I don't think that will be a problem," I said.

"And go down to the ferry bar," he repeated. "Tell them to give you a drink on me."

"You got it," I said.

Satisfied with my answer, Baron started to walk away, but I stopped him, overwhelmed with curiosity, trying to take advantage of his drunken state, and the fact that we were alone. Zanz was still over at the edge of the roof, with a bladder, it seemed, the size of a zeppelin. "Baron, do you mind if I ask you a serious question?"

"Go ahead," he nodded.

"I think I just got somebody," Zanz yelled proudly. "He's more than pissed off. He's pissed on!"

"This puts me in a very awkward position," I continued. "You saved my life, but I'm still a bit nervous about something, and I think if I knew the answer then I would be able to rest easier about the whole thing."

"What's on your mind, Toby?" He stopped and leaned himself against the base of the radio tower.

"I just want to know what was in the steamer trunk that we buried in the woods? Actually I don't want to know. I have to know."

"That's still worrying you? I thought we forgot all about that."

"It's been a burden ever since."

"You could've asked before."

"Well, you know, out of respect for Zanz I didn't want to come off too heavy."

"You shouldn't let it get to you," he said.

"For my own piece of mind," I said.

"There were a lot of 'things' in the trunk," Baron shrugged, itching at his head. "I don't even know everything that was in it. It doesn't make a whole lot of sense."

I wondered if Baron was trying to beat me with semantics by his use of the plural. There were a lot of 'things' in the trunk. The case could be made that while there was only one body in the trunk, within that one body there were a multitude of 'things'. Two hands, two feet, ten fingers. The torso itself could be divided into the thoracic and abdominal cavities. I think there was a pelvic cavity too. There were thirty-two teeth in an adult's head, two hundred and eight bones in the body. The skin itself had three layers. There were two kinds of connective tissue, countless muscles, organs, miles of blood vessels, smooth, striated, cardiac. Gray matter. White matter. Billions of cells.

"Just name the predominant thing, Baron, please."

"The predominant thing?" Baron brushed his hand through his beard and then adjusted the brim of his hat. These were nervous mannerisms. A sour look came across his face. "I'd rather not say Toby because you will probably take it out of context."

"Please? I promise I won't rush to judgment."

"Well, for starters I'm sure there were some clothes."

"Okay, that's a good start, some clothes. What else?"

"A pillow. A blanket, maybe. Soft things, mostly."

"Baron if I were to open that trunk and glance inside, what would be the most conspicuous thing that I would see? Imagine the top pops open, and I am forced to look inside. What am I going to fixate on first? What is the main thing?" Baron puffed his cheeks out then let the air whistle through his teeth slowly.

"I'll tell you, but I'm warning you that it will give the wrong impression."

"Go ahead, try me."

"If you opened that trunk up the first thing you'd probably notice, I mean if we are talking about striking characteristics here, the thing that might catch your eye, I suppose, if one were to really pay attention is... I guess...a human head."

Check please!

PART 3

# WET BRAIN

# CHAPTER 20

The plane ride up the eastern seaboard of the United States was especially turbulent. Every tiny bump the plane hit sent heavy reverberations through my tortured head where I had successfully, the night before atop the Kadore Hotel, replaced the interstitial fluid surrounding my brain with peach brandy. This hangover was its own monster—a creature of such despicable mercilessness that to cure the pain I might in fact need a formal exorcism by an ordained man of the cloth.

I looked out the window, studying the fluffy folds of the cumulus clouds spread out below, giant cotton clumps of empty real estate. When I was a child (a younger one than I am now) I used to study these serene air masses from below for any signs of angels, believing as I did at the time that the winged seraphim lived atop, frolicked gaily, played harps and such. The first time I flew in an airplane I was so excited to finally get a glimpse of them, but when we got above the clouds nothing was there despite my sharp searching. When I inquired to my father about this he murmured between irritable, semi-sleepless tosses and turns from the seat next to me that the angels were all hiding in disgust because I had been irresponsible and negligent regarding my house chores.

"Something to drink sir?" the flight attendant asked me as she came down the aisle handing out snacks and coffee to most of the early morning flyers.

"You wouldn't happen to have an intravenous bag in that wheelie cart, would you?" I asked.

"No," she clipped callously.

"Well then I'll take two beers, please." She gave me a look of disdain before handing them over. I paid for the beers. The plane hit another bump. I sat back and dug my fingernails into the armrests, trying in vain to steady the whole aircraft by holding my breath and clutching the seat. The hangover was so bad I thought it might be a good idea to come up with another term for it. A bend-over? A buried-under? A brain-killer?

The girl next to me was young, maybe ten years old or so. A cursory conversation at the beginning of the flight informed me that she was flying alone, and that we were indeed flying to the same place. Our chitchat, mostly due to my brandy blitzkrieg, had taken on a bit of a lull after that. But upon my strange order of two beers so early in the day I was now being scrutinized. She had a cruel maturity about her. She was relaxed and confident, operating on the assumption that the world was perfect and just getting better. She had ordered hot water with lemon from the flight attendant.

"I'm going to be on holiday in the Hamptons for the weekend," she told me with just the slightest hint of a British accent as she pulled from her travel bag her own personal herbal tea pouch. She set about steeping.

"Are you from the South?" I asked.

"Are you trying to find out something about me from where I live?" she replied. "If I tell you where I am from you may have some false impressions."

"Holy shit kid!" I exclaimed. "How old are you?"

"The same goes for age," was her precocious response. I took a big chug off one of the cans of beer. I was in no shape to cleverly joust with this sprightly soul. I was in no shape to babble to an infant. I sighed and turned to my window. I looked down the length of the plane wing and imagined it snapping off and hurtling upwards, while the fuselage performed a harrowing barrel roll earthward.

"Are you okay?" my little travel companion asked, placing a comforting hand on my forearm.

"No," I said. "A case of brandy is good. A case of brandy-head is bad."

"You look nervous," she gave.

"I think I either need to fly more or fly less."

"You need to fly more," she assured me. "It is the safest way to travel. Would you like to talk a little bit? It might relax you. We can discuss your favorite subject. Go ahead and start it up."

I again had the itch, as I suspected on my date with Star about a million years ago, that my smart confabulator had asked me this only to cleverly redirect the conversation to *her* favorite subject—possibly ponies, teen idols, the rude and smelly characteristics of most boys her age. However I decided to give her the benefit of the doubt.

"Well kid, my favorite subject is a little thing I like to call...Where It All Went Wrong," I began. The girl crossed her legs towards me, arm-rested her elbow and propped her chin in the palm of her hand. Her eyes widened a bit. They were gentle and understanding eyes, indicative of what the mystics might call an old soul. She was ready to take whatever dilemma I threw at her, gather up the smashed bits and pieces, straighten and un-mangle the parts, reconstruct it and hand it back to me in a usable and pleasing form. She had to be older than she looked. "When I was younger I thought it was all going to work out so easily in my favor. But now I find myself falling away from my intended destiny."

"Which is?"

"I don't know exactly," I confessed. "But I know it has something to do with being happy."

"Happy doing what?" she persisted.

"I don't know."

"How can you be falling away from your intended destiny if you don't know exactly what it is?" she put together quite easily, and furthermore without any accusatory sarcasm.

"I guess I'm looking for that exact moment in which my childhood dreams and aspirations turned into a backward slide away from the pinnacle of my own possibility." I said, wondering if this was too much to drop on a prepubescent.

"What did you want to be when you were a kid?" she asked, taking a sip of her tea. "Let's start from there."

"Growing up?" I shrugged. "Normal stuff. Astronaut. Surgeon. The garbage man that gets to hang off the side of the truck as it speeds away. The high profile gigs, although I realized I only wanted these jobs when I saw other people doing them. When I tried my hand at obtaining the entry level criteria for any of these occupations I was completely turned off."

"I know what you mean," she nodded, reaching back down into her travel bag and pulling a couple wedges of biscotti from a side compartment. She held one towards me in silent offering but I declined. "I used to want to play the piano because I'd be so emotionally moved when I saw someone else playing beautifully. I wanted to control peoples' emotions the way I was being controlled. But when I actually sat down at the piano I lost all interest. That's when I realized that I just wanted control. I didn't really want to play the piano. It was an important distinction."

"So what? You are not musically inclined. There are other things," I said.

"Actually, I eventually learned how to play the piano. My teacher says I'm somewhat of a prodigy. But I could only play the piano after I gave up the need to control through it. That is my own personal thing, though. I know we were talking about you. I'm not trying to burden you with my troubles."

"Are you kidding?" I sighed, annoyed. "Kid you are going to be president of the world somewhere down the line." I drank some more of my beer. "It doesn't really matter anyway," I continued. "I get a little touchy and emotional whenever I head back to my hometown." My young psychiatrist nodded sympathetically and took a bite from her biscotti. "It is just the nature of the place to remind me of all that I wanted to do and never did."

"You talk as if your life is over," she retorted, now stirring her tea with the biscotti to soften it up. "You still have a pulse. There is always time for reinvention. No wait, that's not right." She tapped her head, a gentle self-reprimand. "Reorientation," she clarified. "That is what I meant to say. Don't try to be somebody else. Just try to be you at your best, which is better than somebody else, because it is all yours. Impossible to steal."

"Do you suffer from some kind of reverse-progeria?"

"Hush up," she said.

"What is your name?" I asked. "In case I ever needed some kind of presidential pardon."

"I'd like to tell you, but familiarity breeds contempt," she dismissed. "We are getting along very nicely because we are strangers. Why mess that up?"


The plane began its initial descent, to my disappointment, because it broke my new friend's concentration. She began to clean up her little tray, consolidate wrappers and napkins into her little teacup. She took my empty beer cans, crushed them into neat dwarves of their former selves and when the stewardess came around she threw it all away. "In the meantime try to enjoy yourself this weekend," she advised before adorning a set of headphones. "Be happy with what you've got. Try to soak up some of your immediate life that, due to future concern, tends to be ignored."

"Don't take this the wrong way," I put in quickly, "but would you perhaps like to go out on a date in about eight or nine years?"

"That is future concern," she said. "You really need to pay more attention."


Once off the plane I proceeded to baggage claim. I trundled through the airport, taking in the old familiarity, the thick suburban accents, heavy faces and strong language. I was largely ignored, since I had developed into something quite distinct from this archetype—maybe for the better, maybe for the worse. I cast a few quick glances around for my Uncle Jimmy, knowing that he would not be there, but wondering if by some magical circumstance he had decided to surprise me and pick me up, but there was no sign of the short, bullish, broad-shouldered sociopath with similar, matured features. Just as well, I thought. Let me enjoy these remaining moments of peace and quiet. I watched the bags on the conveyor go round and round. The same ones seemed to go around forever. Who were these people that could afford to neglect their bags like this? I caught a few glimpses of my young seatmate on the other side of the conveyor. She had been retrieved by an overly refined, white-collar couple with obvious addictions to champagne and valium. The young girl showed no sign of recognition towards me. Our time with each other up in the sky had come and gone. To make further mention of it would cheapen the experience.

I grabbed my bag, caught a cab and headed for Uncle Jim's bar, known in these parts as The Last Stop Saloon because it was located across the street from the last stop of the northern line of the Long Island railroad. It was also known as the Last Stop Saloon because for most of the customers that is exactly what it was. They weren't going anywhere else. It was the end of the road. But as long as there is a fully stocked bar at the end of the road it can't be so bad. Ambition is a malady of the ungrateful. There was nothing that bred hostility so much as failed ambition. If you took the odds, probably one person out of every thousand actually accomplished what they set out to do and was happy about it, so why play such slim chances, especially when happiness could be found right then and there with a minimal amount of time and effort.

These trips home were a form of time travel. Only in the explicit surroundings of my youth did I ever recall that I had a youth, and thereby experience significant parts of it again, step outside the man I was usually trapped in. These two distinct spheres of existence brought about two distinct characters within myself, almost as if I had two souls stuck in two separate cities and my body was a hollow vessel that only became animated when plugged into the specific air space, and then could operate with its unique set of behavior variables.

My New York behavior that day was quiet, fidgety, and high-strung, particularly because of what I knew I had to do. The time for confession was nigh. There was no escape. Today was going to be a day of serious reckoning, and by the end of it, Jimmy would know the truth. I craved another beer, told myself not to get so upset. A lot of respectable people have met their demise on Long Island. Fitzgerald's Jay "Great" Gatsby for instance. He went down like a dog after having a good run. Hell, at least that prick was *rich*.

I was deposited at the front door of the Last Stop Saloon. I took a deep breath and held it. The much anticipated moment had arrived. I decided to take my plane companion's advice and meditate on the time spent looking forward to an event and the event itself. The time in between did seem to have disappeared right out from under me, lost in the grand, sweeping funnel of it all. No sense worrying about it now. I walked through the doors. The place was good and crowded for a Friday afternoon. The place was good and filthy for a Friday afternoon. The customers were good and twisted for a Friday afternoon. A couple of the old timers did double takes at me, perhaps because they recognized me or perhaps because I bore a strong resemblance to my Uncle Jimmy. Two of them in particular, Mr. Amico and Mr. Genovese, called me by name from the far end of the bar where they were always seated. These two were as permanent a fixture at the place as the cash register, the ceiling, or the jar of briny, pickled eggs sitting on the back bar. They never worked yet they always complained about their jobs. They knew the *real* reason behind every scandal—entertainment, political or otherwise. They always had some major connection to a valuable resource through a brother-in-law. They both looked like they had medicine balls shoved into the front of their leisure pants and were inveterate chain smokers.

This Long Island drinking saloon was its own bracketed, unique experience. All of the conversation was basically one category with many subcategories: How to screw the government out of money. How to screw your job out of money. How the government screws everybody out of money. How jobs screw the worker out of money. How families screw each other out of money. How wives try to screw husbands out of money. How trying to screw people out of money sometimes screws other people out of money. Oh, and also glorifying and debunking paranormal activity seemed to be high on the conversation list. My Uncle Jimmy's place always attracted the blue-collar crowd—plumbers, electricians, carpenters, railroad engineers and shady mechanics, the last of which were the type to suggest rebuilding an entire car engine to fix a loose clutch, and even then they couldn't make any promises.

"Hey it's Jimmy's nephew," Mr. Amico said.

"How is it going...Toby right?" Mr. Genovese added, gloating a bit because he had actually remembered my name.

"Mr. Amico, Mr. Genovese, how are you guys doing?"

"Don't just stand there, give us a faulkin hug," they shouted, now that they had properly figured out how I was connected to this whole thing. I supposed their sudden eagerness to see me was motivated by an essential loyalty towards Jimmy and his bar. Maybe they thought they'd get a couple of free ones if they were nice to me. Nevertheless, I dropped my bags and embraced both men in turn, then proceeded to stand there in front of them. The conversation was now in danger of coming to a complete standstill.

"So, your uncle tells me that you are a faulkin doctor?" Mr. Amico asked.

"I'm still studying," I explained stiffly. This filled them with an agitated happiness. They called for the bartender to get me a beer. They were good men. The bartender came over and dropped a pint glass down, overflowing with foam and beautiful pilsner. I grabbed and quaffed. For this moment, at least, it was great to be home. I finished the beer in record time.

"You should go be a consultant for those medical television shows after you graduate," Mr. Genovese suggested. "My brother-in-law knows a guy that does that. He makes a lot of faulkin money."

"Is my uncle around?" I asked them.

"Yeah, he's around here somewhere," they both responded in a confused fashion, craning their heads from side to side. "Where's Jimmy? Where's Jimmy? Hey has anybody seen Jimmy?"

"He's in the back office," somebody yelled acerbically. Mr. Genovese and Mr. Amico then suggested, as if I would've never thought of it on my own, that I should go say hello to my uncle because it would be a shame to come all this way and not spend time. I agreed that it was a good idea and thanked them for my beer, gathered up my bags and headed down the back hallway, passing as I did a table at which a man and woman were busy shouting at each other over some detail of their inharmonious existence together. The argument was rather repetitive. The woman just kept repeating that she was sick of his shit. The man just kept repeating that he was going to rip her faulkin hair out.

Uncle Jimmy was in his office, at his desk, sipping on what I suspected was a rum and diet coke, because that is what he always drank. He drank about sixteen of them a day and, like his customers, didn't really drink to get drunk. They all drank simply to maintain their hostility. The office was in complete disarray, too small to accommodate the overflow of liquor invoices, sales reports, marketing brochures, swimsuit calendars and whatever else. Jimmy was smoking a cigar and studying a soldier of fortune magazine. I knocked on the door. His head shot up. I could tell he was about to beat silly whoever had caused the disturbance, until he realized that it wasn't some haggard lush trying to find the men's room. It was family. His expression changed from violent rage to violent excitement.

"Toby! You little shit!" he bellowed, jumping from his desk and coming around to embrace me. "How's my medicine man doing?" He took the wind out of me with his hug. "Sit down, let me get a good look at you." He cleared off a chair and pushed me into it. He then settled back down, noticing that I didn't have anything to drink. He picked up his phone and yelled into it, "Get me a beer for my nephew!" He slammed the phone down. "When is the last time you relaxed with a beer eh?" he asked jokingly with a nudge to my knee. I refrained from answering. We sat face to face, studying each other.

I was growing more like this man by the day. There were only a couple minor adjustments I would have to make, like giving myself a crew cut, going entirely gray-haired. Cultivate a bushy mustache and start smoking cigars. Jimmy's head was more square than round, almost developing edges. His neck and chin had gotten a little thicker since I last saw him. He also seemed to be shrinking as the years went on. The bartender ducked his head into the office and handed me my beer.

"So how are you feeling? You look great," Jimmy smiled, grabbing his rum and diet coke from his desk and offering me a cheers.

"You just say that because I look like you," I answered as our glasses clinked.

"Yeah, I guess so. I've been spending a lot of time at the bar. I don't like to be home too often because I know that they are watching me. They've got the place completely under surveillance."

"Who are 'they'?" I asked my uncle.

"If I knew I'd probably already be dead," he answered with an uncomfortable frown.

"Are you sure you are okay, Jimmy?"

"I feel fine," he shrugged with a big swig of his drink. "My doctor had me switch to diet coke in my rum because he says I need to lose some weight. That's why I need you to be a doctor, Toby. I need a doctor who appreciates me just the way I am." His mustache twitched a bit. "I've got it all planned out. After you graduate you can come up here to practice. Mr. Amico's brother-in-law knows a guy that is a doctor for a television show."

"I think that is Mr. Genovese's brother-in-law," I corrected, uncertain myself.

"What's the faulkin difference?" Jimmy exclaimed. "What I'm telling you is that we got connections up here." We settled back into silence again. He was trying to stop himself from smiling, fighting off the vulnerability associated with overwhelming emotion. "So, when are you graduating?" he asked. I paused, trying to get myself to speak the truth. After all, he needed to know. But for all the man's toughness there was something too fragile in his demeanor. For the moment, I couldn't destroy it. I ended up mumbling something about how my clinical rotations were busy, the doctors abusive, and how I liked surgery and psychiatry but was uninterested in obstetrics. I added that it was more gratifying to move from classroom theory to practical application. To work with an actual patient made the whole endeavor worthwhile. To bring health to the infirmed was a miracle, and I was just lucky to be a small part of it. Jimmy coughed his approval.

I shifted the conversation so Jimmy would be on the receiving end. I asked him how the bar was holding up. He said it was giving him joint pain. The whole joint. The joint was giving him pain, perhaps in his joints, perhaps not. He said that he was thinking about selling the bar. I asked him what he would do afterwards. He said he wanted to get into boating full time. I asked what was stopping him. He told me that he would probably have to buy a sailor cap and grow a beard first. He then asked if there was a special woman in my life. I told him that my work prevented me from forging any serious relationships at the moment. At last, I thought. I have spoken the truth. Jimmy studied me with a look of peculiar proprietorship, like a piece of furniture or a car he has owned for many years and now, due to some trick of shade, light and nostalgia, he has come to see in an entirely new way.

"I don't know why my brother named you Toby," he said finally. "It's a child's name."

"At the time I was a child, Jimmy."

"But you give somebody a name like Toby and they never grow out of it."

"I don't know quite what to say to that," I shrugged off.

"I'm not trying to give you a hard time," my uncle soothed. "But you still don't seem like an adult to me. And you certainly don't strike me as a doctor. You don't look like a doctor. You don't act like a doctor. I can't put my finger on it but something doesn't seem quite right."

"Maybe I should wear a stethoscope and carry a pocket full of tongue depressors," I suggested on my own behalf. "Scrawl illegible instructions on little slips of paper and instead of shaking hands I could check for a hernia."

"Oh don't listen to me, Toby. I guess it is just because I've known you since you were an infant. Maybe a child never grows up in the eyes of an elder." I could tell he was fidgety with a growing sentimentality. "I'm proud of you," he confessed finally, nodding over to a picture on his desk that I hadn't noticed before. The picture was of my parents. "And so are they." I watched my uncle choke up a bit. "We got robbed of them way too early," he lamented. "But they are looking down and smiling. They are helping us along, every step." I nodded, looking back to the picture. I suddenly had parents again. Jimmy excused himself, ostensibly to get another rum and diet coke but probably more to pull himself together. I studied the two familiar strangers.

There they were, looking so young, almost too young to be believable, staring out of a grainy picture in outdated clothes. Memories came back, none clear or complete. The fragments were dreamy. My dad showing me how to work a gas grill, particularly the importance of drinking a beer while doing so. My mother showing me how to open bottles of wine so she wouldn't have to get up for refills, tailoring me for my future vocation. These memories that seemed to grow elements of fiction the older they got. My father playing catch with me even though we never played catch. My mother cheering me at a school play I was never in. I realized my memories were forming a life separate from the one I had experienced. They were plotting subtle improvements. I remembered small bits of advice that my dad would rattle off during hockey game commercials, little tidbits that just seemed to be tossed back and forth on the waves of beer crashing through his brooding preoccupations.

"Son, if you are ever able to simply drink an afternoon away while listening to Ray Charles, or make love to a beautiful woman after only knowing her for a few hours, by crumb happiness is yours."

"But dad, I'm only twelve."

"Yeah. Sucks."

I remembered their fights, many times with myself as the intermediary, as they pleaded for me to pass their arguments back and forth, even though they were both within earshot of each other. "Tell your mother to get dinner going. Tell your father if he's so damn hungry to start it himself. Tell you mother to go work ten hours a day." So on. One day I got fed up with this, and so I took my mother by the hand and led her into the television room.

"Mom, I'd like you to meet dad. Dad, this is mom."

"We've met," they muttered with downcast eyes.

Then the death. Mom washed away. Dad scorched into eternity. Water and fire. The empty casket. The urn. The crying. The bell toll. The abrupt chiming of my own ephemera. I remember standing in front of my father's urn, the tiny tomb atop a satiny viewing table. Jimmy was next to me. I felt that the people behind us waiting to pay their respects were watching us for any signs of insincerity.

"Now what are we supposed to do, Uncle Jimmy?"

"Pray."

"What am I praying for?" I asked.

"What do you mean? Pray for anything."

"Anything?" I repeated.

"How about pray that your father gets into heaven."

"Wouldn't that have already been decided by now?"

"Pray for yourself then."

"Pray for myself? You mean I should take this time, since I am standing so close to the death example to put myself in some good standing with the Lord? I feel that is an abuse of the situation."

"Pray that you get out of this room without a good hard slap from me."

Family and friends had placed small odds and ends on the table around the urn. A flask, a deck of cards, a pack of cigars, a ticket stub for a hockey game, some dice, a butane lighter, a fishing pole--so at the time of some formal resurrection he'd be able to rise from the ash, ascend into heaven, have a nice drink and a good smoke. Then he could do some gambling. The fishing pole insured he'd have something to do in the event that there was a body of water in heaven. I remember wondering at the time if there was a heaven for fish? Maybe from the boats of heaven fishermen throw their hooks into the rivers of fish hell. Fish heaven would have to be located in fishermen hell, where no fish are ever caught. Then I remembered wondering what the fuck was wrong with me. Then there was silence. A rupture or break, a part of me left in that moment, and the rest of me just dwindling into the future, unwilling or unable to choose, because to choose was to choose life, and life was too linked to death to be an option.

൦

My attention lingered and waned, searched Jimmy's small office for other points of interest and that is when I noticed something else. Something I had completely forgotten about and now seeing again, was hit with a renewed puzzlement at an odd possession of my mother's. There was a painting on the wall of Jimmy's office, a painting my mother had done. It was the only one she had ever attempted, as far as I knew, and for good reason. It was artistic gibberish--part of some half-assed, creative compulsion of her failed college experience. The painting was just a collection of odd decorative shapes placed in an arrangement with a vacancy of sorts in the middle. In later years my mother would spend hours looking at that picture, just off in some kind of musing space trance. Of course she was doing it while she was drunk, and so could probably have been staring at a peanut with that type of look. Jimmy came back into the office.

"Where did you find that picture?" I asked my uncle, pointing towards the wall.

"Oh that," Jimmy said. "I found it when I was cleaning out my basement. I figured I'd put it up in memory. That's a funny bit of art. Never really knew what it meant to her. She would've never made it as a professional painter but there is something about that picture that strikes me. It grows on you after awhile." We perused the abstract doodle like we were serious collectors before Jimmy suggested we get out of the stuffy office and into the stuffy bar area. I agreed.

We walked out into the developing mayhem. It was steadily getting busier as afternoon made way for evening. More of the same customer kept arriving, an ever-expanding house of mirrors. I went around to where Mr. Amico and Mr. Genovese were still sitting and took up a spot next to them. Jimmy was about to go back behind the bar when a scream rang out from the other side of the room. Apparently, the man whom I had overheard before was making good on his promise to rip his woman's faulking hair out. He had a good solid grip on both sides of her head and was shaking

208

it back and forth. My uncle ran over, caught the man in a half nelson, grabbed him by his own head of hair and dragged him towards the door. The place went crazy, shouting and cheering while Jimmy fought off not only the man he was holding, but the man's wife who had suddenly turned on my uncle and was beating him about the shoulders to get him to lay off her man. The three of them burst out the doors into the front parking lot.

"Atta boy, Jimmy," Mr. Amico shouted.

"It is starting already," agreed Mr. Genovese.

Uncle Jimmy came back in dusting his hands off. Never missing a beat, he walked back behind his bar looking annoyed, exasperated, fatigued and sexually stimulated all at the same time. "Can you believe that? That crazy broad actually accused me of assault. She said she was going to sue me for every penny. I told them both they were banned from this place for one month."

"What did she say to that?" I asked.

"She said that I called her bluff and that she was sorry. She made her old man apologize and begged me to let them in next weekend. Faulking people. I can't figure 'em out. Why do some people have to be so faulkin stupid?"

"It is all a law of nature," Mr. Genovese pointed out loudly. "You got your people who are at the top and you got your people who are at the bottom. It's all a matter of density. The denser you are, the lower you are. It is like faulkin Earth—one big centrifuge. It spins us around and separates us into layers. The idiots settle at the bottom, the smart guys like us settle on top. That's the way it is. You can't change it." He drank his beer.

"You got a point," Mr. Amico agreed.

The strange demographic multiplied through the restaurant like sewer flies, as if a whole larvae had broken open right outside the door and were now looking for a place to nestle in and feed. I was studying one man in particular. In a roomful of bad news this guy looked like a national disaster. He had come in and took up a seat in the corner, alone, in order to carefully watch the rest of the patrons, prowling for the right fusion of weakness and inebriation. He had a horrific pair of eyes, hardened, mean, jaundiced. There were jagged scars across his face. He exuded the vengeful sadism of a prison queer. The tough guy con that for a time is queer out of necessity until he realizes that he just generally prefers it.

Nobody else seemed too bothered by him, but most of the crowd stayed away from that corner reflexively, their primitive warning signals tingling cautiously. Elsewhere in the bar a couple of shoving matches took place, as well as impetuous blasts of laughter or some drunken expletive. "Faulk that! Faulk you! Faulk me!" Uncle Jimmy was back behind the bar sipping his rum and diet coke, making the occasional drink, sharing a little conversation, and then coming by my seat to further tell me how proud he was to finally have a family member in the doctoring business, while I worked at quietly repeating my confession until I became confident enough to put my full-throated voice behind it.


"Beer caught Jeffrey Dahlmer!" Mr. Amico bellowed to us all, reaching as he had that point of intoxication in which such topics became acceptable. "If it wasn't for beer Jeffrey Dahlmer would've gotten away."

"Bullshit," Mr. Genovese waved off, lighting a fresh cigarette from the cigarette he had been smoking.

"It's faulkin true, I swear. My brother-in-law was on the Milwaukee police force for twenty years. He told me that two of his fellow officers were dispatched to Dahlmer's apartment on the night he was finally caught. One was a senior cop and the other was a rookie. The rookie was standing with Dahlmer while the senior cop went looking around the place. Now, what was the first thing he found in the apartment?"

"It was a severed head, as I recall," I said.

"And where was the head?" Mr. Amico pressed on.

"Wasn't it in the refrigerator?"

"Exactly!" Mr. Amico shouted. "Now why the hell, during a disturbance call, are you going to make the refrigerator the first place you look? Because the senior cop was looking for a beer! He figured he might as well have a chug while he was looking around the place. What do you know, ta-dah, there is a human head staring back at him. Hooray for beer. Beer saves the day!"

"That can't be true," I said.

"Of course it is true. My brother-in-law said so."

"Speaking of beer and brother-in-laws," Mr. Genovese put in, not to be outdone. "My brother-in-law was running a plumbing business out in Amityville back in the Seventies. One day he gets a call to a barn style house on Ocean Avenue to replace a hot water heater. Once down in the basement he starts to get a faulkin weird feeling coming over him and that is when he hears a voice. It is coming from the hot water heater. It's a gurgling, raspy, shaky voice, like from somewhere beyond this life."

"And yet still in the hot water heater?" I asked, trying to follow along.

"My brother-in-law leans in to listen. He can't faulkin believe it, but the voice is rattling off one name over and over. Butch. Butch. Buuuuuuuuuuuutch. The hot water heater won't stop saying it. So my brother-in-law tells the owner of the house that the water heater keeps saying the name Butch, but there is nothing else wrong with it. The only problem is the name Butch. Then he gives him the bill for the house call, a standard fee. The homeowner tosses my brother-in-law out of the house and shouts that he would pay the bill over his dead body. Two months later, they found his dead body, along with the entire family. All shot to death. Shot to death... by Butch Defeo."

"So the hot water heater knew there was going to be a murder?" I said.

"My hot water heater makes all sorts of faulkin noises," Uncle Jimmy dismissed skeptically. "That doesn't mean shit. Your brother-in-law has a faulkin screw loose. Maybe there was a gas leak in the basement and that's why he heard what he heard. Did you ever think of that?" My uncle grew good and agitated, which was a highly desirable state to be in, since arguments around these parts were decided many times simply by roaring incoherently.

"Mr. Genovese, I thought you said that your story had something to do with beer?" I reminded.

"Shit yeah!" Mr. Genovese exclaimed. "It had everything to do with beer once my brother-in-law heard about the murders. He sold his plumbing business and moved to Florida. He got a job installing pools and working at Busch Gardens for the benefits."

"Medical? Dental?"

"Free beer."

"Oh."

"Atlanta is pretty close to Florida," Mr. Amico pointed out, steering the conversation back towards the rough, yet shallow waters of my own duplicitous existence—waters in which it was dangerous to navigate, for fear our collective rudder would be caught in the muck and the filth of my ongoing deception. I shied away from the comment reflexively. Both bar fixtures and my uncle sensed this and pressed in towards me, ready for the opening gambit in what would inevitably become a supplication for free medical advice. I was in no mood. In fact, my inner narrative kept scrambling my pitiful answers with a kind of thoughtful recapitulation of the bizarre summer that I had endured. From the corner of the bar the man with the yellow eyes was silently screaming his existence at a world that had wronged him.

"Atlanta," Mr. Genovese mused. "What's it like down there?"

"The streets are lined with peach trees," I said. "All of them. It's a law. At noon everyday people must flood the streets and sing 'Georgia on my Mind'. Also a law."

"You are a little shit, Toby," my uncle condemned as he sat behind the bar sipping on his rum.

"I hear that there are a lot of good nudie bars," Mr. Amico furthered. "Full nudity and a full bar. I'll have to go down sometime for a visit," he nodded to himself, knowing damn well he would never do anything of the sort. "I don't know if I should be traveling these days, though," he added slyly. "I haven't been feeling too well."

"You!" Mr. Genovese shouted. "I'm falling apart as we speak."

"Guys," Uncle Jimmy rebuked. "Don't start all that again."

"Come on Jimmy," Mr. Amico pleaded, gesturing toward me with splayed out hands. "The kid is almost out of medical school. He can help."

"What's wrong with you Mr. Amico?"

"I'm having pain on my left side, Toby. Shooting pain. What should I do?"

"Go see a doctor," I advised.

"Is it my appendix?" he said, holding his left hip.

"That is usually the lower right side," I told him. He moved his hands to his right hip.

"Is this psoriasis or skin cancer?" Mr. Genovese asked, throwing his arm under my chin. "Right here, see!"

"I couldn't say for sure. By the way, I dressed up like a clown last week and chased a man halfway through the city. The other clowns I was with beat him senseless in an alleyway."

"I can't piss at all," Mr. Amico lamented. "A couple of drops, then nothing, but I feel like I always have to go."

"I strongly suspect an acquaintance of being involved in felonious activities. Could be a urinary tract infection. I helped him bury a trunk in the woods, you know."

"I'm always hungry, always thirsty, and I piss constantly," my uncle complained.

"Polyphagia, polydipsia, and polyurea," I responded. "You might want to check for diabetes." All three men straightened up and regarded each other with silent reproach, nonplussed at the sudden severity of illnesses. They were now engaged in a no-holds-barred standoff as to who was dying fastest and in the most agonizing manner.

"I can hardly walk because of bone spurs," Mr. Genovese griped. "It is like having a campfire at the bottom of my leg."

"I woke up last week and couldn't move the right side of my body," Mr. Amico said. "Do you think that is something to be concerned about?"

"Being an accessory to a capital murder charge, now that is something to be concerned about," I told all of them.

"I've been gaining a lot of weight, do you think it is my thyroid?"

"It could be coulrophobia," I warned. "We probably won't know until all the tests come back."

"I've been having dizzy spells and fatigue," Mr. Genovese said.

"Aspirin or ibuprofen, Toby?" my uncle said. "Which do you recommend?"

"Soju. But only if it comes with a dead cobra snake soaking in it."

"I've been having trouble getting an erection," Mr. Amico confessed.

"Consider yourself lucky. I had an erection for twelve hours straight," I answered. "It was a nightmare."

"High blood pressure is the silent killer," my uncle told us.

"Nobody ever caught the original Zodiac killer."

"Speaking of pissing," Uncle Jimmy announced before disappearing out from behind the bar. "I've got to go piss." Mr. Genovese and Mr. Amico lapsed into silence, understanding that if Jimmy wasn't around to hear their complaining, then it really wasn't worth going through it all. My attention turned to a man sitting down on the other side of me. He appeared to have been in some kind of accident recently. His left arm was in a cast from his shoulder to his wrist. Both his eyes were black and blue and he had a white bandage over his nose. He smiled pathetically at me and ordered a beer.

"Toby, don't take this the wrong way," Mr. Genovese offered, turning my attention away from the man in the cast. "But you look a little skittish. Is everything alright?"

"No Mr. Genovese it is not," I sighed. "It is everything derived from one particular thing. The world that I exist in, the world that I have created for myself all hanging on one thing that causes everything else to be out of wack. I have trouble interpreting my experiences because of this. I'm always feeling self-conscious, unworthy, guilty."

"I don't understand what you're saying."

"For instance, last week I was putting gas in my car," I said. "When I was done I shook the nozzle to clear away the excess drops. A woman at the pump next to me was watching me do this, and she looked disturbed by it. I suddenly became incredibly embarrassed, like I had my dick right out there, swinging it dry. She sensed this and with an offended look on her face, peeled away at an unsafe speed. I felt bad about it the rest of the day. This is only one example but I could give many more."

"There is something bigger involved," Mr. Genovese nodded, catching on. "I see. There is an issue that you don't want to face and so you start to feel bad about other stuff."

"You are right Mr. Genovese!" I exclaimed, pounding my fist on the bar. "There is something weighing on my mind. Do you want to know what it is?" I took a deep breath and looked straight at him. "I'm not in medical school!" I had finally said it. This was not just a silent admission to myself. I heard it with my own ears. The wind strummed my vocal chords into a clear tenor. Unfortunately, Mr. Genovese didn't register my confession at all. Neither did Mr. Amico for that matter. They both just kind of stared at me with waxed despondency. I had turned them into a couple of statues. I waved my hands at them. Still nothing. I had, I supposed, completely jumped the boundaries of the situation, particularly in reference to their general awareness and assumptions, like introducing particle physics to pre-schoolers. Finally, Mr. Amico's mouth twitched a little. He was ready to speak what was on his mind.

"Do women give the nozzle a shake?" he asked.

"What?"

"When they put gas in the car. I was just thinking that I shake the nozzle too because I am a man and used to the shaking process. But women aren't. I don't think I've ever seen a woman shake the nozzle when she is filling her car up with gas."

"Exactly," Mr. Genovese supported. "It's a faulkin scientific fact that women do not give the pump a shake to clear a couple of drops away. It's not in their...what do you call it...makeup."

"The gene for shaking your pecker is on the Y chromosome?" Mr. Amico said.

"That's what I faulkin said," reiterated Mr. Genovese. They settled back into their normal positions and continued drinking, talking something or other about a person that owed both of them money. I felt good about telling the two of them that I wasn't in medical school. The warm up would make it that much easier to unload on my uncle. The man with the arm cast was still sitting beside me. I wondered what had happened to him and contemplated asking. Unfortunately I wouldn't get the chance to, since what happened next was completely unexpected and would be shrouded in dense mystery for some time to come. The sadistic looking man who had been sitting in the corner of the bar had gotten up out of his seat and was fast approaching the man with the cast on. He had fury in those yellow eyes. He let out a banshee shriek. This startled all of us, particularly the injured man on the bar stool next to me. He turned uncomfortably and when he saw what was coming after him, tried to make a jump for the door but was too slow due to his arm cast. The scarred man with the yellow eyes got his hands around him, threw him to the floor and proceeded to beat the snot out of him, all the while repeating, "How do you like that... How do you like that..."

The place erupted in a new rash of hot jeers and applause. I was mortified. The crippled man's hysterical cries from the floor where he was being pummeled were enough to wake the dead. A tooth came flying from his mouth. His wounds opened with fresh gook and blood spilling from them. I jumped from my bar stool and ran to the back to get my uncle, who was just coming out of the men's bathroom.

"Uncle Jimmy," I yelled, tugging at his arm, pulling him towards the main room, towards the carnage, towards the murder. "A guy is out here beating some poor, helpless, crippled man in a cast. You need to do something or else he will be killed!"

Uncle Jimmy followed me into the main room. I pushed through the boisterous crowd, aroused as they were by the smell of blood. Jimmy was rolling up his sleeves, ready to dole out brutal justice, but when we arrived at the scene of the slaughter he stopped suddenly, sizing up both the man in the cast and the wiry sadist holding him by the collar of his shirt, a shirt that was tearing away from his body as the injured man jumped out of it to escape his attacker. To my disbelief, my uncle turned and walked back towards his office.

"Jimmy," I yelled, hot on his heels. "What are you doing?"

"Don't worry," my uncle assured me darkly. "It will all be over in a second."

"He has done this before."

"Yup," Jimmy shrugged. "I think it is about the fourth time."

"Beating up the infirmed?"

"Yup."

"You can't let him do that. This place is noble when it comes to matters like this. The fights have to be fair. No beating of women. No beating of the elderly. This guys is breaking the rules."

"Toby mind your own faulkin business."

"This is an injustice."

"Hey! This is the way things have to be handled sometimes. If you don't like it go take a walk around the block. By the time you get back it will all be over."

"Are you scared of that man out there, Jimmy? Is that what this is all about? You are scared of the man with the yellow eyes."

"Medical school has softened you up, kid," Jimmy replied with a don't-push-your-luck tone in his voice.

"Damn it Jimmy, I'm not in medical school!" I shouted at him.

"What the hell did you just say?" he shouted back, shocked as he was into bug-eyed paralysis. I let my body sag, fell against the wall.

"I don't know anything about being a doctor, Jimmy," I confessed. "I never made it into medical school. I didn't even make it to the end of college."

"Is this some kind of joke?" he growled.

"I know rudimentary health tips and vague biology terms that I picked up along the way. Take a multivitamin. Fruits and vegetables—good. Fried food—bad. Don't smoke. Eat fiber. I know that ligament connects bone to bone and tendons connect muscle to bone. I know that gastric juice bubbling up out of the cardiac sphincter causes heartburn. Arteries carry blood away from the heart and veins carry blood towards it. Mitosis occurs in somatic cells, meiosis occurs in the reproductive cells. Mitochondria provide energy, along with ATP, but exactly how this happens I have no idea. Knowing these paltry facts doesn't make me a doctor, Jimmy."

"It can't be true," he murmured, but I could tell from his voice, coupled with his mangled facial features, that he knew it was true. It was almost as if he had known it all along. "What do you do then?" he asked.

"I'm a bartender." This admission crumpled his entire skeleton. He buried his face in his hands.

"I can't believe it," he whimpered.

"I'll prove it to you," I promised. "Ask me what is in a negroni? Gin, vermouth and campari. What about an old fashioned? Muddled fruit, bitters, soda, and whiskey. Godfather? Scotch and Amaretto. Godmother? Vodka and Amaretto. Alabama Slammer—sloe gin, southern comfort, amaretto and orange juice. Ask me any drink and I'll tell you how to make it. What else? How about underage drinkers? How do you spot them? If they ask for the mixer before the booze, or if they obsess over prices, or if they think all liquors are the same, then you ask for identification." Jimmy was staring coldly at me through his fingers. His large hands hid the rest of his face. "When somebody tells you they are going to leave you a big tip they never do," I continued towards my uncle. "Dry martini gets a twist. J&B stands for Justerini and Brooks. A dirty martini means olive juice is added. Cocktail onions for the Gibson. A lime for the Gimlet. The yeoman warder on the Beefeater label holds his pike in his right hand. The best bottle to knock someone over the head with is the Galliano bottle because it is shaped like a bat. The Catholics drink Jameson. The Protestants drink Bushmills. Jimmy, look at my hands. The cuticles have bar rot all through them. These are not medical hands. Face it. I'm a fucking BARTENDER!" I held my hands up in front of me. Jimmy raised himself slowly from his slump, stared at them, and then at his own hands. There was nothing scholarly or academic about either pair. They were identical. His hands, though, began to shake. Then the rest of the man trembled like a mountain above shifting bedrock. I expected plaster, wood and concrete to start raining down. I expected the whole building to collapse.

My bags were ejected through the front door first. Then it was time for me to go. With a powerful toss, my uncle threw me street-ward. Jimmy was standing in the doorway, smoke and heat billowing from his nose and mouth like a dragon, heaving, panting, insane with humiliated anger. He wanted to rip me apart limb from limb, somehow get his hands on my soul and choke it out of its misery, but unable to properly assimilate and utilize his overwhelming rage, he simply shouted down to me, "Don't come back until you've got some goddamned sense into yourself." Then the doors were slammed closed, banging loudly, a thunderous boom of heavy finality. I pulled myself to my feet, grabbed my bags and went in search of a cheap motel.

# CHAPTER 21

The low, bellowing horn of the Bridgeport ferry sounded off three times, sending the seagulls out from their perches atop the thick, creosote logs of the docks to the gray, rolling mist blanketing the Long Island sound. The birds' thin, high-pitched squeals echoed across the water as the barge shuddered and lurched forward into the fog. The low visibility made it as though we weren't crossing state to state, but past epochs, eras, into other dimensions of suspended cause and effect. Flip a coin and somebody dies of heart failure. Kiss your wife and the person sitting across from you begins to age uncontrollably—all of this keenly interconnected, but exactly by who or what is anybody's guess. Points of green and red lights were slightly visible in the opalescent distance. These were the buoy markers, but I imagined they were lanterns being waved by some ghostly type, standing at the bow of a slim rowing vessel carved into the figure of a sea creature, waving us along with a bony hand.

Some folks found it more stimulating to stand on the upper deck and lean over the railing to watch the jellyfish float limply around the hull. Others sat below in the covered area by the snack bar. I had taken up my position in the front part of the bow, which was the bar and lounge area, of course. I had decided to waste some time during my brief weekend stay by riding the ferry across to Connecticut, then riding right back to the Long Island port, where I had started from, none the wiser and all the drunker. I felt that my life was a lot like this ferry trip. There was a whole aquatic world out there, seas, rivers, oceans, vast possibility and adventure, but here I was just going back and forth on a relatively tiny body of water, back and forth in a straight line between two points. I was drinking boilermakers--beer and a shot of whiskey. It just seemed appropriate.

To be honest I felt good about the whole disaster with my Uncle Jimmy the night before. I had predicted his reaction with reasonable accuracy, and although he would need some time to cool off from his hotheaded disappointment, I still maintained the belief that his wishes for my medical career were not exactly authentic, and that he would eventually accept me wholeheartedly for who I was. It was a great load off my conscience to confess that I hadn't spent the better part of five years prodding corpses, weighing organs, looking down the gullets of the elderly, wearing white jackets and all that. I was proud of myself, even if, for the moment, my only living relative was not.

Problems, for me, never really went away. Better yet they shifted forms. As I had cleared away the issue of my Uncle Jimmy, like the head of the Hydra, another had immediately sprung up in its place. I had been nagged the whole sleepless night before as I tossed on a lumpy mattress wrapped in a watertight rubber sheet in some pay-by-the-hour motor lodge. I just couldn't shake it. Why the hell did my uncle just let some weasely, drunken derelict beat up the man in the arm cast the night before? Of course my anger over the whole injustice had actually precipitated my confession that I was indeed *not* a medical student, but that was, I decided, beside the point. My uncle's reluctance to break up the fight was in no way keeping with his usual form and style. He had a strong set of values when it came to bar fights. He would always intervene if he felt the match up was unfair, and as far as I could tell from my own personal observation, there was never a more uneven battle. I knew my instincts had served me correctly in identifying the problem customer—the man with the yellow eyes. I wanted to see my uncle beat him silly, a task Jimmy could've accomplished with ease, but there was something in his face when he finally came upon the scuffle that said he wasn't going to get involved. Was it fear? Did the man with the yellow eyes have something over him? It made me doubly mad that this thin, splenetic scoundrel had beaten my uncle without even laying a hand on him. My Uncle Jimmy—the bruiser of the block. It eclipsed all my previous understanding. It had cut into my faith. To bear witness to this level of absurdity—senselessness in its purest form—devalued the rest of my existence. I was good and drunk by the time we had reached the Connecticut side of the voyage, pleading my case to a rather apathetic bartender standing in front of me while polishing a glass. He looked irritated that I was not disembarking but going back to the original port. He was now stuck with me for at least another hour and a half, provided he didn't throw me over the side midway across.

"A man in an arm cast...a pathetic looking guy...he's hurt," my rambling eddied, whirled, retraced itself, lost, found itself and came back to the beginning, tossed like driftwood on the whiskey current. "...He comes in...comes in and sits down quietly at the bar. He orders a beer. He drinks his beer...the beer that he ordered...that he came in to order... his cast plopped on the bar pitifully. He looks beaten up bad, real bad, and he is obviously easy prey—a hard luck guy, drinking a beer quietly. He drinks his beers quietly, mind you. You can't help but feel for him. Suddenly a man...a vicious, heinous looking man, probably just paroled for pedophilia or necrophilia approaches. He wants a fight but he wants an easy one. He is looking to take out his aggression but he doesn't want to suffer the consequences. He gets his hands around the injured man... the injured man...drinking his beer...who tries to escape...but he can't. He is thrown to the ground and beaten. I tried to have it broken up...but apparently this guy is allowed to do this. It wasn't even the first time. It was the fourth time he had beaten up on a crippled man. I mean what the hell is that all about? A yellow-eyed thug suddenly has an uncontrollable urge to beat up on a cripple...a guy who just is looking to exercise his God given right to get drunk...to attain a quiet decency, and here he has to worry about a psychopath who likes to beat up cripples. Why does he pick on the cripples?"

"I guess he just don't like cripples," the bartender shrugged, and for him that was the end of it. "It doesn't sound like any of your business, anyway. What's the big deal?"

"The big deal? How would you like it if because of this your only living relative tossed you out of his life?"

"Three!" the bartender responded after mulling it over.

"What do you mean, three?" I asked.

"Well, on a scale of one to ten—ten being the things I absolutely love and cherish, and one being the things I truly detest, I'd say it would be about a three...you know, if my only living relative tossed me out of his life."

"May I please have another whiskey?"

"You want another whiskey?"

"Yes."

The bartender went about pouring me a fresh drink, and didn't look none too pleased about it. He looked as old as the battered ferryboat that employed him. He probably lived in a one-bedroom apartment over an old delicatessen and paid women to avoid him after the first night. An old world bartender skilled in tricks, jokes and sports statistics. Any icon of the past hundred years would not be immune to his insightful badgering, except maybe Sinatra.

"How long have you been here?" I asked him.

"This is my first run of the day," he answered dully.

"Have you occupied this position for a long period of time?" I rephrased, trying to establish some decent communication.

"Standing up?" he said. "Since about eight this morning."

The rest of the crowd in the boat's lounge, sparse as it was, all looked uniquely worn out. For starters pretty much everybody was drinking alone. There was one other man sitting at the bar. He was staring into his glass like a peephole into some better part of his life, making the present moment that much more miserable. Out at the tables things were equally grim. A woman with a veil over her head and a glass of wine in her hand sat facing the wall in anonymity. Her glass periodically disappeared under her veil, only to return to the table a little less full and with another red lip mark around the rim. A rubicund man in argyle sat facing us all. He was so heavy that he was no longer able to position his legs under him, but rather they were forced to jut from his sides like a beetle's. Other than that there was a table with two men sitting at it, both with very different mannerisms regarding each other. The one facing me seemed mildly put off, while the one with his back to me was bent forward in an imploring attitude. There was something on the table in between them, apparently, that needed to be considered. After a few moments the man with his back to me stood up from the table, collected something in his hands and then proceeded to sit down at the heavyset argyle man's table, imitating the same mannerisms as at the previous table. Maybe he was selling something. After a few moments the giant, red-faced man began to shake his head in the negative, his jellied jowls shimmying from side to side. As the last man had been, so was he being asked to regard something sitting between them on the table. It was no use. The man sitting in his own fleshy prison of argyle plumpness could offer no assistance to the thin, pale man across from him. Despondently, he moved on to the veiled woman.

"I think I know a fellow who used to work here," I mentioned to the bartender during one of his sweeps past me.

"Oh yeah?" the bartender said. "Who might that be?"

"Baron Corley. He told me he worked here a couple of years ago." A look of specific corrosiveness seized the bartender's face. I could tell there would be no free drink, as Baron had promised me that night atop the Kadore Hotel. In fact, there might be some type of ass-whipping involved. The bartender threw his dishrag over his shoulder and squared off at me.

"Next time you see that son of a bitch tell him that Ernie is asking for his money." The bartender, Ernie apparently, pointed a hairy thumb at himself. "Will you give him that message for me?"

"No problem," I said, cowering a little. Ernie the bartender slackened his shoulders and spread a reluctant grin across his face. Feeling relieved to get the money issue off his chest he now seemed content to reflect on fonder memories of Baron.

"Where is he living these days?" Ernie asked with a shake of his head—a sign that wherever Baron was would do little to break him of his dissolute behavior.

"Atlanta, Georgia."

"He has been all over the place," the coarse bartender admitted with a sigh, staring out at the green waters that stretched into the horizon, waters now visible due to the lifting of the fog. "Always running from something."

"Don't get me started," I said.

"Me neither," Ernie said. To my surprise he poured me another whiskey and set it down next to my beer. "To deal with Baron Corley you are going to need all the help you can get."

I thanked him and took the drink. I decided to head for the airport after docking back at the Port Jefferson harbor. No sense sitting around this sleepy seaport for any longer than necessary. I had actually accomplished what I came here to do, and decided that in a week or so I would place a follow-up call to Uncle Jimmy to see if he had come around, or if he was still gargling his own bile. I was anxious to return to Atlanta, but for what purpose I wasn't entirely sure. There was a basic, unconscious impulse to get back into a routine, something to be trusted amidst the chaos of ample time and directionless behavior, which when combined was the equation whose solution always added up to alcohol abuse—an inevitable, fixed value like Planck's Constant or Pi.

Ernie the bartender was leaned over about midway down the bar, his ear pointed at the thin, pale man who had visited all the lounge tables with some mysterious petition, and who had now cornered the barman himself in order to make some inquiries. He was showing Ernie a few photographs. At this short distance I could make out some finer details concerning this strange person. He looked to be in his mid-forties. He had wire rimmed glasses on and was wearing a cheap suit in desperate need of some ironing. His hair was brown and curly in an outdated way. He was shorter than most and probably had a worldwide grudge because of it. Ernie was studying the picture in the man's hand with his lips puckered. He then nodded, looked up at me and pointed in my direction. The man holding the pictures locked his eyes on me. He adjusted his crumpled suit and mismatched shirt and made a beeline. As he grew in proximity so did he intensify. His desperate feverishness swelled as he approached. He had a shattered glass demeanor, prickly with the rogue shards. He was familiar yet I was sure I had never met him. He smelled of something that wasn't patchouli but spicy and pungent just the same.

"You are here to assist me!" he said. "You have been delivered!"

Finally, I thought to myself, a purpose. He angled the pictures he was holding into my line of vision. I looked at the one on top and immediately got a bad feeling. Something told me I didn't want to be involved and didn't want to know what this man had to say, but it was too late. I had already given myself away to the bartender with my admission that we had an acquaintance in common in order to get a free drink, but now it had backfired. The acquaintance I had spoken of was now staring out at me from a fluttering photograph, trembling perceptibly in this stranger's slender hands—a figure all too familiar. Fedora. Battered sport coat. Tinted glasses. The same exact outfit that he always wore. In the picture he was standing on a sidewalk, in front of a diner window under some twilight sky with an inebriated grin on his face.

Baron Corley.

"You know this man?" he asked, nodding towards Ernie the bartender for corroboration.

"I do know him," I admitted.

"Have you seen him recently?" he whispered.

"First let me point out that I've only known him for a short time," I defended. "He is a friend of a friend. But the last time I saw him was about…two days ago." My information sent the man falling into a bar stool with a look of relief mixed with anguish, a bitter anguish that had replaced the nebulous anguish he had been harboring moments before.

"My name is Jonas. I need some information," he said, placing the photographs he was holding down onto the bar.

"Jonas?" I echoed.

"My wife has been kidnapped," he said. "Kidnapped by this man."

He again pointed at the picture of Baron that was lying on the bar. "Kidnapped," he repeated, "by *this man*." He hammered his index finger right in the middle of Baron's face.

"Have you contacted the police?" I asked.

"Of course I contacted the police," he exasperated. "But I'm from southern California. Do you know how many murders they have to deal with, much less a missing persons report in which there are no signs of foul play? Heck, even getting a case reviewed out there is like winning the lottery. I live in a marginalized community. We don't have the big resources, the funding—the police power to initiate a national manhunt. The police don't respect us. I knew if I was going to find my wife I would have to do it on my own. Luckily I had the help of my community. We put up flyers, held candlelight vigils, prayer services, took donations." He wrestled an unmarked bottle out of his jacket pocket, threw a few pills into his mouth, crunched them up and swallowed them.

"What happened?" I asked, holding out on a last chance possibility that there might've been some mistake with this whole thing, although I knew from my own experience with Baron that it wouldn't take very much convincing.

"It was a little over three months ago," Jonas said. "This man arrived at our cultural center down on his luck, looking for work. He called himself Billy Crowley, a clever alias. Our small town is a friendly, welcoming town, tending to get drifters heading out of the city, usually northeasterly to the national parks. We always give people the benefit of the doubt, a bed and a meal for a few days in exchange for some help on our renovations, usually with positive results, although I never thought it would end up like this. It was with our normal show of good faith that we took this man in, this Baron Corley."

Jonas brought one of the photographs up from the bar and showed it to me. There were two people in the photograph, one was himself, the other was a short woman with long, wavy brown hair and a broad, contented smile across her face. Her right hand was in a salute gesture as she tried in vain to block the sun from her eyes.

"This is my precious wife," Jonas proclaimed sadly. "Her name is Brady Mae but we call her Lily Lou for short." I took the picture in my hands, perplexed at the fact that his wife's shortened name and her real name contained the same amount of syllables, but decided it was neither the time nor the place to point out such peculiarities. I did notice though, her long, wavy brown hair and the fact that she couldn't have been over five foot. Everything came rushing to me at once. The trunk in the woods. The woodsy location of Baron's hideout. The secret, rural location of the buried trunk. The blood all over him, his admission that there was a head in the trunk, the hair stuck to the tape in Baron's car—hair dreadfully similar to the woman's in the picture. It was so obvious, and here I had been living in a pathetic half denial, cowardly willing to accept obvious lies and vague explanations. Jonas studied my reaction. "Have you seen her? Have you seen her with him? Has he mentioned her? Above all else... WHERE IS HE?"

"I...he's...difficult to find..."

"You must help me!" he cried, grabbing me by the shoulders. "I'll come to Atlanta! You will help me find her!"

"Alright, alright," I placated, trying to calm him enough to give myself a little thinking room. His plea sounded genuine. His claim certainly fit Baron's general pattern. In the grocery list of psychotic tendencies, Baron's shopping cart was certainly at least half full. Narcissistic. Guiltless. Impulsive and antisocial. "So let me see if I have this right, you gave him a place to stay for a few days and he kidnapped your wife?"

"A trucker dropped him off on the highway. He made his way to our town, giving us a story that he was down on his luck. Said he had recently come away from a bad divorce and was trying to get back on his feet. He is a very charming man when he wants to be. We offered him a room with a bed over the garage. In exchange he was supposed to help us in our ongoing efforts to rebuild the roof of our community center. For the first few days everything seemed to be working out. He worked hard during the day and would keep us entertained with stories about his life at mealtime. But then he began to spend more and more time away on errands, and when he returned he smelled of liquor. He began to sleep late and he grew belligerent towards some of the other men involved in the construction. Then there were the inappropriate advances towards my wife. She caught him staring at her in odd ways for long periods of time. She grew afraid. I was getting ready to tell him that he had to be on his way. That was when the fire erupted."

"The fire?" I asked.

"The roof renovations had been set on fire in the middle of the night. I got the call and was there as soon as I could. By the time the fire was out it was dawn. The whole thing had been turned to ashes. I thought that it couldn't get any worse, but when I returned to my house the real nightmare began. My wife was gone, nowhere to be found. Lily Lou had vanished along with our car, an old Fleetwood Brougham."

"Oh shit," I moaned.

"I was inconsolable. I wondered why God had done this to me? Why had I been made to suffer in this way? Then I realized it was because I was meant to triumph over this. I was meant to smite this evil, to win back my wife and to see this degenerate punished for his actions. With the help of friends and neighbors I scoured southern California. Every place I heard Baron mention during his stay with me is where I looked for him—bars, halfway houses, the L.A. basin. I talked to hundreds of people. I vowed I would never give up. That is when I remembered him talking about his time working on this ferry and that is why I came here, all the way across the country and found you…I'm sorry, I haven't gotten your name?"

"Toby."

"Yes, Toby. You are here Toby. You are here and you are meant to help me. Toby. You must align yourself with what is good and right, Toby. Together we will destroy this evil defect. He is dangerous. Hostile thought patterns. No emotional connection. He is a terrible deviant. I just hope that I am not too late."

The ferry came to a shuddering stop. We were docked. This infected a fresh wave of urgency into Jonas's body. The passengers around us began to gather their things up and shuffle slowly towards the stairwells, a disgruntled herd slowing each other down with their cumulative impatience.

"How fast can you get back to Atlanta?" my new acquaintance asked.

"As fast as the plane takes me," I answered.

"Good," he said. "You will take your flight. We will meet you in Atlanta. Give me some way to get in contact with you and await my call."

"You said *we*," I pointed out as I jotted down my phone number. "Does that mean you aren't alone?"

"I have a few members of my church with me," he said. "They are combing the bars along the dock for any information about Baron." He looked down at my feet and noticed my bags. "Are those yours?"

"Yes," I said.

He picked both of them up and made his way towards the door. I paid the bartender and ran to catch up with Jonas as he made his way towards the metal stairs leading to the bottom of the ferry where the cars were parked.

"Now I see the man for what he truly is. He is a monster. He is pure evil. He is a creature without a soul, and he has my wife."

A family of four was spread in front of him, walking slowly as families do. He pushed through, using my bags to split them down the middle like bowling pins. I gave them a look of apology and passed by the space that had been created. We crammed ourselves into the line of people descending the metal stairs down into the collection of cars in the ship's lower hold. The vehicles were all coming alive as the ferryboat lowered its gates and began waving the drivers down onto the dock. Jonas went out of his way to push a couple of people aside. I tried to keep up. The harrowed husband kept reiterating his hatred for Baron in bits and spurts. I tried to pay attention to him and still negotiate the path. His language was brutal yet suppressed by his refusal to use any explicitly bad language. His tirade ended up becoming a colorful condemnation, filled with imaginative word choices that expressed his rage yet still kept him rated PG.

"...When I finally get my blessed hands on him I'm going to tear his ever-loving gemstones off. I'm going to separate his peas from his potatoes. I'm going to wax my woodwork with his gray sponge. By Lucifer's beard I will stack his deck. Liberate his alpha from his omega, his wheat from his chaff, his meat from his gristle. Then when all is done, I will stand over his empty vessel and unleash my holy waters upon his funeral pyre."

"Wow," I said.

I followed him off the boat and across the parking lot to where two men were standing. When they saw Jonas approach they raced toward him. The two men were tall and plain looking. One asked Jonas why he had stolen someone's luggage.

"This is Toby," Jonas said. "He has information that will help us. I have located Baron Corley. He is in Atlanta. We will leave immediately!"

The men's eyes grew into a state of wonderment.

"Amazing!" they agreed.

"We must prepare for the last part of the journey," Jonas told the two men. "We are so close. In another day we'll have him and her. Everything will be as it should. Get everything ready."

"Glorious!" they agreed.

"I'll do what I can to help," I added. "After all I can't have this woman's blood on my hands. I tell you that I have been suspicious of Baron ever since I met him, but he is very elusive. After I get to Atlanta you'll just have to give me a little time to..."

"You will be eligible for the reward," Jonas announced.

"…Talk to some people, maybe get Baron to let his guard down a little, find out exactly what…did you say reward?"

"Yes. A great reward."

"Reward?" I spoke the word slowly, carefully.

"You will never want for anything again," Jonas promised.

I felt a deep rumbling below my feet, as if the ground itself was fissuring and a huge billowing geyser of green notes legal tender was whipping up through the cracks, swirling around me like a sandstorm. It was everywhere—a verdant landslide. Never want for anything again. That's a lot of money. I could re-upholster my furniture in fives and tens, make fifties into origami, or hang the hundreds from a Christmas tree as decorations. I could use Andrew Jackson as toilet tissue or smoke Abe Lincoln with a fine Balkan Sobranie tobacco. Use Ben Franklin the non-president as a welcome mat. I wondered if I should inquire about the actual amount, but decided that it was in poor taste for the time being.

Jonas confirmed that he had my contact information and suggested I get along to the airport. The two men next to him gave me a blank head nod. Jonas said that he would get in touch with me as soon as he was able. I caught a cab out of town.


I arrived at the airport, but my impatience was off the charts. I wanted my body to sprout wings and take off. I headed towards my gate. As I walked past some of the airport gift shops I marveled at all of the things it would be possible for me to buy with a Great Reward…luggage, coffee cups, cologne, watches, bumper stickers, air purifiers, souvenir shirts, massage chairs, international best selling hardcover novels, admittance into club rooms, digital alarm clocks that ring with the gentle sounds of nature, ties with various parquet designs on them. I had never noticed any of this crap before and now I was hungry for it all. It could all be mine.

After some skillful explanation to the airline representative and a small bureaucratic fee I boarded an early plane. The engines revved up. We took off. The aircraft pointed its nose south.

"Fasten your seat belts," the flight attendant ordered. "We are expecting turbulence."

"I don't doubt it," said I.

# CHAPTER 22

I was back in my apartment. It somehow seemed messier than when I had left it. I was sitting in my kitchen trying to calm my nerves with the rest of Zanz's peach brandy. My date for jury duty was the next morning. It had completely slipped my mind, because even though my life was filled with emptiness (a deft oxymoron) I wasn't so pathetic as to embrace, eagerly anticipate, cherish, send cards about, put up decorations for, celebrate and lament the inevitable passing of a dry, civic responsibility. I had to be at the courthouse very early in the morning.

The carriage house creaked and groaned. It was either the wind or the strange, young ghost living in the wall. I walked around the meager apartment several times. It was a desolate experience. I looked out the window at the Koi fish pond. There were no signs of any fish. I went to the refrigerator, pulled out a chunk of stale bread and tossed it from my window into the water. They all appeared within seconds, out of the murk, almost waiting for me to coax them with food. They knew I was a pushover. The silence of the backyard was broken only once, when Nona and an old man in a suit, after lobbing an inaudible argument back and forth, began fighting over an African fertility stick on her back porch. She screamed at the man in Tagalog, a confusing and shrill assault of high-pitched pins and needles. I shut the window and waited for Jonas to call. He would be calling any minute. Two hours later he still hadn't called. I drank more peach brandy and changed my clothes twice, throwing the clean clothes I had been wearing in the hamper instead of folding them and putting them back in the dresser. I went and got some water from the kitchen sink. I then got some ice out of the freezer and dropped it into the glass. I decided that I should've put the ice in first because putting the ice in second diluted the water too much. This made sense even though it didn't. The ice reminded me of Three-a-Day Ray Corley. I changed my clothes a third time then sat at my desk and flipped through my serial killer scrapbook.

I was caught in the confines of a feedback loop. Two mental images, round and round, each doing its best to neutralize the other. There was Baron dragging me out of the road, both of us dressed as clowns. There was Baron with his hands around the neck of Brady Mae. There was Baron dragging me out of the road, both of us dressed as clowns. There was Baron with his hands around the neck of Brady Mae. What was all this? Whatever it was, it was inescapable. It was either one or the other. The man named Jonas had yet to contact me. The carriage house was silent. When the phone rang I almost jumped out of my chair. I picked up the phone.

"Hello Jonas," I said.

"YOU... LITTLE... SHIT!" Uncle Jimmy thundered.

"Can't talk right now Unk," I said. "I'm waiting on a call."

"What the hell is the big idea telling me you were in faulkin medical school all these years?" he slurred. "You know how faulkin stupid that made me feel? Pretty faulkin stupid, that is for sure. I oughta fly down there and break ya faulkin head open."

"Jimmy you sound like a dumb drunk. Can you sound like an intelligent drunk?"

"How can we talk about this intelligently when you've been lying for four faulkin years? That ain't intelligent. That's the stupidest faulkin thing I've ever heard of."

"Let me explain," I said.

"You ain't gonna tell me nothin' that is gonna make me change my mind," he said.

"I'm not trying to change your mind about anything. If you feel the same way after I'm done talking to you then that is fine."

"You little shit," he repeated.

"First I think it is a testament to my concern for your feelings that I began this little lie. But there was a second lie that was supposed to make my medical career go away, and that was to tell you I had dropped out. It was true enough, the only catch was that I had never gone in the first place. I am apologizing for this second lie that never manifested. I am apologizing only for this and I am apologizing only once."

"Why bother at all?" Uncle Jimmy asked. "If you put half the effort into your studies as you did into your lying you'd be pretty faulkin successful."

"I wanted you to think I had at least tried. I didn't want to quit before I started because I thought you might feel you had screwed me up somehow."

"Better to have me feeling like a screwup than have me walkin' around like a faulkin idiot tellin' everybody I know that... 'My nephew is gonna be a docta, my nephew is gonna be a docta, hey everyone did you hear, Toby is gonna be a docta.' You made me lie to everyone that I know, all those no-good rat bastards. How am I supposed to look them in the face now when I've been lying to them all of these years?"

"Jimmy how could you have lied if you didn't know what the truth really was?"

"Don't be a smart ass, Toby."

"Look I promise I'll never be dishonest with you again. That is a sacred promise. Be careful of the loopholes that a promise like this can have."

"And if it couldn't get any worse," he said, "you are a bartender."

"Jimmy for you to condemn your own profession is so absurd that had I been a doctor I would've certainly committed you."

"But you got the brains, kid. I ain't got the brains. If you got the brains you gotta do it. That is the way it goes."

"I didn't want to do it. Plain and simple. The idea is nice. The work isn't."

"WHO GIVES A SHIT WHAT YOU WANT TO DO?" Jimmy shouted. "That is why God created amusement parks, cruise liners, miniature golf, regular-sized golf, skiing, camping, ballroom dancing and tropical islands. So you can take vacations from the shit you don't want to do."

"Vacations erase tedium," I countered. "Anything can be tedious. A bottle jockey can feel tedium."

"A bartender gets paid to drink," he said.

"It is easy for you to stand behind a bar and talk shit. How ridiculously easy and useless like all bar talk. Why are you getting all worked up? Why drive yourself crazy like this?"

"My health is failing Toby. Here you are only thinking about yourself instead of your poor uncle dying slowly. I was counting on you to tack a few extra years onto my life, but instead you shaved off close to a decade when you told me the truth about yourself. Good luck with the funeral, slick. Pick me out a nice suit."

"You know something Jimmy, don't throw your misguided disappointment at me."

"Toby you ain't a docta, and if you ain't a docta then you ain't a shrink, so spare me the analysis. Who needs mental analysis when I got a prostate the size of a buckwheat doughnut."

"I tell you what, Unk, you might be disappointed in me, but I'm also disappointed in you," I said, ready to wallop him.

"Disappointed in me?" he gasped defensively. "For being the innocent victim of your con? Yes how could I? I should be ashamed of myself for actually believing my brother's only son."

"I'll tell you exactly what I'm referring to," I said. "When I came to visit you I witnessed something so deplorable and outrageous that it still haunts me. You could've stopped that guy from beating up the man in the arm cast but you didn't. That wasn't a fair fight and you know it. You were afraid of the man with the yellow eyes."

"Don't be ridiculous," Jimmy said.

"Why didn't you stop him? I want to understand this. You owe me this explanation."

"Toby, you don't need to understand shit. This life will pass you by with a thousand unanswered questions. The best thing you can do now is open your own bar, stockpile some money, get a large television and a plump wife and spend your weekends getting drunk and fixing some kind of automotive vehicle." He pondered this further. "I suggest an El Camino or a Chevelle. As long as the thing is from the Seventies you'll have your work cut out for you."

"I am shocked at your cowardice."

"I don't have to take this shit from you..." he said as a blast went off on the other end of the phone. Silence.

"Jimmy! Jimmy! Are you alright?"

"Yeah, yeah," He finally muttered into the phone, and then to himself in a tone of sincere confusion added, "I guess it *was* loaded."

"You are too unstable to have loaded weapons lying around the house," I said.

"A fella has to be ready because one of these days the shit is going to go down!"

"What shit? Down where?"

"It goes all the way back to the war. I know things and they know I know."

"What do you know? Who knows what you know? You don't know!"

"They were watching me through the electrical sockets. I had to cover them up with my trusty silver tape."

"Uncle Jimmy your mental health will fail long before your physical health does. I'm going to be the one to have to take care of you so you better be nice while you still have the ability to make it to the toilet by yourself."

"That's what you think!"

"Jimmy, you tell me why you let that wiry bastard beat up the poor man with the cast?"

"No."

"Tell me!" I demanded.

"No," he spat petulantly.

"Because you were afraid? Because you were afraid of him?"

"I'm not afraid of nothing!"

"Double negative!"

"Damn it Toby you are driving me faulkin crazy. Smarten up, come to your faulkin senses, do something with your life and stop being SUCH A PAIN IN MY GODDAMNED ASS."

The phone slammed down with such intensity that I was sure he had broken it. I hung up my end as gently as I could to counterbalance the smoldering wrath on the other end. In my mind I could see the particular telephone wire that had carried this vitriolic conversation hundreds of miles, burning a thin, incandescent red line from telephone pole to telephone pole along a desolate highway, and the innocent birds who had been resting on this piece of ignited wire now falling singed and dead to the ground below.

I never heard from Jonas.

☙

I got to the jury room at the ungodly hour of eight-thirty in the morning. I was given my 'juror' sticker and told to have a seat by a woman who regarded me with troubled concern. I had tried to dress decently, a button down shirt and all-purpose sport jacket, but it was impossible to conceal my situation. My anxiety was apparent.

"Are you okay Mister...Sinclair."

"Yes ma'am. I'm just a little...on edge."

"Don't worry. You are here to be on the jury. Not at the defense table."

"Tomorrow is another day," I said.

I found a decently vacant row and sat down. Another woman, severe and warty, told everybody to move towards the seats in the middle. I scanned the other potential jurors, a random cross section of people from the county, and realized just how ugly most people are. I guess I was ugly too. The beautiful people are all on television. The ugly people congregate in jury rooms.

Something about being in the courthouse aggravated my reflexive sense of guilt. I kept thinking that some court official doing a casual, visual sweep of the crowd was somehow going to recognize me as someone wanted for something serious, something that I didn't remember at all doing, and only when it was too late would I be reminded of some tragic set of circumstances that I had played a marginal role in.

As part of the justice system's infinite kindness, us jurors were afforded ample time for a quality nap, as they turned down the lights and played an interesting and highly informative video about who-knows-what, although in the darkness of my half sleep, with my intermittent head lolls that bounced me awake, I kept hearing one phrase repeated—Voire Dire. Apparently it means to speak the truth, however as a bartender my primary training was in prevarication and falsity. I wondered if that would be enough for my dismissal. "I know that I'm supposed to speak truthfully your honor. Understand that I'd like nothing better than to succeed at that very task. However it will be with some difficulty that I can overcome the years of habitual lying, verbal deceit and circumlocution that I have cultivated during my time as a bartender. I lie to myself, I lie to women, to friends, to the people I love. I lie just to make it through the day with some semblance of self-respect and decency. My compass of veracity spins wildly, your honor. There is no point of reference. I'm lost in a sea of deception, so badly tossed and thrown about that I wouldn't recognize honesty if it took on the form of a nervous bartender, whacked on peach brandy, answering to the name 'Toby'."

Eventually the lights came up. They began to call people by name. We were ordered to form a line and after a certain line got to be about twenty long or so, they snaked us out of the initial waiting room, up a set of elevators and down a hall leading to various courtrooms. Our line stopped outside of one such door. Our guide explained that it would be a short wait, as the docket was particularly crowded that day, and we would have to wait for the current room to be cleared. I immediately plopped down on the hallway floor and put my head between my knees, still agitated about being in the midst of this building—a building designed to punish and incarcerate. Damn Baron Corley and his steamer trunk that I had helped bury. There was a human head in it and presumably a human body. Brady Mae's head? Her petite body callously shoved into a makeshift coffin and put into the ground. What if those hikers filled out a report? If Baron gets pinched he'd turn on me in a second so the punishment would be more evenly distributed.

Suddenly panicked, I jumped to my feet and asked our line leader if I could get a drink of water. She told me that I could. The fountain was around the corner. I dashed quickly and found it, although it was occupied by a lawyer-ish type trying both to work the water flow handle while maintaining a grip on the mountain of paperwork he had cradled in his hands.

"Would you like me to hold that for you, sir?" I asked.

"Why thank you, young man," he spoke appreciatively, handing me the stack. He took a long sloppy drink, like a young teenager practicing for a first kiss. After he was done he thanked me again and extended his hands to take back his burden.

"Excuse me sir, are you a lawyer?" I asked as I handed his papers back to him.

"You betcha. I'm with the District Attorney's office." He began to walk away, but my pleading mannerism made him pause.

"Do you mind if I ask your opinion about something?"

"Sure," he said. "I'm always happy to talk to people who are interested in the law."

"Out of curiosity," I began, "I was wondering about a possible scenario."

"Scenario?"

"Yes, a scenario. Let us imagine, hypothetically of course, that somebody helped somebody else transport an item that turned out to have felonious contents in it. Would or could I...or the person in question—this hypothetical person—be held responsible or accountable in any legal sense?"

"Well now," he said with a confident smirk as if he had me right where he wanted me. "I'm going to need some more specifics about this whole thing in order to give you a proper answer." He motioned for me to step away from the water fountain. He then placed the stack of papers he was holding on a nearby windowsill and turned to face me with his arms crossed. "First of all who exactly is this person?"

"Nobody. Like I said he is a faceless hypothetical figure put forth to illustrate a general situation."

"Have you ever met a person that didn't have a name?" he said. "Everyone has a name. Come on…just give me a name."

"Manfred Fredman," I answered.

"Where is he from?"

"Grimalta."

"Never heard of it."

"That is because this place, like Mr. Manfred Fredman, does not exist."

"So you are saying that this Manfred Fredman thinks that he aided in a crime?"

"Yes," I nodded, happy to be back on track. "But he's not sure."

"What did he do?" the lawyer asked, pulling his tortoise shell glasses off and polishing the lenses with his cuff, an action calculated to undermine my guard.

"He helped bury a steamer trunk in the woods. The contents, mind you, are unknown to Mr. Fredman. Now is it possible that if the trunk is ever found to have criminal objects inside of it that Mr. Fredman could see jail time?"

"You better believe it, sonny," the lawyer nodded as if it were a no-brainer. He replaced his glasses to his face. "Crimes with multiple perpetrators are not uncommon in the judicial system. We aren't just a collection of bumbling fools whose attitude is that if we have one guilty person then we are satisfied. Let me tell you something, we are NEVER satisfied until everybody has been rounded up and brought to justice, which is usually easy once we have one of you."

"Although you wouldn't have me," I corrected, "you would have Manfred Fredman, who is if you will remember the subject of our discussion."

"Once one person is implicated," the lawyer went on, "they usually sing like Pavarotti to save their hides. They will give up their own mother if it means keeping them from the electric chair. Just imagine the convict's screams, see the convulsions, the smoke, watch those lights flicker, believe me they would be willing to turn on the gas station attendant who pumped the gas into their car on the way to the murder if it meant being able to live out their days. I tell you one thing, if there turns out to be a dead body in that steamer trunk, Mr. Manfred Fredman is going to fry like bacon." The lawyer appeared pleased with his analogy. "Have you ever seen a man killed in an electric chair? His fingernails shoot off. His eyeballs pop out. Blood pours from every orifice. He shits himself. It is not uncommon to catch fire. How do you think Manfred Fredman is going to feel when his eyes come scorching out of his sockets? Or will he not be so concerned with that because his organs will be blistering and splitting apart inside of him?"

"But what if Manfred Fredman legitimately wasn't aware of all the circumstances? What if he was called out by a friend to help a stranger and doesn't know anything else about it?"

"Why wouldn't this Fredman freak report it to the authorities because of its highly suspicious nature?" the lawyer countered in normal, lawyer style. "Right there was his first mistake and let me tell you it was a big one." He paused for effect. "Imagine if it can be determined that a person was in the trunk and the person died while being transported against their will? That is felony murder, which put simply means that a person like Manfred Fredman could be tried for the death without even being the one who actually committed murder."

"Great Mercy! You are saying that I could...I mean good old Manfred could be charged with murder just for being there? Just for carrying some shovels?"

"Smarten up kid. The primary perpetrator doesn't want to go to jail. If the shit comes down on him he'll say that you were the one behind it. It will be his word against yours and you'll both be in jail till you rot."

"Manfred. Not me."

"Nobody named in complicity with a crime is ever completely innocent. Are you going to tell me you had no idea that anything odd was happening? Digging a hole. Dropping a trunk in it. Burying it. What if a child is in that trunk? An innocent child—and you are just going to sit there playing in the dirt like you are planting a Norway spruce? I tell you one thing when this whole deal comes to light Manfred Fredman is going to be hung up like a Christmas stocking. Do you know what happens to a body when it is hanged? Rarely does the neck snap. Most of the time death is from asphyxiation, which could take up to five minutes. Have you considered that? Five minutes of purple tongued, spasmodic suffocation."

"But there has to be some mitigating circumstance?" I implored, ignoring the rather vivid imagery.

"Like what? Don't tell me that you want to plead insane." He let out a festal laugh. "The fact alone that you covered up your crime so meticulously means that you knew the difference between right and wrong and therefore you would be judged sane and then judged guilty."

"I meant," I said quietly, trying to ease the lawyer's zeal, "that the police are usually savvy to the main culprit, the mastermind, the one in control of the situation. I'm…Manfred is a humble law abiding citizen with no criminal record. The prime suspect has a significant rap sheet. Manfred could possibly be used as a witness for the prosecution. After all he wants to see justice served. Who knows, Manfred probably fears for his life from the real criminal if he ever comes forward to the police."

"We had us a 'snowdropper' recently," the lawyer recalled. "That is the term for a man who steals women's undergarments off clotheslines and pleasures himself with them. Harmless right? Victimless crime you say? Not when he meets up with a career criminal—a soulless drifter. The two partner up. The 'snowdropper' owns a van, not surprisingly. He and the drifter go cruising. While they are out the drifter starts luring women into the back of the van. He then orders his friend the 'snowdropper' to drive to a deserted location. Once there the drifter tell the 'snowdropper' to go for a walk, which he does for about an hour or so—takes in the sights, gets in touch with nature, feeds the chipmunks, tries to find some discarded undergarments to whack off in—innocent, outdoor activities, right? When he comes back he gets into the vehicle and drives his new best friend back to his house, realizing that the woman he had picked up earlier is conveniently absent from the van but doesn't bother to inquire about it. This goes on for a couple of months. The women are there when he leaves, gone when he gets back. Eventually the drifter is caught when a woman he is trying to strangle gets free and finds help. The 'snowdropper' is arrested as well and his van is impounded as evidence. Can you guess what the 'snowdropper's' defense was? That the drifter exhibited a deep, psychological control over him and he was powerless to act freely lest he be the victim of his partner's homicidal rage and after all, he never actually *saw* anybody being killed, so what's the harm. You know where that 'snowdropper' is now? On death row, awaiting the same fate that awaits Manfred Fredman, who will be run through with enough pancuronium bromide and potassium chloride to kill a herd of elephants."

I was not getting the answers that I expected. I wanted my faith in my innocence reinforced, not stripped and smashed. My heavy perspiration and twitching were conspicuous signs of distress under the prosecutor's strong stare. I should've asked a defense counselor for advice—but now it was too late. I was being worked over. My flippant inquiry had put me right into the hot seat.

"I understand what you are saying," I said. "Trust me I believe that the guilty must be punished. But I don't think Manfred's situation is the same as these other criminal situations."

"Everybody thinks that they have special circumstances," the lawyer waved off. "But these circumstances usually fall apart come trial time. Manfred's story is close enough to hundreds of other death penalty cases that it won't matter—especially when the gas-masked orderlies come in to the chamber and shake the cyanide crystals out of the hair on his corpse."

"I don't think he's guilty of anything," I disagreed.

"That will be up to a jury of his peers," the lawyer countered.

"I'm thinking it's apples and oranges," I said.

"Yes," the lawyer nodded. "But if your apple is rotted, brown and oozing, and the prosecution's orange is big, fresh and juicy, then guess what—that robust and vigorous orange is going to kick the shit out of your filthy, diseased, criminal apple." We stared at each other in silence for a bit.

"This is all hypothetical remember."

"I'm not so sure," the lawyer disagreed. "You've got a guilty look to you, young man. Remember, I do this for a living. I've seen your type. You go look up some case studies involving two or more criminals. Hardly anybody gets away with it. If I were you I'd take a good look at the Leopold and Loeb case, which is the godfather of multiple perpetrator/capital murder cases. They both kill a child because they think they are so damn smart and wealthy that they can fool the police. They put the plan together, go over the alibi, and when they are caught Leopold blames Loeb and Loeb blames Leopold. Both of them get nailed, spared the death penalty by the likes of the legendary Clarence Darrow. But what does it matter? Loeb is sliced up like a Thanksgiving Turkey by his cellmate and Leopold is cornholed by psychopaths for the next thirty-odd years."

"I would like to thank you for your time," I told the attorney.

"Number Twelve," our group leader yelled at me, leering her head around the corner. "You are holding up the rest of the potential jurors. Would you please get in line!"

"I have got to be going," I told the attorney.

"I might be seeing you soon," he winked.

I slid back into my place in the row of jury candidates. I was between an elderly woman with a dog-eared romance novel under her arm and an oversized man with a hip pack. We marched into the courtroom. I realized that I hadn't even gotten a sip of water from my trip to the fountain and now my mouth was doubly parched from the opinions and descriptions of the man from the District Attorney's office. I decided that as soon as I was done at the courthouse I would drive myself out to Zanz's cabin and confront Baron.

It was a standard courtroom set up. The judge was at his post. The stenographer, a tall, ashen fellow, was speaking into a funneled voice recorder. It made him look like he was feeding on a bag of oats. The defense's table was in front of us and off to the right was the prosecution, three no-nonsense individuals perusing some last minute documents. The defense lawyer was a beautiful piece of Southern regalia. He had a formidable cowboy hat atop his head, one of those bolo string ties held together by a large replica of a buffalo coin. His belt buckle was bigger than my kitchen and his steel-toed cowboy boots had been polished to a fine sheen. The unfortunate creature with her back to us was, I suspected, the defendant.

The judge thanked us again and told us some shit about how we were the most crucial part of the American Justice system and that the state was getting an incredible deal for us since we earned two dollars something cents a day to dole out the wisdom of Solomon. He then asked us a few preliminary questions, which basically boiled down to inquiring if we had any outside familiarity with himself, the prosecuting attorneys, the cowpoke at the defense table or his client, who swiveled in her chair so us jurors could get a good look at her.

To properly convey the shock that blew through my ribcage as the defendant whirled around to face us, let us imagine a couple of possibilities that would provoke a similar reaction. Let us suppose that the woman in the chair turned to reveal the face of an elderly Adolph Hitler, almost unrecognizable because of transsexual surgery, picked up recently for vagrancy by a rookie cop in a neighborhood known for its heavy prostitution.

No?

How about this one: as the woman in the chair turned towards us, deafening blasts ripped through the walls and floor, and we all went plummeting down into the dust and rubble, because, as the survivors would later find out, the building had been blown up by a right wing extremist group angered at governmental abuse and corruption.

Dissatisfied?

How about this one: instead of a normal face on the defendant in front of us there were just two butt cheeks and a puckered asshole right in the middle of where that face should've been.

I digress.

The oversized man with the hip pack who was sitting next to me let out a hungry whistle as he gazed at her, Star, the girl who had taken me home that night only to never talk to me again. The ex-wife of Doctor B. Right, motivational speaker and jealous husband. She had told me that she felt like doing something illegal as part of her divorce.

I guess she had.

Her hair was up and she was wearing glasses in order to look honest and forthright. Try as she might, though, she could not keep her plenitude from overflowing her suit jacket. Added to the fact that she was on trial for some wanton cunning of the mind, her dangerous physical beauty made the scene significantly pornographic. I tried not to lapse into another dreamy stupor. Her eyes met mine--grew wide, then narrow. What was she trying to convey to me? Did she want me to feign ignorance about my knowledge of her, carnal or otherwise, so that I could maybe infiltrate this jury and sway it on her behalf, forever solidifying her allegiance to me? If she got acquitted we could pick up where we left off, get married and sire a long line of little felons, aiders and abetters, corpse-hiders, drug and alcohol abusers, people who gave our judges, attorneys and police force something to do during the day. Sensing I was already in enough trouble, I raised my hand and asked to approach the bench.

"You may," said the judge. Star leaned in and whispered something to her lawyer who nodded, put his hand on her back, and then approached the bench along with one of the prosecutors. The judge toggled a switch on his desk and a light hiss kicked up from some nearby speakers so nobody would overhear us.

"I know the accused," I said. "I met her at a bar. We spoke at length. She took me home, had her way with me and then never called me back. Then her ex-husband beat me up. I think, because of this, I would have a hard time being impartial. You see, your honor, I feel that all girls who don't call me should go to jail."

"My client states that this information is true," the prodigious defense attorney added as he adjusted his cowboy hat.

"Well then you will have to be dismissed," the judge said over the artificial static noise.

"Sorry hoss," the buckaroo defense attorney said. "If she had known the way it was going to turn out, I mean, I'm sure you would've heard from her."

I turned and walked slowly out of the courtroom. There was nothing I could do for Star, but I could still help myself. It was time for action. If I didn't fix this Baron situation I could soon be sitting right where Star was. As I walked past the defense table her eyes met mine and she gave a small, mournful smile. "Sorry," she mouthed.

Me too.

What kind of perverted, sadistic joke was the universe having at my expense? I could see him now…some wizard fellow sitting in an easy chair in a silver palace above the exosphere, watching the events of my life unfold through his crystal ball, laughing like a lunatic, holding his side, brushing the jubilant tears from his eyes while he watched me get put down like a sick mutt time and time again. Why didn't he just turn me into salt? I suppose that might've been too easy and certainly wouldn't be as much fun as witnessing a prolonged floundering.

# CHAPTER 23

The drive down south turned rural rather quickly. The artificial heat and light of the city fell away. Its luminous conurbation was replaced by a natural, darkened solemnity of the wild where the normal rules of proper civilization were bled dry amidst the unforgiving harshness of pure survival. Anything could happen out here and I knew it. From alien sightings to cutthroat games of BINGO, I needed to be prepared for the worst barbarity.

The comforting glow of skyscrapers had all but disappeared into the forest, only visible from their very tops, and soon even the iron apexes would be sunk into a lush infinity of pine trees. A kudzu shroud blanketed the woods.

I was driving out to Zanz's cabin. I had a rough idea of how to get there, put together from periodic trips, not a strong enough memory to explain the route, but I could feel it as I went along, inspired to find the way because of the weight of the circumstances.

I was spooked at what I was doing. I had serious reservations about approaching Baron's hideaway unannounced like this. So spooked, that I had knocked on my landlady's door after arriving back home from the courthouse to ask her if I might borrow a gun that I knew she kept in her office in order to keep her marriage proceedings orderly and respectable.

"You want my gun? Are you pushing my leg?"

"Neither pushing it or pulling it. Yes I need your gun."

"No, Dung Face. I forbid it," she had said.

"But Nona, you have to let me borrow your gun. I am in danger and I need something to protect myself."

"Dung Face, you are always in danger. You are a danger to yourself. If

243

I give you my gun you will shoot yourself. I will feel responsible for killing you. I can't have that on my consciousness."

"You mean *conscience*, Nona."

"Go to hell."

"You have to let me borrow it. I will only use it in case of emergency. Only to protect myself. Last resort."

"No! It is out of the question. You are no good to me dead. You are hardly any good to me alive, but even your normal dung face behavior is better than death."

"Please, damn it. I'm begging you."

"Beggers can't be choosers."

"Well Nona, you've finally got a saying right. Now we'll have to work on context."

"If you don't get out of my face you'll be working on finding another place to live."

"For the last time give me the gun."

"No!"

This desperate attempt to get her to submit had gone back and forth. I had gone through various strategies. Different pleas, appeals, outright begging. I told her I would clean her house for the remainder of my lease. She said she didn't even believe I could clean my underarms.

"I had a goldfish," Nona explained to me from the other side of her screen door. "While I was feeding the goldfish one day the lid came off and too much food fell into the water, spreading along the top surface. I watched that little goldfish eat and eat. He just watched me and ate and ate and ate. I tried to scoop some of the food out, but it was no use. I told him that he was going to make himself sick, but he just looked at me, tiny bubbles coming from his little mouth that worked and worked. Pretty soon there were no more bubbles and he pushed his little, bloated belly up to the ceiling so God could see what I had done to him. I do not want to see your bloated belly pointed up at God, Toby. I learn my lessons. You may not have my gun. I wouldn't even loan you a butter knife."

I should mention that there was a tiny Filipino girl standing behind Nona. She was wearing a dress patterned with orchids. She seemed genuinely interested in my dilemma, and rather patient about it all.

"By the way," I asked, pointing over my landlady's shoulder. "Who is that?"

"Her name is Yolan Mi," Nona said, her eyes following the direction of my finger to the thin girl standing at her heels. "She is here on a travel visa and wants a husband. She enjoys television."

"Do you mean construction of, or programming on?"

"*Ito ba ang lalaki?*" Yolan Mi squawked, which, even though I didn't understand a lick of Filipino, Tagalog or whatever, seemed to just about sum it all up.

"Now, if you aren't interested in getting married to this girl, you should leave me alone," Nona dismissed. "I have a very busy evening ahead of me." She slammed the door shut. I was left standing hopeless and frustrated with a stinging bleakness, an effusive chill, like watching the great golden nimbus of a floating utopia disappear over the horizon, leaving me stranded and alone.

The door opened back up.

"By the way, a man named Jonas came by here asking for you. He left you a message to meet him at this diner tomorrow." Nona slipped her handwritten message out of the door to me. The note gave the name of the diner and said to be there at noon. It thanked me in advance. The name Jonas was printed at the bottom.

I continued driving--straight down the two-lane road, toward the setting sun, and as these things go I swore I could hear the plangent whine of a harmonica rising up around me. It wasn't long before I was cruising past quiet fields of brown grass, farmhouses and the occasional unincorporated town that, after passing the church, the gas station and the antique shop, were gone almost as soon as I had entered them. I went over a railroad crossing that conspicuously lacked the cautionary black-and-white gate arms. There were no formal billboards as such, just hand painted ads for various goods and services—boiled peanuts, pressure washing, auto parts and feed, free dirt, as well as miscellaneous information signs such as 'Glad to see you', to the more condemning, 'People who litter are garbage'. There were also small, plastic campaign signs along the side of the road, pleading for votes in the next sheriff election. "Elect Elwin 'Shooter' Macdonald, odds are you're probably related to him, and how could you turn your back on family?"

I shut the car radio off and rolled down the windows, concentrating on the final mile of my trip. Night was setting in and the strange sounds of the forest echoed throughout my car, insect buzz, bird calls, animal cries. My car struggled over a steep rise, after which the road turned to dirt.

I wondered what was in store for me when I arrived, surprising Baron? Something terrible. A veritable bloodbath—a storage facility of missing

245

and mutilated women out in the middle of nowhere. A secret so cold and cruel as to defy comprehension. Baron's callous urges. He would show me it all, try to make me understand the cruel imperative involved. Then maybe he would hack me to pieces.

I turned slowly onto a thin pathway and followed it to its end, where a small cabin emerged in a semi-circular clearing. The Fleetwood Brougham was parked in front. I pulled up next to it, shut my car off and walked to the door. As I knocked it swung open easily. I stepped inside, through a vestibule and into a larger main room. I considered what it must have been like for the authorities in Plainview, Wisconsin to enter the condemned farmhouse that was Ed Gein's ghoulish factory of horrors. The famous search of the notorious murderer, grave robber and skin collector back in the Fifties turned up all sorts of rank perversity. I envisioned some sort of re-creation on Baron's part, an ode to one of his heroes--the crooked, old, stubble-faced man in flannel. Baron would create a painstakingly accurate tableau of carcasses, garbage, furniture upholstered in human skin, craniums used as dishware, an array of organs, perhaps a clever back scratcher made out of vertebrae.

Much to my surprise the room I was standing in was rather neat and tidy, with rustic sensibilities. It was a quaint, quaintly decorated, quaintly comfortable little bungalow in the middle of the woods. There were no signs of overt death. Old signs for bait and tackle were hung on the walls, as well as decorative fishing equipment, a largemouth bass. A crackling fire danced in the hearth. Along a nearby shelf sat a refurbished stereo with a library of old records next to it. I stopped to flip through the collection. The titles were peculiar—all aging, post-hippie soft rock. Mungo Jerry, Mac Davis, England Dan and John Ford Coley. It was the type of harmless, non-abrasive music a white guy might want to listen to in his quaint, rustic cabin after strangling and mutilating a hooker in the woods or the basement.

I heard a door open behind me. I turned, figuring it was Baron, but jumped as I realized it was a woman, watching me carefully. She was short and cherub faced with brown, wavy hair and warm eyes. She was wearing a modest knee-length skirt and a plain blouse. Both her wrists were bandaged. Even though she looked young there was a certain motherliness about her, something I was immediately drawn to, an undeniable, nurturing energy. There was a meaningful familiarity about her, somehow deeper than the surface familiarity of me recognizing her from her pictures. It was none other than the elusive Brady Mae, kidnapped wife of Jonas, looking healthy, radiant, and particularly young. There was no way she was over twenty-one. I could tell these things. I'm a bartender.

"I'm sorry," I said. "I am a friend of Baron's."

"Oh," she said. "I'll get him for you."

"Sorry to just walk in but the door was open. My name is Toby."

She brightened up. "Oh yes. Toby. I'm Brady Mae, but you can call me Lily Lou if you would prefer it."

"Brady Mae works for me."

"It is nice to meet you. I've heard good things about you, Toby. I feel like I know you already...like you are part of my family." She crossed to my side of the room and shook my hand, holding it still in both of hers for a few extra moments. "Sometimes you can just see a person's kindness, and it is as plain as the nose on your face."

"Thank you," I said.

"You look a bit tired. Was it a long drive? Of course it was. We are out here in the middle of nowhere. Baron and I had a long drive too—an incredibly long drive. Actually it was more of a journey." She paused, considered if she should divulge anything further. "Actually it was an escape. We escaped, and our drive here that was more of a journey or more of an escape...you see..." she paused again. I could tell she was looking for the best way to express some important point, or a sentiment of such overwhelming emotion that it smothered any attempted description of it. It was as if I were a blind man and she were trying to explain to me the color orange, or the shape of laughter.

"Imagine," she said, "that you find yourself on a deserted island because you know that everybody in the world hates you, and that you will be safe alone on that island, and you stay on that island for a long time because you fear what people would do to you if they got a hold of you. But after a few years you decide, out of the nameless obligation that goes to the heart of life itself, to venture out to sea and you swim till you think you are going to drown, but you don't drown and you hit another piece of land, much larger than the tiny one you were deserted on and when the inhabitants find you they welcome you as if you were the most cherished thing on Earth, and then you have to wonder, why or how you ever convinced yourself they would act otherwise. Does that make sense?"

"I think it does."

"I am going to get Baron," she said, leaving me alone for a moment. I walked in a small circle around the room. In a matter of minutes I heard his voice coming towards me from somewhere in the house. When he came into the room I hardly recognized him without his fedora and eyeglasses. He was surprised, to say the least. He offered me a seat on the couch and asked if I wanted anything to drink.

"I am okay, for now," I said. Brady Mae came in and sat next to Baron. he put his arm around her and she cuddled into him. This wasn't the type of behavior I would expect from somebody held against their will. Baron kissed the young girl on the forehead.

"What brings you all the way out here?" Baron asked.

"I need to talk to you," I said.

"How was your trip to New York?"

"That is what I need to talk to you about."

He turned to Brady Mae. "Why don't you go get the guest bedroom cleaned up in case Toby is too tired to drive back home," Baron said.

"That is a good idea," Brady Mae said. She returned a kiss to Baron's forehead. Baron smiled at her. The young girl seemed happy, the bandages on her wrists notwithstanding. She went gliding out of the room, but not before she performed an odd compulsion. On a low shelf was a set of Russian *matryoshka* dolls, seven porcelain figurines of descending size. Brady Mae carefully placed each doll in the next larger one so that eventually only the largest one was visible. Once this was done, she left the room.

"I've got to give her household chores and little games to keep her mind occupied," Baron said in a low voice. "I don't want her thinking too much about *him*."

"Who?" I asked.

"A man who calls himself Jonas."

"That is the reason I came out here to talk to you, Baron."

"How do you know about Jonas?" he asked, his voice pitched in alarm.

"Remember when you told me to get a drink on the ferry? Jonas was there."

"Shit!" Baron said, jumping up and pacing. "I should've known he would go there. I forgot he knew about that." He then turned to me, his body rigid with fear. "What did you tell him?"

"I didn't tell him anything. But I have to let you know that he is in Atlanta, Baron," I said.

The old man collapsed back onto the couch. "I told you not to say anything to anybody!" he said with hushed alarm so Brady Mae wouldn't hear.

"He told me you kidnapped his wife," I said. "That is why I am here.

248

To find out the truth. That is why I've come all this way. I need to know what this is all about. If you are on the level then I am going to have to get rid of this guy. I am going to meet him tomorrow and I need to know the angle." Baron put his face in his hands and breathed deeply. Then he looked around to make sure that Brady Mae wasn't anywhere near him.

"It all started with the kidnapping," Baron whispered.

"You kidnapping Brady Mae?" I asked.

"*I* was kidnapped," he shot back. "Seduced out of a bar in Torrance, California, just outside of Redondo Beach. I was drinking at this bar, minding my own business when three young girls come in and sit next to me. It wasn't long before we got to talking. They were flirty, coy, snickering between each other as if they were taunting me with their own private joke. So I bought them a round, and then another, and then another. When it came time for last call the one girl who seemed in charge asked me if I knew why they were there? I played it cool. I told them it wasn't their fault. I had been plagued for years with this type of charisma and irresistibly aggressive facial contouring." As Baron was telling the story the rumble of a dryer kicked up somewhere in the recesses of the cabin. Baron acknowledged the sound and continued. "They told me that I was going to be a religious experience. I told them they were damn right. They said there was a place we could go that was open all night long. So we finished our drinks and off we went. One girl had a camera. She kept taking pictures of me, saying she wanted to remember me as a stranger, which for some reason made sense at the time. We jumped in the car and took off. While we were driving the girls kept feeding me this strange whiskey. The last thing I remembered was heading east towards the desert, drinking with the radio blasting and the girls and the anticipation, and the big-hearted screaming of my soul like on those nights when everything just seems to be going so right that it is criminal. But I never could've imagined what was going to happen. I ended up passing out. When I woke up I was blindfolded and tied upright in a chair, bruised and aching. I didn't know if it was day or night, how long I had been there. I only knew I was going mad. It was the voice. The voice got into you like a disease."

"What voice?" I asked.

"The voice echoing through the room. A looped tape of caustic, bombastic, exhausting sermonizing, hours and hours of it blasting at me. It was crazy talk--all about something called Abraxas, a mystical star enshrouded in the Oort Cloud, the wicked and the chosen, a final pilgrimage, an ultimate departure, on and on and on and on." Baron sat back, legitimately distraught. "Eventually I fell into merciful sleep, but not for long. I was soon awakened by the recorded sounds of animals being slaughtered. My blindfold was taken off and a blast of light was shone into my face. Cold water was poured over my head. I received a painful injection. Eventually I could make out in the dark room about half a dozen hooded figures. The room itself was red and black, too dark to figure out much. I myself had been strapped to what looked like an old electric chair. In front of me was a makeshift altar. Standing behind the altar was, I guessed, the leader--a scraggly little thing, pale and maniacal, his face rife with all the trappings of delusional megalomania. In the center of the altar sat a bell jar with, of all things, a severed head floating in murky green liquid. So we've got me tied up, about half a dozen hooded figures milling around, an altar, a leader and a preserved head. That was the situation at that point." Baron's ragged and weary honesty fell upon him. From somewhere in the back of the house a faucet came on.

"The leader wanted a word with me," Baron continued. "He told me that I had been chosen for a great purpose, by their God Abraxas, to fulfill a prophecy and that I could rest in the fulfillment of true death through pain and torture, something that would provide me with everlasting peace, of course after the pain and torture part were all over. He said that in two days time I would be purified through fire. I tried to get him to talk reasonably but I was again beaten, blindfolded and given another injection. I heard the men file out of the room and the recorded sermons began to play again." Baron kneaded his forehead with his fingers, grappling uneasily with the memory.

"Sounds terrible," I said.

"Please let me get this off my chest."

Just then Brady Mae returned to the room. Baron and I straightened up into postures of guilty composure. She walked over to the low shelf and pulled each doll back out, one by one, until all seven were lined up in a row. She did it slowly with ritual precision, a smile on her cherub face. Then she came up behind Baron and began to rub his shoulders. Baron smiled up at her and patted one of her hands with his. She returned his warm gaze with one of her own.

"How is everybody doing in here?" she asked. "Do you like my dolls?"

"They are very nice," I said.

"Baron got them for me. I can't walk by them without stacking them or separating them. It makes me think of Baron. Then I'm happy." She looked at me. "Are you sure you don't want anything to drink?"

"I think I could use that drink now," I said.

"Me too," said Baron.

"I'll bring you something," she said. "It is good to keep busy, after all." I nodded. She disappeared out of the room.

"So back to me stuck there in that filthy room," Baron continued. "Just sitting there, counting down the seconds until my execution, dehydrated and drugged, still trying to keep my mind clear enough to wonder about my fate, the big 'why' the big 'what for'. A person never thinks it will end like that, strapped to a chair, blindfolded, held captive by a murderous cult, presided over by a severed head in a bell jar."

"You are right. It is a shame that people aren't more aware," I said.

"I wondered what I had done to deserve this," Baron pondered, "but regrettably there were too many reasons. I had led a beautiful, wasteful life. Instead I just tried to figure out a way to escape. That is when she arrived." He motioned his head toward the direction of Brady Mae.

"She wanted to help?"

"At first it was just a voice in my ear, since I was still blindfolded. She was telling me not to be afraid. She was one of the leader's wives, and had been planning her escape for some time, she said. She promised to take me with her. She told me that if I wanted to survive I would stay quiet and do exactly as she instructed. She had secured a safe house just over the Nevada border. We would be leaving the following night. I asked her what the hell I had gotten mixed up in, but she said there was no time. She would come back later, when it was safe to talk. Before I knew it she was gone. But with the disappearance of that sweet voice came hope. At that point a wave of optimism washed over me. The tape recorded loops of propaganda being fed to me disappeared from my consciousness. I was being granted an introspective gift, something to weigh against my life in order to change it, to better it, but above all to survive, to survive."

"Did you find yourself in a bargaining game with the authorities of death?" I asked. "Were you called to righteousness?"

"Yes," Baron answered. "Although these measly contracts are often rendered void upon being safely reinstated into one's own comfort. I decided I wouldn't let that be the case. I vowed to make sense of this situation, if I made it out alive. Again, because of my anguish and exhilaration, I fell into a dreamless sleep. It wasn't until she returned, some time later, that I came awake. This time she wanted to talk extensively, but she wanted me to talk about myself. She wanted me to tell her everything. She wanted to know that she was saving a worthy soul and so I let it all go. My life, my mistakes, my desires, I poured it out--a boundless confession. When I was done she removed my blindfold and there she was, staring down at me with God's radiance, my saviour, Brady Mae. She told me it was going to be alright. If I trusted in her I would have nothing to fear. She would be back when the time was right. I was frantic. I wanted out then and there. I told her to find me a weapon, something I could use to defend myself if we were caught. She told me not to worry, she had taken care of everything. I asked her where I was, what was happening, who was responsible for this? That was when she explained about the cult. I had stumbled into the west coast chapter of a millennium extremist group known as the Gilded Dawn. The leader was known as Father Jonas. He had recently seized power of this desert society because he felt that the end of the world was coming soon, but that the chosen few would be rescued by a mighty alien known as Abraxas. This Abraxas was living on a far planet with an army of highly evolved alien penitents at his side. He commanded a paradise of orgy and drug use for thousands of years and he was going to visit Earth soon before it was destroyed."

"Why was Earth going to be destroyed?" I asked.

"Because if it wasn't there would be no reason to leave it," Baron said with a frustrated sigh as if I hadn't been paying attention. "It was all planned. He had written out his own personal prophecy. He even had another name for himself as the main delegate when Abraxas finally came to Earth to collect the Gilded Dawn members."

"What was the name?"

"Abraxas."

"Not very imaginative," I said. Brady Mae came back in with two drinks. She gave them to us, smiled at us again, stacked her *matryoshka* dolls and left the room. The sound of a vacuum came on.

"There are strict rules governing these types of things," Baron said. "It is like baking a cake. You need the right ingredients. First start with some controversial figure. Then isolate a group of young, desperate types and convince them that this controversial figure is a deity, a space alien--something remarkable. Inculcate your recruits with an apocalyptic dogma—tell everybody they better watch their asses because this space alien deity is coming, the sooner the better. He's going to rescue some folk, and destroy some other folk. Give a comprehensive criteria for pissing your new God off. Avoid independent thought among your loyal few. Send them out to recruit more of the desperate and the lost. Meanwhile talk your shit all day long. The less sense you make the better. Try running in circles for ten minutes Toby. You'll be on your ass, nauseous, disoriented, wondering where the fuck you are and who the fuck you are. Do that enough and you'll be ready to believe that the world is run by a homosexual brotherhood living in the center of the Earth, magic spiders whisper the circumstances of our own lives to us while we sleep, or that flushing a toilet removes sin. Father Jonas had all the drug-addled followers at his compound convinced that he was being given instructions by Abraxas from his distant planet through a 'Hierophant'--or an interpreter of sorts. In this case it was the human head that was placed on the altar, floating in the bell jar. Decapitated cranium of the old leader. It is believed that Abraxas speaks through this to the new chosen one. It is a severed head soaking in formaldehyde. Deceased leader of the west coast chapter of the Gilded Dawn. There is a new leader. It is all part of the ritual, dating back to the beginnings of the movement. When a leader dies they keep his head. They believe their God can speak to them through this. Creepy fucking thing, let me tell you. They call it 'Wet Brain'."

"So every time a leader dies, they cut his head off and preserve it?"

"Yes. It's an important part of their spiritual apprehensions. They can't talk to their God without Wet Brain."

"What do they do with the old...Wet Brain?" I asked. "The head of the old leader?"

"Play kickball with it, I don't know," Baron shot back. "So now I knew what I was dealing with. Brady Mae told me that, although she was betraying the congregation, she felt that she couldn't condone the sacrifice of an innocent person like myself for the glory of the group. I must admit that I was in total agreement. She then replaced my blindfold and told me she would be back when it was time to escape. That was the longest wait of my entire life. I imagined she would be caught, or have a change of heart, or suffer a stroke, anything was possible at that point. But she returned as promised, and we made our escape."

"Just like that?" I asked. "You didn't have to fight your way out, or sneak around, crawl on your bellies, create a diversion?"

"That was the thing," Baron answered. "Our escape was simple. She untied me and we just walked out of the room, down the hallway out the front door, got into the old Fleetwood Brougham that was parked outside and drove off. The steamer trunk with the 'heirophant' in it was in the back seat. We were taking Wet Brain with us, she said. I asked her what possessed her to steal that sickly head in the jar. She had no reasonable answer. That was when I knew something was wrong. Our escape was way too easy. The place was deserted. That raised the question...where was everybody? So I asked Brady Mae about this. I could tell she was fumbling for an answer. Now this girl is an impressionable twenty years old..."

Twenty years old, I thought to myself. I knew it.

"...She's just too brainwashed to think the whole thing through. But I kept badgering her and eventually she slipped up, telling me how excited she was to be a part of The Great Prophecy. I asked her what the hell The Great Prophecy was? That was when she got quiet, so I pulled the car to the side of the road and told her that I wasn't going anywhere until she told me everything that was contained in this so-called Great Prophecy. After awhile I got it out of her. Father Jonas had written a prophecy and entitled it 'The Great Prophecy' because obviously he suffers from a terrific imagination. I'll spare the laboring details, but basically the prophecy stated that a stranger would come along and force one of his wives to betray him. Together they would steal the sacred Wet Brain and flee, at which time Father Jonas in his great wisdom would find them and retrieve his sacred object. Well, since no stranger had come along Father Jonas, in order to secure the all-knowingness that he predicted about himself, had sent some of his harpies out to find one, to steal a man that 'nobody would miss'. That man was me." Baron radiated a kind of warped pride at the thought. "To further hedge his bets, he drafted one of his most loyal women, Brady Mae, to befriend me. She was cast as some type of Judas figure, because every good prophecy needs one. He then let us escape, knowing that Brady Mae would deliver me right back into his hands, with his congregation there to witness, and from that point on his glory would be pretty well secured." Baron leaned back haughtily. "But this idiot didn't count on the strong reasoning capabilities of old Baron Corley. I knew what I had to do. I had to snap her out of her brain fog, get her thinking again. I pointed that car directly for Atlanta. This got Brady Mae very worked up. She said we needed to go to Nevada. I told her that if her leader was as powerful and knowledgeable as he claimed to be, wouldn't he be able to find us anywhere? She had to admit that was the case. So I bought myself some time. We drove straight for Atlanta. As we made our way across country I kept trying to get her to come around, to have a clear grip on the situation but she was too far gone. I considered just leaving her on the side of the road but unfortunately, I couldn't just ditch her. I had, alas, fallen in love with this girl. And so what? Jonas had about ten wives. He wouldn't miss one. It was around Arkansas that she started to get a little violent, knowing that she was violating this very specific, clearly planned prophecy and so although I'm ashamed of it I had to tie her up and gag her." Baron hung his head. I could sense now the undercurrent of his unreasonable behavior, his need for secrecy, his general stress. It was like finally mapping the layout of the bedrock at the river bottom to figure out how it underscores the character of the rapids above. He had been driven to the point of madness and as a result the irrationality of the situation required unsound measures.

"When I got to Atlanta I came to see Zanz. I had to put Brady Mae in the trunk of the car. Funny enough, it was at her request. She agreed to lay in the trunk quietly, assuring me that if she meditated hard enough her Father Jonas would be able to find her within the hour. So Toby, you and I went drinking. When it was obvious Jonas wasn't going to be showing up, I buried the trunk with the Wet Brain in it and took Brady Mae out here in order to unscramble her mind. I didn't want any distraction--didn't want anything around Brady Mae that would remind her of her old life. She needed to be deprogrammed. Finally, as you can see she is coming around."

"She seems all right," I agreed.

"Understand that I didn't feel right about taking Brady Mae against her will," Baron continued. "But I had to. She was putting herself and me in a very dangerous situation. She was unthinking, unfeeling and uncomprehending. She had been under the spell of this Gilded Dawn for too long. I didn't have much experience with this type of thing. I got her down to this cabin and held her here. I tried to show her that I loved her. I loaded her up with sedatives. I encouraged her to think objectively about the whole thing. I bought her stuff. Got her concentrating on little games, like her dolls over there. She was a mess for a few weeks. I had to cuff her to the radiator if I wanted to leave. She was a jumble of zoned-out bliss, hatred, fear, sadness and exhaustion. I had to keep it a secret from you guys, from everybody, because what I didn't realize was that when I had told her all about myself she had actually taken the information back to Father Jonas. I had confided my life to her. I figured he might try to track me down in Atlanta so the less everybody knew the better. Plus, little by little, Brady Mae started to come around. The time away from the compound was really doing incredible things for her. She was watching television. She was reading magazines. She would take walks in the woods or go swimming in the lake--under close supervision of course. But then that awful day arrived when she cut her wrists. Luckily I caught her just in time, got her stabilized and to the hospital. That was why I was covered in blood when I got to Zanz's that day."

"I knew there was no Red Cross bus accident."

"Of course not Toby!" Baron chided. "That was a ridiculous story." He shook his head to clear it of my dumb comment. "When I knew she was okay I came to Zanz's place. I was so pissed off, frustrated, at the edge of it, that I knew I needed to blow off some steam. Beating the crap out of that asshole motivational guy that day really helped me out. But then, after I got her back here, I could see it in her eyes. That brush with death had brought her out of it, not all the way, but she had hit a realization. She was coming back into herself. There was a person behind those eyes, and that night we promised we'd never leave each other again, and I knew she meant it. Now here we are, ready to start the rest of our life together." The vacuum cleaner had shut off. Brady Mae came back into the room, performed her small but important ritual with the dolls and sat down next to Baron.

"Brady Mae, can you give Toby and I just a few more minutes?"

"No problem. I was thinking about cleaning the lint out of the dryer," she said.

"Good girl."

"I am going to go meet with this Jonas freak," I said quietly after Brady Mae had left, of course after doing her thing with the dolls. "I am going to tell him that you have left the city."

"Toby this man is dangerous."

"Baron, it is just him and two of his geeks," I said. "I am meeting them in a public place. What are they going to do? You have to stay here and watch Brady Mae. Make sure she is safe. I'll bargain with him. I'll tell him that I can get his Wet Brain back to him, but you and Brady Mae are gone. I'll have Zanz go dig up the steamer trunk. These men know where I live. I don't want to chance them following me. I won't be coming back after I leave here tonight."

"This nut Jonas needs Brady Mae and I to complete his Great Prophecy," Baron said. "But he needs that head in the bell jar even more. It is the treasure of their whole religion."

Brady Mae came back into the room. Again, the thing with the dolls. Then she smiled and asked me if I wanted to hear her play the guitar. She said she had written a song for me within the last five minutes. She told me it was about Love and Springtime and being Naked and Frolicking in the rain. I made her promise me that she would play it for me when I saw her again. She said she hoped it would be soon. I bid them both goodnight and drove hellfire back to the city.

# CHAPTER 24

There is an old philosophical principal, or argument, or whatever you might want to call it, that suggests a kind of mathematical paradox for a philosopher. It suggests this mathematical paradox for a philosopher and only for a philosopher because nobody else in their right mind would bother with these ridiculous, hypothetical principals, arguments or situations or whatever you'd like to call them. I don't remember exactly which philosopher was responsible for this mathematical argument, but I am going to try and recount the philosophical problem...

A philosopher attempts to walk from one side of a room to the other. There is no need to bother with questions about why he might want to be on the other side of the room, although I may give a few reasons why *I* might want to get from one side of a room to the other side. (To escape lingering flatulence. To avoid sniper fire. Because there is an ice cold beer on the other side of the room.) Anyway the philosopher decides to walk across the room using the particular method of halving the distance he travels each time he moves. So in a twenty foot room he would first walk ten feet, then five feet, then two and a half feet, then one and a quarter feet, so on and so forth. Theoretically the philosopher never reaches the other side of the room, unable to close the distance because there is no way to get to zero, his point of terminus, by this type of division and so he doesn't escape the disagreeable body odor, never gets his ice cold beer, or eventually gets shot by the sniper in his thick head. Try as I might to avoid the cruel fact, I found myself guilty of this very idiotic method of travel. I had been experiencing this diminished movement for too long. I had been defined by it and up until now the movements were such that I could trick myself into believing that I would eventually make it to this other side of the room, so to speak. But I was grinding to a frustrating standstill, or movement so minuscule that there was hardly any difference. It was time for full-scale action. I was going to walk right across that mother-fuggling room, up to the wall, then through the wall out to the other side—snipers, flatulence and ice cold beers be damned. Well, maybe not ice cold beers.

I had gotten Zanz on the phone and told him that he needed to go back to the woods and dig up the steamer trunk. He needed to break into it, grab the bell jar with the severed head in it and keep it in a safe place until I got in touch with him again. Baffled almost to the point of having an embolism, he made me explain the plan to him a few more times--the reason, the context, the fact that there was a severed head in a bell jar. I told him it was very simple. Weird, but simple. I had met the person that Baron was hiding from while I was in New York. He was now in Atlanta. I told Zanz we needed some leverage to make sure Baron was safe. It was his job to go get the bell jar. I told him to bring Skid Row Paul. He had been dying to break into the steamer trunk anyway. The head in the bell jar is called Wet Brain. You might get along with it better, I said, if you address it by its proper name. It is the lynchpin of a millennium cult's belief system, so be careful with it. Don't take it out drinking with you to try and impress the ladies. Zanz asked me how this man who had been hunting Baron had known to come to Atlanta from New York. I admitted that I had told him to. This made Zanz none too happy, and my characteristically relaxed friend became uncharacteristically unhinged.

"You did *what?*"

"This man named Jonas approached me while I was on the ferry, Zanz," I said into the phone. "He said his wife had been kidnapped by Baron."

"And you believed this perfect stranger?"

"Given Baron's behavior it seemed like a strong possibility. The guy seemed legitimate."

"You double-crossing traitor!"

"That is why I went to your cabin when I got back--to confront Baron. When I met Brady Mae I realized that she wasn't in trouble. So now I have to go meet this Jonas guy and give him the brush off."

"Don't you realize it might be too late!" Zanz condemned. "Shit Toby where is your sense? You'd turn God over to the Devil for money! You'd throw your firstborn into the smoldering volcano. You'd kiss your savior, take your thirty pieces and wouldn't even have the decency to hang yourself in the temple. What kind of heartless, cheap, thoughtless piece of shit have I been calling a friend for so long? What type of sharp-clawed beast have I been working next to for all these years? What kind of black heart thumps in that chest of yours Toby? What poison pumps through those veins? How can you look in the mirror? How can you stare at your hands, your fingers, the tip of your nose—how do you look at one square inch of yourself without getting sick to your stomach for putting people at such risk? For not believing in them?"

"Don't you throw that shit at me!" I shouted back. "You don't remember anything except to refill your peach brandy. Don't you remember the blood on Baron, his violent comments, his weird secrecy, his ex-wife with no arm? A damn steamer trunk in the woods? Did you know that when we lifted that thing out of his car I found duct tape next to it with hair stuck all over it? Like someone had been bound and gagged, you know like, against their will? What did you expect me to think?"

"I expected you to trust, not think."

"Trust is fine, but I'm not ready to donate my brain to science just yet because the damned thing gets in the way of charming simplicity. It goes down like this...a guy approaches me on the ferry up on Long Island. He says his wife has been kidnapped. He shows me a picture of her. He shows me a picture of Baron. It is obvious he knows Baron and compared to all of the bullshit I listen to at the bar, his story seems alright. I told him Baron was in Atlanta but I didn't draw him a map to the cabin. Baron is alright and he is going to stay alright."

"Are you going to try and convince me that you are some impartial judge of character?" he said. "For years you were just looking for some homicidal maniac to come into your life and turn it into real shit. You needed it in a way and you found it in Baron. You are the only person I know, Toby, that feels guilty when you have it good because there are a lot of people out there that don't. Well that is none of your business either way. There are always going to be people who have it better and there are always going to be people who have it worse, but your willingness to be some kind of victim because you don't feel you deserve your own decent circumstance is foolish and has led to much more harm than good."

"I'm only trying to say that there were at least indications of something bad happening," I reiterated. "You want to talk about trust? You now have to trust me that I was only doing what I thought was right. As a friend you need to stop misinterpreting my mistake for some sinister intention."

"There are two types of friends, Toby. War time friends and peace time friends," Zanz sighed. "Peace time friends are plentiful. War time friends are not. Both are okay. The only danger is to get them confused. I confused you Toby. I thought you'd have my back when the shit got rough and the enemy was at the gates. I thought you'd have Baron's back. But instead you left it exposed. Hell you painted a bulls-eye on it."

"Even if this Jonas hadn't met me how do you know that he wouldn't have come to Atlanta eventually?" I said. "He knew that Baron has spent a lot of time here. This is better. Now we know exactly where he will be."

"I am going to do what you ask," Zanz said. "In the position we are in right now it makes the most sense. But," he warned, "you better have a damn good idea of what you are doing."

"You just go get Wet Brain out of that hole in the ground. Leave the rest to me," I said and hung up the phone.


As I drove to my meeting with the man known as Jonas, I realized I had another valuable commodity at my disposal that I had completely overlooked, which was my own sharp understanding of a deviant like Jonas. I had read hundreds of killer profiles, reviewed hours of television programs on the subject. I had studied the glossy inserts of true crime books, the ones that show the victims, the killers, the scenes of the crime. I knew the childhood indications of shame, rage, parental apathy, domestic imbalance and hatred. The psychological torment of reform school abuses. I knew the finer points of the Helter Skelter philosophy of demented social revolution. The need to embrace apocalypse as a dependable and absolute criteria for opportunity. It wouldn't be so hard to manipulate a man like Jonas. My confidence grew. Any argument he made I would be ready for. I would be several moves ahead of all his contentions. I could not be blindsided by this man's irresponsible logic. What was I worried about? By the time I was done with him he'd be asking me to take his place in *his own* organization, offering me my own franchise in the Gilded Dawn syndicate. I was overcome with a rare sense of arrogance, of merited hubris. To imagine that I could somehow be outfoxed by somebody who probably didn't even have a high school diploma was laughable. A man who preyed on weak-minded and helpless young adults because he didn't have the capacity to match wits with a master thinker.

I walked into the greasy spoon of a diner. From the looks of the place all the utensils were sure to be equally as filthy. The place was good and busy, especially since there were only a few cars in the parking lot and an

261

old bus that smelled as if it had a gas leak. Two clunky cowbells tied to the handle of the door signified my entrance like a clumsy bovine. The diner was full. Almost every seat taken. A long, formica countertop stretched the length of the room. A short order cook was behind it, overseeing a flat grill loaded with heart disease, for the most part. Various pies spun insipidly in the glass display case next to the jukebox. The posters on the walls advertised cigarettes, lard and red meat by showing slim, rosy-faced teenagers at a sock hop or going off to war.

Jonas was sitting at a table in the middle of the dining room with the two men I had met in New York. I walked over and sat down at their table. He looked different. Not as helpless. His demeanor was a little more intense. He smiled at me.

"Glad you could make it," he said.

"No problem."

"Has there been any news about my wife?" he asked, although there was no alarm in his voice. "Do you know where Baron is?"

"I do. But I'm not going to tell you. See, I heard about your little cult out there in the desert. I heard about how you sent some girls to kidnap Baron so you could put your sleazy plan of greatness into effect."

His eyebrows raised. He smirked and began turning his coffee cup slowly on the table.

"So here is the deal. I will give you Wet Brain. Your freaky head in the jar. Then you can take your asses back out to where you came from. Brady Mae is not your wife. Not in any literal sense. She is done with you. She told me so herself."

"That is where you are wrong," Jonas said with an easy laugh. "Soon you will understand that this is all a smaller part of a bigger experience." He looked at his watch. "Nothing is going to stop it."

"What are you going to do?" I asked. "This is a public place." The two men sitting with Jonas started to laugh, until Jonas shot them a look and they quieted down.

"You three aren't going to be able to do shit," I said. Now Jonas produced a giddy laugh. The two men cautiously echoed it.

"This is the way it has to be," Jonas said, tensing up with impatience. "Something incredible is going to happen this evening and you should just consider yourself lucky that you will be able to witness it."

"What am I witnessing?"

"If I could promise you," he said, "that I could show you a bona fide miracle...would you be eager or fearful to witness?" He looked at me

262

coldly. It was a look that I somehow recognized, although I was sure that I had never received it from him.

"I would be skeptical," I said.

"That is because his heart is not pure," one of the men at the table said. "Evil elements are afraid of miracles. The righteous have no need." Jonas kept his eyes squarely on mine.

"There is a miracle on the horizon," he promised. "And boy are you going to see it. It will be the key to your everlasting preservation. You will understand the nature of sin and glory. You will understand your own salvation."

"You sound so sure of yourself," I said.

"We are in a state of becoming, on our way to a great place," he continued. "Not everybody will reach it. But the chosen ones who do will experience a clarity never before imagined, a new set of values, a purging or cleansing of old paradigms and it will be led by the one true Abraxas."

"Who?"

"A prophet," one of the men at the table said. "From another world. The world we'll be going to."

"The only place you'll be going is back out to the desert," I said.

"Abraxas is ours," Jonas declared. "He has been a great deal misunderstood throughout history but we are here to present a clear portrait of his greatness. Your friend Baron has unknowingly played a significant part in the revelation of the great Abraxas, who will reveal himself at the conclusion of the Great Betrayal, which will be directly followed by the Great Arrival. Your friend, before he suffers the ultimate fate of being purified by fire, will have brought about a rare and wondrous development in the spiritual understanding of the new millennium."

"Bullshit," I said. "You know where to find me. Let me know if you want your Wet Brain back." I stood up to go. The man seated next to me grabbed me.

"I wouldn't be going anywhere," he said.

"There are a lot of men in this restaurant," I said, looking around, realizing in fact it was all men. "If I yell they'll want some words with you."

"I think they'll want some words with you," Jonas said with a snap of his fingers. A great shudder went through the restaurant, as if the establishment itself had suddenly come alive. My heart sank as I realized what was happening.

"What...the..."

I fell into silence.

As Jonas rose from his seat the whole diner got quiet and everyone... every single damned one of the men in the restaurant began to stand up around him. This produced a rippling effect as from table to table, man by man, they all began to gather their things up, first the ones closest to us and then out towards the edges of the restaurant--like dominoes in reverse. Jonas had enough men with him to fill an entire diner. The crowd gathered around me and, like an army of ants carrying an apple core, swarmed on me and dragged me out to the old bus that was sitting in the diner's parking lot.

I overheard a waitresses say, as the men cleared out of the restaurant, that she could only imagine all the toast she could make with all that white bread. The mob filed onto the old bus. They took their seats and stared blankly at me through the grimy windows of the jalopy. I was being held against my car.

"My two followers will ride with you," Jonas said. "They will inspire you to take the quickest route possible. Drive carefully and considerately now. Remember--Speed Kills."

"I'll try," I mumbled, dumbstruck, all the eyes from the bus staring down at me with emotionless abandon, raining their gaze like a firestorm.

"To try implies failure," Jonas shouted as the jump start roar of the diesel engine on the bus kicked up a cloud of smoke around us. "If I were you I wouldn't fail."

# CHAPTER 25

My waning, whining car did its best to cope with the rumbling vehicles in whose wake I was constantly steadying against to keep from being blown off the road. The pick-up trucks, the Harleys, the old muscle cars, the family cars with kids staring at me from the back--their gawking, disheartened faces pressed against the window, almost pleading for freedom. I also had to steer clear of an old station wagon, unable to make up its mind as to which lane it actually wanted to travel in while the driver's left arm periodically ejected an empty beer can from the open window. Alongside these private motorists were the normal commercial trucks—the 'wide right turns' truck, the truck that launched large strips of tire rubber at my front bumper, the chemical truck (refrigerated nitrogen), the gravel truck that pelted my windshield with rubble, the 'oversized' load truck carrying a mobile home to some future tornado victim.

I mention the traffic because it was all a secondary entourage to the rusted grill of the old bus shuddering, swaying and barreling at my bumper behind me. Jonas, along with his bus full of generic men. A big hunk of scrap metal and brown smoke in my rearview mirror. Between that and my two car companions, things were looking bad. After the two Gilded Dawn members had taken up their seats in my car they had continued a rather tedious quibble about who should have been 'chosen' to sit in the front, the man next to me defending his arbitrary superiority against his sulky partner's weak complaining from behind.

"Father Jonas says we are all equal," said the man up front.

"Then what would it matter if I sat up front?" said the man in the back.

265

"Because you obviously have a strong desire to sit up front. Father Jonas says if you desire something you must renounce it to remain pure."

"If you're so pure then why don't you be selfless and let me sit up front," said the man in the back.

"I would be enabling your desire," said the man in the front. "Then we would both be sinning."

"It is all very convenient that you get to sit up front by being selfless," said the man in the back.

"If you see the world through the eyes of desire you won't be able to see clearly. Thus, you don't appreciate the situation."

"Father Jonas likes me better than you," said the man in the back. "He would've wanted me to sit up front."

"If he wanted you to sit up front he would've given us explicit seating arrangements. Since I didn't care either way and I could see you really wanted to sit up front, I decided to put you in the back."

"If we are all equal," continued the man in the back, "why are you making the seating decisions?"

"I'm trying to save you from sin!"

"You're just jealous because Father Jonas hand washes me," said the man in the back in a sophomoric tone.

"I harbor no jealousy," said the man in the front.

"And he gave me a soapy water enema," said the man in the back. The comment made the man up front stiffen a bit. I wrinkled my brow and continued driving.

"That doesn't mean you are entitled," said the man in the front, getting a little edgy.

"And he calls me into his office and dresses me up," said the man in the back.

"All the more reason," said the man in the front.

"He tells me to be thankful I'm not a woman because women are dirty and meant for procreation..."

"Enough!" I shouted. They both lapsed into thankful silence for the better part of the trip. There were only two exceptions.

"Boiled peanuts sounds like peanut soup," was the only thing the man sitting next to me had to say after I admonished them, as he read a handmade advertisement for the snack on the side of the road.

"What do you think they called Grandma Moses when she was a child?" was the only thing the man in the back had to say.

"Maybe Little Moses," was the only thing I had to say.

There was so much wrong with this situation. I wracked my brain for a way out of this massacre that was on the horizon. Whatever happened I had to do something. I had promised Zanz and Baron. I would not be the one to organize a slaughter. It was time for an evaluation of this predicament. It was time for a miracle.

I got off the highway and turned onto the road leading to Zanz's cabin. The bus was a few feet away from my bumper. I decided to do an incredibly desperate thing. I decided to petition the universe for assistance in this matter. I was pleading with the entire vault of heavenly sky to help with my situation. What I needed was some divine manipulation that would give me the proper circumstance with which to display my capabilities, as the surfer prays for the perfect wave or the rainbow needs the right combination of mist and sunlight in order to arc its majesty. I made a quiet pact that should any mystical powers provide me with the right opportunity I would pledge my undying allegiance to them. I needed to give my tail the slip, although I scoffed at the use of the word *tail* since an organism as miniscule as my car having a tail as big as Jonas's bus was like a whale fin on a deer tick.

"Something is wrong," the man in the back of my car said, looking out of the rear window. "The bus is pulling over." Sure enough, the old bus came to a halt on the side of the road.

"Stop the car," said the man next to me. I pulled over, watching in the rearview mirror, trying to make out what was going on. I could see some commotion, but it was impossible to interpret. A minute went by. Two minutes.

"Go see what the problem is," said the man in the back seat to his partner. "I'll make sure everything is alright here." The guy sitting next to me got out of the car and swung the door closed, although it wasn't closed all the way. The latch had not caught.

"Do you mind if I step out of the car to stretch my legs?" I asked the man in the back seat.

"Sure."

I got out of the car and stood up straight. The man who had been in my car had reached the bus. He was standing at the door. He motioned fore and after of the big vehicle then gestured up to where I was parked. A truck full of chickens sped by. There was an abandoned gas station up on the right. Not much else to the horizon out in these parts. A few old houses. A confederate flag or two. A ghost of a windmill. A gloomy looking factory in the distance pouring white smoke, probably a rendering company, melting down livestock and roadkill. Death hung heavy in the air.

"Hey," I called to the man in the back. "This might be a fine opportunity to take the front seat away from your buddy."

The man in the back seat's eyes got wide with opportunity. He looked at me like I was the smartest man alive. Quickly, he climbed up to the front seat and plopped himself in with an expression of victory across his face. I decided to get back into my car--using a very peculiar method. I opened the driver's side door as far as it would go. then I gripped both my hands on the roof of the car and thrust my feet at the man in the passenger seat in a forward mule kick. I was dead on. He hit the other door and, because it hadn't been closed properly, he went bouncing out of the car and into the soft shoulder of the road.

I repositioned myself as fast as I could and hit the gas. My car jumped forward. The man who had been lying on the ground had gotten up and was trying to make it to the passenger door, but staggered and fell into the middle of the road. Sweating and hyperventilating, I looked into the rearview mirror. All hell was breaking loose. The bus had pulled back onto the road and had slowed only momentarily to pick up the man I had ejected out of my car. Once he was in, it was full speed ahead.

As I raced down the road I could see, in the distance, the railroad crossing lights flashing. A vast field spread out on either side of the intersection. I could see the train approaching. It was a rumbling freighter that looked like it ran the length of the whole state, into infinity, the caboose completely hidden in the horizon, moving slow enough to dare and fast enough to kill. The heat and buzz now boiled up through my entire body. This was it. I had asked for a miracle and here it was, goddamn it all, unmistakable and urgent, a veritable flashing, blinking, twinkling miracle. What was even more miraculously preposterous was that due to whatever county I was passing through's lack of traffic, or funds, or concern, there were no gate arms to block the road from the train tracks, just the flashing lights and a smaller sign that (once I got close enough to read it) stated it was forbidden by law to stop on the tracks. It didn't say anything, though, about flying maniacally right over them. I checked my rearview mirror. Jonas's bus had been gaining, and now, sensing what I was about to do and understanding that if they got caught behind this impenetrable moving barrier then all their strategy and ambition would be completely wasted, began to close the distance. No matter how many men, or how many busses, or how many men in busses, the whole crew would be stranded impotently in the middle of nowhere, for probably a good fifteen or twenty minutes if they got stuck behind the train. My foot mashed the gas pedal to the floor. The only thing I couldn't figure from the distance was if I could make it over the tracks before the train made it across the road. My eyes met my own in the rearview mirror, both of us having a pleasant, silent dialogue, a tacit argument of calm rationality that belied the general rigid horror at being killed by a train.

"Up ahead, watch out," my rearview mirror self told me. "There is a train coming. It might be best to decelerate." I kept my foot on the gas. All the dials on the dashboard were pinned to the far right side. My engine gave a bestial cry. I glanced in the rearview mirror and saw the occupants in the diminishing bus behind explode in a fury of gesturing and head shaking. The train was coming fast, faster by the moment. I gripped the steering wheel like I was trying to choke it to death and leaned forward, watching the gridiron cowcatcher on the locomotive speed rapidly towards our mutual intersection.

"We are in no real hurry," I heard myself say casually. *We are going to be smashed to shit*, is what I meant. My car shook like it was coming apart as the train's pulsing procession of grinding steel came rushing forward to slice through my path.

"We may want to reconsider any rash decisions," I continued. *Stop this fucking car right now you psychotic bastard.*

"I've got it," I wheezed.

"This type of erratic behavior is acceptable in some situations, and not so in others." *Stop you idiot, stop!* The old bus was falling back. They would not make it. But would I? The road inclined up. To stop my car now would've skidded it to a dead halt on the track and, like I said, there was a sign saying that was strictly forbidden.

"You may want to consider that there are some things that we *both* want to accomplish in this life." *You are going to die.* An urgent horn exploded from the locomotive. I could see the engineer waving out of his window frantically, and kind of in an advanced apology for hitting my car. In the stark moment before impact I noticed he had a mole on his nose.

"I understand you may be feeling a little down, lately," my rearview mirror self said as it braced, "but I assure you it can't be so bad." *Suicide is not the answer.*

My car came off the road and went sailing over the tracks, dipping back down towards the opposite pavement. By the time I hit the ground my rearview mirror was flooded with freight car after freight car flying by. I struggled to get control of the tires as they did a jelly dance across the road. I fishtailed left, then right, and after the smoke, the whine and the pealing, steadied her back to the normal cruising speed. My shirt was soaked around the neck and underarms. My breath had to catch up to the car. I had survived death, I thought. Then I laughed. Nobody survives death.

*

"Good going," my rearview mirror self said. "You pushed your car to the limit and now you have no gas."

I was right. The needle was leaning down on the fifth letter of the alphabet, capitalized, foreboding. In my heart-pounding hurry I did not want to waste any time on unnecessary errands. I needed to get to the cabin immediately. But running out of gas and having to proceed on foot would be a disaster, and by the way I figured it I had a good ten minutes at least to get out of sight. At that point there was no way Jonas's big bus and his small brain would be able to pick through the web of unpaved roads to the secluded cabin, especially with nothing to go on. I decided to try my luck at an abandoned-looking gas station on my right. The sign said that it was open for business. I ran in, slapped a twenty dollar bill on the counter and told the man in overalls, asleep behind the counter, that he could keep the change. He answered with a long, growling snore. His mouth hung open and a nice glistening thread of drool had descended from his mouth. How incredibly tensile drool is, I thought. The drool was stretched so far to the ground that it looked like it was making a conscious effort to escape the man's lipless old mouth. If it was a calculated endeavor then the drool could not be blamed. As the man snored the drool vibrated. What an amazing and overlooked evolutionary substance. I realized that time was wasting so I forced myself to break the hypnotic trance the drool had me in. I made a dash for the front door.

The gas pumps were not computerized. They were the old, odometer-style numbered wheels. This too, was mesmerizing. A world of small wonders, right here in the middle of nowhere, I thought. I was so taken again that I didn't realize a woman standing about ten feet from the front of my car. She was sizing me up, beckoning me with her hand to approach her.

"What?" I said. "I am in a hurry."

"What do you mean?" she said.

"Why are you waving me over to you?"

270

"I am not waving you over to me. What type of woman do you think I am?"

"The back of your hand is facing me," I pointed out, "and you are moving it towards me then towards yourself rapidly. What other meaning does that gesture have?"

"For your information," she said haughtily, "it is hot out."

"I know."

"I am fanning myself to cool off," she said.

"Oh," I said, pausing for a moment. "Don't you know that you make yourself hotter when you fan yourself."

"What are you, stupid?" she said.

"I mean that the activity involved in fanning yourself actually makes you hotter regardless of the breeze you create. Haven't you ever heard of that?"

"You are a smart city boy. If you are such a smart city boy, why do I feel cooler?"

"I am talking overall."

"Well I'm not. My hand might be getting hotter but my face is getting cooler."

"Then," I explained, "overall you end up being the same as before."

"My face is more important than my hand!" she said, growing agitated.

"I am just saying it doesn't matter."

"If someone gave you a choice as to whether you wanted yer hand chopped off or yer face, you wouldn't care one way or the other?"

"You've got a point," I said. "Sorry I brought it up."

"Where you heading, city boy?"

"The lake."

"Which one?"

"I don't know."

"There is only one."

"I guess I'm going to that one, aren't I."

"You just gave the nozzle a shake after you got done filling up yer car," she pointed out. "What's that all about?"

"I don't know. My oppressive mother. Is that what you are thinking?"

"She beat you for the yellow pee-pee spots in yer underwear. I bet you feel as shameful as a sodomite every time you have to put gas in yer car."

"I've really enjoyed our time together," I said as I hurried to the driver's side. "Happy fanning."

"I'm just freezing out here," she said flatly, her hand going back and forth in front of her face, watching me carefully as I drove off.

ᔕᔓ

I bounced down the dirt road that led to Zanz's cabin. Night was falling. I switched on the headlights, but with the sudden illumination I had to slam on the brakes as I saw Brady Mae come running at my car. I stuck my head out the window.

"Brady Mae, what's wrong?" I shouted. "Where are you going?"

"Toby, she is going to kill him!" Brady Mae screamed, running past my car and down the dirt path. I considered going to get her but decided to get to the cabin to see what was going on. As I pulled up alongside it I could hear the incredible struggle, the different sounds associated with the destruction of different materials rang out through the air in symphony. The shrill shattering of glass, the mid-range pitch of ceramic and tile crashing throughout, the low percussive boom of wood and timber cracking, two voices shouting at each other. A chair came flying out of one of the side windows along with a lamp and a suitcase that ejected, in mid-flight, all sorts of defenestrated, random clothes. The destruction rumbled, sizzled, sawed, crashed, and crumbled, each sound trying to overtake the other, metal on glass, metal on metal, wood on metal, wood on glass, everything pulverized into a pile of unrecognizable raw materials. No more records, no more electronics, no more picture frames, no more dishware, mugs. The contents of the house were now reduced to its source materials—copper and tin, glass and plaster, plastics and polystyrenes.

I walked into the house and had to duck as a brick went sailing through the air. It lodged itself in the wall. The place was destroyed. There was a cloud of plaster running through the house and the stench of some electrical burning. When I got back to the kitchen I saw them wrestling on the ground. Baron and his ex-wife, Three-a-Day Ray.

"I told you I'd find you!" she screamed. "Now I am going to kill you."

"You bitch," Baron said. "I should've never gotten you those karate lessons!"

She had her one arm gripped around his neck. Baron was in danger of passing out or just a general heart attack. His face was purple. I ran and got my arms around Ray, trying to remove her.

272

"You ruined my life!" she yelled.

"Toby," Baron said. "I want you to remember this scene any time you have the notion of getting married!"

"Come on Ray," I said. "You can't kill him."

"The hell I can't," she raved, letting him go and then turning on me. She grabbed me by the throat. "I can kill him and I can kill you too if you get in my way. Nothing personal." She wrestled me to the ground. Now I was on bottom, with Raylene on top of me and Baron pulling at her. She let me go and turned back on her husband. I rolled into a pile of pots and pans and broken ceramic.

"You tell me how many!" she shouted. "You tell me how many women? How many broken nights? How many lies? How many broken promises? You owe me. Confess before you die!"

"All of them!" Baron shouted. "I had them all." I ran and started to peel her off her husband again.

"Look," I told them both. "This is not the time. We have to get the hell out of here! Jonas doesn't just have two men with him. He has fifty men with him. They are in the area. I don't know how long it will take them to find this place." Ray let go of Baron and started to attack me again. Baron got up and jumped on his wife's back.

"One thing at a time, Toby," Baron said as he grabbed a hold of Ray's hair.

"Did you hear me?" I said. "Fifty men!"

"Fifty men?" Ray screamed. "I am going to fuck them all! All fifty. HAVE A GO, BOYS! You can watch. See how you like it you lying, cheating, abusive..."

"Baron get her off me!" I wheezed. He pulled her pink bathrobe off. Ray sunk her teeth into my arm. I screamed murder. Baron threw the bathrobe aside and began prying his loving wife off me.

Finally we got her to the ground. Both of us had her pinned there. She looked back and forth at both of us calmly, as if she wondered why we would be so rude to have her lying on the ground in the cabin. She was, after all, a guest.

"If we let you up, do you promise not to kill us?" I asked.

"Yes," she said.

"Are you lying Ray?" asked Baron.

"Yes."

"We can't sit like this all day," I said. "Don't you understand. We have to get the hell out of here right now!"

"Why did you leave me?" asked Ray.

"Because I needed some peace and quiet."

"Didn't work out so well, did it?"

"Let's just get out of here," I said. "I promise that once we are out of this place, if you still want to kill him Ray, I won't stand in your way."

We let her up off the ground. I stood in between her and Baron, who was holding his back and panting like a dying animal. He staggered off to find his fedora while Ray picked up her pink bathrobe, shook the debris out of it and put it back on.

"Raylene," I said. "You go wait on the porch." She scowled at me and walked out of the room. I went to find Baron. He was picking through a pile of broken glass. he pulled his eyeglasses out from the bottom of this pile. He found his crumpled fedora, punched it into its proper shape and put it on his head.

"I don't know what I am going to do about this mess," said Baron.

"When all of this is settled I'll help you come back and clean it," I said. We walked into the main room. Ray was standing in the middle of it. I had never seen a look on anybody's face like the one I saw on that woman's at that moment. It was pasty and beleaguered, a rich discomposure. It was a look that suggested for once in her life she had no idea what to do, what to say, or how to proceed in any fashion.

"Would you two please join me out on the front porch," she said calmly to Baron and I. "This is something we are going to have to deal with together in order to balance the odds a little bit." With careful step Baron and I walked to the front porch. Raylene followed.

# CHAPTER 26

In certain dangerous situations the human mind, faced with assured destruction, still to its credit may very well run through a list of absurd possibilities, slim hopes, mad attempts and unlikely solutions to keep its frail vessel from finally entering into that permanent, irreversible, no refunds or exchanges, can't-go-out-the-way-you-came-in, thanatological, rather long-lasting mystery that we would be glad to let someone else take the credit for solving, condition known as death. Such was the power of my own basic, instinctive survival mode that in the blood boiling, spine chilling seconds before we were all brutally murdered I had come up with an absolutely perfect plan of escape that consisted of turning myself into dust, coaxing a mighty wind to come racing through the trees, at which time I would ride the tempestuous air current up over the mountains, gently rain my sediment down into the parking lot of a warm saloon, put myself back into my recognizable human form, walk into said saloon, order a beer and ask the prettiest cowgirl in the place to join me out on the dance floor. Sounds easy, doesn't it? But for whatever reason, I remained exactly where I was.

Baron, Raylene and I stood looking out from the front porch at the sea of faces spread before us in the clearing. These faces completely obstructed everything in the immediate area—my car, the Fleetwood Brougham— everything except the outer rim of forest and the old bus that had somehow found its way up through the woods to its objective. The bus was parked broadside at the far end of the clearing. In the back, through a grimy window, I could see Brady Mae's face staring out at us with crumbling despair, her features sunken, quivering, defeated. Just behind her, in the dark, murky interior of the old jalopy, surrounding male shadows walled off any possible escape route. We watched each other for the briefest of eternities, before she was pulled away from the window, trapped in the grip of a hopeless farewell, not knowing who or what to believe now.

The congregation had come prepared. Lining the outer perimeter of glassy, zoned-out men were half a dozen stakes of timber. Atop each of these a magnificent fire blazed, giving the state of affairs a ritualistic, primitive, sacrosanct atmosphere. Some of the men were holding video cameras, for posterity's sake. At the center of it all was Jonas--leader of the Gilded Dawn. He was cloaked in a bold, crimson robe. His hands were held outstretched, palms up, as if he balanced the whole grand firmament of heaven between them. Around us all the blank yet sinister faces, still though they were, danced in the flames of the tall torches.

"The gang is all here," Baron murmured.

"ABRAXAS, KING OF ALL HISTORY," Jonas bellowed, "KING OF ALL WHO RULE AND WHO HAVE EVER RULED, LET IT BE WITNESSED BY YOUR AND FROM YOUR INFINITE POWER THAT YOUR GREAT SERVANT DID GO FORTH, IN ALL-KNOWING GLORY TO FIND THE INFIDEL TRAITORS, MARK THEM IN THEIR INIQUITY, RETRIEVE TRIUMPHANTLY THE SACRED 'WET BRAIN', AND LASTLY DID CONSECRATE THESE IMPENDING MOMENTS WITH HIS LOYAL FOLLOWING TO WIT, DID RAISE UP IN GLORIOUS HONOR AND FROM WHICH FUTURE DISCIPLES WILL OBSERVE AND CELEBRATE."

Father Jonas moved towards the porch, away from the center of his disciples, but still the collective attention remained focused on him, grimly, as he stood in front of us and raised an accusing and disdainful finger at Baron's forehead.

"DID YOU REALLY THINK YOU COULD GET AWAY? DID YOU THINK YOU COULD ESCAPE THE SCOPE OF THE ALMIGHTY ABRAXAS, WHO HAS SEEN FIT TO GRANT ME A SMALL PORTION OF HIS ALMIGHTY WISDOM TO LEAD ME TO YOUR WICKED SINFULNESS, YOUR CRIME OF TRYING TO STEAL MY WIFE AND SOIL HER FOREVERMORE IN THE EYES OF THE CONGREGATION. YOU HAVE BEEN THWARTED, EVIL ONE."

"Can we talk about this in a logical manner?" Baron offered.

"NEVER!" thundered the reply. "THAT YOU WOULD THINK, WICKED ONE, YOU COULD JUST ELUDE AND DELUDE OUR PROPHECY, IN YOUR LOWLY SCRAMBLING, TRYING VAINLY

TO OUTWIT THE GREAT MASTER ABRAXAS'S ASTRAL OMNISCIENCE, HIS WRATH, HIS POWER AND HIS WISDOM. THAT YOU THOUGHT YOU COULD THIEVE WHAT WAS NOT RIGHTLY YOURS. SHAME!"

"There has to be an intelligent way to settle all of this?" Baron proposed quietly.

"IMPOSSIBLE," bellowed Jonas. "THE PROPHECY HAS SAID THAT THERE WOULD BE A BETRAYAL AND THERE WAS," Jonas continued. "THE PROPHECY SAID THAT I WOULD FIND YOU AND SMITE YOU. WELL CONSIDER YOURSELF SMOTE. THEN THE PROPHECY SAYS THAT YOU WILL UNDERGO A PURIFICATION THROUGH FIRE. AS GOOD AS DONE. THIS IS ALL WHAT IS GOING TO BE AND IT CANNOT BE OTHERWISE."

Nobody said anything. We simply stood, us three prisoners, still as a grave, on the small porch. Verbal resistance to this man's unhinged ranting would not help us in the least. It would only infuriate him and furthermore we would have to listen to more of his self-righteous harangue, already a properly torturous experience. He was dangerously worked up, and given that he was in possession of madness and a small army we all decided to submit.

"SILENCE!" he shouted, even though there was nobody speaking. He paced crescent shaped patterns in front of us, kicking up a dusty nimbus around himself, his arms stretched to their breaking point. "HOW DARE YOU THINK THAT YOU COULD OUTFOX THE MIGHTY ABRAXAS. HOW DARE YOU TRY TO ROB ME OF A SMALL PIECE OF MY CONGREGATION, MY PRECIOUS BRADY MAE AND EXPECT HER TO FALL FOR YOUR DECEPTION. HOW DARE YOU TRY TO MEDDLE WITH MY AUTHORITY. HOW DARE YOU ATTEMPT TO SOIL AND PERVERT OUR SACRED BELIEF SYSTEM. HOW DARE YOU...(at this point I am going to modify his tirade, or interpret, by filling in what I strongly believed Jonas was actually trying to say to Baron.) "...HOW DARE YOU USE SENSIBLE JUDGMENT, BRAZENLY RESIST OUR KIDNAPPING AND ATTEMPTED MURDER OF YOU. HOW DARE YOU ACT CLEVERLY, ENGAGE IN FREE THINKING. HOW DARE YOU FAIL TO SUBMIT BLINDLY, TO NOT TAKE ME SERIOUSLY, TO MAKE ME LOOK STUPID, TO HELP AN OPPRESSED YOUNG WOMAN GAIN HER INDEPENDENCE. HOW DARE YOU FUCK

WITH MY PLANNED SPONTANEITY, THE CONTROL OF MY ENVIRONMENT OVER ALL OF THESE FEEBLE-MINDED VICTIMS. HOW DARE YOU QUESTION MY ARBITRARY AUTHORITY. HOW DARE YOU THINK YOURSELF WORTHY OF YOUR OWN OPINION. HOW DARE YOU CONVINCE MY IMPRESSIONABLE, UNDERAGE AND ILLEGAL BRIDE THAT I AM A TERRIBLE FAKE AND HAVE WHAT BOILS DOWN TO A HAZARDOUS CASE OF LOW SELF-ESTEEM. HOW DARE YOU IMPLY THAT I AM A SELF-SERVING, EGOTISTICAL, HUMAN NIGHTMARE WHO MANIPULATES SENSITIVE PEOPLE'S FEAR AND SELF-DOUBT FOR PERSONAL GAIN BECAUSE I HAVE TROUBLE GETTING AN ERECTION AND HAVE REPRESSED FEELINGS OF HOMOSEXUALITY. (And it is here that I return to his literal rant) IT IS BECAUSE OF ALL OF THESE HORRENDOUS CRIMES YOU HAVE PERPETRATED, FOR THIS HIGH TREASON AGAINST THE MIGHTY ABRAXAS AND HIS HUMBLE SERVANTS THAT YOU WILL DIE A DEATH MOST PAINFUL, YET HIGHLY NECESSARY TO PURGE YOU OF YOUR OWN ATROCIOUS AND MONSTROUSLY DEGENERATE SIN."
Jonas dropped his arms and approached us. The crowd of men behind him slowly started to spread, closing in on the porch, ready to engulf.

"You are overlooking one little thing," Baron bartered sharply. "Your prized possession, your hierophant, your sacred object, your Wet Brain--is not here."

"But I trust you know where it is," said Jonas. "And he knows where it is." He pointed to me. "That is all that counts."

Jonas stepped back a bit and the crowd moved with him, a ripple effect outward. He watched Baron in silent calculation as the flames danced at the edge of the forest and the three or so men holding video cameras dipped and swayed around their high priest, looking for just the right angle to properly convey his magnificence, his messianic capabilities, the powerful essence that had endeared him to all of the rest of these men. After some consideration Jonas apparently made up his mind. He furtively motioned for his cameramen to position themselves equidistant around him, one on his left profile, the other on his right, the third in the middle, all cameras pointed up at him from a crouched position. When he was satisfied with all the angles he raised his hands again and addressed his congregation, his face tight, his eyes bulging.

"MEN," Jonas cried. "THE GREAT TIME IS UPON US. WE HAVE

COME SO FAR BUT OUR TASK IS NOT COMPLETE. SEIZE THE INFIDELS AND BRING THEM ON THE BUS!"

The mob screamed, knocking together in exaltation.

"GO FORTH, MY CHILDREN!" Jonas commanded and with a mighty roar the crowd charged at us. We were grabbed and dragged towards the old bus. Baron's fedora was knocked off. His glasses knocked crooked on his face. Ray fought as hard as she could with her one good arm. We were pulled onto the bus. Our hands and feet were taped together. Our mouths were taped shut. Baron and I were thrown in the back, stuffed behind the last seat and driven away. Ray's one good hand was incorporated into the taping of her two feet, folding her in half. She was balled up and rolled into the space across from us.

The bus ride was mostly a silent one. The gang of men sitting in the seats appeared to be lost in deep meditation. There was a low hum, like a Gregorian chant, but that was it. Baron and Ray stared at each other in silent accusation, tears in their eyes along with anger, hatred, love. If they could've yelled at each other through their noses they would've.

After about twenty minutes the bus stopped. Jonas, in his crimson robe, came to the back and announced that one of us was not needed. With that, he picked up Raylene, opened the emergency back door and rolled her down into the road. As the bus started up again I watched through the window as Ray jerked herself free, picked up a sizable rock and hurled it at the back window, cracking it into a spider web pattern that ran the length of the panel. The bus kept going, the powers-that-be not concerned with a wretched one-armed spinster swallowed up in the darkness.

We drove through the night. I wondered what they were going to do to us. Were we heading, at that moment, all the way back to California? Even though, in the position we were in, all fears and possibilities being valid, the only reason I knew we weren't was because by all accounts Jonas and the Gilded Dawn were missing one thing. The Wet Brain. It was far off in the woods, buried next to the Flint River. Baron and I would be tortured until we confessed to its location. This was something I looked forward to, because by the time I freely gave them the information they needed Zanz would have retrieved it. It was the only source of hope.

The air in the bus was somehow familiar. There was a sour, festering quality to it. If air could've been furry, then this air was just that. I had been in the midst of this stale odor before. Not the bus. the physical surroundings had been different. But the air had been of the same dead stillness.

Then I saw him. He was sitting a few seats up. I hadn't recognized him at first, since most of the men were physically similar to him. What made him stand out was that he was the only person on the bus who was studying me. His was a look of silent disappointment. A terrible miscalculation. Everyone else faced forward. At that point it all became very clear. It was Zephyr, the guy who had brought me to his art community. Then it suddenly fell into place. A fraternity of rural establishments. We weren't going to California. We were going back to the compound in the woods outside of Atlanta. The one I had been brought to in order to meet Father Jeremiah.

Father Jonas. Father Jeremiah. The leaders of separate chapters of the Gilded Dawn. They looked the same. Spoke the same. They had the same surface frailties. Same bombast. Two fanatics operating in the iron grip of extreme isolation. It was all so simple, and not too weird considering the devouring indulgence of historically precarious societies. Yahweh Cult. Solar Temple. Heaven's Gate. Unarius Society. The parade of hysterical mythos. Sacred perspiration, cowboy hats, white jumpsuits, comet-space ships, alien welcome centers, arson, castration and cyanide. When I thought about it, the Gilded Dawn had pretty far to go before things started to get really weird.

Half an hour later I caught sight of the dilapidated compound at the end of the long dirt driveway, watching it grow larger through the dirty windows of the bus as we approached it. The bus went around to the back of the compound. Off to the left it looked like a covered pavilion was being erected for some formal get-together. I figured I would not be welcome at the festivities this time around. I was no fountainhead.

They would not be happy to see me, was all I could think of. Father Jeremiah was standing out in front of the bus with ten or so of his followers, a grim look on his face. Behind him there was an open set of cellar doors and beyond that a stone stairway leading to a basement.

No, they would not be happy to see me.

# CHAPTER 27

Six years of life as a bartender. I had spent the last six years plying the trade, plying an insensate life, plying people with heavy drink. Plying. Six years. Six years and now this, lying, no longer plying, lying in some godforsaken concrete room underneath the Gilded Dawn compound. So this is what gurgled below the harmless facade of Jeremiah's art colony. This was where Jonas knew he would be safe, where he would be provided asylum--a different chapter of the same, sickly fraternity. A manifold, multiform, motley organism.

Baron and I were moved off the bus last, after the rest of the drones had marched down and out. I had seen Brady Mae for an instant, her mouth taped shut, her eyes big with fear. Then it was our turn. Jonas commanded two of his lackeys to cut the tape from our feet and our mouths, although our hands were still bound. He told us we better be quiet and then, looking around at the vast spread of emptiness outside the bus, shrugged and said we could scream our heads off if we wanted to. Not wanting to give him the satisfaction, we remained quiet.

Baron and I were taken down a stairway and into a kind of bomb/tornado shelter. There were a few dirty mattresses laid out on the ground. A pile of old clothes. A naked light bulb hung from the center of the ceiling. The walls had all sorts of crazed ranting scrawled on it. Abraxas this and Abraxas that. There was a portable lavatory in the corner that smelled as if it had served its purpose well. Baron and I were thrown to the ground, each landing on a dirty mattress. It was unclear whether we were supposed to land on the mattress or whether it was just a lucky accident. Jeremiah and Jonas were standing over us.

"Well," said Jeremiah to Baron. "I see we have the Great Traitor here with us today. It is nice to meet you. I have heard so much about you."

"I will try," said Baron as he lay there on the floor, "depending on what you've heard about me, do my best to either live up to or downplay the reputation."

Jeremiah turned to me. "And you? What a small world. Did you know Jonas that we have a pervert in our midst?" Jonas shook his head as he stared at me. "A filthy monster. He couldn't wait to expend himself on our sacred ground." Jeremiah knelt down, "but don't worry. We are going to put you on the path to righteousness." His expression grew dark. "After it's all over you'll feel like a new man."

"How the hell did you find that cabin?" I said to Jonas.

"This is not a question that a superior being can properly answer," he said. "Why don't you ask me how I know my own name?"

"It was the woman at the gas station, wasn't it?" I said.

"I did have a chat with her," Jonas said. "She gave a rough description and a rough direction. It was more than enough. I had already seen you with my mind. I followed your being. It was a question of mere minutes. I can go into my mind and see anywhere."

"Impressive," I said. "Especially when you stick your head up your ass and brag about the view."

"Save your strength," Jonas told me, then turned to Baron. "But for now we need Mr. Corley for a little question-and-answer session. There is still a very important item that needs to be retrieved. If you will be so kind as to accompany us." His lackeys picked Baron back up and marched out of the room through a metal door that I had not noticed until it had been used.

"Don't go away now," Jeremiah had warned me with a wicked smile. The door slammed shut.

I lay there for what felt like an eternity.

I always believed I would have some kind of interaction with a bona fide serial killer. Who knew that my brush with danger would actually be from a cult leader, some self-appointed messiah in a burgeoning sect for the new millennium. I didn't see it coming. Jonas was no Monster of Venice. He was no Rostov Ripper. No Butcher of Kingsbury Run was he. A small, nervous man who believed in the destruction of the world. Harmless and dangerous all rolled into one.

Six years as a bartender. As I lay there in the dim light I couldn't get that out of my head. Why had I been wasting myself? All the other things

I could've possibly been doing (wasting myself in other ways). If I knew I was going to die tonight I would not have spent the last six years as a bartender. I would've run for president, seized control of Hugh Hefner's castle, invented immortality.

Six years leading up to this. But what did six years mean? With all the time on my hands, lying there on that filthy mattress, I did some calculations. I had been a bartender for two thousand, one hundred and ninety days. I had worked nine hundred and thirty shifts. I had cut approximately nine thousand, three hundred sixty limes. I had courteously lit approximately fourteen thousand cigarettes. I had poured approximately thirty thousand martinis. I had drunk (at least) approximately three thousand, seven hundred and forty-four shots of peach brandy (the accuracy of that number subject to blackouts, of course). I had swiped approximately twenty one thousand five hundred credit cards. I had mopped the floor about seven or eight times. It was difficult to come to this mad realization, that a whole life, and what's worse—mine, was just an accumulation of a handful of repetitive actions. There was no deeper meaning. I was a machine with the capacity to worry.

I heard something scurry in the darkness.

In the trap of frustrating hindsight I found myself considering anything that could've been done differently on my part, knowing or at least strongly believing that I hadn't singlehandedly orchestrated our demise. I should have known that this Father Jonas would have more men with him. There was too much for him to lose. This, after all, is his shining moment. The time of the 'Great Arrival'. His one chance to actualize his self-constructed and tightly manipulated prophecy. It was his chance to make a God of himself.

I had only witnessed the tip of the iceberg in New York, and had sunk myself like the Titanic. There were circumstances, both observable and unseen. How could I have known? I was unaware of the cause and effect. Who knows what is happening just below any surface—what type of situation we may fail to understand due to the limits of our perception. It is like quicksand to a person who has never seen it and therefore could easily fail to recognize quicksand. How do you explain why you fell, ass over teakettle, into a big stinking thing of quicksand? How do you explain, as it engulfs you and you sink to your death, how it could've been avoided? All I'm trying to say is that I had fallen into a quicksand-type situation, plain and simple. That is all I'm trying to say. All I'm trying to say is that sometimes natural forces are outside one's ability to predict. That is all I'm trying to say.

I fell into a disturbed sleep, only to be awoken by the opening of the metal door at the end of the room. Baron was brought in and thrown onto a nearby mattress. The door closed. Baron was coughing and moaning.

"Baron," I said. "What did they do to you?"

"Torture," he wheezed.

I should have known. Stupid question. Did I think they would parade him around in appreciation, give him a back rub, feed him peeled grapes. I must say that while he was gone I had clung to the slim hope that he was in serious negotiation with the leaders of this place--Jonas and Jeremiah--and due to his wisdom and cunning, had worked everything out. I imagined that Baron would return triumphantly to this dark room that smelled of accumulated shit-rot and declare that he, myself and Brady Mae now had a full release, and the cult leaders even threw in the old Fleetwood Brougham to send us on our way, as well as some nice pastoral renderings by a young member of the congregation with artistic promise in such areas. All we would have to provide in exchange would be: one rhesus monkey, one Thompson submachine gun with silencer, a pledge of absolute secrecy concerning what Baron and I had seen, half a pound of high grade psilocybin mushrooms, a video surveillance and recording system for protection against government infiltration, and a promise to never travel west of Dodge City, Kansas ever again for the rest of our natural born life. But no. In Baron's utterance of that one word I knew that things weren't good. I knew they would only get worse. Torture.

"The other night I had a thought," Baron murmured. "It wasn't a dream. I was awake, but even at that time of night, a person awake will have thoughts like dreams. Brady Mae was sleeping next to me. Everything was quiet. I had never been so happy. In this thought I saw myself acting out every aspect of my existence up until this point, although I was doing it alone, out in a nameless stretch of arid land. Everything. Being born, crawling, walking, running, eating, drinking, lying down, sitting in class, going to work, playing sports, screwing. Nothing but me. Everything reduced to simple gestures and postures. I was struck by the meaninglessness. It hit me that our lives are our surroundings. The people we find value in. The scenery and the circumstance. Without that, it is a meaningless dance."

"Save your strength, Baron." I said. "We are going to need it to get out of here."

"I am not getting out of here," he said. "My only request is that they let you and Brady Mae go. I'm not too optimistic. We really don't have a shot at this point. At least, I don't. I'm resigned to it. But I want them to let you go."

"I am not going to leave this place with you here," I said.

"Yes you will!" Baron demanded. "It is not your decision."

"Is it too late to try and join the Gilded Dawn?" I suggested, in the darkness, a prisoner. "Let's try to convince them that we've seen the light." Baron produced a coughing laugh. "We could have all the privileges and rights afforded to these people," I continued. "We would become The Devoted. We could have the pleasure of one alcoholic beverage a month, an extra half hour of sleep a week, limited carnal relations with a wife of the leader's choosing, we could have pride in intense physical and mental labor and in the event of an unexpected mass suicide we could have the option of going first."

"It hurts to laugh like this," Baron said, continuing to cough his mirth out.

The metal door at the end of the room was jerked open and Jonas's lackeys went back to Baron. They got him up off the mattress and dragged him back out of the room.

"No," I screamed. "You sons of bitches don't hurt him. Take me out there."

"We'll get to you," one of the men promised before shutting the door.

Again, I lay there for what felt like an eternity.

We had to do something for ourselves. Nobody, not Zanz, not Skid Row Paul, nobody would ever find us out here. There were no clues. No trail to follow. Time was running out. I thought about Brady Mae. She had been kept separated from us during the bus ride and now she was being held as a traitor herself, in some part of this compound, probably being pounded with the old beliefs, the world she had known. There was the distinct potential for her mind to fall into numb submission again. How easy would it be for Jonas to convince her that he actually was an all-powerful God? He had, after all, found her, and not even where he was supposed to find her. It was the Wet Brain, I thought. His prophecy could not come together until he had the Wet Brain. It was critical that Jonas never get his hands on it if Brady Mae was going to have a future as a reasonable woman. I knew that, when I talked to her at the cabin, she was in control of her mind, that she was a real person. Baron had made her strong. She loved him of her own freewill. That would save her.

After hours of being alone, the metal door opened and again Baron was thrown onto his mattress. The metal door banged shut. He was crying out in pain. It took him awhile to quiet down.

"These bastards won't quit," he gasped. "They are getting desperate. They want that head in the bell jar."

"Baron, I know Zanz has it. Let them take me out of this room so I can get in touch with him. I'll fix this whole thing."

"They want to have their fun. I am not going to tell them shit." He pointed his mouth toward the ceiling. "DO YOU HEAR ME? I'M NOT GOING TO TELL YOU ANYTHING!" He was immediately exhausted from the energy involved in this declaration.

"Baron, what the hell? You know what I mean? What the hell? That is all I am really trying to get at. It is the general, overriding question that contains under its umbrella all the other smaller questions. I could go on about pondering existence versus essence, empiricism versus rationalism, the interplay of opposites, deconstructionism, categorical imperatives and all that crap, but right now I'm going for the big question. The one that has all that other stuff contained in its simple mystery. What the hell Baron? I repeat WHAT...THE...HELL?"

"It is not always easy," he said, breathing heavily. "We have certain understandings. There are lines that are not crossed. Remember Toby, that idealism is just something that aggravates a person while they are acting out what will inevitably be the only thing they will ever have. Right now we can't have any idealism. Right now it is pure survival. I like you Toby. You are one of the good ones. I am going to get you out of here. I just need a little imagination. Sometimes imagination is good for showing us what we don't know. But sometimes the imagination is very good at showing us things that we have completely overlooked. There is something I am overlooking right now."

"I need to talk to Zanz," I insisted. "It is the only way."

"Zanz," Baron reflected. "That is a good man right there. I would do anything for him."

"He would do anything for you."

"I remember when we dug that body up," he mused.

"What?" I said.

"That is why Zanz believed he owed me a favor," Baron said. "It ate him up inside to know that this man known as Munchik had assaulted Zanz's friend, beaten her bad, and he got away with it."

"Ah yes," I said. "Evelyn Goss. I always suspected Zanz might've killed Munchik himself."

"No," Baron said. "By the time Zanz had caught up to him he was already dead. But Zanz wanted the world to know. He wanted it on history's record exactly what happened. So he got me to help him. It was a warm night. We scaled the wall of the cemetery. Found the fresh earth where Munchik was buried. Dug for a few hours. Luckily he wasn't entombed in some kind of sealed concrete. Nobody was going to spend the extra money for something like that on a piece of shit like Munchik. We pried open his coffin. Filthy looking man, in life and in death. You could tell from the expression on his dead face that Hell had been the last thing he'd seen in this life, and the first thing he'd seen in the next one. We lopped his hand off with an axe and planted his fingerprints."

"That is disgusting," I said.

"But effective," he said. He adjusted himself on the mattress and I heard him give a little wince.

"Are you holding up over there?" I asked.

"Don't worry about me."

"How do you make it through the torture?" I asked.

"I play pinball," he said.

"What? How?"

"In my head. It has always helped in disagreeable situations. I played pinball in my head for the first six months of my third marriage."

"I always thought it was a stupid, primitive game," I said.

"Oh no," Baron said. "Beautiful and simple. There is an art to it. So much going on and all you have to combat it are two buttons that work the flipper paddles. The odds are against you. That is what is so compelling about the game. I pull the knob with the coiled spring and the little ball goes launching out."

"Then what happens?"

"The first one always goes directly into the gutter, down into the innards of the machine. That's just life. But I launch another ball into the game. The lights glitter, the music plays, the ball whizzes and arcs and caroms through all of the little traps, holes, secret passageways. It disappears through a little door. A futuristic impulse sound erupts. The ball comes out from a totally different part of the board. I hone my game. The flipper paddles work independently of one another. Sometimes

287

the compulsion is to trigger them together, but this is wasted energy. Sometimes the compulsion is to work the flipper paddles when the ball is nowhere near them, but then you can't appreciate the part of the game you have no control over. The magic results of chance. There is timing involved and where there is timing there is also patience. I win another ball and the machine goes into a great mechanical seizure. Waiting. Timing. Know when *not* to do anything. These are all important lessons. Of course when the time is right...BAM, knock that little metal sucker as hard as you can. Playing pinball is like being the Catcher in the Rye. Salinger should've named his book 'The Happy Idiot at the End of the Pinball Machine'."

Baron's hypothetical pinball game was interrupted by the metal door again. The lackeys dragged him out. His muffled howl from the other side of the door became less and less audible and finally dwindled into silence.

Again, an eternity passed.

# CHAPTER 28

If Zanz had reported the kidnapping of Baron and I, the police were sure to be skeptical, especially since the clock was running. I didn't know how long I had been lying in that murky, tenebrous dungeon, but it felt like years. I hadn't had a drink of water or food since I had been down there. My skin itched like mad.

If I had been down in this hole for forty-eight hours then the chances I would ever be found alive were grim. The odds decrease exponentially after the first forty-eight hours. The emotionless clerk at the police station would be telling Zanz that we were as good as dead. She would then tell him not to abandon hope, but that he shouldn't rely on it either. Of course we could be part of that slim category of survivors, but let's not kid ourselves, eh. However miracles can happen, but the police clerk would tell Zanz that she didn't have the phone numbers of any saints handy. She would advise him to keep his fingers crossed, and while his fingers were crossed it wouldn't be a bad idea to look into funeral arrangements.

I also considered the possibility of a police detective in the missing persons unit running Baron's name through a computer and realizing that one of Zanz's missing persons was himself wanted in connection with some type of fraud, emptying out some poor widow's bank account, bigamy, as well as other lesser charges. They would tell Zanz not to worry because in a sense Baron was already being pursued. The detective would ask Zanz if he had any information leading to Baron's whereabouts, at which time Zanz would explain that it was for this very reason that he had gone to the police in the first place. The detective would give Zanz his number and tell Zanz to get in touch with him if he heard anything more about Baron, which would be a clever reversal of the initial dynamic.

Baron had been dropped back off next to me. The old man had held on for as long as he could, but the Gilded Dawn had broken him. He was simply crazy. He wouldn't answer me any longer or talk reasonably. He would just mentally dawdle and whisper any nonsense that entered his head.

"Did you ever notice how thoughtful trees are, the way they wave goodbye to the wind," he said calmly from his spot over on the mattress.

"Come on Baron," I said. "Keep your head straight. Don't go Wet Brain on me."

"When you eat a squirrel the other squirrels seem to know and are understandably cautious," he said.

"Your name is Baron Corley. It is the twenty-first century. You are in Georgia. You love Brady Mae. We are going to get out of here."

"A flock of witches once performed a palo stick ritual in my garden," Baron murmured. "I was living in Massachusetts. They told me they were going to kill me for the potency of my organs and I've never known witches to lie about such things. I guess I'll just have to wait and see."

"Where were you born Baron? How old are you? Do you believe that love conquers everything? Play pinball, goddamnit. Play pinball for me."

"I once saw the city of Atlantis rise up in the middle of the river behind a house I used to own. A couple of men spoke to me from the rim. Said that some of their houses were suffering water damage. Did I perhaps know a good hammer-and-nail-smith, an all around chappie with a mind for creative repair? I suggested they watch out for harmful mold buildup."

"Sing me your favorite song!" I said to him. "Tell me about Brady Mae. Tell me about the best time of your life. God, tell me...tell me about your first wife. Do you remember? All ass and tits and ass?"

"Did you know," he said lazily, "that the Green Language is also known as the Language of the Birds? I once deciphered it. Interesting to note that all these birds do up in the trees is insult each other all day long." Baron gestured in a complete circle over his head. "It is a terrible thing to have to hear. So much negativity. But they will never tell you when they are going to shit on you. That is all I'm going to say concerning the subject of the so-called Divine Language of the Birds."

I let him go. At this point I just hoped he was beyond pain.

"Have you ever seen the way a crack prostitute kind of hugs herself when she walks down the street? Not when she is tricking. When she is maybe walking from one trick to the other... I have always refused to be led around by the strings that Freud operates over all of mankind from the comfortable quarters of his grave. That being said there is something absolutely thrilling about making love to the barrel of a well-oiled gun."

The metal door opened.

"Please don't take him out again," I said. "He can't handle anymore."

"It is your turn," they said. I was picked up and made to stand. My legs buckled. They caught me and helped me through the metal door. I was taken and dragged down a hallway, up some stairs and dropped into Jeremiah's office. I was shaking and I had to squint from the sunlight. Behind the desk was Jeremiah. Jonas was standing over his shoulder. They were both staring at me. They offered me some water and I drank it gratefully.

"What day is it?" I asked.

"How long do you think you've been down there?" Jonas asked.

"Four days?"

"More like seven hours," Jeremiah said.

"Are you getting desperate?" I asked them.

"What do you mean?"

"You have tried the strong arm approach with Baron and it hasn't worked. I don't think you are any closer to your Wet Brain then when you started. You," I said, pointing at Jonas. "Every day that you are stuck out here is a day that you lose a little more control. Each day that you are stuck out here is a day your carefully planned destiny goes unfulfilled. I think you understand that now is the time for a little compromise. Just between us."

"The stated prophecy says that the Great Traitor can't be sacrificed until we have retrieved Wet Brain," Jonas said.

"You let me make a phone call and I'll get you the Wet Brain. But you will have to let me go. You have to let Baron go. You have to let Brady Mae go."

"You want my wife?" Jonas said.

"Yes. I care about her. I want her to come with us. Then I promise I will have your Wet Brain delivered."

"Out of the question!" Jonas declared.

"Understand that by losing your Hierophant," I said, "your Wet Brain, your interpreter of sacred mysteries, your connection with the mind of Abraxas, and your proclaimed bond with the supernatural, that you are losing the bond you have with the men of your congregation. Right now, moment by moment, hour by hour, your followers are waiting for you to exercise your powerful intuition to find this sacred centerpiece of your whole belief system. I'm sure their confidence is already starting to dwindle. You can't afford to lose your grip." Jonas's face hardened.

"It has been foretold that I am going to return to my compound in the desert with the traitor, my wife and the Wet Brain. This will bring on the arrival of the Master with his floating ship that will take the chosen to the Great Land. The prophecy states this exactly. There is no ambiguity in it. All my wives must come with me. Brady Mae included."

"But you wrote this prophecy, didn't you?"

"Well," Jonas admitted. "Yes."

"You wrote it to suit the conditions of your own greatness, right? If you wrote it you can change it." A look of surprise came over Jonas's face. He began biting his nails in vexation. Jeremiah drummed his fingers on his desk.

"Change it?" Jonas said. "The Great Abraxas will not allow me to change it. It is his word that I have written down."

"So you are saying that *he* can't change his mind?" I said. "He is your All-Powerful Being, an immortal affixed with the vast power to travel through time and space. He can wave his hand and move planets, rain death upon anybody he chooses and he is not even afforded the simple capacity to change his mind? Your Man is afflicted with the limitation of not being able to modify his strategy? A five-year-old can change his mind if he knows it will suit him. Your supreme leader is not equipped with this rudimentary mental capacity?" Jonas looked at me like I had just slapped him hard across the face.

"You better watch how you speak," he warned.

"Come on, we can figure this out," I encouraged. "Damage control is becoming a hobby of mine. Let's hammer this thing out right now. The Great Abraxas, ruler of your people, space traveler, cosmic auteur has exercised his awe-inspiring faculties and restructured his expectations of you. It is like a test to see if you can follow through. Any idiot could see this."

"Don't patronize me!" he yelled. "I have forty men just waiting to carry out my will, which doesn't bode well for you."

"Good luck returning to the desert without your Wet Brain," I said. "That is a long trip. Plenty of time to explain to your followers about how you just couldn't figure why your wisdom failed you. Your whole foretelling goes to pieces. Then your illusion of power will be compromised. You will slowly lose your grip, increase your drug usage, delve deep into moods of extreme paranoia, all the while these young disciples are beginning to form some unsavory opinions of you. All it takes is one with power aspirations to rise up against you. Then they'll cut your head off, stick it in some bell jar and dance around it, have orgies on holidays or whatever it is you do in the name of all that is good and righteous."

"NO!" Jonas shouted nervously, his hand unconsciously shooting up to massage the front of his neck. "They wouldn't do that to me. I'm their leader."

"That is a temporary job. Leaders are meant to be overthrown. Sooner or later they all topple. I don't even want to scare you with historical examples. Nobody rides the gravy train forever. For some people it only takes the wink of an eye. There are probably already plans, talk, murmurings. How long will they wait while you fumble around in the backwoods here? Each day that goes by is a day that your status gets a rung knocked out of it."

"So you are saying that Abraxas has used this as a test for me? Let one of my wives go, have mercy on the traitor, retrieve the Wet Brain?"

"Of course," I said. "You'll be going home triumphant. You had to sacrifice one of your wives. Big deal. To be able to give up something cherished shows strength. This alien deity of yours will be proud to have you as an interstellar representative."

"I don't know about that," Jonas said, nibbling on his lip in cautious deliberation.

"Take a tip from the Big Book," I told him. "Haven't you read the story of Abraham? Ready to sacrifice his only son to please God. In the end God changes his mind. Tells him not to. Thinks better of it. It is the mark of a great mind--malleability, compassion, wisdom. The talent of re-evaluating strategies in the midst of shifting circumstance. Take the leap of faith. God catches you in his hands."

"But I enjoy having all my wives," he said.

"You have plenty of them," I said. "Giving up one won't hurt. When you get back to California you can put forth a campaign of heavy recruitment. You'll be fresh on the heels of a big victory. Your Wet Brain could've been anywhere in the world and you found it and brought it back. Think about it? I'm even impressed you got this far. You found the needle in the haystack. Women will be drawn to you. Membership will soar. You won't even be able to remember what Brady Mae looks like after you are swimming in all that young, impressionable tail."

"But the Great Abraxas would not want me to release any of my women into this wicked world. He needs to be worshipped. He smites those who turn away from him."

"So you are saying that your deity has imposed ego limitations and feelings of inferiority?" I asked. "This is a Grand Being who travels in a space ship and has survived immortality, but he's got low self-esteem?" Jonas looked like I had kicked him in the groin.

"I want you to know how much I would like to kill you right now," he said.

"It is a simple solution," I told him. "You know what you have to do. Let me make the phone call."

He hung his head. Suddenly, his head came up. He had a thoughtful expression. He stood up and actually smiled. It was a light-switch moment, but I couldn't tell if that was a good thing or a bad thing. One thing I knew, it was the only thing. He whispered something to Jeremiah, who nodded.

"Yes," Jonas said. "You call your friend. We'll arrange the trade."

I was amazed I could be so convincing.

"Okay," I said. "Let me have the phone." I dialed Zanz's number. Jonas and Jeremiah looked pleased.

# CHAPTER 29

We were driving away from the compound. I watched it disappear out of sight from the back seat of the Fleetwood Brougham. Jonas was driving. One of his lackeys was sitting next to him up front. Baron and Brady Mae were with each other in the trunk, which I guess was good and bad. Good they were with each other. Bad they were stuck in the trunk. Brady Mae, at least, had to be getting used to it by now. I had seen her briefly when she was brought out of the compound and put in the trunk. She didn't say anything and had kept her eyes to the ground. Jonas had joked that it was kind of him to let Baron and Brady Mae have this quiet time together. The trunk was probably big enough for a conjugal visit, I thought. I was unclear about the details of the trade. Zanz had worked out the particulars with Jonas after I had been removed from Jeremiah's office.

"Your friend Zanz is very stubborn," said Jonas. "I kind of like him. He seems like a real leader. It would be a shame if he gets you all killed." The two men in front of me laughed.

"He is pretty precise when he wants to be," I said.

"I was impressed that he was so prepared," said Jonas. "He is familiar with this area. The town we agreed to meet in is not far. Main Street and Nightingale. I have the instructions."

"You seem pretty confident and relaxed," I told him. "That makes me nervous."

"What... don't you trust me?"

"I just want to make sure you aren't pulling anything deceptive," I insisted. "I mean other than your whole way of life."

"You think you are so clever," he said with a humorless laugh. "You condemn me as cracked and insane and you ridicule my religion and my people. But we are happy while you are miserable. Misery pours out of your lonely body. You hate us because we live with conviction. There is strength and support in our numbers. We live for something bigger than ourselves. You are only comfortable avoiding your decision for God. We trust in the organization. We are guided by a bigger phenomenon, bigger than any one person. Your so-called individualism will turn to dust. The rogue thinkers never make it. They are angered and destroyed by their own skepticism. I take comfort in the fact that you are doomed."

"I see some desperate frauds sitting in front of me," I said to both men up front. "If you really trusted in yourself you wouldn't rely on such heavy manipulation. What are you hiding from out there in your isolated compound? Are you afraid that your carefully constructed demagoguery would crumble under intelligent analysis? You had to script the fulfillment of your own prophecy, for heaven sake. That is a cheap stunt."

"Every school of thought, every religion starts out as heresy," Jonas said. "The chosen are always marginalized. That is their power. They fully realize something far beyond this world and are satisfied to be a part of it. It is the beauty of the secret. The smaller the secret the more valuable it is. You don't understand and you never will. That is your own personal tragedy. Mankind needs to be led. It takes a man to lead mankind, to save him from the perils of his fear and ignorance. To show him a new path to salvation. I am the visionary. It is a rare gift and the only ultimate sin is for me to ignore it."

"I just don't care for disillusionment," I said. "I keep myself open to progress. Every single fundamental truth can be subject to multiple criticism. That is where its strength comes from. If you don't test the integrity you'll never know the breaking point. You discourage this process and your truths become brittle truths, and eventually they will be too weak to even be considered that, and finally you will be left in the rubble of something that should've been condemned long ago."

"You wouldn't know what to do with my power if you had it," he said. "It would destroy you. Even at this point I know you are never going to forget me, to forget the power that I held over you. You will fear me for the rest of your life. You will know that I am just over your shoulder. That I am the man who made you see and feel how deprived of manhood you really are."

"Don't think that you are going to get away with any of this," I said. "When the time comes, the important entities are going to flounce you good for so shamelessly cultivating your own splendor. Honestly, Jonas, if it was there in the first place why would you have to go through so much trouble?"

"It is Father Jonas."

"I just see a Jonas," I replied with a shrug. "I see a Wet Brain."

Jonas turned the car onto a quiet thoroughfare. It was Main Street. I felt as if I had traveled back in time. Small country shops lined either side of the street. The sidewalks were immaculate. The store windows sparkled in the setting sun. People waved to each other, called each other by name. One of them waved to us and we all waved back. I imagined the townsfolk would be talking about what was on the old Ed Sullivan Show the night before. 'Get a load of them June Taylor dancers!' Or the hot new fashions from the Montgomery Ward catalogue. There was a barber shop. There was a toy store. A music store. A candy store. A pet store. A post office. A dental practice. Gus Bradley. Owner, Proprieter. Steven Jacobs, D.D.S.

A little girl was bent down on one knee and tying the shoelace of an old lady. I was instantly fond of the little town due to a secondhand nostalgia I harbored for an era too deep in the past to be tarnished by my own personal idiocies.

We reached the corner of Main Street and Nightingale. There was an antique shop on the left. From the looks of the rest of the town the store's inventory would probably be considered state-of-the-art. Jonas turned left on Nightingale and then swung the old boat into a short alley. The area was quiet. The sun was setting. The alley was deserted. We got out of the car. Jonas went to the back trunk. His lackey kept an eye on me. Jonas swung the trunk lid up. Seconds later Brady Mae appeared. Then Baron was helped out of the trunk. Brady Mae stood off to the side. Baron was pushed to a sitting position on the ground. His sparse hair going in every direction. The old man was still bombed-out looking. He didn't seem to realize what was happening.

"I hope you two had fun in there," Jonas said. He went over to Brady Mae and freed her hands. He then whispered something in her ear. She still wasn't making eye contact with anybody.

"Now," Jonas said to me. "I am going to send you and Brady Mae around the corner. You will walk to Main Street. Brady Mae, you continue across the street. A man will approach you. You are to go with him." Jonas turned to me. "You will let Brady Mae cross the street but you will not follow her. Instead, you will walk into the antique shop, stop at the front counter and talk to the woman there. The woman will ask you to tell her something sweet. You will tell her...chocolate. That is the code. After that she will know what to do. You have five minutes to get back to me with my Wet Brain. Then I let you and Baron go."

"Okay," I said.

"There is just one more thing," Jonas said. He pulled a gas can out of the trunk of the Brougham. He uncapped it and began to douse Baron with gasoline.

"What the hell are you doing?" I cried, rushing towards him. His lackey stepped between us and pushed me back. Jonas was holding a shiny, silver lighter in his hand.

"If you aren't back here in five minutes your friend goes up in flames."

Baron looked around. He was so disoriented that he didn't even notice that he was soaked in gasoline. "The whole space program is just a big Hollywood hoax," he said from his spot on the ground. "Everybody knows that if anyone was dumb enough to try and pass through the inky vellum of space you would be lodged in it like a fly in the ointment."

"Get going," said Jonas.

I took Brady Mae by the hand and walked around the corner towards Main Street. I told Brady Mae not to be afraid. We would be out of this place very soon. She nodded, studying her stride. Even though I had told her to not be afraid, I was troubled. Had Zanz made it? There was no sign of him. We reached the corner. A middle-aged man strolling by us commented on what a lovely day it was. I told Brady Mae that everything was going to be fine. We were going to get her away from her old life and into her new one. I told her that she was going to be happy. Truly happy. She was happy with Baron once and she was going to be happy with him again. I encouraged her to take the final steps. I told her to walk across the street. With that one simple symbolic movement she would have her life back. Her eyes finally met mine. She said that she understood. I watched her look both ways down the empty street and walk across to the other side. She turned and gave me a wave. I waved back and walked into the antique shop.

"Well look at what we have here," the old woman behind the counter said, picking up a magnifying glass and staring at me through it. Her one eye became grotesquely larger than the other. "A stranger."

"I am a customer," I said, wondering if she was studying the pores of my skin with her magnifying glass.

"I know what you want," she said. "It does no good to lie to me. I knew you would be coming here today."

"How did you know that?"

"I am an old woman sitting in an antique shop, get it? A touch crazy but that only adds to my intellectual sensitivity."

"Alright."

"Before we proceed," she said, putting down her handheld lens, satisfied with whatever nuance she had been searching out on my face. "I want you to tell me something sweet."

"Chocolate," I said.

"Behave now," the woman said. "Follow me please." She led me into the back. We walked past old televisions, bicycles, paintings, lanterns, rugs, furniture. A collection of old coke bottles. Wrought Iron everything. A large tome on Operative Gynecology and Modern Drugs was sitting upright in an old rocking chair. Published 1956. A five pound canister of Lightning Red Chief's linnament and Brain Tonic was in the Native American section, next to the dream catchers and the cigar store Indian.

"Got a lot of interesting doo-dads around here," the old woman said, moving deftly through the mess in a septuagenarian shuffle. "That there was dropped off by Ted Reilly. And Old Betsy Grace, after the stroke, never needed her leg brace."

"Yes, of course," I said, moving towards the back of the store and thinking that if we didn't hurry up, Baron was going to go up in flames like a straw man.

"Those drawings of the German city of Hamburg were done by little Jenny Hopkins--the autistic girl who lives on the hill. Beautiful girl. God's child." She motioned elsewhere. "That fishermen's tackle is filled with a veritable pauper's trove. Discarded objects of the highest beauty." The woman stopped at a table. "And this...oh this is something special..."

"Lady," I said. "If we could hurry this up..."

We stopped at a set of black drapes. The old lady leaned forward and drew them apart. I gave a heart-stopping jerk as my eyes caught hold of what had been concealed behind it, as if the face of death had come to rest right in my line of sight. Unmistakable. One of a kind. A human head floating in a murky green liquid—all enclosed in a sealed bell jar. The Hierophant of the Gilded Dawn. Abraxas, the Wet Brain. The skin all over the face was wrinkled and green. Its mouth hung open in ghastly shock. Only a few wisps of hair floated lazily atop its head. Its eye sockets were dark hollows. It was terrible and yet, mesmerizing.

The old woman's hand came to rest on my shoulder. "You get along now," she said, motioning to a hallway beyond. "Use the back door."

Remembering that Baron had just a few minutes before he was set afire, I wrapped my hands around the bell jar and carried it down the back hallway like an infant. The head of the Wet Brain was gently shaking its head in a 'NO' gesture, as it rocked in its murky green current in my arms. I stepped out the back door expecting to see Baron ablaze like a protesting monk. But he was still sitting next to the car, the strong smell of gasoline coming off him in waves, a puddle around him as if he had pissed himself.

Jonas was smiling, turning his cigarette lighter around in his hands. The other man was sitting on the hood. When they saw the Wet Brain their faces melted into a somber form. They stood up straight, came over to me, took it out of my hands and stared at it. Jonas fell to his knees, ran his hand over the glass. Put his forehead against it in quiet consultation.

A car pulled up at the mouth of the alley. Zanz was in the driver's seat of an anonymous sedan he had no doubt borrowed. Brady Mae was in the back.

"Come on," he yelled through the window. "Let's get the hell out of here!"

I got Baron up and trundled with him toward the car. Zanz swung the passenger door open. I pushed Baron into the front seat and got in the back with Brady Mae.

"Phew," said Zanz. "What is that gasoline smell?"

Baron mumbled something.

"They were going to light Baron on fire if I didn't come back with the Wet Brain."

"Sons of bitches," Zanz said, producing his billy club from under the seat. "I should go split their heads open."

"No!" I said. "We're safe. Let's cut our losses and go."

Zanz pulled a quick U-turn then hooked a right on Main Street, cruising along slowly.

"Peggy really came through," Zanz said. "The woman that runs the antique store. I've known her for years. We used to have a weekly game of Mahjong going."

"Where did you meet her?" I asked.

"Prison. Long story."

The exhaustion finally overcame me. I had been through a lot. We had all been through a lot. I didn't know if Baron would ever be the same. Maybe with some therapy and the love of a good woman he could put his mind into a functional shape. I turned to Brady Mae. She was expressionless.

"Now you are safe Brady Mae," I said to the docile girl sitting next to me. I patted her knee. "Now you can be with Baron. He saved you. He saved you from a life you couldn't pull yourself out of. That guy Jonas is a crook. Not what he claims to be. You have to know that."

"Yes," she said. "I am glad to be free. I have a real life now. A happy one."

She said the words but her tone was unmoving and kind of flaccid. I watched as her hand went behind her dress. I assumed it was going back there to scratch an itch. Zanz hooked a left onto a side street. As the car was turning I saw the flash of steel out of the corner of my eye. Brady Mae lunged towards the front seat and sunk the blade of a concealed knife into Baron's neck. Blood shot out everywhere.

"Holy shit!" I yelled, trying to grab Brady Mae's arm. She was a slippery one. She dislodged her knife and lashed out again at Baron, hitting him in the shoulder. Baron screamed, no longer locked in a state of catatonia. He flailed his arms. As he moved blood spattered all over the car. Zanz yanked the steering wheel and hit the brakes. Brady Mae jumped onto the seat in a crouching position to get another shot in. The car swung hard. The rear end whipped around and smacked into a brick wall. I was thrown into the side door and a terrific pain shot through my arm as I felt a smart crunch. The back window blew out and Brady Mae was sucked backwards with the momentum. She rolled out the back window, skipped along the top of the trunk and hit the pavement hard, knocking her out cold.

Steam poured out from the hood of the car. Zanz opened his door. He grabbed Baron and pulled him out of the car and into the road. Baron's neck was still running blood at a dangerous rate. I climbed from the back seat into the front and out the door, my right arm hanging limply at my side. I knew that it was broken. I bent over Baron and used my one good hand to apply pressure to his wound. The sight of the blood and the smell of gasoline were making me sick. It was as if the old man was half man/half machine, with red gasoline pumping through pig iron veins. It would explain how he had survived as long as he had.

"Get him back up to Main Street," Zanz ordered. "Get a doctor."

From around the corner the lackey that had been with Jonas appeared. He stood for a moment, looking at us. Zanz straightened up and grabbed his billy club from out of the car. The lackey produced a knife. They stared at each other for a moment before running headlong at one another.

301

I got Baron up out of the road and started walking him back to Main Street, but it was hard to hold him because I couldn't use my right arm. Zanz and the lackey were squaring off. They took turns taking a couple of empty swipes at the air--the lackey with his knife, Zanz with his billy club. Baron and I kept a safe distance. Once we were on Main Street I looked up and down the road for anybody that could help. There were a few scattered people around but nobody seemed to notice us. The place was too serene for the sight of a blood spattered, dying man.

What I did notice, to my terror, was the old Fleetwood Brougham idling in the middle of the street, about a hundred yards up from us. Baron, wheezing and crumpled, noticed it too.

"Come on Baron," I said. "We have to find a doctor."

He was now staring the car down. I tried to get him to walk but he pushed me away. With the last of his energy, all that he could muster, an adrenaline-charged death march, he staggered out into the middle of the street. I could see it in his face. He wanted to use up the last ounce of his strength. He would never be needing any ever again.

"Baron!" I yelled. "What are you doing?"

Baron stood there, in the middle of the road, staring at the car, facing off. Now some people were noticing. They came out of stores and stood on the sidewalk, too shocked at the scene to do anything. I noticed Peggy the antiques lady hanging herself out of the front door of her shop. Somebody yelled to call Jim Shepard. I imagined that was the small town version of yelling to call the cops.

With one final gesture Baron stuck his hand in his pocket, pulled out a lighter and easily set his gasoline-soaked clothes on fire. He then, with a nameless strength that he should not have been able to harness, went running down the road towards the car. In response, the Fleetwood Brougham's engine roared like a King Lion. The car took off headlong at Baron, who kept his sprint going as hard as he could. The flames, aided by the wind, grew higher and higher around his shoulders and head. Baron had turned himself into a charging fireball.

A wild collective scream ripped through Main Street at the moment of impact. Baron had gone flying over the hood of the car and had crashed himself through the windshield. The inside of the car came alive in an orange dance of licking flames. There were shouts of horror as Baron threw himself around Jonas's body. Instantly it was impossible to make out the difference between the two men. They had been joined in a common conflagration. The car itself swerved and turned sharply, jumping the sidewalk and smashing through the toy store window. Luckily it was closed, although from some kind of kinetic, thermal reaction from the car the entire store came alive. The alarm went off. Lights were flashing. Toy robots and cars started marching and racing around. The big car was lodged in the center of the toy store but its wheels were still spinning, smoke pouring off them, fire raging out of the windows.

"Oh my God!" screamed a woman. Quickly, what few spectators that had been on both sides of the street all regrouped down the middle of the road as they watched the Fleetwood Brougham, like a one-machine tank squadron, finally catch its wheels on something solid. It went lumbering over the checkout counter and crashed through the wall, pushing its way through the middle of the adjacent candy store.

"Oh no!" someone screamed. "Not the candy store."

The inside of the Fleetwood Brougham was a roaring inferno. Baron and Jonas had to be dead, but the car itself, perhaps because something was lodged on the gas pedal, perhaps because it was possessed, continued to lurch forward, a few feet at a time. It was as if the big car was being digested through the innards of the shops.

There was intense heat spewing out of the candy store. A great plume of black smoke now covered the immediate sky of this town that had, moments before, been as pristine and pure as a snowflake. Burnt marshmallows, popcorn and other assorted treats were flying out of the store and into the air, raining down. A few children, keeping a safe distance, went to gather up these singed treats until they were admonished by some of the older townsfolk.

The inside of the car was raging with flames, spitting and spewing, and still the car lumbered on, taking shelves and displays down as it crawled like a dying man. It would momentarily get snagged on some debris in the store, and then it would shoot forward like a comet through the next wall.

The music store was about to be destroyed. It was the last in the row of shops. The car lunged through the wall and a hellish symphony rang out in the sky as pianos, guitars and drums all exploded, twanging and whining. A great backdraft of wind blew the store windows out and the horn section came to life, trumpets, trombones, saxophones, in a great cacophonous screeching. The Fleetwood Brougham's grill came to the final wall. If it broke through this one it would be free to drive down the road.

That was when I noticed Zanz on the ground. I was so taken with the destruction of the row of stores that I didn't realize that the Gilded

Dawn lackey was on top of Zanz, trying to drive his knife into his chest. Zanz was holding him back with the billy club. The car, if it went through the final wall, would crush them both. In a tangle and tussle they rolled back and forth on the sidewalk, mostly oblivious to the unrelenting slog of the car against the brick barrier, separated by just a few feet. The car's grill pushed against the wall and it started to buckle towards the two men, swelling over them like a large pustule on the groaning and swaying infrastructure. It was just like Zanz, the son of a bitch, to openly flout like this, in a dangerous situation, putting himself in the middle of unnecessary risk in order to overcome it.

I ran across the street to help, but I knew I wouldn't make it in time. With a terrific, thundering quake the burning Fleetwood Brougham broke through the last wall, its tires catching on some firm piece of foundation. It rocketed forward just as the cult member, in a move of amazing strength that would doom him, gave Zanz a donkey kick that ejected him out of harm's way, leaving the Gilded Dawn man hopelessly in the remorseless path of the fiery Brougham. Like the sacrificial victim of a medieval monster he was sucked up under the grill and, in a mangled mess, carried across the street to be pulverized into the next immovable object, in this case the brick facade of an old pharmacy, on which was plastered a faded advertisement for the health benefits of skunk oil.

The Fleetwood Brougham finally died, as did, I imagine, the lackey smashed under it. I ran across the street to see if Zanz was alright. He was sitting at the edge of the devastation, shaking some plastery residue from his hair. He would later claim that the kick he had received to his chest that ended up saving his life was his own precise maneuver, a controlled gambit to use his opponent's strength against him.

I walked across the street towards him with a meandering limp, convinced that there was no more looming danger. I should've known. Completely off guard, I wasn't prepared for a fast moving figure coming at me from my left. I felt the sting of the knife in my side as Brady Mae lashed out at me, slicing up the side of my love handle. I pressed my arm to my wound. Blood poured over my hand. Brady Mae was standing in front of me with murder in her eyes. That was when I realized that she had always been under Jonas's spell. He had made her do this and now she was carrying it out faithfully--Kill them All! Leave no Trace of Them! She had the blank stare of a killer. My killer. Right in front of me. I should've known. I now remembered Charles Manson's army of women--Lulu, Katie, Sadie Glutz, Squeaky, Capistrano, Ouisch, Gypsy--I was staring them all in the face, all in this little woman's murderous, frenzied gaze. The pain in my abdomen was getting worse. Brady Mae swung her knife at me again, missing by inches.

I loped down the street. My arm was screaming in pain. A warm circle of blood spreading across my shirt. I searched for safe haven, and that is when I saw a sign for a bar. Somebody had to be in there. I ran up the stairs and into the room but it was empty. Of course it was! Everybody had gone outside to watch the flaming car destroy one whole side of their small town.

Brady Mae was coming up the steps after me. I headed towards a back hallway, staggered into the wall. I pushed myself along the wood paneling of the old hallway, streaking blood from the gash in my side as I stumbled and tumbled away, a fevered glance over my shoulder. My killer was behind me. I was actually going to have one. A killer. A person who sings my doom, satisfied with the subtraction of myself from this absurd world--hungry for it. A human being, not the specter of death, but fused for a moment, in the eyes of the dying, all blade and hunger and empty murder in her eyes. I fell forward again, escaping through a doorway. I found myself in this old bar's storage facility. The bottles stared down at me from the shelves, all lined up like a jury, or a chorus of angels, their liquid souls beckoning me. This might as well be where it all ends, I decided, looking around. Bottles of bourbon, vodka, whiskey, Scotch, brandy, beer, cheap wine. Goodbye Johnnie, goodbye Jim, goodbye Jack, goodbye Jose, goodbye Evan. Thanks for the fun Grand Marnier, you orange devil. Sorry we never got to know each other Pernod. Mr. Beer Keg, do you remember me? The first time we met. You were all foam at first. Don't worry, it was the tap's fault. We did handstands while we drank from you. We had funnel races. A friend's older brother had gotten you for us. And you champagne, you wily bitch. Getting me sick on New Year's Eve. All of you--friends, foes, lynchpins of all the noteworthy events of my whole life. You sly manipulators of all the pivotal moments, the parties, the funerals, the occasions, always present, never letting me down, providing in times of frustration and tedium an alternative of majesty, of soaring magic, of things as you would most wish them in the heart of your biggest dreams. It has been a good run. I would like to thank you all. You've been more than a family to this broken boy, making this bleak reality something special, something beautiful, something to be embraced and celebrated, something to keep the loneliness out, the heartache, putting a sharp and shining edge on this dull frontier. This is where it ends. I turned to the doorway, the only doorway leading out of the room. I could hear Brady Mae's footsteps, audible, tentative yet excited, savoring the moment of knowing that her prey is trapped. I needed a drink. Which one of you... This may be the last time I ever get the chance. Who will it be...

I grabbed the nearest bottle of whatever and slumped down next to the beer keg. I got the cap off and chugged it, waiting for the inevitable. Brady Mae's little body was in the doorway.

Now she moved in for the kill. Think of Tate, Sebring, Folger, Labianca. Close your eyes. Forty-seven stab wounds. I probably wouldn't feel past six or seven. No sense pleading...but

"One last little bird," I begged her.

"What?" she asked, knife in the air.

"One last swallow." I took another long drink.

"You have to die," she said. "It is the will of Father Jonas." The knife came down at me.

From behind her a figure darted into the room, moving with an awesome fluidity, an animal mastery--like a flash and before I knew what happened, Brady Mae's head shot forward and she fell in a small heap to the floor. The knife flew out of her hand and came to rest in the corner. Zanz was standing over me, his billy club gripped in his triumphant hand.

"You got here just in time," I said.

"It was nothing," Zanz said as he slumped down next to me, covered in sweat and gasping for air. "You might not know this about me Toby but I was actually the one who clubbed that skinny bitch Richard Ramirez over the head in Los Angeles, 1989, as part of the vigilante mob that chased the notorious serial killer through his brother's barrio. I've got experience with these types of situations. Of course I was eighty-five years old at the time."

We sat for awhile, not saying anything. I handed him the bottle I was holding. Sirens were approaching from somewhere outside.

"That will do," he said, taking a long drink.

"Yes," I said. "It will."

# CHAPTER 30

I had made the whole thing up.

Or so it felt. After all, life trips strangely dreamlike at times of crisis and injury. I had been a little too bold, a little too clever in this most recent matter, a little too competent to enforce my will over a large and imposing opposition. I had been a little too fancy. It was a simulation, a choreographed struggle, a rehearsed confab, after which the muddled components of illusion and reality form complex and enchanted ruins for future generations to marvel at and dismiss.

I remembered bits and pieces of the drama, like staring into those abyssal eyes of that ghostly, wrinkled head. But what if that was just a fictional construct of the inevitable mortality that haunts us all? In the face of something distant and bad why not create something present and worse. A little perspective keeps a mind sound. My battle with the Gilded Dawn was the fear of my own susceptibility to the appeal of dangerous charisma. I had been wounded by a woman with a knife, but I was always being wounded by women. I find this preferable to the longing absence. I had seen the blood from the cut flow over my hands but that could've been a form of stigmata. No one can hurt you if you've already sacrificed yourself. A fiery ending? Very convenient. A wishful fabrication of a mock goodbye to a serious addiction to alcohol? They all knew I wasn't going anywhere. Zanz was busy working at being his favorite thing, a bartender. Skid Row Paul was busy bumming around. As far as I can tell Baron never existed.

The important thing to remember from this point on was that I had broken my arm and sustained a puncture wound. Maybe from the way I had told it, maybe not. Maybe from a drunken fall. Maybe I had been reaching for a jar of something and slipped off the something I had been standing on to reach the jar of something. I might've wandered into an industrial-sized air conditioning unit and been knocked over by a blower wheel and then impaled on some exposed ductwork. I could've been bitten by a snake or a dog, or a snake being chased by a dog and then, all three of us being in some mode of pursuit, I fall in a very elegant manner down an exposed manhole cover. I have a terrific lawsuit against the city, if that is indeed what has happened. My temporary fear of serial killers has vanished, by the way, simply because that is what temporary things are supposed to do. My primary goal is to entertain, to provide fuel for the Big Machine. I am taking some time off from any physical labor because, like I said, I broke my arm.

Since my arm was broken and I needed a few stitches I went to see Doctor Eddie, who attended to both of these things. He sewed me up and then wrapped my arm in plaster netting, slowly and methodically, a confident sculptor working in reverse, adding layers, concealing the subject.

"How stupid of me to do this," I told myself.

"Yeah," he echoed a bit absently. "You'll be alright. I mean, you'll be structurally sound."

"It was all so clever and dramatic but in the end nothing really changed," I said, again more to myself than Doctor Eddie.

"Things do happen, as they say," he replied, continuing to turn the wet plaster around my arm, applying mild pressure to the bandage to make sure it didn't wrinkle. "Sometimes things don't happen. You just have to take both as they come along."

"I could've killed myself," I continued. "One little slip up. It doesn't seem fair that we have to survive everyday of our lives but it only takes one moment to die."

"Probably not a good idea to really think about it," Doctor Eddie said.

"Should I be forced to ignore the deeper issues?" I asked him.

"The air is nice on the surface. The sun is out. You dig down and you get frustrated and tired in the darkness and what is worse, there is no sun. You suffocate in the tunnel of your own making. It collapses on you and then you are stuck. Even if you find the truth. What good is truth if there is no air and no sun?"

"You don't seem to have much of an affection for the grander mysteries?"

308

"I'm a medical professional. How I feel personally about these abstract, non-medical issues is unimportant. I am here to fix what is wrong with your body. As you can see I am in the process of doing just that. Then I am going to play golf. That is the substance of my ontology, if you want to put it in those terms. I need to improve my handicap." He turned to soak more of the bandage, running his hands smoothly down the length to remove the excess water. He worked with an enviable fluidity, unaware of himself in regards to the process. He was the process, entrenched in his performance, as unconcerned with the possibility of error as the bandage was. I hated that about him and fought the temptation to tell him so.

"I wanted a happy ending to this whole thing," I said.

"Life isn't about happy endings," he said, choosing to ignore the obvious and crude comeback. "Life is about putting off the ending for as long as you can." That was a good point. I took the time to study him, being that I was so close to an actual doctor creature in its natural habitat and wouldn't know when I would be again. Musky smelling. Impeccable hair. A man committed to action and results. I wondered if all that was learned or innate. If I asked him he'd probably come back with some glib response that would only frustrate me.

"I was supposed to be you," I said.

"Be glad you don't have my nicotine habit."

"What's it like to be you?"

"Not so bad. I've got a family. I've got a mistress. I have money market accounts. I own real estate. I like to go parachuting. My children take their lifestyle for granted. We spend a few weeks of every summer in Martha's Vineyard. I go to Vail for my ski trips."

"I don't do any of those things," I told him. "I couldn't imagine myself doing them. Better you than me, I guess. I don't think I could pull it off quite right."

"You are pinned against the wall of your own existence," he assured me with a shrug. "Luck of the draw. When you slink out of your mother it is already all planned out according to the parameters of that particular time and space in history. You die at this particular time or that particular time. You die now. You die later. You've died a million times before, and you will die a million times again." He shrugged. "Have a drink. Live out your days. Go fishing. Don't worry about your path. It is already in place. You are a bartender. In your case you help people get drunk. Nothing wrong with that. If you were me you would save people's lives, for the time being. You allow them to put off death. You tell the grim reaper to take a hike, for now." He shrugged again. "Let me know immediately if there is any pain or discomfort. Keep it clean. Don't get your cast wet and make sure you check the bandages on your stitches. Get some rest. Last but not least DO NOT put yourself into any physically dangerous situations."

The phrase *physically dangerous situations* held some kind of appeal for me. It had triggered an idea that at first seemed crazy and quite honestly never settled into the category of a particularly good idea. But there was something about surviving a broken bone that inspired a sense of strength and invincibility in me. I had never broken a bone before and now felt I had crossed over into a tougher, more manly state of being. I was a survivor. My injury had earned me a sense of entitlement to other risky situations. There was one last thing that I had to do. It could've been one of the most important things I had ever done in my life or would ever do. I say this only because it is the end of my story, and things that happen at the end of stories should be the most important things ever done in one's life.

I had flown up to Long Island. I was now in a cab on my way to my uncle's bar, The Last Stop Saloon if you will recall. Today it may very well be. I was studying my arm cast. Yes, this was the reason I had broken my arm. It was a means to an end, an opportunity to solve a frustrating mystery. The man with the yellow eyes was going to have to put up or back down. It was to be a showdown of the righteous versus the wicked, bone fracture versus jaundice, the protagonist versus the villain.

I knew that my Uncle Jimmy would not be at his bar because it was a Monday. Uncle Jimmy hated Mondays with a passion. Everybody hated Mondays but Jimmy's rage towards the day made the rest of the world's attitude seem a reluctant form of delight. Mondays for Jimmy were the start of the whole terrible cycle. From its desolate vantage point the end of the week seemed a million miles away. Mondays were the worst for him. Mondays were the worst, yet they weren't as bad as Tuesdays. Jimmy hated Tuesdays with a passion. At least Mondays didn't try to hide the fact that it was the start of the work week. Mondays did not give out false impressions. But Tuesdays were sneaky about it, giving the illusion of being better because it was closer to Friday than a Monday was, but still so far back in the week that the difference was negligible. Now Wednesdays, according to Jimmy, were the big phonies of the group. This so called 'hump day' designed to give people the idea that the rest of the week is an easy, downhill slide, is actually one of the most diabolical days ever invented. If one were to view a typical work week as a swim out into the ocean, then Mondays and Fridays were spent in comfortable, shallow waters, but Wednesdays were the furthest point out in the cold, deep, murky and merciless waters where dangerous sea creatures abided, making Wednesdays more treacherous than ten Mondays combined. Now Thursdays were terrible. Jimmy hated Thursdays because they never had any personality. They were just there. It was like a big fat carcass getting in the way of the weekend. If Thursdays didn't exist the weekend would arrive that much sooner. Fridays for Jimmy were always a letdown. All that buildup and expectation. For what? He never had any fun on Fridays. Saturdays were the loneliest night of the week. It was widely known. Songs had been written on the subject. Now Sundays were the worst for Uncle Jimmy. It was the day he associated with death. The calendars tried to trick humanity by listing Sunday as the first day of the week, but Jimmy knew better. It was the end. It was a weekly death tutorial that swallowed him up and dropped him right back into Monday, which of course was the worst day of the week and the one he usually spent at home.

The cab stopped. I paid the driver and walked into the bar. There was a good afternoon crowd in there. Plenty of spectators. I walked to the bar as if I didn't have a care in the world, looking indifferent to any possible violence that may be directed towards me for no good reason. I took a seat at the bar and placed my cast arm on top of the bar in plain view of anybody who cared to view it. Then I ordered a beer from a bartender that I didn't recognize. He must've been new. Mr. Amico and Mr. Genovese were nowhere to be seen. Perhaps they had finally succumbed to their laundry list of maladies.

I was drinking casually. There was no reason to rush any confrontation. Everything would proceed in a normal fashion, at the normal tempo, to the steady beat of life's circulatory system. The path was already laid out, as Doctor Eddie had said. I just needed to be present for it. Well, here I was, arm cast and all. I could tell that the people around me were curious about it. How did it happen? Was it a simple fracture, compound, triturated maybe? Everyone certainly had their own opinions on the matter. Was I the heroic star of the girl midway across the room's daydream, where she saw me as some racing phenomenon flipping around and around in my sponsored car, over the wall, crash/ bang/smoke, as I pull myself from the wreckage and walk away casually, giving strong waves to the cameras with my one good arm. Or how about the fella next to the jukebox, admiring my handicap, admitting to himself that he wished he had the guts I had, to fight off that whole gang of angel-dust smoking, prison escapees as they tried to take that entire day care center hostage. I let them play in their haphazard guesswork. The real show was not what I had been through, but what I was about to do.

As I sat there sipping my beer, the skin under my cast began to tingle, a clear indication that somebody had taken a serious and not necessarily kindhearted interest in it. I glanced around, eventually setting my sights at the corner booth and sure enough, there he was. The man with the yellow eyes was staring right at me, his gaze so intense that he held off blinking for fear that one microsecond of missed sight would rob him of the whole delicious experience. The smoke, the noise and the people drifted off into the wings. It was only him and I, now fully locked on each other's being. I could tell he was being turned on by my weakness, he was sensing an opportunity for an easy beating. Wasn't there some sort of sexual fetish associated with people wearing casts? This could've been part of his problem. A sadistic subsection of an illicit, overwhelming desire for sexual release in the presence of splints and bandages. I had seen grown men run from the sight of clowns. Anything was possible.

The man took a sip of his drink through his snarled lips. He dropped the glass to the table and pushed it aside. With that he stood up and walked towards me. I took a deep breath. Be strong. Don't let him detect fear. That is what he wants. Stand your ground. Everybody in the place got quiet. He stepped right in front of me, rubbed his stubbly chin with his worn, wrinkled hands, nails chewed down to the nub. From close up I could see that he had, what palmists tend to call 'murderer's thumbs', flat and stubby, a sure sign of a violent individual. He raised his hand in the air and I flinched.

"Two shots of whiskey!" he called out. The bartender brought them over and put them down between us. The man with the yellow eyes then stuck his hand out towards me. It seemed that he wanted me to shake it.

"You are Jimmy's nephew, right?" he asked. His yellow eyes glared at me above some menacing facial scars.

"Yes," I eventually spit out. He looked down at his hand, which caused *me* to look down at it. I realized that I hadn't shook it yet and placed my good hand in his firm grip. I gave it a few pumps.

"Good to see you again," he said. "I didn't get to talk to you the last time you were up here. I feel like I know you so well because Jimmy always brags about you. Everybody in this place is really proud of you. You are living your own life. Don't you let anybody tell you what to do with it." He

312

then took up one of the shot glasses sitting on the bar and implored me to take up the other one. I grabbed it and held it high in his direction, as he was holding his shot in mine. Cheers, he said, then we put them to bed.

Fresh off the heels of my mystifying victory over the sadistic, yellow-eyed man (nice guy, really) I decided it was just a short cab ride over to Uncle Jimmy's house where I could use all the momentum from my dangerous encounter (that turned out to be not so dangerous and quite pleasant, really) to inspire and convince the old stubborn screwball to grant me some family clemency, to restore me back into his ill-tempered good graces. I didn't for a moment dwell on the possibility of failure. It was as if the whole concept was just an old, broken down superstition. My arm cast was a blinding, triumphant emblem in the feverish blaze of the sun. I wanted to wear it forever.

Jimmy's house was a farcical kind of low class panache. Some aspects of its upkeep were completely ignored while other details were obsessed over. To start off with there were a pair of ironic, stately marble lions on either side of the entrance to his driveway. Half of his roof was covered in blue tarp. His small boat, parked atop the trailer at the side of the house, was freshly washed and waxed. His front screen door had always been broken and always would be. He had put three additions on his house over the years and none had ever been completely finished, making it look less like a house and more like a set of unrelated rooms with embarrassing mutations growing out of them. The front lawn was groomed and edged. There was a pile of treated lumber and five bags of wood chips always stacked on the porch, no longer waiting to be put to some kind of use, now its own landscaping design. When I arrived at the door I could tell from the abrupt shouting inside the house that he was embroiled in some sporting match.

I knocked on the door anyway.

"Screw off, the game is on," my uncle's gruff voice rang out.

"Uncle Jimmy, it's Toby," I yelled.

"Who?"

"Your nephew." The television went off.

"What are you doing here?"

"I came up personally because I didn't want you to be able to hang up the phone on me," I yelled through the door.

"Hold on a second," he said, his voice filled with irritable surprise. I let out a sigh and took a seat on the porch steps, my back to the door.

I was glad to be on the front porch. The front porch was the perfect setting for our reconciliation. Front porches were where all the serious discussions were held in my family. Even as a child I remembered that when the grownups had to talk serious they moved to the front porch. As I grew older I found myself called to this location, usually to be told some overwhelming but regrettable truism about the modern world and what I could expect it to inflict upon me as time went on. Family tragedies, inside rumor, domestic concerns, issues of sex, the guile of hazardous women were all hashed out on the front porch, usually sitting down and facing out into the street, with pauses and intonations designed to effect a serious and profound wisdom.

From inside the house the various rumbles and creaks continued, evidence of a high degree of movement. I playfully mused, as is the curse of a strong imagination, that Jimmy was rooting around for one of his handguns which he would load, say a small prayer of absolution, then come out the front door, put the cold steel to my head and really show me how he felt about my unforgivable years of lying. Then he would curse my limp body (a couple of twitches here and there, but for the most part) pack me off in garbage bags and start hosing off the front walk.

I did not think this was really going to happen.

So it was strangely alarming to experience the corresponding sounds and sensations associated with my mock theory. The door behind me opened and closed. I could hear Jimmy's struggled breathing, a sound which in and of itself was a mode of surly complaint. Something cold and hard was being pressed against my head.

"Jimmy!" I said, stiffening up. "What the hell are you doing?"

"This is the only way I know how to make peace," he grumbled. The barrel pressed harder into my head. It was cold. In fact, it was freezing. I turned slightly and saw that Jimmy was holding a cold bottle of beer up against my temple. "Well are you going to just sit there or are you going to have a drink?" he asked. I took the bottle from him. He had one for himself. We cracked them open. For some reason it was one of the best tasting beers I ever had. Jimmy hiked up his leisure pants and sat down next to me, staring passively across the street.

"How are you doing Jimmy?" I asked him.

"Not bad, you know, for a faulkin Monday," he answered.

"Look at it this way," I said. "Tuesday is almost here."

"Don't even get me started, Toby." He then did a double-take at my arm. "What happened to you? Are you alright?" He looked from my arm to either side of the street as if to catch whomever did this to me before they could get away.

"I broke my arm. Don't worry. It is one of the best things that has happened to me recently."

"How did you do it?"

"I was just being fancy."

He made a deep-throated sound, a shamed, grunting plea for my forgiveness. Whatever obstinacy he had been harboring against me was crumbling fast. How could he forsake his crippled nephew? Any frustration or anger he now had was a weak form, an emotion he was holding onto if only so he could ceremoniously discard it in front of me. It was a ritual purging. I felt that again the cast was my catalyst and wondered how long I would be allowed to wear it. He put his arm around me and pulled me towards him, kissing me on top of my head. He let go of me. A thoughtful silence followed.

"You know," he said, taking a drink of his beer. "My father never gave a shit. He didn't want to waste his time with me. I was just trying to give you some direction because I never had any."

"Maybe he just wanted to let you choose for yourself," I said.

"I could've thought of it that way," Jimmy admitted, "but then it would've been harder for me to dislike him. I couldn't have blamed him as much." He cracked a smile in fond reflection. "For awhile I really had him on the run. Guilty for having him feel like he had screwed up with me. But you are a sneaky one, Toby. I didn't count on you kicking me in my own ass while my back was turned." He patted me on the shoulder.

"Look at it this way," I said. "I followed in your footsteps. You can hold some pride in that. At least I'm maintaining, holding down a job, paying my way. I could've been a lot worse."

"You could've been Gerald M. Funchess," Jimmy remarked distastefully.

"How did you know about him?" I asked.

"You gave me the book to read when you were done with it."

"You know, I had occasion to think about that guy recently," I told him.

"You must've been in some strange situation."

"Jimmy, I can't even begin to tell you."

"You had the potential, Toby," Jimmy assured me with a slap on my back. "Even if you didn't do it, know that you could've."

"Jimmy, quite honestly I am comfortable as a bartender," I said. "I understand it. I am content with the peculiar form of intelligence it requires. There are certain forms of intelligence that I find much too terrifying. The medical field is one of them. I like to keep my wisdom frivolous and not a matter of life and death. I will look into the watery eyes of a drunk and not the frozen eyes of the deceased. I will treat death by encouraging life instead of encouraging life by treating death. They will do their job. I will do mine. We will stand together, in the face of the great immensity of knowledge, methods and means, the impossible collection, and ply our trades to the best of our ability and at the end of the day we will all gather around the mighty bar and talk of many things--princes, paupers, sons and daughters, as we drink the blood of the kings."

"You are a little shit," Jimmy said, taking a drink from his bottle. He was then hit by some errant thought, a critical memory that he would do well to act on before he forgot it again.

"That reminds me," Jimmy said. "I wanted to give you something last time you were here but you left too quickly."

"You told me you wanted me gone," I pointed out.

"You tell me I look better with age," he said. "There, we both lie."

He disappeared into the house and returned with a picture. It was my mother's picture, the one that had been hanging in Jimmy's office, the weird one she had painted, full of meaningless shapes and figures with the patch of odd negative space in the middle. "I want you to have this," he said. I took the picture into my hands and admired it. Maybe it wasn't much. Maybe it was great art. Maybe it was just something that needed to be done. I pondered the visual omission. The gap. That might've been the key to it. The negative space. By placing all of the observable crap in life in just the right way it was possible to get something redeemable in the empty space, in between the borders, shapes and curves, maybe it spelled something.

I looked closer. Son of a bitch it did spell something. It was a name, a four letter name, unfamiliar to me, so subtle and inconspicuous and somehow powerful because of it. I supposed if it was overt it might've served as an insult to the seeker. Like I said, the name meant nothing to me, but obviously it meant something to her. It was right there in the middle of the picture. A four letter name. The scholars might refer to it as the Tetragrammaton, but it was her own personal one, her proper name for IT, the undefinable IT. The whole deal--stars and molecules, water and fire, mountain and ocean, flux and stillness, ash, bloom, soot, soil and rose petal. City and sand, crumble and rebirth. Her four letters, this whole time. I was in possession of a secret thrill, something I couldn't even convey if I wanted to, especially to Jimmy, who was sitting next to me, off in his own absent space and time. I put the picture beside me and stared at it for a long while, longer than I could've ever imagined anybody would look at it for.

"Danny Fusilli," Uncle Jimmy said.

"Who's that?" I asked.

"You asked me about him before," Jimmy replied. "He's the guy that, from time to time, has to beat the crap out of the men who step out in front of his train."

"What do you mean, step out in front of his train? Are you talking about that mean looking, scar-faced, yellow-eyed, upstanding, gentlemanly fellow who beats up the guys in the casts?"

"Danny Fusilli is a conductor for the Long Island railroad. Policy states that if somebody steps out in front of the train to commit suicide and gets hit, then the train has to stop and wait for the police to come and process the scene. It is especially time consuming if the person gets caught under the train, because then they get mangled. It can take awhile to find all the pieces that way. But if the stupid son of a bitch standing on the tracks succeeds in killing themselves then the conductor gets three days off paid, as kind of a grievance period. If the stupid son of a bitch standing on the tracks thinks better of it and steps off the tracks, maybe he just gets clipped or something, the train still has to stop and go through the whole ordeal of police coming, taking the injured away and now the train is late and people are angry and worst of all the conductor doesn't get his three days off with pay. That guy you saw in the bar a few weeks ago had tried to step out in front of Danny's train. He was struck in the arm but managed to avoid being killed. It ruined Danny's whole day and worse, Danny doesn't get his vacation. When the guy had the dumb luck to show up to the bar, I guess Danny figured he was going to get him one way or the other. My attitude is that if you are trying to kill yourself, do it without inconveniencing others. If you don't--you get what is coming to you."

"I'll be damned," I said, looking up at the sky, pleased that at least two things in this world finally made a little more sense. "It is a near perfect day," I remarked because it was a very pretty day and because I was hesitant about anything that was 'perfect'.

"It is a near perfect day," he agreed. "Now if the goddamn C.I.A. would stop monitoring my every movement and leave me and my Omega Machine alone, then it would be a perfect day."

Later on, we stopped in at his bar.

"What you going to do now, Toby?" Jimmy asked, pouring himself a drink.

"I think I'm going to try doing some writing."

"I didn't know you wanted to be a writer. Since when?"

"I've wanted to be a writer ever since I discovered that Arthur Miller married Marilyn Monroe."

"That is a good reason."

"I know."

The whole experience had left me feeling playful and a bit sneaky. It was my job now to manipulate this journey, to filter the experience to understand somehow in the negative space of it all, what I was looking for, the quiet territory that would reveal myself at the highest potential.

*I wanted an intense testament, ever dramatic, powerful and timeless, invoking elements noble, trenchant, learned. Yes, freedom of righteous thought halts everything luckless or readily doomed. A new dream! Hope, even if nothing's certain. Love, it now escapes defeat. Uplifting narratives to overcome my ephemeral anxieties, nagging demons, harrowing emptiness aimed right down my yearning, crying, rallying youth.*

Yes, I decided. The acrostic was sound.

Closing time. The last of the dregs drifted out of the bar. It was just Uncle Jimmy and I. I wiped the bar down with a rag. Uncle Jimmy lit his cigar and began stacking glasses. I pulled the mats from the floor and ran a dirty mop across the tiles. Jimmy stacked the bar stools. I shut the lights off. When everything had been taken care of we walked to the front door.

"Are we ready?" Uncle Jimmy asked.

"You know it," I said to him.

We walked out the doors of the darkened establishment and headed into the night in order to soak up some of the immediate life that, due to future concern, tends to be ignored.

THE END.